PRAISE FOR FAR

Jana Goes Wild

"A beautiful, compelling romance celebrating second chances and forgiveness."   —*Kirkus*, starred review

"*Jana Goes Wild* is an enchanting story of love, family, and self-acceptance set against the vibrant backdrop of Tanzania. I was swept away by Jana and Anil's emotional whirlwind and cheering for their second chance at love. It was the perfect swoony escape. I can't wait to read what Farah Heron writes next!"   —Sara Desai, author of *The Singles Table*

Kamila Knows Best

"An endearing cast led by a Bollywood-loving hero and a fashionista heroine set Heron's retelling of Jane Austen's *Emma* apart from the pack. Both Austenites and movie fans who fondly remember *Clueless* will be delighted."
                   —*Publishers Weekly*

"There's nothing better than a book that warms your heart and your belly. This Bollywood-inspired retelling of Jane Austen's *Emma* is a fun, lighthearted binge from page one."
                   —*USA Today*

"Heron's sensitive insights infuse this romance with both immense charm and emotional depth."   —*Booklist*

Accidentally Engaged

Entertainment Weekly Best Romances of the Year
USA Today Best Rom-Coms of the Year
NPR Best Romances of the Year

"Voraciously readable...fresh, warm, soft in all the right places...both its comedic and emotional moments sing. We dare readers not to devour it. Grade: A."
—*Entertainment Weekly*

"An engaging read with authentic characters who continue to surprise you."
—*USA Today*

"A mouth-watering romantic comedy...This book is undoubtedly what Heron would pull out during the Showstopper Challenge on a literary version of *The Great British Bake Off*."
—*BookPage*

"Full of heart and humor...Farah Heron balances the ingredients for a charming romance: a heroine finding her way, a swoon-worthy love, a complicated but loving family and a happily ever after."
—Shelf Awareness

"*Accidentally Engaged* does what all good romance novels do best: It's full of emotion, fun, and family, with that ultimately satisfying HEA that will settle in your stomach like a home-cooked meal."
—*Vulture*

Just Playing House

Just Playing House

Farah Heron

FOREVER

New York Boston

Forever
Hachette Book Group
1290 Avenue of the Americas, New York, NY 10104
read-forever.com

First Edition: July 2024

Forever is an imprint of Grand Central Publishing. The Forever name and logo are registered trademarks of Hachette Book Group, Inc.

The publisher is not responsible for websites (or their content) that are not owned by the publisher.

The Hachette Speakers Bureau provides a wide range of authors for speaking events. To find out more, go to hachettespeakersbureau.com or email HachetteSpeakers@hbgusa.com.

Forever books may be purchased in bulk for business, educational, or promotional use. For information, please contact your local bookseller or the Hachette Book Group Special Markets Department at special.markets@hbgusa.com.

Print book interior design by Marie Mundaca

Library of Congress Cataloging-in-Publication Data

Names: Heron, Farah, author.
Title: Just playing house / Farah Heron.
Description: First edition. | New York : Forever, 2024.
Identifiers: LCCN 2023052692 | ISBN 9781538725474 (trade paperback) | ISBN 9781538725481 (e-book)
Subjects: LCGFT: Romance fiction. | Novels.
Classification: LCC PR9199.4.H4695 J87 2024 | DDC 813/.6—dc23/eng/20231121
LC record available at https://lccn.loc.gov/2023052692

ISBNs: 9781538725474 (trade paperback), 9781538725481 (ebook)

Printed in the United States of America

LSC-C

Printing 1, 2024

This book is for all my fellow BRCA genetic mutation carriers.
We are worthy of happily ever afters, too.

CHAPTER ONE

Marley

When Marley Kamal was a young girl imagining her future, she pictured fabulousness. Gorgeous clothes, tons of friends, and the most glamorous job in the fashion industry. She wasn't too upset that reality came nowhere near those lofty expectations, since as an adult she discovered that *peopling* wasn't all it was cracked up to be, anyway. But she was surprised so much of her adult life would be focused on *breasts*.

Talking about breasts. Looking at breasts. Worrying about breasts. And *corralling* breasts was the most challenging of all.

"I need my boobs to sit here!" said Angel Durand, Marley's customer in fitting room one, with her thick French-Canadian accent. "Center ice! Maybe blue line! Not end zone!" Angel was currently topless with a black vegan-leather jumpsuit unzipped and hanging at her waist, and her long, nude nails were indenting dimples into her ample breast flesh. Marley was skeptical that Angel's bosom had *ever* seen that particular gravity-defying resting place since puberty, but Marley had been selling dreams, aspirations, and illusions—otherwise known as luxury fashion—for almost a decade now. She knew how to make the customer happy.

Marley tilted her head with feigned sympathy. "We can try adhesive supports again. We just got a new line—"

Angel made a face of disgust. "Absolutely not. My nipples were on *fire* the last time I wore pasties. Pink nipples are fine, but mine looked like maraschino cherries!"

Great. The last thing Marley needed now was the painful image of cherry-red nipples in her brain. "I think that jumpsuit might be challenging without shoulder support. Maybe something with transparent straps?"

At that, Angel whipped a strapless underwire bra at Marley's head. Thankfully, ten years of working with spoiled sports wives had given Marley reflexes as impressive as those of Angel's hockey defenseman husband.

"I want my boobs to be like yours!" Angel's hands reached out, ready to grab Marley's own breasts in her slim white blouse, but again, Marley's quick reflexes got her out of the way before contact was made.

"I'll see what I can find," Marley said, closing the fitting room door. She plucked the expensive bra off the floor. If Angel knew a thing about Marley's breasts, she wouldn't want them. Even if they were full and round, no one would want breasts that were silently plotting to kill their owner. Which was why Marley's breasts were going to be ousted from her body very soon.

Marley twisted the ring on her index finger, reminding herself she was almost done for the day. It had taken six years at this job, but she was officially burnt out from working on the selling floor and dealing with invasive comments and abrasive customers.

She checked on her other customer in the fitting rooms, Paris Mousavi. "How are you feeling in that Armani?"

"It's too big," Paris said. "I look like an overcooked eggplant. I *cannot* be seen in court like this." Lawyers in Ontario wore robes in court, so no one would be seeing Paris in the eggplant-esque suit in the courtroom. And the suit fit fine, anyway.

Marley smiled sympathetically. "These Armani suits are not meant to be worn off the rack—they always need tailoring. I'll send someone up."

Marley left the ladieswear fitting rooms, her black patent stiletto heels echoing over the marble floor of Reid's Department Store, and headed toward lingerie while calling alterations to send someone to Paris.

Tova, another sales consultant, caught up with her as she hung up her phone. "Did Angel Durand really tweak your nipples in the fitting room?"

"Of course not," Marley said. "Angel is lovely." She knew Tova was waiting in the wings to steal the customer out from under Marley the moment she disclosed that things weren't rosy in the salesperson-customer relationship.

"Oh god," Tova said, looking toward the customer service desk. "I'm pretty sure Aubrey Ashton got implants while she was on vacation in Mexico."

Marley's head shot to Tova. Aubrey was a sales associate in the store, not a customer. It was highly inappropriate to be discussing the body of a coworker like that. Also…Aubrey didn't have implants, did she?

"I can smell the silicone a mile away," Tova said. "Highly suspicious that her Insta didn't have any beach pictures in Cancún."

Marley took a quick right and straightened the YSL blouses on a rack, mostly to ditch Tova. She really disliked her. Actually, Marley was at the point where she didn't like most of the people who worked on Reid's selling floor. Bunch of snooty vultures. Marley was one of the biggest sellers in the store, which meant most other consultants frothed at the thought of dethroning her.

Ruby Dhanjee was working at the lingerie counter. She was Marley's cousin and easily her favorite person at the store. Ruby had just returned to town six months ago after years away, and Marley had referred her for the position at Reid's.

Marley gave Ruby a pleading look. "Please tell me you have a bra in a 42G that won't show under the Alice and Olivia jumpsuit."

Ruby shook her head. "Impossible. That's backless and strapless. Why don't you show her some other jumpsuits? The green Stella McCartney one or the Vivienne Westwood."

Marley chuckled at Ruby's suggestion. "You know we do carry lines that aren't from the UK, right?" Ruby was obsessed with anything from England. Except colonialism, of course.

"I'd put her in Halston," Tova said, appearing seemingly out of nowhere.

"Tova," Ruby said sweetly, "there's a woman over there looking at formal dresses."

"On it," Tova said, rushing away. She didn't even thank Ruby for giving her the customer. Marley raised a brow once Tova was gone. Was Ruby handing Tova commissions now?

Ruby snorted. "I saw the girl looking up each dress on her phone on a designer dupes site. She's not going to buy anything. Erin Prichard was just here with a message for you." Ruby put on a fake British accent. "Her Excellency has requested your presence in the personal shopping suite at five o'clock sharp."

Marley's jaw nearly dropped to the counter. She checked her watch. That was in twenty minutes. "Why?"

Erin was Reid's personal shopper. She worked by appointment only in her gorgeous *private* office. There had been rumors in the store for months that Erin was pushing to expand her department and hire a second personal shopper to work with her. Marley would give her left arm for that job, just like every other consultant in the store.

Well, actually, Marley probably shouldn't be even *thinking* about removing *more* healthy body parts.

"Apparently, Her Excellency needs you to consult with a client," Ruby said.

Erin was notoriously protective of her customers and never allowed anyone to assist her, other than the personal shopping assistant. And Erin was extremely difficult to get close to—she didn't socialize with the rest of the staff. Marley had been trying to cultivate a friendship with her, but she wasn't getting anywhere. She wasn't even aware that Erin knew her name.

But maybe Jacqueline, the store's general manager and Marley's boss, finally agreed to hire a new personal shopper, and Erin was testing out the top consultants. Marley nearly shook with the excitement of that prospect. Moving to personal shopping would mean her own office and her own dedicated assistant. She could be selective with her clients. No more hockey wives whipping undergarments at her. No more staff waiting for Marley to lower her guard so they could steal her customers. No more gossip. After Marley had had the absolute crappiest of years, it was high time something went well for her.

Marley knocked on the door of the personal shopping suite at five sharp. Erin's assistant, Ernesto, wearing a perfectly tailored

Thom Browne suit along with his normal bored expression, let her in. As the city's premier luxury department store, Reid's was expertly designed, but the personal shopping suite was the flagship. No expense had been spared in the fixtures and decor. Gleaming white walls with colorful designer chairs and the softest white leather couch imaginable. And a pink feature wall that made everyone's skin glow.

Erin stood to kiss Marley on each cheek. "You're here. Wonderful. You look radiant as always. Utterly flawless."

Marley smiled. Erin herself was the flawless one. Wearing black wide-legged pants and a frilly, puffy white blouse, Erin somehow looked both luxurious and effortless. With Erin, the devil was in her details. The silver charm bracelet. The oversized vintage brooch. The immaculate platinum-blond hair with nary a millimeter of dark roots showing. Marley knew not to get too excited by this warm greeting, though. Erin treated everyone exactly the same—with polite praise. "Come. Meet Lydia Chambers." She indicated a small woman sitting on one of the designer chairs. The client in question, Marley assumed.

Lydia stood, eyes narrowed, shrewdly sizing Marley up. She was white, with smooth pale skin and wavy brown hair reaching her shoulders. She could have been anywhere between twenty-five and forty-five, but Marley assumed midthirties, and she was dressed in slim ankle jeans paired with an army-green T-shirt and a black blazer with the sleeves pushed up. And she had her phone clipped to her belt with a hideous leather harness.

Marley put on her client smile and held out her hand. "Marley Kamal. Are you looking for something for an event, or a new wardrobe?" This client would be easy enough. She seemed unassuming and had a proportional figure, if a little small. She would be a breeze to dress.

"Oh, no," Lydia said, shaking her head and sitting back down. "This isn't for me."

Erin sat gracefully at her glass-topped desk and indicated for Marley to sit next to Lydia. "Lydia is a *celebrity handler* with a film studio. She's come to contract with Reid's to exclusively style a VIP for several upcoming appearances, but you'll need to sign her NDA before we go any further. Ernesto and I have already signed. You must also sign the standard Reid's NDA for personal shoppers."

Marley's brows furrowed. She served wealthy clients all the time, and she liked to think she had a reputation for professionalism, maintaining privacy, and of course, making the impossible happen. But A-list celebrities...*true VIPs* who needed NDAs—those were usually brought in through the secret back door straight into the personal shopping studio. Marley had never signed an NDA in her six years at Reid's.

Lydia immediately slid a thick agreement to Marley, and Marley started reading it while adjusting her initial impression of the celebrity handler. Lydia was actually formidable. Her agreement was terrifying. The clauses and stipulations were... intense.

"Do I need a lawyer for this?" Marley asked.

"There isn't time," Lydia said, voice dripping with impatience. "This is a standard agreement. You sign this or we go elsewhere. There are still *plenty* of stylists in this city."

"Of course, there are more consultants in this store, too," Erin added. She gave Marley an annoyed look. Marley bit her lip. If Marley ever wanted to move to personal shopping, she needed to play along.

Marley flipped to the next page. The actual VIP's name wasn't on the agreement—they were only called *the subject*. "Will I find out who the VIP is before signing?"

Lydia shook her head. "No."

Marley read the next clause, which was about the use of recording devices. Marley's mind was racing. Who could the VIP be? Whoever they were, she kind of felt bad for them. Imagine having to go through all this to buy a pair of jeans. The verbiage about big lawsuits, fines, and even employment termination if Marley broke the confidentiality agreement was alarming. She looked at Erin, but Erin's expression was blank.

"Any questions?" Lydia asked once Marley was on the last page.

Marley nodded. "Yes. There are separate clauses here for before and after an event. What, and when, is the *event*?"

Lydia shook her head. "You will be told after you sign."

This could be a problem. Marley had *surgery* scheduled in a couple of weeks...Would she even be able to take this client?

She reached the final page and noticed it had been printed with her legal name, Mahreen, instead of Marley. Lydia had done her research.

"The studio has a considerable wardrobe budget here," Lydia said. "If this goes well, we'd consider bringing more talent to Reid's."

The situation was crystal clear to Marley. If she refused to sign and Lydia walked, Reid's would lose thousands of dollars in sales. And Marley would likely lose her job. If she signed, then learned the timing of this *event* didn't work with her surgery and recovery, Marley might not be fired, but it would be unlikely that she would get promoted to personal shopper anytime soon. If she signed it and *was* able to take the client, she'd have to work her ass off for what sounded like the biggest client of her life. If she failed, she could expect never to get an opportunity like this again.

But if she succeeded...this could be amazing.

"He's waiting outside," Erin said.

Marley looked up from the contract of doom with one brow raised. "*He*? I'm a ladieswear specialist."

"We'll be needing menswear for this," Lydia said.

Erin frowned, crossing her arms in front of her. "Marley, personal shoppers are specialists in all areas of the store. You can learn what you don't know."

Marley exhaled. She didn't have a choice. She needed this job—and, importantly, the health benefits and paid sick time that came with it. With a shaking hand, she signed both copies of Lydia's contract, then opened the Reid's NDA. It was considerably shorter—and simpler. It basically said she must keep the identity and any private information about any personal shopping client confidential, or she would lose her job. Marley signed it as well and slid both agreements across the desk.

Lydia took one copy of each agreement and handed the others to Erin. "Excellent. Looking forward to working with you, Marley," Lydia said. "Now that you've all signed, I can give you more information. The primary event we need wardrobe for is in just under two weeks. He'll be needing at least three distinct looks for the event and for a press junket following it."

Whoa. That *was* fast. Marley nodded along, but her mind was reeling at how the hell she could become a menswear specialist so quickly. But also...this wasn't going to get in the way of her surgery in two weeks. Thank goodness.

"Tailoring that quickly might be an issue," Marley said.

Erin waved her hand. "You'll be assigned a dedicated tailor."

Marley nodded. "Is there anything else that might make him a challenge to dress?" There wasn't time for any made-to-measure bespoke pieces.

Lydia snorted at that statement. "Oh yes. He is *definitely* a challenge. This is our biggest issue—he's a little...*resistant*."

"Spoiled celebrity bad boy?" Ernesto asked.

Lydia gave away nothing with her smile. "This is why we need confidentiality. The person you will be styling has recently been cast in a starring role in an upcoming blockbuster."

Ernesto whistled low. "An A-list movie star?"

Lydia shook her head. "No. He's not a movie star...yet. That's the problem. Movie stars already have stylists. They know how to present themselves to the press. They know when to shut up and listen to experts. But God only knows why the studio has cast a complete nobody in easily the most coveted role of the year."

"My god," Erin said, her hand going to her mouth in shock. "This is for *Ironis 3*, right? You're talking about the *Bronze Shadow*."

Marley wasn't really into superhero movies or comics, but she'd have to have been living under a rock to not know how popular the Ironis movies were. Based on a comic book franchise, two huge blockbuster action films had already been made, with more expected.

Lydia nodded. "Simon DeSouza, otherwise known as The Bronze Shadow, has been a fan favorite from the comics since day one. There are Vegas bookies taking bets on which Chris will be cast in the role. Many are sure it will be Tom Cruise, or Daniel Craig, despite them being much too old. This role should be going to someone like Pattinson. Cavill would be amazing. Hell, there is a whole email newsletter out there stating that fans will accept none but Timothée Chalamet as the Bronze Shadow. This role *should* be going to an A-lister. Not a nobody Canadian. And especially not a nobody Canadian who dresses like coastal-grandma-meets-frat-boy."

Marley frowned at that image in her head. "Yay Canada, though." She had no idea which Canadian would be up for such a huge part. Keanu Reeves? Maybe he'd be too old, too. Marley didn't exactly keep up with Hollywood.

Lydia made a disparaging noise. "Suffice it to say that there will be *a lot* of disappointed fanboys when the casting is announced. We are attempting to mitigate that by relying on hometown advantage and announcing at Toronto Comicon—before filming. We've been working our asses off to get him ready, but this man needs *help*. He's *fired* five stylists so far, and he's on his third personal trainer. And we're not even going to talk about dentists."

"A diva?" Erin asked.

Lydia nodded. "I would *almost* feel sorry for the guy—he's about to walk into a media zoo. But he accepted the role. He knew what would happen. And honestly, existentialism is *so passé*. No one cares about his impostor syndrome. We all have our own to deal with."

Marley wasn't sure she felt a whole lot of sympathy for him, either. He was probably being paid a fortune for this role. He'd already fired five stylists. He sounded like an insufferable, inexperienced man-boy. "Why did the studio cast him?"

Lydia shrugged. "I'm not in casting, but there are reasons the studio wanted to move in this direction. It's my job to turn him into a movie star whether he wants to be or not." She sighed. "Fans haven't embraced every Ironis casting decision, but everyone knows the backlash here will be exponentially worse."

"Well, if he's dressing like Chris Pine during the pandemic..." Ernesto said.

Lydia shook her head. "No, it's not because of his lack of fashion sense...It's because the Bronze Shadow is the *fan favorite*. No one is expecting a South Asian actor in the role."

Marley inhaled sharply. Of course he was having an existential crisis—he knew he was about to be put in front of a firing squad of racist neckbeard fanboys. Poor diva boy. Her heart kind of broke for the man. And that was probably why they'd requested Marley—they wanted to work with a South Asian stylist so he'd have someone with the same skin color as him on his side. And Marley was the only South Asian sales consultant at Reid's.

Marley nodded. "Okay. When can I meet him?"

Lydia stood. "Right now. My assistant is with Nik at your back door." She pulled out her phone. "I'm telling them to come in."

Marley stood and stepped toward the door, putting on her shopgirl smile to greet the VIP. She wasn't going to be the next stylist he fired. Her job was depending on it—but also, as a South Asian, she was already protective of him. And weirdly proud. It was amazing that a desi had been cast in the biggest action role of the year.

When the door opened, first a small white woman with honey-colored hair walked in—Lydia's assistant, presumably. Behind her was a tall, brown-skinned man—clearly the VIP. The first thing Marley noticed, of course, was his clothes. A faded, stretched-out Superman T-shirt with an oversized cream cable-knit cardigan over it. And a pair of wide-legged ripped jeans...wait. Were those painter pants?

Finally, Marley looked at his face and frowned. It wasn't just his clothes that resembled Chris Pine's pandemic look, but also that beard. That was *not* a good beard, and neither was his halo of frizzy black hair reaching his shoulders, or his lopsided smile. It wasn't lopsided like in a sexy, cute romance-hero kind of way, more like…half his face was paralyzed. And he was drooling from the slacked half of his mouth.

This was the VIP? How in God's name was she going to turn this slack-jawed man into an international movie star?

He put his hand up and waved. "Hi, Mahreen!" he mumbled through the mobile half of his mouth. He winced. "Chit. Dorry. I wad at de dentitht."

That's when Marley realized she knew the half of his face that still had muscle tone. Even under that unkept beard. This was her scrawny class-clown grade-twelve chem lab partner. Also, the second person she'd ever had sex with. The guy who fucking ghosted her *and* kiss and told. *Nikhil Shamdasani.*

"Marley, Meet Nik Sharma, the new Bronze Shadow," Lydia said.

Marley shook her head. "No. Are you being serious right now?"

CHAPTER TWO

Nikhil

Nikhil Shamdasani was having the most surreal day of his life. It started when he woke up and saw a Google alert for his name from a tweet from New Zealand. That was good. Free publicity.

Then he read the tweet. It said that Nikhil Shamdasani, the co-star of the short-lived comedy show *Commuters* (which was still in syndication and strangely popular in Polynesia), was dead. Maybe that wasn't good. Nikhil was definitely exhausted and, to most people, a *nobody*, but he was 100 percent alive. In fact, he was about to become one of the most hated men in Hollywood. Alive and despised.

He let his talent agency know about his untimely Kiwi death, since they presumably had a necromancer process to resurrect celebrities wrongly mourned on social media. That's when he heard from Lydia, his handler, who informed him that they were going to another dentist that afternoon.

Nikhil hated dentists, but the studio insisted on having his front tooth fixed that had been missing its left corner for over a decade now—since Oren Glassman punched him as he was walking out of grade-eleven cooking class. Nikhil had *never* considered fixing that tooth. As far as he was concerned, the chip was a part of his identity. But apparently, *superheroes* needed to be *flawless*. But two different dentists took half a look at his mouth before recommending a full set of veneers, which Nikhil did not want. He liked his real teeth, thank you very much. But finally, today's dentist agreed to repair only the chipped tooth. Seeing himself with an intact tooth after the procedure was the second surreal thing of the day. He looked like himself and a complete stranger at the same time.

But the third surreal thing that happened topped the two before it. While Lydia was paying for the dental work, he thumbed through a three-year-old magazine and saw the breathtakingly beautiful face of the very goddess who caused the chipped tooth in the first place. Nikhil remembered the day well. He had been walking out of cooking class and asked his crush, who happened to be Oren's girlfriend at the time, how she'd liked his coq au vin. Oren assumed another meaning of the phrase and promptly socked Nikhil in the mouth.

Mahreen Kamal.

Nikhil lifted the magazine closer to study the picture. Yeah, that was her. His cooking class buddy, chemistry lab partner, and prom date. He'd fucked things up so monumentally with Mahreen that he still felt nauseous whenever he thought of her. His fist clenched as he read the article. It was about Toronto's top luxury sales associates, and the little profile about her didn't say anything about her personal life, only that she was a consultant and stylist at Reid's, this fancy store in Yorkville. Mahreen was standing behind a counter looking into the camera with the same nonsmile smile she'd perfected back in high school. She was even more stunning than she used to be.

It made sense. Nikhil had gone to an arts-focused high school for their drama program, and Mahreen had been in the fashion program there. He examined her eyes: rich brown with pale green striations. Warm and cool at the same time. And they often had the same detached expression on the surface. Nikhil used to study her eyes more than the periodic table in chemistry, trying to decipher the minuscule changes that gave away her true emotions. He spent most of grade-twelve chemistry trying to get those icy-warm eyes to flash with pleasure… pleasure because of him. He'd once made it a personal goal to make her smile at least once a day—and he could tell which of her smiles was real. But he couldn't read her eyes in this picture. Since he couldn't resist—when Lydia was done with the receptionist, Nikhil told her that he wanted Mahreen as his next stylist.

Which was how he'd ended up here now. In a moment that outsurreal-ed all the surrealism of the day: Nikhil was standing in front of Mahreen Kamal with his face still partially frozen from the dentist, and Mahreen was giving him the same unimpressed glare she'd given him a decade ago when he'd suggested he wear his dad's wedding kurta to prom. By this point, he should have been used to stylists being disappointed in him.

"Mahreen, let me explain," Nikhil said. Or rather, mumbled. He probably should have waited for the numbness to wear off before this reunion.

She looked…amazing. It had been ten years since he'd seen her. He was in show business now—living in LA, where he was regularly surrounded by women who looked like they'd just stepped out of *Vogue* or a *Sports Illustrated* swimsuit issue. But those women weren't like Mahreen. She wasn't just pretty…she was, like, *otherworldly breathtaking*.

She was wearing shiny black pants that perfectly skimmed her long legs. Her hair was in a sleek, high ponytail that cascaded in waves down her back. Her white blouse accentuated her narrow waist. And her breasts...full, round, and generous. Nikhil had fantasized about her body for months before getting a chance to see it in the flesh on prom night. Spectacular. Mahreen still being as beautiful as she'd been at eighteen was immaterial right now, but man...it was messing him up to see those eyes looking at him again.

"You're drooling, Nikhil," Mahreen said.

He wiped his mouth. This was officially the first time they'd spoken since prom night, and he was making a complete fool of himself.

Lydia gave him a scolding look. "He just came from having a chipped tooth fixed. Marley, do you know Nik?"

Mahreen raised a brow. "Nik?"

He nodded. Mostly because he was afraid if he said something wrong, she would run away. Or that spittle would fall from his mouth.

"Is it the tooth Oren broke?" Mahreen asked.

Nikhil nodded again. He tried for a disarming grin, but with only half his mouth working, he wasn't sure he was disarming anyone.

Mahreen chuckled. At his expense, but that was fine. It gave him the same rush it did ten years ago.

She glanced at the two people standing near Lydia. One, a tall, fiftysomething white woman who looked like she'd stepped out of her summer home in the Hamptons, and the other was a burly man with light-brown skin and a goatee wearing a shiny blue three-piece suit. "May I speak to him alone?" Mahreen asked them. Burly Guy stepped forward a bit. A bodyguard? "Nik and I went to high school together," Mahreen said quickly. "I'd like to catch up a bit first. I can handle him."

Yes, she could handle me a decade ago, too.

Nikhil squeezed his lips together. Or half his lips, at least. This was a mistake. *He* was the movie star here…or soon-to-be movie star. *He* was the one who'd fired five stylists. He should have the upper hand. But it had somehow slipped his mind that he would *never* have the upper hand with Mahreen Kamal. That look…she had all the power over him. She always had.

"We'll be in the fitting room." Mahreen smiled, then took Nikhil's hand in hers. Smooth and soft. Long, slender fingers. Perfect round nails almost the same brown as her skin. She guided him to a smaller room and dropped his hand immediately. It had been a decade, but she clearly hadn't forgiven him.

This room had a desk with a computer terminal on one side and a massive three-way mirror with a shiny little white platform in front of it. There was also a pink privacy screen in the corner. He stood awkwardly in the middle of the room as Mahreen closed the door.

She stepped in front of him. "Nikhil, you could have *called* me instead of doing this your-people-call-my-people thing," she said, irritated.

In the small room, he could smell her perfume. Lightly citrusy. Floral. *Expensive.* He didn't know what to say, so he said something ridiculous. "The studio asked me to take a stage name."

Her gaze flicked upward in exasperation before focusing on him. "Do you want *me* to call you *Nik*?"

The shortened…Anglicized version of his name coming out of Mahreen's lips didn't sound right. He shrugged. "No, I really don't. I just thought…Am I supposed to call you *Marley*?"

She nodded curtly with her arms crossed over her chest. Nikhil tried very hard not to peek at the enhanced cleavage that presented. "Yes, please do. May I ask why you *insisted* on me as your stylist?"

"I'm sorry," he said. "It's complicated. Everything happened so fast, and Lydia's big on secrecy."

"Her NDA gave that away. I'm not going to have sex with you."

Wait...was that even an option? "What?"

"If you asked for me to style you because you want to have sex with me, then you may as well walk right out the door, because that isn't going to happen. Reid's doesn't tolerate sexual harassment of the sales staff."

"Why do you think I'm here because I want to have sex with you?"

Her lips pursed. "Maybe you're looking for a stylist with benefits. And with our history...Did you forget about prom night?"

"I don't think anyone has forgotten their prom night. It's an important life event, right?" He cringed the moment the words were out. That was definitely the wrong thing to say. Maybe he should apologize for the past? Would it make a difference after so many years?

She glared at him. This was definitely a mistake. But the truth was, he *wasn't* here because he wanted to sleep with her again. Hell, he wasn't even here to make amends for getting scared and avoiding her after they hooked up on prom night. He was here because he wanted Mahreen to be his savior... only, she didn't want to save him.

Nikhil took a deep breath. "I've had five wardrobe stylists, three personal trainers, two hairstylists, and three dentists in the last two weeks," he said.

"I know. Your handler told me."

"Lydia is really more my babysitter than my handler. The studio flew her in from LA—she's like a Hollywood bad-publicity fixer. They only bring her out for the difficult cases. Apparently, I'm not...adapting well." He ran his hand over his hair, shoulders slumping. "I'm high-maintenance. Difficult. But all those people talk about me like I'm not even there. They see what they can turn me into, not who I am." He shook his head. He shouldn't be saying this. He didn't need to be unloading all this baggage on his *stylist*.

He looked down. "They want to chemically straighten my hair, fix my tooth, and tell me what to wear even when I'm not on set or promoting the movie. I've been working out with a buddy in LA since I got this role, but as soon as I got to Toronto they hired all these boot-camp-style trainers who clearly think I've been wasting my time. Things are intense for me right now, and it's going to get worse. I saw you worked here, and I wanted at least one friendly face on my team. Someone who'll make sure I'm still *me* after this movie star transition."

Nikhil looked up to see Mahreen—*Marley*—staring at him. All of him. From his Brown dad sandals to his shoulder-length hair falling out of the hair tie he'd twisted around his man bun in the morning. What was she seeing? The new Bronze Shadow body (he wasn't quite there yet, but he was leaps and bounds buffer than he'd been in high school)? The old thrift store clothes?

The crisis of confidence? The crippling impostor syndrome?

It felt like her eyes bored into Nik Sharma, soon-to-be international superhero, straight through to Nikhil Shamdasani, one of a handful of desi kids in their suburban high school. The guy who'd convinced her to go to prom with him, who'd *slept* with her at the after-party, then never spoke to her again. Why did he ever think Mahreen Kamal would give him the time of day?

She shook her head, expression still unreadable. What was he doing, pouring his heart out to *Mahreen*, anyway?

"Your family must be proud of you," she said suddenly. "This is quite a role."

He exhaled, looking down. He *thought* his family was proud. But that was also complicated. "I'm sorry to blindside you like this. I understand if you don't want to work with me… because of our history…but…it's great to see you. I mean, you look amazing, which you always did. I'll go." He headed toward the door.

"Wait. Nikhil."

He turned back to look at her. Mahreen had always been posh. Sophisticated. Worldly. He'd never thought she was snobby, although he knew others saw her that way. She was just…reserved. Until she wasn't.

"I'm going through some stuff right now," she said. "Here at work, and…personally." He knew she wouldn't tell him what she was going through. She hadn't told anyone her problems back in high school, either. Except him. "But I can help you. I'll be there for you for that first event Lydia talked about—"

"Comicon and the press junket afterward."

"Yes. But not after that. I cannot work with you past March twentieth. I'm going on a leave of absence." Her gaze shifted to the pink privacy screen, but her expression didn't change.

"I understand. Thank you," he said, trying not to sound too eager. She looked at him again and smiled. A *real* smile that made Nikhil's entire body relax with relief. He wanted to hug her, but he knew she wouldn't want that. And maybe it was best if he kept things as professional as possible…because the memories that came crashing in when her floral-citrus scent hit his nose were probably best buried deep. He put out his hand to shake hers. "Deal. As old friends," he added.

Mahreen nodded as she shook his hand. "As *colleagues*. Let's keep it professional." She motioned toward the door to the main personal shopping office. "Okay, let's get out there before rumors start," she said, heading toward the door.

He snorted. "No worries there. The ironclad NDA prevents gossip."

When they got back out to the main room, Mahreen apologized for her shock at seeing him and explained to the others that she would be happy to work with Nik for the next couple of weeks to get ready for Comicon. Nikhil smiled and nodded along while she spoke.

Everyone sprang into action. Lydia outlined what he'd need for Comicon, and Mahreen said she'd send inspiration pictures to her the following day for studio approval. Nikhil himself wouldn't be doing any of this approving. Once that was settled, a septuagenarian tailor came in and took Nikhil's measurements.

When they were all done, Mahreen smiled her professional smile and said goodbye. The glimpse of warmth she'd had in the fitting room a few minutes ago was long gone. Clearly, she'd meant it when she said that she would keep things professional between them. Maybe he wasn't getting his friend back. Maybe all he'd done by finding Mahreen was add a touch more humiliation to his life now that his high school crush, one-time lover, and the most beautiful person he'd ever met also thought he was a man-baby diva.

He shouldn't have come here. Nikhil wished he could go back to this morning when everyone thought he was dead.

CHAPTER THREE

Marley

Angel Durand's bra-whipping incident was clearly cosmic foreshadowing for all the strange twists fate was throwing at Marley's life. Of course, the strangest twist had to be the reemergence of Nikhil Shamdasani, her chemistry lab partner who was now apparently a soon-to-be Hollywood superstar. Marley honestly didn't need the reminder of that time in her life, *especially* now.

But today's moment might be even stranger. Marley was now standing in a hospital examination room, and a fifty-something silver fox of a plastic surgeon was sitting on a chair in front of her. The doctor's eyes were inches from Marley's naked breasts, and he was inspecting them with a thoroughness that no hookup of Marley's, male or female, had ever come close to matching. He even lifted each breast to inspect the underside. That wasn't the weirdest part of this experience, though. The weirdest part was that none of this felt weird at all.

Dr. Andrew Abernathy was considered one of the best plastic surgeons in the country for breast work—both augmentation and reconstruction. And being the subject of his full attention now was a relief more than anything else. Marley had been waiting over a *year* to have a prophylactic double mastectomy with reconstruction, and finally the surgery was two weeks away.

"We've decided on a one-step direct-to-implant procedure, right?" the doctor asked.

Marley nodded. One step—remove her natural, healthy, and very-much-appreciated breasts and immediately replace them with silicone facsimiles. Everyone told her she was so lucky she was a candidate for this procedure. That it was so much easier than tissue expanders or using tissue from elsewhere on her body to create new breasts. They said she was lucky Dr. Abernathy would be the one operating on her.

Marley didn't feel very lucky about any of it.

After the examination, the doctor explained the process while Marley sat on the table with her gown pulled shut. It sounded so...simple. And terrifying. She dug her fingernails into the flesh of her thigh.

"I'll order implants in several sizes and see what fits you best when we're in there," he said. Just like Marley bringing dresses in several sizes to a customer in the fitting room. "Do you have a size preference? We can't achieve a drastic size change with this procedure, but if you'd like to go a hair larger or smaller, I could accommodate that."

Marley liked her body shape just fine. "I'd like to stay the same if possible."

He nodded, then turned to get something from a cupboard behind him. It was a round, clear water balloon–looking thing. Marley knew this was a breast implant. "This is the model I'll be using on you. I think this size will fit best." He handed it to her.

The implant was large in her hand, and the plastic-like shell felt smooth while the inside was soft and squishy. It was cool, heavy, and it felt so fake…so not like a body part. Marley squeezed the implant with trembling fingers. She handed it back to the doctor. How could something that felt so sterile ever feel like a part of her?

"How much time will I have to take off work?" she asked.

"What do you do?"

"I'm a retail sales consultant. Luxury fashion."

"Oh, like at Saks Fifth Avenue?"

"Reid's."

He smiled. "My wife's favorite store. I assume you're on your feet a lot? I'd say you'll need at least six weeks. Could be longer. You can apply for unemployment insurance if your employer doesn't offer sick leave."

"We have short-term disability."

"Excellent. The nurse will provide you with a note. I'll have her give you all the pre- and post-op instructions. Do you have any more questions for me first?"

Marley did not, so Dr. Abernathy left. After Marley put her clothes on, an RN came in to give her a huge packet of instructions. She showed Marley the drain tubes that would be inserted into her body during the surgery to drain excess fluid and showed her how to empty the bulbs twice a day. Her stomach churned as she squeezed the empty bulb. Marley remembered helping her mother with her drains after her mastectomy. Marley wasn't squeamish…normally. But she'd never had surgery before and had no idea what to expect.

"Do you live alone?" the nurse asked.

Marley shook her head. "No."

"Good. You'll need help for the first few days…especially overnight."

The nurse went over bathing instructions and the medications Marley would be prescribed after surgery for pain and to prevent infection. It was a lot to remember, and her mind kept wandering. She was glad it was all written down.

I can do this. Marley tightened her fist on the paper covering the examination table.

The nurse handed her a pamphlet. On the front of it were a few women sitting around a table, clearly a stock image, and the words *BRCA Peer Support.*

"What's this?"

"A support group meets near here once a month…Jaime, the group facilitator, is fantastic. Her contact information is there. Oh, and you'd be eligible for this, too." She handed Marley another pamphlet, this one for a charity that helped women who had breast surgery and/or cancer treatment with clothes, makeup, and wigs.

Marley took the pamphlets, adding them to her pile of paperwork, even though she doubted she'd use them. She wasn't really a support group kind of person, and she certainly didn't need help with clothes and makeup, considering she worked in luxury fashion. She opened the clasp on her bag to slip the paperwork in.

After finding out that she carried the BRCA1 genetic mutation that put her at an 80 percent breast cancer risk, Marley had seen countless surgeons and specialists and dealt with torturous mammograms and breast MRIs. Now she just wanted the surgery to be done. She didn't want to be living with this anxiety anymore. Every day until her surgery, the chance of cancer coming for her like it had for her mother and her aunt just went up. Marley had ticking time bombs attached to her chest.

But that didn't mean Marley wasn't *completely terrified*

about the surgery itself. Or about what her life would be like afterward.

Marley straightened her spine and swung her Chloé bag over her shoulder. Being scared helped no one. All Marley could do was plow ahead. She had no choice.

"Hey, handsome," Marley said as she walked into her east-end two story. "I missed you. I should have stayed in bed snuggling you this morning." Her cat, McQueen, responded with a long meow as he came to greet her, his fluffy tail standing sky-high behind him.

"You don't say," Marley responded, leaning down to pet McQueen on his soft, tan head. McQueen continued to meow conversationally, telling Marley all about his day. As Marley caught up with her cat, she heard a distinct rhythmic thumping on the floorboards. Marley rolled her eyes, intending to ignore the summons. It was Shayne, her roommate and ride-or-die best friend forever, but she wasn't in the mood for his antics right now. She wanted to sit with her cat and a hot ginger tea and mentally process that doctor's appointment. Alone. She put a pot of water on to boil and took out her tin of black loose tea.

Loud thumps reverberated through the floors again. *Ugh.* Why had she agreed to this ridiculous communication system when they moved into this house last year? They were renting from Shayne's grandmother, who'd just moved to a senior-living apartment, which was the only way Shayne and Marley could afford a whole house in Toronto. Even an extremely narrow house that had barely been upgraded in thirty years. But they both loved the vintage seventies and eighties furniture and decor and had added even more houseplants and macrame after moving in. Shayne was a fashion photographer and his office/studio space was in the basement. He'd developed this code system to communicate with Marley when he didn't want to come upstairs. Why he didn't text like a normal person was anyone's guess.

Marley ignored the thumping as she grated fresh ginger and swirled it into the hot water and black tea. She added milk after it came to a boil and was soon curled up with her big orange mug on the goldenrod-yellow sofa with McQueen. She was inhaling the scent of the sweet ginger tea when Shayne finally gave in. She could hear his heavy footsteps as he climbed the basement stairs.

"Did you forget our code?" he said the moment he opened the basement door.

"I don't know Morse code, remember?"

"Neither do I. That's why this chart is here." He tapped the laminated card stuck to the wall. Shayne was dressed in white ankle pants and a fuzzy pink sweater that glowed against his warm-brown skin. He looked like he could comfortably fit in both on a Paris runway and on Sesame Street. Shayne was biracial, with a Black Jamaican father and a white mother, and was an absolute *savant* at picking the perfect shade to complement any skin tone.

Marley made a mental note to surreptitiously have Shayne help her with menswear trends. She just had to figure out how without violating the NDA. Shayne knew Nikhil from high school, too. And knew everything about Marley and Nikhil's history. Shayne had even offered to chip another of Nikhil's teeth when he didn't call her after prom.

"Sexy," Marley said, indicating the fluffy sweater. "With that thing on your upper lip, you look like you just arrived from Copacabana." Marley was not a fan of his recent thin mustache. Just like she wasn't a fan of Nikhil's mountain-man beard earlier.

"Stop flirting—you're not my type," Shayne deadpanned, plopping next to her on the sofa. Which made McQueen hop from Marley's lap to Shayne's, purring. There had *never* been any *actual* flirting of any kind between Marley and Shayne. Marley was bisexual, but Shayne was strictly into men and had informed her of that the day they met in grade-nine art class. Before Marley could put her own preferences into words, actually.

"What was your coded message, anyway?" Marley asked.

"I said, *Put something cute on. People are coming over. Maybe that yellow floral romper with a wide green headband.*"

Marley snorted. "There's no way you said all that in Morse code with a broom handle on the ceiling."

Shayne gave another deadpan glare. "I said the important parts." He looked at his watch. "Be quick. They'll be here soon."

"Who is *people*, anyway?"

"Ruby and Reena."

Marley frowned. "I don't have to dress up for my *cousins*."

"I want to take pictures. We have a surprise for you."

Marley knew better than to argue, so she hopped off the sofa to change. Reena was Marley's cousin on her dad's side while Ruby was her cousin on her mom's side. The two were also Marley's closest friends, other than Shayne. These three might be her favorite people in the world, but she would have preferred the alone time tonight.

But a knock on the door stopped Marley while she was still on the stairs. Shayne let them in. Ruby was carrying a bunch of colorful tote bags, and Reena was carrying a large cake box, which wasn't out of the ordinary for her—Reena owned a bakery.

They dropped their things on the dining table.

"I'm confused. Did we have dinner plans?" Marley asked, watching Ruby unload Thai takeout and wrapped gifts from her bags.

"It's a surprise party!" Shayne said, clapping. "Your ta-ta-to-your-tatas party!"

Ugh. She should have known. Only a handful of people knew Marley was having a mastectomy. And other than her parents, all of them were now in this room. She gave Ruby a concerned glance, but Ruby was still unloading the Thai food, looking unbothered by this party's theme.

"Look what I made!" Reena said, opening the cake box with a flourish.

It was a boob cake—an iced cake in the shape of round, brown breasts with a purple piped buttercream bra. And because Reena was an excellent cake decorator, it was beautiful.

Thanks for the Mammaries was written in cursive across the cake's cleavage.

Marley's eyebrows rose. "My surgery isn't for two weeks… Why are we celebrating *now*?" Actually, why were they *celebrating* at all? She was literally having body parts removed—not really something to celebrate. But clearly, the three had gone to a lot of work for this get-together, so she didn't want to complain.

"We're celebrating all month!" Shayne said. "I mean, I took you to that Scandi spa for your bikini photo shoot last week."

True. Shayne had surprised her with a trip to a Nordic spa where he'd insisted on taking about a million pictures of her in a swimsuit so she would have a record of her body pre-mastectomy. She wasn't sure she'd ever look at those pictures, though. Why would she, when she could never have that body back?

None of this was how Marley would prefer to cope with her upcoming surgery. And she was pretty sure Shayne knew that. He knew she was a *very* private person. It almost felt like Shayne was "performative best-friending" and making a big show out of supporting her even though he knew this wasn't the way Marley would *want* support. But that was ridiculous. Planning this party was thoughtful. She should enjoy it.

Shayne again insisted Marley change her clothes, and soon they were crowded around their tiny dining table eating Thai red curry noodles, fish cakes, and mango salad while sipping bright-orange Thai iced tea. It was all delicious. Thai was Marley's comfort food.

"Hey, question for you," Reena said as Marley slurped some noodles. "My friend Andrea wants you to take her shopping. Any chance you'll have any time before surgery?"

"Yeah, absolutely," Marley said. On top of owning a bakery, Reena had a pretty popular YouTube cooking channel and lots of content-creator friends. Marley had gone shopping with a few of them to help them find looks for their videos. "I'll send you my work schedule."

"Marley, you should be *charging* these influencers to style them," Shayne said.

Marley shook her head. "Nope. No interest in that—I could *not* manage working for myself." All the freelance stylists Marley knew did a ton of content creation of their own and hustled to get clients. Marley preferred to be behind the scenes.

"Reid's will suck your soul right out of your body. I can't believe you *want* to stay there." Shayne would know. He'd only lasted a year as a menswear associate at Reid's.

"It won't be as bad if I move to personal shopping," Marley said. "I could be more selective of my customers." That, and she could have a private office. And not have the likes of Tova Kaplan trying to steal her commissions.

"How's that going?" Shayne asked. "Any word of them opening up a position yet?"

Ruby raised a brow. "Ooh, is that why Erin wanted to see you yesterday?"

Marley reached across the table to get the container of mango salad. "She needed my help with a client. Can't really talk about it." She piled more salad on her plate.

Reena beamed. "Is Erin the personal shopper? That's awesome!"

Marley nodded. It was awesome. But it could also be a disaster...if she screwed it up. Or if Nikhil really was the man-baby that his handler thought he was.

Marley was still not sure why she agreed to work with him. He just looked so...small, despite his new superhero muscles. He said no one really *saw* him. And that reminded Marley of when she was eighteen and her favorite aunt, Maryam Aunty, was going through cancer treatment.

Marley hadn't told anyone at school that the woman who was more like a mother to her than her actual mother was sick. But somehow Nikhil, the never-serious, wisecracking guy who sat next to her in chemistry every day, saw that she wasn't happy. She eventually told him everything, and he turned out to be a great listener. Nikhil had been there for her like no one else. He let her vent, or cry, or whatever every day. When he convinced her to go to prom with him instead of staying home like she wanted to, she agreed.

And of course, it all ended in disaster. Nikhil told everyone what they had done at the prom after-party, and Marley realized he'd only been nice to get her in bed. Marley left school soon after prom because her aunt got even sicker. And she never saw or spoke to Nikhil again.

But even if his motivation back then was only to get into her prom dress, he *had* helped her. He made her laugh every day at the worst point in her life. She wasn't sure how she would have gotten through it without him. She said yes to styling him now so she could repay him.

But this time she would keep her boundaries up. She had no intention of growing attached to Nikhil in any way, even as a friend. She simply didn't have the bandwidth for that right now.

Marley, her cousins, and Shayne continued talking while eating. Reena told them about how her newest YouTube video was outperforming the others, and she couldn't figure out why. Shayne told them about a fashion shoot he'd done for an up-and-coming designer who wasn't even twenty yet. And Ruby steered the conversation toward her favorite topic: her longtime dream of moving to England.

Marley hadn't loved the idea of a party to celebrate losing body parts, but this was nice. She didn't have a ton of friends—in fact, these three were her only true friends left in the city. And it suited Marley perfectly. These people knew her…She could relax and be herself with them.

After dinner, they sat in the living room.

"Okay, before cake, we have presents!" Shayne said. They each handed Marley a gift—it looked like Ruby had wrapped them all in Reid's wrapping paper.

Marley opened Ruby's first. It was two soft rayon knit shirts in pale pastel colors with snaps down the front.

"They're specifically made for post-mastectomy," Ruby said. "There are hidden pockets for your drain bulbs inside. I wish I'd had ones like these after my surgery. I kept my drain bulbs in a Home Depot tool belt."

She smiled at Ruby. "Thank you so much. They're lovely."

Reena's gift ended up being some hi-tech microwave cookware and an IOU for homecooked meals after surgery—also very thoughtful. Shayne's gift, on the other hand, was a set of bird-pun coasters. Some said *Boobies* on them and had the names and pictures of several species of booby birds. There were also coasters that said *Tits* and *Hooters*.

Marley raised a brow. "Seriously, Shayne?"

"I ordered some *cock* ones, too, but those are for me. Anyway, your real gift is coming tomorrow. I found a secondhand recliner for you to use while you're recovering. It's *hideous*. We'll burn it after you're recovered."

Marley chuckled. Shayne then took about a million pictures of the cake and of Marley holding it. He wanted a picture of her cutting the cake, but Marley refused. She looked away while Reena cut and served it. It was delicious, at least.

"I made your favorite lemon curd cake so you'd talk," Reena said.

Marley frowned. "What am I supposed to talk about?"

"Your pre-op appointment," Reena said. "How did it go?"

"It was fine."

Shayne exhaled dramatically. "Marley, please say something

other than *fine*. Don't make me bring out my *Hammer into Marley* free pass."

Marley rolled her eyes. "Shayne, I don't think *Hammer into Marley* means what you think it means."

Everyone was quiet, while Shayne hopefully reconsidered his choice of phrasing.

Reena finally gave Marley a pointed look. "Marley, you need to *talk* about what's happening to you."

"I'm talking now, aren't I?"

"Has Jacqueline approved your time off yet?" Ruby asked.

Marley shook her head. "No, but I just emailed the request today. I have a doctor's note, so she doesn't really have a choice."

Shayne snorted. "Oh, believe me—Jacqueline will find a way to make this harder for you."

"Look at everything coming up roses for y'all, though," Reena said, changing the subject because she clearly sensed Marley's discomfort. "Ruby has plans for her future, Marley's finally having surgery and hobnobbing with the personal shopper, and Shayne's career is exploding. Maybe you guys will break your love curses, too."

Since getting married, Reena had been irritatingly preoccupied with everyone being as in love as she was. Marley didn't think it was possible to achieve relationship *perfection* as epic as Reena and Nadim's.

"Reena, there is no love curse!" Shayne said emphatically.

"Then why have none of you had a date this year?" Reena asked smugly.

Ruby frowned. "I had a date two months ago."

Shayne rolled his eyes. "You told me about him, Ruby. He was *literally* a clown. Like, he works at the circus."

Ruby nodded. "He was remarkably dull. That's the last

time I swipe right on someone just because they were born in Liverpool. He sounded like John Lennon and looked like Ronald McDonald."

"Wait—he didn't show up to your date dressed in a costume, did he?" Reena asked.

Ruby nodded solemnly.

Shayne snorted. "I do agree that Marley needs someone, though. *Cat lady* isn't a relationship status."

Marley scowled at Shayne as McQueen hopped onto her lap.

"See? At least have a hookup. You've been celibate since Celeste," Shayne said.

Marley had plenty of reasons to not want to date right now. The main one was, of course, dating before a mastectomy sounded like a terrifying prospect. Dating after a mastectomy seemed even worse. In fact, everything was a terrifying prospect lately. She took a bite of the cake. At least she still had good food.

What Marley's friends didn't get was that she couldn't exactly look for a committed relationship when she had no clue what would happen to her, healthwise, in the future. And casual hookups had never worked well for her. She rarely felt any sexual draw until she had an emotional connection with someone. She scratched McQueen's chin as he started purring loudly. Being a cat lady was so much easier.

"You need a *one last time* for sex," Shayne said.

Marley stared at him. *One last time*s were another of Shayne's brainchildren—basically, he insisted there were things Marley needed to do one last time before her surgery. One of them was fly on an airplane, which was why they flew to Montreal for the weekend a few months ago. The bikini photo shoot at the spa was a *one last time*.

"Don't you want to do it one more time with your old body?" Shayne asked.

Ruby nodded. "You really should. I had wild monkey sex with a French professor right before my mastectomy. You won't have any sensation in your boobs afterward, you know." Ruby poked her own breast. "Can't feel a thing."

Yeah, Marley knew. She had no intention of being in a relationship now…but she was sad she'd never have *that* sensation again.

"And don't be picky," Reena said. "All three of you need to be more open-minded."

"We *are* open-minded," Shayne said.

"Have you even been on one date since Anderson?" Reena asked.

Shayne glared sharply at Reena. "We're not supposed to mention that name."

Anderson was *the one who got away.* Marley wasn't even sure what happened between them, but she knew Shayne was nowhere near being over the man. It didn't help that Anderson was a host on *The Confab,* a live afternoon TV talk show. She knew how much it stung for Shayne to have to see Anderson's face on billboards and bus ads across Toronto.

Marley didn't consider herself *irrationally* picky. If she were willing to date, she'd have only two requirements for potential partners. One, they couldn't run away scared when they heard the c-word. *Cancer.* Marley was having this surgery so she wouldn't get sick, but she didn't know what the future held for her or her family with this defective gene running through their DNA. And two, they had to be comfortable with whatever choices Marley made with her own body for her health without sticking any of their own unwanted opinions in.

But those two requirements seemed huge. Who'd want to sign up for that?

After a bit of awkward silence, Marley shrugged. "It's more important for us to focus on our careers right now. Shayne, didn't you say you wanted to get more runway work before anything else?"

At that, Shayne looked at Reena. "Yeah…about that. Um…"

Marley frowned. "What's going on? What haven't you guys told me?"

"I had a call yesterday," Shayne said. "From Philip Tanaka."

"Holy shit. *Really?*" Philip Tanaka was Shayne's idol, a photographer who'd moved from the fine art world to the fashion world.

Shayne nodded. "We'd been emailing back and forth since you made me send him that embarrassingly gushy email. He invited me to join him as his assistant for spring Paris Fashion Week. I'd learn all about runway work from one of the best."

Marley's eyes widened. "*Shut. Up.* Seriously?" This was amazing.

Shayne nodded.

Marley hopped out of her seat to tackle Shayne in a tight hug. Shayne deserved this so much. He'd been trying to break into major runway work for so long.

"Okay, okay," Shayne said, gently pushing her away. "You might not be so happy when you hear the details."

Marley frowned. "What? Why?"

"Paris Fashion Week is soon. Like, in two weeks."

Marley fell heavily back in her seat. *Shit.* Her surgery was in two weeks. Shayne would be deserting her right after her mastectomy. But this was too amazing an opportunity to turn down.

Marley forced a smile. This news was probably why he'd planned this party. To soften the blow. "It's fine. I'll go to my parents' to recover."

Shayne shook his head. "You *cannot* go to your parents'. Your dad will, like…pretend whatever is happening to you isn't happening, and your mom will tell everyone on the family WhatsApp every detail about your recovery. No. Your friends will help."

Reena nodded. "Yeah. I can come over every day. I just hired a new part-timer and—"

Marley shook her head. "Reena, you can't come all the way here every day!" As a baker, she was up making bread at three a.m. daily. Marley couldn't ask Reena for help after that. "My mom is home all day. It will be fine."

Shayne shook his head. "What if we got a bunch of people to take turns coming? Grams too. We'll set up shifts."

Marley hated the idea of putting that many people out. "Maybe I can put the surgery off…" She was pretty sure she couldn't. Dr. Abernathy had a long waiting list.

"You cannot put it off," Reena said. "It's lifesaving surgery."

"It's not lifesaving," Marley said. "My last mammogram was fine."

Shayne put his hands on his hips. "Mahreen Abigail Kamal, you know that with your family history and genetics, this isn't a case of *if* you'll get breast cancer but *when*. Do you really want to go through what your mother went through?"

Marley frowned. "*Abigail*?"

"You don't have a middle name—so I'm loaning you my sister's. If you'd rather, you can borrow mine, but Beauregard is *horrendous*, and it's bad enough that I'm saddled with it."

"Marley," Ruby added after being silent for a while. "Think about my mother." Ruby didn't have to say anything else.

Marley leaned back in her chair, looking up as tears filled her eyes. No one needed to remind Marley to think of Ruby's mother. She was always thinking about Maryam Aunty.

When Marley was clashing with her parents on just about everything, Maryam was the *only* one who understood. Marley had even told Maryam Aunty and Ruby about her first girlfriend when Marley was fourteen, and they had kept her bisexuality a secret. Marley and Ruby's passion for clothes and fashion came from Maryam, who worked as a seamstress from her home. Honestly, Marley wouldn't be the person she was now without her aunt. Maryam Aunty died of breast cancer when Marley was eighteen, right after Marley graduated from high school, and Marley still wasn't over losing her.

When Marley's own mother was diagnosed with the same cancer two years ago, Mom's genes were tested because of the family history of cancer. First Mom, then Ruby, then finally Marley were all found to carry the BRCA1 genetic mutation, which gave them an 80 percent lifetime chance of developing breast cancer and a 40 percent chance of ovarian cancer. Mom had a mastectomy after chemo and now wore external prosthetics. Ruby had been living in Montreal back then, and she had a prophylactic—a preventative mastectomy—there soon after.

And now it was Marley's turn for surgery. The timing sucked, but she needed to do this.

Reena's voice lowered. "It's your decision to make. We'll support you either way. I can't imagine how hard this is, Marley, but we got you. I'll come every day. And Nadim, if you want him. We got you, Marl."

"I can help, too," Ruby added.

Reena maybe could help, but Marley wasn't going to let herself be a burden on Ruby. Ruby had already been through enough thanks to this stupid gene.

Marley smiled at her friends. "Don't worry about me. I'm *having* the surgery. No matter how hard it is," she said softly. She had no choice. She couldn't go through what her mother went through. What her aunt went through. She blinked away the tears. "I'll figure it out." *Hard* seemed like the biggest understatement right now.

"I'm already planning your one-month-post-mastectomy party," Shayne said. "I'll get streamers. Now, how about lychee martinis to wash down that Thai?"

CHAPTER FOUR

Nikhil

Nikhil was one hour into his first styling meeting with Mahreen, and his self-esteem was even lower than before. Why had he thought all this pressure and impostor syndrome would miraculously go away by having someone who *knew* him pick out his clothes? Ridiculous. They were just clothes. Lydia and Kaelyn, the studio publicist, were right now arguing about his outfit while Mahreen was looking back and forth between them like it was a tennis match, and Nikhil felt as invisible as ever.

And of course, Mahreen was still *so* beautiful that he didn't know what to do with himself when he was in the same room with her. Just like when they were in high school and he'd discovered that sitting next to the hottest girl in the school wasn't the windfall he'd thought it would be, especially if he wanted to actually pass the class.

At least in chemistry Mahreen had been focused on the teacher, or whatever chemical warfare they were cooking up. Now her attention was 100 percent on *Nikhil*. She narrowed her eyes and bit her lip as she eyed him in his newest getup—black pants, a casual-ish white shirt rolled up at the sleeves, and a funky black asymmetrical vest. Nikhil thought the outfit was cool, even if it wasn't something he'd normally wear. Too monochromatic and stiff. But Lydia said the studio had requested dark colors to move him away from his goofy comedian image.

"That looks too Indian inspired," Kaelyn said, shaking her head. "We're going for mainstream looks. The pants are good, though."

Nikhil snorted. Because God forbid anyone reminded people of Nikhil's homeland. It was one thing to hire a nonwhite actor—but apparently it was important that his skin tone be the only *foreign*-looking thing about him.

Nikhil inspected himself in the three-way mirror. A Nehru collar didn't automatically make something Indian, anyway. He thought he looked vaguely sci-fi, which should work for a comic convention, right?

"The pants need to be taken in," Ernesto said. He was poking and prodding at Nikhil's waist, which should have tickled, but apparently, he was immune to tickles by grouchy men who didn't look him in the eye. Nikhil had tried to make a joke about how he expected someone to shove five-dollar bills in his underpants after undressing so many times, and Ernesto had only frowned and pointed him in the direction of the changing room with a new pair of pants.

The tailor, Fernando, shuffled in front of him and started pinning his waist.

Lydia shook her head. "Not too much! He still needs to increase muscle mass before the announcement! He *should* have done it by now." There was no way he could increase his muscle mass that much in a week. Lydia clearly didn't think Nikhil was working hard enough.

Fernando nodded but still pinned the pants, poking Nikhil in the process. Nikhil wondered if it was on purpose.

"What do you think, Mahreen?" Nikhil asked. Mostly because he wanted to say something to remind the others that he was a human, not a mannequin.

"It's Marley," she reminded him, looking at his lower half. She still smelled citrusy…like a fancy lemonade he'd had in LA with lavender and thyme in it. She stepped closer, and the smooth skin of her neck made him swallow.

Nikhil pictured Fernando putting five-dollar bills in his pants. That helped.

Mahreen suddenly pulled her phone out of her jacket pocket and made a call.

"Ruby, can you run into menswear and get me the Borealis and Sons sage pants, jacket, and vest? Bring them to the personal shopping suite and text me when you're at the door. I'll come out and get them." She named Nikhil's size, then also asked for a black satin scarf.

"We said no suit for Comicon. And sage as in *green*?" Lydia questioned.

"I want to try something…" Mahreen frowned, her perfect eyebrows knitting in concentration. She was wearing a black knee-length skirt today that hugged her curves like it had been painted on. Nikhil had no idea how she walked in it, especially in three-inch heels—these in a shade of tan that perfectly matched her warm brown skin. Her cream blouse was looser today, fine silk skimming over her figure. Her hair was up again, this time in a sleek bun at her neck.

He needed to stop staring at Mahreen, but maybe she needed not to be standing half a foot away from him looking like…her.

"I'm all for some color," Nikhil said. "I'm not sure this emo-vampire look is really me. Unless you can make me sparkle."

Mahreen finally looked at his face, and there was the faintest *real* smile in her eyes. So faint that Nikhil was sure no one else noticed it, but it was the same smile she used to give him when he showed her the silly doodles he'd drawn in his chemistry textbook. He looked down, flustered. Yeah, this was a mistake. He'd hoped Mahreen would make him feel like himself again, but he forgot that the self Mahreen made him feel like was usually somewhere between mortified, aroused, and sheepish.

Everyone started discussing whether a green suit was appropriate for Comicon, when the door to the personal shopping suite suddenly opened wide. Mahreen immediately rushed to it to prevent Nikhil from being seen.

"Tova," Mahreen said, "I thought Ruby was bringing..." She was clearly struggling to keep this person from entering the suite. Lydia motioned Nikhil toward the changing room, so he rushed there to hide. After a few minutes, Mahreen came in.

She held out the green suit. "Sorry about that. Apparently, people are gossiping about who this supersecret VIP is."

"Who do they think I am?"

"Current prediction is either Harry Styles or the Weeknd."

Nikhil snorted as he took the suit. It was made of the softest buttery fabric, and the green was light and a little washed out. It wasn't what he expected. "I'll look like celery in head-to-toe green. Are you hoping someone will hire me as an Indian Hulk?" He made an angry Hulk snarl.

Mahreen almost smiled again. "Put it on, then come out." She left the changing room.

He put on the suit, then stepped out into the main suite and stood in front of the others on the box facing the three-way mirror.

And holy hell, he was surprised at what he saw. The suit was a touch big, but not that bad. And the color—he would have thought the pale green would make him appear sickly, but the shade made his skin glow. He actually did kind of sparkle. He didn't look like himself anymore. Not Nik Sharma the chiseled, plastic superhero, and not Nikhil, who preferred loud, bright clothes. He seemed like a whole different person.

Was this the person Mahreen was imagining when she studied him just now with intensity?

Kaelyn stepped closer to the mirror. "That's unexpected." She eyed him with narrowed eyes. "It's pretty good, actually. Still a suit, though. A bit too conservative."

"I think we can break it up," Marley said. She called someone again to bring a gray vest. The person brought it without trying to push their way into personal shopping, so that was good.

And the green suit with the pale-gray vest and white shirt—plus, weirdly, a black scarf—all looked amazing. He looked cool and sophisticated. Like Shah Rukh Khan in the nineties. The slim cut of the jacket showed off his superhero physique, but the color prevented him from seeming too alpha-male buff.

And amazingly, even if he didn't look like himself, he *felt* like himself. Or at least a person he would want to be.

"Winner, winner, chicken dinner," he said under his breath, mesmerized at his reflection. He was sure he saw the barest hint of a smile on Mahreen's face behind him. Nikhil felt warmth flow through his body.

"I agree," Lydia said. "I think we've found our Comicon outfit."

After enduring weeks of preparation, hours at the gym, media trainers, publicists, all those stylists (hair and wardrobe), and of course, Lydia, Nikhil was finally at Comicon. It was all down to this moment—when the casting for the most coveted action role of the year would be announced, and fans would either be thrilled or disgusted.

Nikhil was nervous. Actually, that was a gross understatement. He was alone in a private dressing room behind an auditorium filled with Ironis superfans, with his pounding head in his shaking hands, wondering if the bank would take his parents' house if he ran out the back door.

Well, he wasn't actually alone. Lydia and two people from the studio were right outside his door. Probably there to make sure he *didn't* run after all the work they'd put into their make-a-celebrity project. He was wearing the outfit Marley had picked for him, so it kind of felt like she was here, too. He ran his fingers over the smooth silk of the scarf. He hoped he'd draped it properly.

It had been a week since that meeting in the personal shopping suite when she'd surprised them all by choosing a green suit for him. They'd picked a few other outfits after that, but this was still his favorite.

He assumed he'd see more of Marley after that, but he hadn't. He'd gone back to Reid's once more—after the tailor finished the alterations—but Marley hadn't been there. Just that surly guy, Ernesto, and Fernando the tailor. Who didn't seem to appreciate Nikhil humming the opening bar to his namesake ABBA song while he checked to see if the waist of the green pants fit.

But it was fine. Marley had done what she was hired to do. Nikhil didn't have regrets for insisting the studio hire her—he'd wanted Marley to pick out his clothes because he'd hoped she'd help him retain a little bit of himself. And Marley had succeeded there. He was more comfortable in these clothes than in anything those other stylists had picked for him.

But he couldn't deny that seeing her again—seeing that she was as perfect as he remembered, maybe even more—brought back feelings that were a little inconvenient right now. Feelings of regret for how things had ended between them in the past, and a realization that he was just as besotted with Mahreen Kamal as ever.

The door to his dressing room opened. "Hey, hot stuff," said a voice behind him.

"Esther." Nikhil grinned widely and turned to face his agent. "I had no idea you'd be here."

Esther put one hand on her hip. "What, and miss the *biggest* announcement for my *biggest* star in his *biggest* role?"

Esther Brownstein had been his agent for five years and was one of Nikhil's favorite people in the industry. Though a few years younger than he was, she talked like a stereotypical 1950s old Hollywood agent, thanks to having grown up in the business. She worked at her dad's agency and had no shortage of up-and-coming superstars in her client roster.

Nikhil leaned way down to kiss her on both cheeks.

"Darling," Esther said, squeezing his biceps, "we need to have a tête-à-tête before the big event. I've locked the door. Just had a call from LA: you're going on a press tour before shooting."

Nikhil frowned. "What? Why? More than the junket tomorrow?"

"Yeah. They did some market testing and are worried. So

I said, 'Get him on *Drew*! On *Jimmy*! Hell, send him overseas to *Graham*.'" She reached up and pinched his cheek. Someone had shaved him a few days ago, so the beard he'd had for two years was now gone. "Let them see that this face is cuter than any Ryan or Chris."

"Wait—*you* suggested the press tour?"

Esther nodded, then glanced at the door. "I'll lay it straight, kiddo. I don't like that they're announcing this with such fanfare before the movie even shoots. I think they're using this event to see what they can get away with, if you know what I mean."

What she meant was the studio wanted to see if the racist fanboys would be on board with a Brown Bronze Shadow before it was too late to recast the role.

"You think they'll fire me before we even shoot?"

She shrugged. "Scripts can still change, and they can edit your role to practically nothing if they decide it's not worth irritating their fan base. Which, fine. You and I still get paid. But...we want sequel money. We want *merchandising*."

Nikhil had no idea if he wanted a sequel. Or action figures. The money he was making from this one role was more than enough to pay off his parents' debts. "I'm not sure if I want more than the one film, though."

Esther put her hands on his arms again. "In this industry, you're only as good as your last title." She let go of him and sighed. "Maybe you don't *want* to be an *action hero*, but you do want to work, right? Any role will be hard to come by if this one goes south. Especially with your..." She waved her hand at his face. Esther didn't have to say it. He knew she meant especially with him being nonwhite. "You don't want to be living in your parents' basement forever, right?"

"I'm only *temporarily* living in my parents' basement," he

said. He still had his LA apartment—sublet while he was in Toronto. Before this role, he could only afford that apartment because of his collection of side hustles. He really did not want to go back to driving for Uber or fertilizing lawns in LA.

"Do the press tour, gorgeous. I'll work with them to get it as short as possible. Be charming. Make them fall in love with you like I did. The fans are going to eat up those pearly whites, and I'll have a contract on my desk for a standalone Bronze Shadow origin movie before this one's out. You wait and see."

Nikhil exhaled. It didn't sound like he had much of a choice. "Okay. Fine. But there are only six weeks until shooting, and I'm in training and rehearsals nine to five every day."

"Yep! That's why we're pushing for a short trip. Stay tuned. The cogs are turning."

Nikhil's phone rang then. He looked at the screen. It was an unknown number.

Esther patted his arm. "We'll catch up after the event. I'll be right here cheering you on. Knock 'em dead, hot stuff. They are going to *adore* you!"

Nikhil reluctantly accepted the call the moment Esther left the dressing room.

"Nikhil, are you seriously *living* with Mom and Dad now?"

Fuck. His brother. How did he get Nikhil's new phone number?

"Arjun. Where are you calling from?"

"I have a phone now. I found a guy to come look at the basement tomorrow. Can you clear it out?"

"Look at it? Why?"

"To renovate! Do you know how much Toronto rent is bringing in these days? My guy said—"

"Arjun, I'm literally living in the basement." Plus, the last thing his mother needed was contractors and chaos in the house. Not to mention, who was this "guy," and where did Arjun find him? As if Arjun hadn't done enough damage to the family.

"I thought you were some big shot—why are you living in the basement?" Arjun asked.

Arjun shouldn't be the one talking about less desirable living situations. "It's temporary. Mom and Dad refinanced the house once because of you. Leave them and their house alone."

"I'm trying to get that money back for them! I can act as a real estate broker from here. My guy said we're sitting on a cash cow."

Nikhil's hand fisted. "Money for them...or for you?"

"Look, little brother, not everyone can hit the lottery like you. Maybe you should be thinking about how to support yourself after you're washed up. When you peak at your age, you only fall faster. You'll be a has-been in two years."

"You should talk about *falling*, Arjun. At least I make an honest living."

Arjun snorted. "Honest? Your job is *pretending* to be someone else. If you're not pretending, you're nothing. Who'd you blow to get that role, anyway, *Nik*?"

The door opened and Lydia came into the dressing room, pointing at her watch. Nikhil nodded at her.

"Go to hell," Nikhil said. "And don't you dare call Mom and Dad about this. Cancel your guy." He disconnected the call.

Nikhil looked at Lydia, his heart pounding heavily in his ears. "Sorry. Family drama. Hey, can you get me a new phone number?"

Lydia almost looked like she had a drop of compassion on her face. It could be irritation, though. "Yeah, later. Jason will be done with his intro soon. I'm expecting the signal to get you out there any moment now."

Nikhil nodded. Jason Bruzas was the director/screenwriter of the film, and he was currently on the stage telling the roomful of fans about his exhaustive search for the perfect Simon DeSouza.

Lydia's text tone buzzed seconds later. "Okay. You're on."

They'd done dress rehearsals. He knew where to go. What to say. Nikhil took a deep breath and headed through the door and down the narrow hallway to the back of the stage.

The auditorium was simple. Just a black stage with a large screen. Jason and Sasha Keller, one of the producers, stood in the middle of the stage. All Nikhil had to do was walk toward them. The crowd was cheering. At least that sounded like cheering. It was noise. Nikhil's headshot was projected on the screen behind him. Not his regular headshot, but a new Ironis one they took a few days ago that looked like the rest of the Ironis cast pictures. When he got to the middle of the stage, he shook Jason's and Sasha's hands and looked into the crowd smiling. At least he hoped he was smiling. He couldn't feel his face right now. All his senses seemed blurred.

"Nik Sharma!" Jason said, holding up Nikhil's arm. The stage lights were too bright to see anyone. Did he hear booing? Maybe Arjun was wrong. Maybe he was *already* a has-been.

"Happy to be here!" Nikhil said.

"Wait until you see this one in the Bronze Shadow costume!" Sasha said, squeezing Nikhil's arm.

There may have been whistling then. Definitely clapping. Maybe still booing. Nikhil was sweating and felt lightheaded.

He inhaled deeply. He wasn't going to pass out. He'd been on the sets of plenty of TV shows and even a few movies, albeit not ones anyone watched. He wasn't going to get stage fright now.

He had to pull through. Because if he screwed this up, he could kiss his entire career goodbye. He'd be a has-been before ever being an anything. Arjun would be thrilled.

"Tell me, Nik," Jason asked. "How did it feel when you got the call that you were going to be the Bronze Shadow?"

"Oh. It was great." He wasn't supposed to say that. He was supposed to go on about how unexpected it was.

"This is a big change from sitcoms and stand-up, isn't it?" Sasha asked.

Nikhil nodded. Even though he was supposed to talk about how he'd always wanted to challenge himself physically, and how he was a huge Ironis fan, and how he still couldn't believe this was really happening.

But he couldn't get the words out.

Your job is pretending to be someone else. If you're not pretending, you're nothing.

Nikhil exhaled. He couldn't let his brother get under his skin. Not now.

Jason and Sasha were pros and somehow were able to get Nikhil to relax enough to give more than two-word answers. But when Sasha asked what he hoped to bring to the role, someone in the audience screamed, "*Diversity points,*" and Nikhil lost the ability to speak again.

Thankfully, this announcement wasn't meant to be more than a few minutes. They would not be taking any audience or press questions today—those would be saved for the press junket tomorrow. Nikhil was whisked off the stage so Jason and Sasha could talk about another Ironis project, an animated show that was premiering in a month.

He was led straight back to the little dressing room where Lydia, Kaelyn, Esther, and Harlan Green, one of the studio executives, were waiting for him. He immediately flopped onto the makeup chair, closing his eyes and willing his heart rate to go back to normal. It wasn't working.

"Wow. You bombed that, didn't you?" Lydia said. Direct as usual.

She was right, though. How could he have fucked that up so badly? He looked at himself in the mirror, only it wasn't Nikhil looking back at him. It was Nik, with his slicked-back hair and green suit. He was a pawn that the studio had taken a risk on. A risk that was failing.

"Is he going to freeze at the junket tomorrow or actually answer questions?" Harlan asked.

"I'll be fine," Nikhil said. "I don't like huge audiences. Plus, my brother—"

"You're going to have to deal with audiences bigger than that one," Lydia said. "Talk show audiences are bigger. You going to clam up on a press tour, too?"

"Give him a break," Esther said. "You were the ones telling him everyone would hate him."

"Checking social media feeds," Kaelyn said, frowning. "It's not good. What we expected about the diversity angle, but also people are calling him a grump. Saying he's not charismatic enough to be the Shadow." She scrolled a bit before looking up again. "The green suit is a hit, though. Someone said, *Yes! We stan a superhero who knows his season!* That post has over five thousand likes."

Lydia didn't look impressed at that. She was still scowling at Nikhil.

He tried not to look anxious. "I'll do better tomorrow. I was just…nervous."

"We need to do something," Harlan said, looking at Kaelyn. "What about the pictures of him and Serena?" Serena Vox was Nikhil's co-star in the movie. She'd been in the past two Ironis movies and was a former child star—a huge celebrity. Nikhil saw her briefly in LA a month ago, and the publicity team took about a million pictures of them.

Kaelyn nodded. "Done. We'll release them strategically."

"We should have flown her in for this," Harlan said. "Will he be like this tomorrow? The press isn't going to go easy on him."

"I'm right here, you know," Nikhil said. Esther smiled at him sympathetically.

Nether Harlan nor Lydia acknowledged him. "I don't know. He's unpredictable," Lydia said.

"You'll be with him, right?" Harlan asked.

Lydia snorted. "Yeah, but Nik doesn't like me. I don't put him at ease."

"I like you," Nikhil said. Weirdly, he did. Lydia was like a cactus, but a cactus who cared.

"Someone else, then," Harlan said. "There must be someone on his team that the man likes."

Lydia said nothing for a while. Then sighed. "The wardrobe stylist. We can also get her to bring him something colorful for tomorrow. Since the fans *stan for a man in colors.*"

Nikhil chuckled, still staring at the mirror. Apparently, Marley was going to save him again.

CHAPTER FIVE

Marley

Marley was almost finished with her Friday shift when her phone buzzed with a call.

"You going to answer that?"' Ruby asked. She was wiping the glass counter, bringing it to the mirror shine that Reid's required.

Marley stared at her screen. "It's Jacqueline."

Ruby raised a brow. "So?"

She hesitated another second. Jacqueline had barely said a word to Marley since she'd reluctantly approved her time off. And now the surgery was a few days away. Maybe she discovered Marley was having breast surgery and was angry that it was a nonessential procedure. Even though she was having a mastectomy, not a breast augmentation.

Or was Jacqueline going to yell at Marley for Nikhil's celery-colored suit?

She finally accepted the call. "Marley Kamal speaking."

"Marley, you are needed at the Ironis press junket in the morning. Bring some men's shirts in the client's size...They are asking for jewel tones and pastels." Jacqueline named a downtown hotel.

Marley frowned. Why was she being summoned back to Nikhil? "I have a few customer appointments tomorrow. Can we send the shirts by courier?"

"No. They are asking for you all day. We'll pay your average daily commission; plus, they're including a generous per diem. Another consultant can help your customers here." Jaqueline's tone was crystal clear. Marley didn't have a choice—she *had* to go to this press junket.

"Okay. I'll pick out some pieces."

Marley took an Uber to the hotel in the morning, laying the garment bag of clothes on the seat next to her. She wasn't sure how she felt about this change of plans. She'd assumed that she wouldn't ever see Nikhil again. That the fact that she'd styled him for his big announcement would be a short anecdote she'd bring up years from now when she saw one of his movies or saw pictures of him on the Met Gala red carpet.

She'd given in to temptation and looked him up on social media last night, and apparently, the reaction to his announcement was…not good. As expected, many blamed "political correctness" for the decision to cast a nonwhite actor as Simon DeSouza, but the biggest surprise was that he was called grumpy, surly, and completely uncharismatic. The green suit was a hit, at least.

It didn't make sense. Nikhil was, and always had been, one of the most charismatic people Marley knew. He was *funny*. He could be incredibly charming. He had a boyish appeal, as well as a trusting, down-to-earth vibe. At least he used to be all those things. Marley knew he was going through a rough time now, but she assumed he'd be able to put on the charm again when necessary. Hell, she knew he was more than capable of *pretending* to be charming.

When Marley got to the King Street hotel, she asked for Lydia at the front desk and was sent to the ninth floor. A white man met her outside the elevator.

"Ms. Kamal?" he asked. She nodded, so he took her to a room a few doors away. Marley clutched the Reid's garment bag in one hand and her leather tote in the other. She was in her heels again, and it was hard to walk on this plush hotel carpeting. The room she was guided to looked like a regular hotel suite, only with no beds and some extra chairs. It was filled with people, some on phones, some talking to each other. No one looked at Marley when she walked in.

Eventually, a white woman with long blond hair noticed her. Marley remembered her—Kaelyn, the publicist. "Lydia, that shop girl is here," she said loudly, then pointed to the Reid's bag in Marley's hand. "There's an ironing board near the window. I assume the shirts will need to be pressed?"

Marley nodded. She could press a shirt, of course. But she expected someone would pick one for Nikhil to wear first. She maneuvered toward the ironing board and picked what she thought would look best on him—a deep-teal shirt covered with tiny magenta flowers—and started pressing the creases out of it.

"He cannot wear that," a woman behind Marley said. Marley turned to see another white woman, this one wearing an impeccably tailored tweed suit—either a Ralph Lauren or Max Mara. She looked over to someone on the other side of the room. "I thought we said gray or black."

Lydia came in then from an open door. Finally, a familiar face. Not friendly, but familiar.

"The public responded well to the softer look yesterday," Lydia said.

"The public also thought he was a mute diversity hire," the woman responded.

Marley did not like this tweed woman. She continued to press the shirt. It had an extremely high thread count, was softer than butter, and would bring out the green in Nikhil's brown eyes.

"Why is Mahreen ironing?" That was Nikhil. Finally. Not that she'd been aching to see the man or anything, but as a hired stylist, she should *see* the person she'd been hired to style, right?

Marley turned to look at him. Which may have been a mistake. Nikhil wasn't topless, but he might as well have been. He was in a black sleeveless undershirt. It was…snug. Stretched over chiseled pectoral muscles. The outline of a six-pack was visible. And his arms…goodness. There was even a tattoo on his warm brown skin…a vaguely Indian design that looked a bit like a lotus. Marley's mouth went dry, and she nearly dropped the iron. She quickly looked back at the shirt and focused on pressing out a crease on the sleeve.

"It's Marley!" she reminded him. "And I'm ironing because you can't wear a wrinkled shirt."

He made a sound that resembled a growl. No wonder the media had called him a grump. Did he really *growl* at his team? He was clean-shaven, like the pictures she'd seen from Comicon. She preferred this to the mountain-man look from a couple of weeks ago.

"The wardrobe assistant can iron, can't they?" Nikhil asked.

There was a wardrobe assistant? Why was Marley here, then? A man Marley hadn't seen before suddenly appeared and took the iron out of her hand. "I'll take over from here." He motioned Marley away from the ironing board.

A few people gathered around them to analyze the shirts Marley brought, while someone else grabbed Nikhil and started spraying his hair with something. These people were… a lot. No wonder Nikhil was having a nervous breakdown. *Not my circus, not my monkeys*, Marley reminded herself.

The mystery ironing man made quick work of the flowered shirt and handed it to Nikhil. Nikhil took Marley's hand. "Come on, stylist. *Style* me." He pulled her into the adjoining room through the open door.

This room still had hotel furniture in it but also had people standing around and a makeup artist and hairstyle station in the corner. Nikhil pulled Marley straight to the washroom. It was a large room—they weren't crowded. But still. When they'd been in the fitting room back at the personal shopping suite, he'd changed alone. Not *with* her.

"Sorry," he said immediately as he locked the door. "There is absolutely nowhere else we can be alone."

Marley kept her expression neutral. The last thing she needed was for Nikhil to discover how attractive she was finding him right now. She couldn't believe this was scrawny Nikhil from high school. "And why exactly do we need to be alone?"

He sighed, looking up at the ceiling. Then he looked at her, clearly trying, and failing, to smile genuinely. "Yesterday was a disaster," he said.

"I saw online. It wasn't *that* bad." She pulled out her phone and read him some of the posts she'd saved. "*OMG, a BROWN Bronze Shadow, YUM! Is that melanin I see?* People were trying to find the name of your stylist." Marley felt pretty good about that. There were negative comments, too, but she didn't read those to him.

"What kind of social media accounts do you follow?"

She shrugged. "Fashion people mostly. And some social commentary accounts."

"Any rabid nerdy fanboys?"

Marley frowned.

"I fucked up," Nikhil said, leaning back against the counter. "They're calling me an antisocial snob. I was...distracted."

"Why?" Nikhil was almost too goofy and upbeat back in the day. But she didn't really know him anymore. She shouldn't project Nikhil the boy onto this full-grown man who was wearing an undershirt thin enough to see through.

When he didn't answer her, she pointed at the shirt. "Put it on, Nikhil."

He did. As expected, it looked amazing on him. She watched as he buttoned and tucked it into his gray pants. The deep greenish blue of the shirt brought out the cool undertones in his warm brown skin. And the soft floral on such a burly, masculine body was...well, it was hot. She felt herself flush.

She couldn't let him know what he was doing to her.

"That's perfect," Marley said, reaching to undo his second button.

Nikhil was looking only at her as she smoothed the shirt, his eyes never breaking contact with hers. Had he always been so intense? His expression was pure trust. Not mischief or amusement like it used to be when he looked at her, just... respect. Admiration.

And maybe, just maybe, a touch of heat.

But he *had* been intense before. Marley's mind flashed to prom night. Marley had been in several relationships before then—and had even slept with someone before Nikhil. But Nikhil felt...different from the others. He wasn't awkward that night. He was focused, serious, and surprisingly passionate. She didn't realize it until she'd been with a few more people in college, but Nikhil was much better than average in bed. She shivered, remembering the feeling of his fingertips on her bare skin. It wasn't what she'd expected sex with the class clown to be like. She quickly shook out those thoughts and took a step back. It was a long time ago.

"That shirt is the one, I think," she said. "I mean, of course your team has to approve, but that would be my choice."

Nikhil nodded, running his hand over his hair. It was smooth and sleek and reaching the bottom of his collar.

"Your hair," Marley said. "I figured they'd cut it short."

He shook his head. "The movie Simon DeSouza will have a man bun to hide his secret identity instead of glasses."

Marley chuckled, which brought a small smile to Nikhil's face.

"I'm sorry you got dragged into this today," he said.

"It's fine. I'm being paid well."

He exhaled. "Good. I…They said I needed someone I was comfortable around today. Lydia thinks you're the only one on my team that I like."

Marley frowned. "You don't like anyone else you work with?" Marley didn't have a ton of friends at work, but she had Ruby at least.

"I like my director a lot. The cast that I've met seem fine. My current trainer is fine. He's actually a stunt coordinator on the movie. It's just these publicity people who aren't my favorite. And anyway, yesterday's screwup wasn't because I don't like anyone, just…" He sighed. "My brother called right before I went onstage. He got under my skin. I'd put money on his timing being intentional."

Marley said nothing for a few moments. "Family is complicated, isn't it?" she finally said. She didn't want to pry into his personal life.

He nodded. "Totally. I understand if you want to leave now that you brought the shirts. I'll make sure they still pay you." He glanced at himself in the mirror. "You're right—this shirt is *fire*. I'm going to ask to keep it." He put his hand on his chin in a sultry thinking-man pose, and Marley finally understood why he was on the brink of superstardom.

Nikhil Shamdasani was anxious, a little grumpy, and clearly going through it all, but he was *sexy* now. Like, breathtakingly so. When he was comfortable, that is. And he appeared to be comfortable around Marley.

"It's fine," Marley said. She should distance herself, but she couldn't. "I'll stay as long as you need me. I've never seen a press junket."

He grinned a wide smile that was as heart-stopping as his sultry gaze. Shayne would *love* to photograph Nikhil now. Marley wondered if she was allowed to talk about him yet.

"Let's go, then," he said, opening the bathroom door. "You're my emotional-support wardrobe stylist for the day."

It was another hour before they were finally called across the hall for the press junket. The room was nowhere near as chaotic as the other two. It had been cleared of furniture and transformed into a little TV studio.

An entertainment reporter from Global TV, a Canadian broadcaster, was conducting the first interview, and they wanted to speak to both Nikhil and Jason, the director. Marley,

Lydia, and Kaelyn the publicist were on stools behind the cameraperson. The interviewer mostly had questions for Jason, but eventually, she turned to Nikhil.

"So, the Bronze Shadow! How does it feel to land such an iconic role?"

Nikhil smiled. "I still can't believe it's real. Maybe once I get into the super suit and we start filming I'll start to believe it's actually happening."

"Why do you think the studio went in a different direction from how the character is portrayed in the comics?"

Marley had no idea what that meant. Because Simon DeSouza in the comics had short hair and blue eyes? Because he was coded as white in the comics? "Oh, I mean, I don't know," he stammered. "I auditioned and got the role."

Marley cringed. That was not a good answer. She could practically feel Lydia vibrating with annoyance next to her. But it was a stupid question. Why was he being asked why the studio cast him? Why not ask the director that?

"All right, I'm sure everyone would love to hear your secrets. How does a Canadian actor with little action-film experience turn himself into a superhero?"

Nikhil chuckled, rubbing his chin. "Personal trainers mostly." He needed to give better answers than that. Longer ones.

"Just personal training?"

Lydia leaned over to Marley and whispered, "Get his attention. We're losing him."

Marley agreed. She needed to get him back to the man he'd been in the bathroom a few minutes ago. First step: get him to remember she was here. Marley dropped her large Prada tote to the floor. It landed with a loud thud.

Everyone turned and glared at Marley. The cameraman groaned.

"Whoops! So sorry! I'm such a klutz!" She smiled at Nikhil. And he smiled back. The interviewer asked him the question again. "So, all you needed was a trainer to turn you into a superhero?"

While the interviewer was speaking, Marley leaned down to retrieve her dropped bag. And since the stool was tall, it was a pretty deep bend. That's when she realized she was giving Nikhil and the director a prime view of her cleavage. Welp. That was *unintentional*.

Oh well. Might as well use these while she still had them.

When she sat straight again, Nikhil was looking at her. His eyes were hooded like they'd been in the bathroom. His mouth sultry. He even licked his lips. Marley had no idea if he even realized what he was doing, but it was working. The camera would *love* this sexy Nikhil. Marley beamed at him, and that brought a flustered smile to his face.

"So, your trainers worked you hard."

"Very hard," he said, his expression now hovering between embarrassed and aroused. "I was motivated. I mean, I've always wanted to look like a Ken doll." He chuckled. "But honestly, I can't *wait* to start working on the fight choreography. That will be the fun part."

Marley gave him another reassuring grin as the interviewer asked more about the physical demands of the role. Nikhil was optimistic and easygoing in his answers. He was charming. He did well with the next few interviews, too—without any visual distraction.

After they all took a break for lunch, Marley handed Nikhil a deep-violet shirt to change things up for the afternoon interviews.

Marley smoothed Nikhil's hair after he sat back down. With
the amount of product she saw the hairstylist spray on him, she
assumed it would be dry and sticky. But it was soft. She resisted
the urge to let her fingers comb through the wavy strands as she
pushed them behind his ears. Nikhil's eyes rose to meet hers as
he swallowed. "How am I doing?" he asked.

Marley straightened the collar of the shirt. "You're amazing. The camera loves you."

He didn't break eye contact. And she couldn't look away from
his face, either. His skin looked so soft. She wanted to run her
fingers over his cheeks. Just his eyes meeting hers had her skin
tingling with goosebumps. What was happening right now?

"Oh my god," a male voice behind Marley said. "*Marley
Kamal*. Is that you?"

Marley quickly stepped back and turned. She knew that
voice. And *oh my god* was right. It was Anderson. Shayne's ex.
The one Shayne was still so hung up on that Anderson might
as well be a coatrack.

"Anderson!" Marley said.

Anderson Lin was an East Asian man with a small stature
and a huge, bubbly personality. He'd been on the production
side in TV when he and Shayne were dating, but now he worked
in front of the camera. Marley leaned forward to hug Anderson
because she really did like the guy, even if she'd spent countless
nights helping her best friend drink away his heartbreak.

"Why are you even here?" Anderson asked after hugging
her back. "I'm so delighted to see you! It's been way too long!"

"Oh, I'm here with Nikhil...sorry, Nik Sharma." She
pointed at Nikhil. "I'm his wardrobe stylist."

Anderson's eyes widened. "How amazing! And how is..."
he stuttered.

Marley raised one brow. "Shayne?"

Anderson nodded. He looked invested in the answer. Anderson clearly wasn't as heartless as Shayne thought. Marley wasn't sure what Shayne would want her to say here. She decided to go with *living well is the best revenge*. "Shayne is *fabulous*. Working so hard. He's going to Paris soon for fashion week as a runway photographer."

Marley couldn't be sure, but she thought she saw a pang of regret. But Anderson wiped it off his face immediately. "He is *such* a talent. I've been trying to reach him but..." His voice trailed off.

"Wait," Nikhil said, looking back and forth between Anderson and Marley with shock. "*Shayne*...you never mentioned you're *still* friends with Shayne."

Anderson raised a questioning brow.

"Nik went to high school with us," Marley explained. Maybe that wasn't information the media needed to know. And Anderson was media.

"Let's get this interview started," Kaelyn said, bringing an end to the awkward reunion. She looked at Anderson. "You're from *The Confab*, right? You have five minutes. I assume you read the approved questions and, more importantly, the off-limits topics. Go ahead."

Thankfully, Anderson kept to the script, and Nikhil was fine again, so Marley didn't have to do any awkward pseudo-flirting. When Anderson left, he gave Marley a wave as the next person was herded in.

"That was weird," Marley said to Nikhil as she fixed his collar again. "Shayne's going to flip his lid when he hears about this. He's been pretending Anderson doesn't exist for months."

Nikhil shook his head. "I love that you two are still tight. You were inseparable in high school."

Marley nodded. "We're roommates now."

"I want to hear all about how he's doing," Nikhil said as the next interviewer was taking her seat. "Later, though."

Marley exhaled as she returned to her chair. Was she going to have a *later* with Nikhil? Was he feeling this attraction, too, or was he just being friendly and a little needy? She'd told him that she wasn't going to have sex with him, and yes, she did use her breasts to get his attention earlier, but the fact that it worked didn't necessarily mean he was hoping for something here. Her breasts were nice.

And in three days, she wouldn't have them anymore.

Marley swallowed. Funny how being around Nikhil plucked that major upcoming life event from the front of her mind. But it was back now.

At least she wouldn't be styling Nikhil again. He'd forget all about her after the junket when he got busy with rehearsals and shooting. Marley would be a blip on his radar...He'd be dating supermodels and A-listers soon.

The rest of the interviews were fine. After the last one, Kaelyn pulled Nikhil back to the other room to talk about something. Marley grabbed her bag and followed, stopping near the door. It was past five o'clock— she'd been here all day. Could she just leave now? Lydia looked up from her phone.

"We're done with you now," Lydia said. "Have the store bill the studio for the shirts."

No *thank you*, no *you did a great job*. And Nikhil hadn't even looked at her when he left with Kaelyn.

But it was fine. This was *supposed* to be professional only. She smiled, thanked Lydia, and left the hotel room.

CHAPTER SIX

Nikhil

Nikhil was whisked across the hall by Kaelyn to talk to the suit-wearing publicist, Carmen, the moment his last interview ended. He expected them to ream him for messing up at the beginning of the junket, but they didn't. In fact, the only debriefing he got was a "good job" before they started outlining the plans for the mini press tour.

"We are conscious of your training schedule," Carmen said, "but you will have to be in New York or LA for this. It can't be avoided."

Starting Monday, Nikhil was progressing from a few hours a day of weight training to an intensive six-week program to learn the stunts and fight choreography at a private gym close to the studio. He'd be there nine to five, Monday through Friday. One of the reasons he'd been excited to get this role was that both principal photography and rehearsals were already slated to be in Toronto, and he thought it was a good idea for him to be close to his family for a while. Although Nikhil barely saw his mother since she stayed in her room most of the time. And his father was still sweeping all the family's problems under the Persian carpet in the living room.

Fixing problems reminded him that he needed to thank Marley for her help today. And he wanted to ask her for a drink before she left. He wasn't sure, but he thought he detected a flirty vibe from her earlier. But when he glanced around the room, he didn't see her. "Where's Marley? Is she still across the hall?"

Lydia joined them then. "Oh, she left." She looked at Kaelyn and Carmen. "You can't pull him out of rehearsals for press for too many days. Production could slow if he's not ready for principal photogra—"

"Marley left?" Nikhil frowned. "Without saying goodbye?" If nothing else, he'd thought they were at least friends now. But maybe not.

"I must say that girl has quite an effect on you." Lydia chuckled. Nikhil didn't realize Lydia knew how to laugh. "You sure you two were just *friends* in high school?"

"We were friends. And...prom dates."

At that, Lydia full-on laughed. "Yeah, *prom*. Not surprised. Channel that chemistry when you're with Serena." She turned to the publicists and asked a question about some promo pics of him and Serena Vox they were planning to release, but Nikhil tuned them out.

Did he and Marley really have chemistry strong enough that others noticed? How obvious was he? He cringed when he remembered catching a view of her chest as she leaned down during one of the interviews. He'd been mesmerized. Had she noticed?

He was a pig, and she was *still* so out of his league. No wonder she left.

"Nik...earth to Nik!" Lydia said, snapping her fingers inches from his face. "Glad to see you can be something other than a sourpuss in an appearance. You're free to go now." She turned back to the publicists, and they continued talking about some press releases or something.

Nikhil grabbed his stuff and headed back to the washroom in the adjoining room to change. Was he really a sourpuss? He knew he was struggling lately, but hearing it spelled out like that was rough. Why was all this so hard for him? He was literally living his dream…one that had been a decade in the making. He hated that he was already getting a reputation for being difficult. But he didn't know how to brush off all this pressure and negative press the way everyone seemed to think he should be able to do. And clearly, his family shit was getting under his skin way more than it should.

At that, he sent a quick text to his sister to see how things were going. Nalini sent him a few thumbs-up emojis, then a series of long messages telling him in detail everything that had happened at home all day. It was too much information, but he was able to grasp that his mother was the same today.

On impulse, Nikhil decided not to change. He wanted to stay in the shirt Marley had picked a little longer. He tied his hair back and left the hotel room without speaking to anyone. When he got off the elevator on the ground floor, he headed toward the concierge desk to ask if they could call him a car. But a glance over to the hotel bar stopped him short.

It was Marley. She was alone. Nikhil recognized her by her ridiculously shiny hair, pale-gray blouse, and snug black skirt. He should leave her alone. She left without saying goodbye—she didn't want to see him. And she specifically said she couldn't work with him past the twentieth, which was only two days away. But he was like a moth to a flame—he would always be drawn to her.

And besides, after that day, he could use a drink.

The posh bar was dark-wood paneled with leather seats

and deep-burgundy carpets. He slipped in and stood next to Marley, not sure what to say.

When she noticed him, her reaction made his knees weak. She *beamed*. Not the small Marley smile that still managed to make his skin pebble, and not her fake professional smile, either. This full, wide grin lit up the whole dark room.

"Nikhil! Hi!" She seemed a completely different person from the cool, professional woman upstairs.

"Hi, Marley...I noticed you...I mean, I saw you in here and...I hope I'm not intruding...I didn't get a chance to say thank you and I thought—"

"Come sit," she said, still smiling. She patted the barstool next to her. "Wait—you're probably busy. Are you done upstairs?"

"Yeah. And I really need a drink," he said, sliding onto the leather barstool.

She nodded. "Yeah, I needed this, too."

He ordered a single malt from the bartender.

Marley was drinking something clear with a lime on the rim. "You drink now?" Back in high school, she hadn't.

She chuckled. "I'm an adult now, Nikhil. I wanted one last drink before...never mind. I'm not affected by my parents' attempts to guilt me for drinking anymore."

He laughed. "Sounds like we could compare notes on family shaming..."

Marley only smiled at that. The bartender brought his drink then—a high-end whiskey with a hint of smokiness. It was delicious. He sighed. "Nothing tastes as good as the first drink after a public appearance."

She looked at him curiously. "You really don't like them, do you?"

He shrugged. "It's emotionally exhausting to be *on* like that. If it's a project I'm very passionate about, then it's fun. I did this indie movie a couple of years ago, *The Last Time*—"

"*The Last Time He Cried*...I saw it."

Nikhil's eyebrows rose. Marley had seen that movie? No one had seen that movie. It was a small indie film about four friends who check into a mental health retreat together. It hadn't exactly made waves on the festival circuit. "Seriously?"

She nodded. "Yeah, at TIFF. I was hoping you'd be there for the screening."

He swirled his drink. "I wanted to come, but I had another gig in LA. The director and I are friends, so it always felt like hanging out with my buddies when we promoted it, you know?"

"You're not as passionate about this role?"

"No, I am. It's just different because the big studio is such a machine. And it's hard to be excited about a movie that hasn't even filmed yet. I think the script is great, and I like the changes they made from the comic. Jason, the director, is awesome. I barely know the rest of the cast. I'm sure they'll be fine. But..."

"But the backlash yesterday, right?"

He swallowed another sip of whiskey. "I kind of wished they'd warned me about it. I mean, before I accepted the part." He would have taken it anyway, though. The money was amazing.

"It hasn't all been terrible," Marley said. "I think today's interviews will be well received. You seemed to be...enjoying yourself."

So she *did* notice him drooling over her body earlier. Mortifying. Marley then gave him a look that was pure mischief.

Was he getting a glimpse of the real Marley without her professional mask on? The grown-up Marley? It reminded him of when they'd been back in school. She was usually quiet in class, but whenever it was just the two of them, she was like this. Warmer. Teasing. She laughed more. Now she seemed more confident—she was comfortable in her skin—but he could see how this person tonight evolved from his old friend.

"You're adorable when you're embarrassed, you know that?" she said.

Nikhil exhaled. She called him adorable. She *was* flirting with him. Should he flirt back? Nikhil didn't normally think this hard about whether he should flirt with someone. But this wasn't *just* flirting. There would never be a *just* anything when it came to Marley.

He sipped his whiskey. They were both silent a few moments. "I love hotel bars," she said. "They always feel... private. Everyone in here is just passing through. They seem to exist alone, like not in any place. Time stands still."

He nodded. "I know exactly what you mean. I always make a point to have a drink in the hotel bar whenever I'm traveling. It feels like one of those in-between places."

Marley nodded. "I was thinking about getting dinner here before heading home. Want to join me?"

Yes. Yes, yes, yes, he wanted to have dinner with her. Maybe she'd forgiven him for what he'd done back in school. Maybe he was getting a second chance.

"That'd be great." Nikhil forced a chuckle so she wouldn't hear how eager he was. "Place as fancy as this, maybe they have coq au vin. Wait...you don't have a significant other hiding somewhere who'll punch me for saying that, do you? I *just* got this tooth fixed."

Marley rolled her eyes. "I still can't believe Oren did that. I dumped him that day. Worst relationship ever."

It wasn't lost on Nikhil that she'd sidestepped the relationship comment. Maybe she wasn't single. He knew back in high school she'd dated both girls and guys, which had been quite the scandal for a Brown girl. It never bothered Nikhil, though.

But it was clear she was still a private person. He still didn't know why she was going on a leave of absence in a few days. Which, fine—she didn't have to open up if she didn't want to. But it felt like she wanted to keep this reunion surface level only.

She *did* want to have a meal with him, though. And nothing in the world could make him say no to spending more time with Marley, even surface-level time.

He took his glass and stood, holding his hand out for her. "So, dinner?"

She stood, smiling. "Let's do it."

CHAPTER SEVEN

Marley

M arley had no idea what she was doing. Or why she'd asked Nikhil out.

Had she asked Nikhil out?

The vodka soda had clearly gone straight to her head. But…honestly? She didn't want to go home. Shayne was home tonight, and she still felt kind of weird about him deserting her right after her surgery. And she felt like complete trash for resenting him—she couldn't expect her friends to put their lives on hold because of her defective genes. But staying with her parents was going to be hell, and hearing Shayne talk about his trip to Paris wasn't fun, either.

If she went home now, she'd just wallow and feel sorry for herself. So the moment she saw Nikhil in the bar, she made a decision—forget their past and forget her future surgery for one night. She was going to lower her inhibitions and just be herself. Flirting, even flirting badly, with a movie star in a hotel bar was the escape she needed.

She couldn't deny it—she *liked* being around Nikhil again. He made her laugh. He didn't make her talk about her life, but she knew he'd listen if she did. When everything in her life had been a mess back in high school, the only time Marley could guarantee that she would smile was when she sat next to Nikhil in class. And she needed that right now.

This time he needed her, too. Dinner together would be the escape they both deserved.

They sat at one of the round private booths at the end of the bar. The high-backed seat blocked out the rest of the room in what was already a private space. The small flickering candle added to the feeling that they were the only ones in the world. Nikhil ordered a beer and Marley another vodka soda, and they looked over the menu.

"Alas, no coq au vin," Nikhil said.

Marley chuckled. "Ooh, they have steak frites. That's what I'm having." She closed her menu. "I've been clean eating for months and I need a cheat day."

The server came then, and Nikhil ordered braised short ribs, and Marley the steak frites.

"Everyone in LA is on some special diet," Nikhil said once the server left. "I'm always nervous ordering at a restaurant. I had a date walk out on me once because I was 'triggering,'" he said, making air quotes. "Dating in LA is a trip. Do not recommend."

Did that mean he was single? "Did she warn you in advance that she had food issues?"

Nikhil snorted. "I honestly think everyone in LA assumes everyone has food issues. Hard to be a foodie living there."

"The restaurants in LA must be amazing, though."

He shrugged. "Eh, I prefer Toronto. In LA I cook more than go out." He chuckled. "I'm a bit addicted to cooking shows. I like to re-create what I watch."

"You ever think about moving back to Toronto for good?"

He shook his head. "I don't know. Most big auditions are in LA. But it would be good for..." His voice faded. "You're living in the city now, right?"

She nodded, then told him about her and Shayne's little house in the east end.

"Wow, that's pretty close to the film studio," he said.

Marley frowned. Was he implying they would see each other while he was filming? Have lunch or something? She couldn't tell. Thankfully, the server came with the food then. The steak looked perfect. Juicy, charred, and with a creamy green peppercorn sauce. Marley immediately dipped a slim fry into the sauce, then moaned with appreciation.

"Good?" Nikhil asked, smirking. His short ribs looked amazing, too—a big hunk of beef in a glistening sauce on a bed of mashed potatoes and leeks.

Marley nodded. "So good. Yours?"

He took a bite. "Perfection."

"Your nails look nice," Nikhil said after they'd been eating silently awhile. "I thought they were skin color. But now I see they are like...shimmery. They glow."

Marley smiled. "It's a luster powder over nude. This is about as bold as I'm allowed to do at Reid's."

"That's too bad. Hands like yours should be...adorned. Bright colors and jewels."

She raised a brow.

He laughed. "I like your hands." Should Marley thank him for the compliment?

"It's killing me," he said after a few moments of silence. "Why'd you go see *The Last Time He Cried*? There were much better movies at the festival that year."

She shrugged. "I was looking through the listings and

saw your name." She'd been surprised to see the name Nikhil Shamdasani. She knew he was an actor, and she had even seen a few of his small TV roles. She'd gone to the festival screening alone—even though she knew friends would join her if she asked. Shayne for sure, but even Reena probably would have come, too.

But she hadn't wanted to explain to anyone how she knew the supporting actor or listen to Shayne make cracks about Nikhil being a love-them-and-leave-them fuckboy. She didn't want someone else there when she saw him in person for the first time since high school. But he wasn't even there. Just the director and the lead actor.

Nikhil sipped his beer. "I'm pretty sure that movie was a mistake. Careerwise, I mean."

"I loved it," Marley said. *Objectively* the film was not great, but Nikhil's performance *was*. He wasn't the lead…and it was clear that his role was meant to be a punch line. Comic relief. But he brought so much more to the part. His character had a tragic past, and the tragedy was sometimes played for laughs, but with nuance. He somehow made viewers want to give him a hug after laughing at his one-liners.

Or at least he made Marley want to do that.

"I thought you were great in it," she said. "And I know I wasn't the only one. I read the reviews—they all said you were the only good thing in that film. They said you were going to be a breakout star."

"Yeah, well that prediction was false."

Marley frowned. "Um, the Bronze Shadow?"

Nikhil shook his head. "They said I was going to be a breakout *romantic* star. Another review said I should be doing more dramatic roles. I rarely get auditions for romantic or dramatic roles. I'm not romance-hero material, apparently. Same for dramatic roles. I'm missing a certain something. Probably white skin."

"That new superhero body should help with roles, shouldn't it?"

He shrugged.

"Will you have any opportunity to flex your acting chops in the Ironis movie?"

He nodded. "Yeah, a bit. But it's mostly action. I'll be Serena Vox's love interest, though." He snorted. "Still can't believe I'm going to be working with her. I used to watch her show."

Marley too. In fact, *Lily Lavender* had been her favorite TV show when she was a kid. "What's she like?"

"Don't really know her much. She's *very* professional. Maybe we'll get to know each other when we start rehearsals next week."

"I have no question people will want you for romantic roles after this movie. I mean..." Marley smiled. "That look you gave me in the junket..."

He chuckled, running his hand over his glass. "It's been really weird to see you again."

"Good weird?"

He lowered his gaze and a tiny smile appeared on his lips. "Absolutely."

Yeah, he was going to be a sex symbol. No question in Marley's mind. A tiny little prehistoric part of her brain was screaming, *I had him first!* Because she had. That night, their chemistry had been crackling. She smiled. "Viewers aren't going to have a problem seeing you as a romance hero."

With his still-lowered gaze, he bit his lip. It was a little bashful, and very flirty. And not a ploy...this was all really him.

Or he was an even better actor than Marley realized. "Are you telling me that *Mahreen Kamal* thinks I'm attractive?"

"It's Marley now." Marley was sure she was bright red. She cut her steak to break the spell of that moment.

"Why the new name, anyway?" he asked. Good. He was changing the subject.

But honestly, this wasn't a topic she wanted to talk about, either. About how the name *Mahreen* always reminded her of the person who'd named her. Who'd chosen *Mahreen* because it was similar to her own name, *Maryam*. After high school, she started going by Marley all the time instead of it just being a nickname her cousins called her. It was easier not to be reminded of her aunt anytime someone said her name. She wanted to put Mahreen, and Maryam, behind her because the reminders hurt too much.

Of course, Marley hadn't known that she'd inherited more than just a name similar to her aunt's. They both had the same broken gene. One day, Marley could face the same fate as Maryam. As Marley's mother.

But no. Her surgery was just days away. Marley's breast cancer risk was about to be eliminated. She squeezed her wrist with her left hand until it hurt.

Nikhil's hand reached close to hers on the table. He didn't touch her, but he looked like he wanted to. "Mahreen—sorry; *Marley*—are you okay? You seem…sad all of a sudden."

Marley exhaled. "Yeah. Dealing with some personal shit."

"I'm sorry. Tell me what not to say and I won't say it."

"No, it's fine. You didn't do anything wrong."

"I know we don't really know each other anymore, but I'm still a good listener. I'd even be willing to sign an NDA."

Marley snorted. He looked so earnest. Maybe she *should*

tell him about her surgery. She remembered what Shayne had said, that keeping everything inside would make her explode. Besides, they were in their own little hotel bar bubble right now.

But tonight was supposed to be about *escaping* it all. And honestly, this was all too heavy to tell a random movie star she was having dinner with.

Marley gulped down the lump in her throat. "Nah, I'm absolutely fine. And anyway, you shouldn't talk about name changes, *Nikhil Shamdasani*."

He laughed at that. Deep and sensual. Yeah, he was going to be a superstar one day. He would belong to the whole world. But not right now...Right now he was just hers. "The studio requested I change it. They wanted me to go with Nik Sheffield, but I insisted on an Indian last name at least. My LA friends were already calling me Nik, so it doesn't bother me."

They talked more about his life in LA and about some of his favorite roles. It was all so easy...it had always been.

It felt like Marley had gone back in time to when she was eighteen. She had never admitted it to anyone, but she *did* have feelings for Nikhil before prom night. She'd always thought he was a wisecracking goofball. But getting to know him better in their last year of school changed things for her. He was a lot smarter than she realized. He was kind, and he listened better than anyone else. He was still scrawny back then, but he had the cutest smile. When they danced together on prom night, Marley felt tingles all over her body for the first time.

That night Marley discovered what sexual tension felt like. And here it was all over again, crackling between them. It was remarkable. Attraction was hard-won for Marley—it always had been. As an adult, she realized that she had to know the person well before she had any physical interest in them.

Clearly, she had known Nikhil well enough on prom night... but that was a decade ago. Now? It seemed Nik Sharma was still the Nikhil Shamdasani she knew well.

He told her about some antics his old roommate and he had gotten into when he first moved to LA.

"You've made good friends there?"

"Yeah, actually. My buddy Ty and I lived together for years. He's the best. We have our own little crew going way back from seeing the same faces in auditions for so long. I assumed LA would be cold and, you know, a little phony, but there are some real gems there. I've been there for so long, though. I haven't spent a significant time in Toronto in years." He grinned. "I feel so fancy being bicoastal now."

"Toronto isn't on a coast."

"It's considered eastern seaboard, isn't it?"

"Do you even know what a seaboard is?"

He laughed at that. "Not really. How about you? Planning to be a Toronto girl for life?"

Marley bit her lip. "I don't have a ton of friends here, either. But it's my home, you know?"

He chuckled low. "Well, now we're both here. We can be friends again. Or..." He leaned closer to her, and she leaned in, too.

Marley was playing with fire here. He was looking at her with an expression that somehow broadcasted compassion as well as *desire*. Attraction and...respect. His eyes were intense, and she wanted to climb into his lap and maul him.

There were so many thoughts swirling through her head. Like Nikhil had no business coming into her life *now*, when it was both the worst possible time and the best possible time. Marley was having surgery in *two days*. Her body would be forever changed. And this could be her only chance for another *one last time* with this body.

But also, this was *Nikhil*, the guy who basically ghosted her after sleeping with her. She was honestly over it—it was so long ago, and she was in no way mentally in the right place for a relationship back then. But she still didn't know what had happened. And she didn't want to get hurt again.

Marley took a deep breath. "Remember prom?" she asked.

Nikhil bit his lip. "How could I forget?"

That night, they'd found themselves alone in an after-party hotel room after the group they'd been partying with had all paired off into other rooms. Marley didn't remember who made the first move—but she did remember that she'd wanted him all night. She'd wanted to tune out the world and lose herself in Nikhil.

But after the amazing night, she didn't hear from Nikhil the next day. Or the day after that. When she got to school on Monday, he didn't come to chemistry, even though she saw him from far away before class. When some of their classmates started teasing her about prom night, she realized that he had told *everyone* what had happened. Nikhil wasn't the person she thought he was. The next day Maryam Aunty had been admitted to the hospital, and Marley didn't go back to school again. There had only been a week left, and she wanted to be with her aunt as much as possible.

So it wasn't completely Nikhil's fault—*she* could have called him. And he did call her once—about a week after she'd left school. But Marley had seen his name on her phone and didn't answer. She didn't know how to talk to anyone about her aunt dying.

She exhaled. He was close enough that she could now smell

a cologne...it was subtle. Tropical. His eyes were hooded. "What happened that night?" she asked. "Why didn't you... why didn't we ever talk after?"

The question hung in the air for several long seconds.

He finally sighed, and she saw regret in his eyes. "I'm sorry, Mahreen. I was a dumbass."

Marley shook her head. "I don't even know why I asked. It was a long time ago. We were kids. I didn't call you, either."

"People were saying stuff...like you were out of my league, and I got too deep in my own head. I was planning to move to LA the moment school ended, and I didn't want..." His voice trailed.

"You didn't want me holding you back?" she asked. She sounded a bit bitter.

"No. I mean...maybe? But I should have talked to you."

"You did try and call me once, didn't you? I didn't pick up."

He looked at her for a while, then sighed. "I wish our friendship hadn't ended like that."

Marley squeezed her lips together. *Friendship.* She'd wanted more than friendship back then, but maybe he hadn't. She'd known he wanted to go to Hollywood to try to be an actor, and she could understand him pulling away from her if he thought she'd try to stop him from going. And honestly? It was probably for the best. She was way too vulnerable for a relationship back then.

"We both should have communicated better," she said slowly, looking right into Nikhil's eyes. "We should be *clear* about our expectations this time. If it's going to happen again, I mean."

Nikhil swallowed. "And...what are your expectations this time?" His hand found her thigh, and the friction of his touch through the soft wool of her skirt nearly made her skin combust.

"I'm going through a lot right now. I told you…about my leave of absence. But maybe we need another chance to do it right. As friends." Her eyes nearly closed with the pleasure of his hand making circles on her thigh.

He smiled and it almost made Marley rip that damn shirt off so she could see—no, *touch*—that Bronze Shadow body. "You mean friends with benefits?" he asked.

"*Benefit*," she corrected. "Singular. Just tonight—no more."

"That works for me," he said. "I've got a lot going on, too. I like this…communicating."

He leaned even closer. He was now only inches away. Every nerve in her body was reaching for him, aching to feel his skin on hers. Marley put her hand on his chest, stopping him from closing the gap between them. She resisted the urge to stroke him under that designer shirt. "I mean it. This can only be *one time*. Not more. I am in no way looking for a relationship right now. Especially with a movie star."

He gulped, then nodded. "I'm also not really…in the right place for a relationship now."

Marley swallowed. Maybe getting this…attraction out of their system with open communication could mean they could move on. Maybe even be friends again one day. "I mentioned I'm going through some stuff right now…I would love to turn it all off for a night."

"It would be my absolute pleasure to distract you." He came even closer and ran his hand up her thigh, which caused a full-body shiver and warmed her core. She could feel his breath on her cheek. Her lips were tingling, primed and ready to feel his on hers.

But he didn't kiss her. He just looked at her, his expression pure leading man.

"I'm staying at this hotel," he whispered. "That room upstairs where we talked in the bathroom. Give me about fifteen minutes' head start to make sure the studio people are all gone, then come up. Nine oh seven."

Good idea. "I'll go to the drugstore."

He nodded, then stood, then stared at her for a moment. Intense. When he smiled, it was all Nikhil. "I'll get the dinner bill. See you soon." He left the bar.

Marley bought some snacks and a box of condoms from the drugstore near the hotel. She didn't want to think too much about what she was about to do...mostly because she didn't want to change her mind. And she didn't want to overthink it. Just like Shayne and Ruby said, Marley deserved this last hurrah with this body.

At exactly fifteen minutes after they'd separated, she headed back to the ninth floor and knocked on the door of room 907.

Nikhil opened it, and Marley slipped inside before anyone saw her. And then she just stood in the entryway, looking at him.

He was so gorgeous. Still in the deep-violet shirt she'd picked for his interview and slim black pants. He'd taken off his shoes, his hair was pulled back, and his gray socks had red on the toes. Yeah, he'd grown in the last ten years, but the face was the same. *Her* Nikhil.

"I...um..." He rubbed the back of his neck. "I know...I mean, we were a little chaotic down in the bar. I totally understand if you want to change your mind. No hard feelings…We can just, you know, Netflix and chill or something."

Marley frowned. "Do you *want* to Netflix and chill?" she asked.

He chuckled. "No. I just don't want you to regret this again."

Marley smiled and took a step toward him, kicking off her shoes. "I *don't* regret prom night. I wish we had handled things better after, but I have *never* regretted you," she said. Clearly, he was getting deep in his own head again. She put her hands behind his neck, stroking the soft skin there. It felt so good to have him close. She watched his eyes hood as his lips quirked up in a smile before she pulled him in for a kiss.

There. That was exactly what Marley needed. His mouth. Soft, sensual, and immediately taking over. Wiping all the thoughts she didn't want to be having from her head with one sweep of his tongue against hers.

They kissed softly like that for a long time. Exploratory. Marley would have thought that with all the sexual tension down at the bar and in the press junket earlier, this would be more urgent. Hurried. But Nikhil wasn't the same horny teenager he was before. He was controlled now. And so, so powerful. Marley ran her hands over that broad chest, marveling at the firm smoothness beneath her fingers.

He pulled back a moment. "Come here," he said, guiding her toward the bed. She tossed the drugstore bag and her purse on the dresser. After he sat on the luxurious white duvet, she sat on his lap sideways, loving the strength of his thighs under her. They kissed again. His hands were in the hair at the back of her head, and her arms were around his shoulders. Marley didn't think. She just felt…everything. He was so sexy. Total leading-man material.

His mouth moved down her neck, leaving open-mouthed kisses down to the collar of her blouse. She shivered while his hands grazed her top button. "May I?" he asked.

She nodded. She wanted him to just tear it off her, but she could be patient. One by one, Nikhil flicked open the pearl buttons of her gray silk blouse, revealing her white lace La Perla bra. He whistled low. "Did you wear this expecting someone would see it?"

Marley frowned. "No. This is an everyday bra."

He looked up at her, grinning. "You *always* wear sexy lace bras? Like, all the time?"

"Usually. I like to wear quality clothes."

"Well." He grinned. "If you like expensive things touching you, I'm delighted to let you know I am now very, very expensive." He ran his fingers ever so lightly over the delicate lace. "This is beautiful, but I think the point is to enjoy what's inside, right?"

Marley laughed as she reached behind her and unclipped her bra.

She honestly never expected this would happen...that someone would see her naked (other than a doctor or nurse) before surgery.

And the fact that it was Nikhil was *perfect*. She *knew* him. Their expectations were the same. They'd get this out of their system now with open communication like mature adults; then she'd have her surgery, and he'd go off to Hollywood to be a movie star. Every time Marley saw a movie poster or an action figure of him, she'd probably turn bright red and remember the feeling of his hands on her body. One day she'd tell her nieces and nephews about her torrid one-night stand with a superhero. Two one-night stands, technically.

Her boobies were going out with a bang. Lucky birds.

Once her breasts were exposed, Nikhil immediately leaned forward to lick her nipples. Marley moaned, every nerve ending in her skin going haywire. He continued to stroke, lick, and fondle her, lavishing attention on her until Marley couldn't hold herself up anymore. She lay back onto the bed and he immediately climbed on top to continue worshiping her body. His lips, teeth, and tongue seemed to know exactly how to make her nerves sing louder than anyone else had ever been able to get them to do. He almost brought her to orgasm with just his mouth on her breasts. Marley absently wondered if he somehow knew that these were the body parts that deserved the most attention tonight. She wondered if she should mourn the fact that she would never feel this exact sensation again. But it felt too good to do anything but enjoy it now.

Finally, she couldn't wait anymore. She clutched on to his neck and whispered in his ear, "Clothes. Off. Now."

He lifted his head and smiled. "Yes, I agree."

He climbed off her and finally started removing his clothes. After taking off her skirt, she lifted herself to her elbows to watch him. He was...a god. Perfectly sculpted chest. A real-life six-pack. A narrow waist. And when his pants lowered, she was gifted with the sight of firm, solid thighs and toned calves. A superhero. She was a little overwhelmed at the perfection of his body now.

But he was also Nikhil. Not a stranger. Not a god. Just her friend who was giving her an unforgettable gift without even knowing he was doing it. She scooted to the edge of the bed and ran her fingers over his waist, loving watching his brown skin pebble under her touch. He shuddered. "That feels amazing," he said. "You good? You still want to do this?"

Marley smiled. "Yeah…I'm perfect." She gathered her hair above her head since she preferred not to have it in her face if things got rowdy later. Which she hoped they would. "Crap. I don't have an elastic. Do you have an extra one in your bag?" Considering his long hair, he should.

Nikhil cringed, then smiled sheepishly. "Um…before we go further, I should probably tell you something. I…I have a confession."

Marley looked at him, blinking. Her mind raced…Was he married? In a committed relationship? She took a deep breath. She was alone in a hotel room. No one knew she was here. She was wearing nothing but a pair of expensive lace underpants, and her pricey La Perla bra was probably wedged between the wall and headboard. And he…Nikhil Shamdasani, the class clown who currently had the body of Adonis, was in nothing but Hanes boxer briefs.

Why had she trusted him? She closed her eyes, bracing herself. "What is it?"

She felt him sit next to her on the bed. "Okay. I probably should have been honest with you…but…I…"

She finally looked at him. Whatever confession he was about to make seemed to be upsetting him as much as her. He exhaled. "I don't have a bag here. I was lying when I said I was staying at this hotel."

Marley looked around the room, panicked. "Whose room are we in, then?"

"Oh, the studio has it all night…I just wasn't planning on staying here since I'm living somewhere else in town. I called Lydia while you were at the drugstore to ask if I could use the room."

Marley frowned. Why was this a secret? Was there a

reason she couldn't see his actual home? "Is your place being renovated or something? Or is it in a bad area?" She realized that he'd been a working actor—a *struggling* actor—until recently. He possibly didn't have a lot of money for Toronto homeownership.

"No. I...I'm in Markham. With...my parents."

Marley blinked. He was *living* in the suburb where they both grew up? With his *parents*?

"I mean, I'm only here for nine months or so, and I could get a place in the city closer to rehearsals, but my family's had a rough year and—"

Marley put her hand on his chest, stopping him. And she let her fingers trail over the firm muscles while she was there anyway. "Shhh...It doesn't matter. This is just one night. I don't know why you'd think I'd care."

He shrugged. "Because you're sophisticated and cool...I live with Mom and Dad. Dad wakes me to make me an omelet and rotli every morning, and tomorrow I need to help him check the gutters before spring. It's not very sexy." He smiled, still looking a little sheepish, and took the hair tie from his own hair and held it out to Marley.

She eyed it before taking it. "You clean? I have a friend who got lice this way."

He laughed, then almost tackled her, but she stopped him to put her hair up in a bun on the top of her head. She hadn't had this much fun in bed since, well, a long time ago. She gently pushed him so he was lying down on the bed and straddled his waist, then leaned down to lick *his* nipples this time. "I'll have you know that this sophisticated person is finding you incredibly sexy right now."

He groaned, pulling her down for another bruising kiss

before they broke apart to open the box of condoms. She was on top when they finally joined, and his hands were on her breasts the whole time, which she was incredibly grateful for. She was also grateful for the toe-curling orgasm he gave her. She'd had no idea how much she needed that.

All in all, Marley was so glad Nikhil Shamdasani had come back into her life to give her old body the send-off it deserved.

Marley ended up staying the night with Nikhil in the King Street hotel room. They put a healthy dent in the box of condoms before passing out on opposite sides of the bed. In the morning, Nikhil was still sleeping when Marley snuck out of bed, found her clothes, and went into the bathroom to shower and get dressed. Thank goodness she always had a small deodorant and toothbrush in her bag, and this fancy hotel provided a decent facial cleanser. Also, thank goodness for Nikhil's hair tie, because all she needed was a shake of the head to get her hair presentable.

Nikhil was awake and sitting up in the bed with the sheet over his lower half when she came back. He smiled when he saw her. "You heading out?"

She nodded. "I have to work at twelve." She sat on the edge of the bed. She'd thought that seeing him this morning might be a little awkward, but he was so relaxed that she was at ease, too.

"I can get my car service—"

She shook her head. "It's fine. I'll call an Uber." She hesitated before getting up. She wondered if she should say something— they were supposed to communicate this time. But they'd had the conversation before even coming up to this room. No strings attached. One night only. Friends with a benefit. *Singular.* (Marley was still calling it singular even though she'd had plenty of *benefits* last night.)

"Okay," he said.

"And…" She paused. "Thank you for last night. I kind of needed that."

He chuckled. "I mean, it's not like I didn't get something out of it, so I should be thanking you, too. Should we…" He paused. "I can give you my number? As a friend? Oh, wait. I'm getting a new number."

Marley sighed. She sat back on the bed. "So…I told you I was going through some shit. It's not the greatest time for me to make new relationships. Even friendships." Maybe someday, but there was no way she could be friends with him *now*. What if he texted her to ask how she was while she was drugged out and in pain? What if he wanted to hang out?

He didn't look surprised that she rejected him, though. Or upset. His expression was unreadable. "Yeah. And I'm incredibly busy, too," he said. "It's probably best. I had fun, though."

It was kind of heartbreaking that he wasn't upset. That it was easy for him to walk away from the chemistry that was so strong last night. Because Marley was finding this very hard.

But they had a deal…friends with a *benefit*. One night only.

"Me too," she said. She reached into her bag and pulled out a Reid's business card. It didn't have her phone number on it, but it did have her work email. "You can email me… maybe after your movie finishes filming." He took the card, nodding.

"Okay…bye." She stood. She wasn't sure a hug or a kiss was in order. Probably best to keep things professional-ish again.

"Bye, Marley!" he said. Clearly, he was finding this a teeny bit awkward, too. With one last look at that superhero chest, Marley waved and left the hotel room.

CHAPTER EIGHT

Marley

At around six that evening, Marley was finishing up with a client when she got a message that Jacqueline wanted to see her in her office. Marley couldn't think why. Maybe she wanted to tell her she'd done a good job at the press junket yesterday. Marley headed straight to Jacqueline's second-floor office.

Heart racing, she knocked on Jacqueline's door. Jacqueline's assistant, Kate, let Marley in. Like the personal shopping suite, this space was also luxuriously appointed with a sleek glass desk and a modern light fixture. Jacqueline was sitting at her desk, wearing a pristine suit with a Gucci scarf around her neck. Her perfect black bob was shining under the bright white recessed lights, and her lips, with their perfect nude lipstick, were smiling.

Jacqueline rarely smiled. Maybe excelling with her first personal shopping client meant Marley could get whatever she wanted out of Jacqueline now.

"Marley, *delighted* to see you," Jacqueline said. "And I see you're in our new Celine blouse? Wonderful. You always look so put together when you wear pieces from the store. Have a seat. Kate, can you get Marley a sencha tea?"

Marley sat on the leather chair across from Jacqueline's desk.

"I'll get straight to the point. I had the most interesting phone call today. Apparently, the film studio you have been working with is *smitten* with you. They said they'd never seen anyone please that client more."

Marley did her best not to chuckle. After last night, she'd say that Nikhil was the one who *excelled* at pleasing. "I enjoyed working with him."

"Well, clearly it paid off, because I'm thrilled to tell you that they have contracted with Reid's for a minimum of six months as the exclusive stylist for Nik Sharma. The client said he cannot lose you. You will build his wardrobe for all events and public appearances, and you will be expected to travel with him as needed. Compensation is your average daily commission when you are working with him, plus the actual commission on whatever they purchase. Plus a generous per diem for travel."

Marley blinked. They wanted her to work with Nikhil long-term? "But—"

Jacqueline waved her hand, stopping Marley from speaking. "If this goes well, we can talk about keeping you in personal shopping permanently. The executive team has been toying with the idea of launching a TV-and-film service for our shopping suite. This could be the beginning of a long-standing relationship with the studio."

"But I'm having surgery in two days! My medical leave—"

Jacqueline frowned. "Oh yes, I forgot about that. You'll be off for a few weeks, right?"

"Six."

Jacqueline shook her head. "Well, that can be canceled. This isn't the right time for elective surgery. The studio said the crunch time is the next four weeks before the movie starts filming. You'll have to go to LA with him for some talk shows, and there will be a photo shoot. Talk to the women's lead about working around your schedule on the selling floor." She paused. "You can have your surgery in a month, once filming starts."

Surgery was *Tuesday*. Putting it off a month wasn't possible... not with a surgeon as busy as Dr. Abernathy. After waiting so long, she couldn't be at the end of the queue again. "I won't be able to reschedule. This surgeon has a long waiting list."

Jacqueline scowled. "So, find another surgeon! This isn't an opportunity that comes often, Marley. There are other sales consultants in the store who will take the client if you won't." The subtext was clear—Marley needed to take this assignment, or she'd never move into personal shopping. But if she canceled her surgery, it could be months or longer before she could get another date.

She could get sick during that time. She looked down at her ticking-time-bomb body.

Jacqueline waved her hand in a dismissive gesture, clearly telling Marley she was done with this conversation. "Let me know your decision in the morning."

Marley walked out of Jacqueline's office in a daze. What the hell was she supposed to do now? How could she keep her job and have her surgery? But she had no choice but to push her decision aside for now because she still had an hour left of her shift. Marley put on her practiced shopgirl smile and let her customers berate her, abuse her, and nag her while she was screaming inside. She needed to get the hell off the selling floor.

And she'd just lost the best opportunity to do that that had come her way in years.

Marley texted Shayne as she left the store to make sure he was home. Then she ordered two deluxe chicken shawarma plates from her favorite Lebanese place for delivery. She was going to need some comfort food to make this decision.

Over fire-roasted chicken shawarma with hummus and fluffy pitas, Marley told Shayne all about her meeting with Jacqueline. Of course, Shayne still didn't know who the VIP was. Or that Marley had left him naked in a downtown hotel room twelve hours earlier. She had told him she spent the night at Ruby's.

"Holy shit. I *told* you Jacqueline was a witch," Shayne said. "I can't even. She told you to *cancel* your surgery?"

Marley nodded, chewing her garlicky chicken. After taking a big gulp of peppermint tea, she sighed. "This is the opportunity of a lifetime. I'll have to cancel surgery if I want to move to personal shopping. Jacqueline was quite clear."

"There must be a way you can work with this client *and* have surgery. Tell them you can style them in six weeks after you're recovered."

Marley shook her head. "His film starts shooting in six weeks. And they want me to go to LA for some appearances before that."

Shayne raised a brow. "The VIP is a *movie star*? Shoot, girl, have you been styling Keanu Reeves? Why didn't you tell me! I—"

"What? No! Why do you think it's Keanu?"

"He's in town. He was spotted eating a cupcake on the subway yesterday. So, who is it, then? And what *exactly* did you do to make this person so enamored with you that he's insisting you come to all his appearances?"

Marley quickly dipped a potato in the vibrant-red hot sauce and popped it in her mouth. If she started blushing, then Shayne would know exactly what Marley did to please the client. "I can't tell you. NDA."

"This sounds like a rom-com. But I know you wouldn't get involved with a client. Or a movie star. We went to an arts school—we know exactly how *insufferable* actors are."

Marley didn't say anything. She still couldn't believe Nikhil had done this to her. She may not have told Nikhil the truth about her leave, but he *knew* she would be unavailable. He knew she was going through something hard. She'd been way more open than she usually was with anyone. And he'd betrayed her. Some friend. He really was insufferable.

"Wow, you're turning bright red. That must have been some client."

"I'm bright red because I am incredibly pissed off at him. Why would he sabotage my job like this?"

"You know this, Marley. Because actors are all self-absorbed divas. Except Keanu, of course. The rest are so wrapped up in their own shit that they don't notice, or care, when they put someone out. This is why we stayed away from the theater kids at school. Did you tell him off?"

Marley snorted. "Of course not. He's a *client*." Marley had considered calling him right after leaving Jacqueline's office, but of course, she didn't have his number. Only Lydia's. And she wasn't going to call her. "I *should* tell him off. I know I was just his stylist, but..." She sighed. "It's complicated. I can't say why, but I trusted him." Her voice cracked as she spoke.

"Maybe you should talk to him," Shayne said after a few moments. "It might not be his fault. Sometimes these people have no clue what their team does. He might be able to convince the studio to work with you *after* your recovery."

Was that possible? Marley didn't know if it was Nikhil or his team who'd insisted she work with him.

"I don't have his phone number. Only his handler's." She stood, taking her now-empty plate to the kitchen. "But I *do* know exactly where to find him. I'm going now."

Shayne excitedly got up, too. "Ooh, we're going to tell off Keanu Reeves! Should I wear my *Matrix* jacket?"

Marley rolled her eyes. "It's not Keanu. And you can't come."

"C'mon, Marley. I'm not letting you go alone to confront a movie star. For safety...I'm coming."

Actually, maybe she *should* bring Shayne. As her friend. And as Nikhil's former friend, too. She wagged a finger at Shayne. "If I bring you, you'll keep all of this to yourself. They'll sue me for a million dollars if I break the NDA. This needs to be tighter in the vault than what happened on your twenty-fifth birthday. Okay?"

Shayne's eyes went wide. He knew how secure the twenty-fifth-birthday vault was. "Deal. What happens in... wherever we're going stays in wherever we're going."

Marley didn't tell him who they were going to see, so Shayne was utterly shocked when she started driving north toward their hometown of Markham. He made a disparaging sound when Marley got off the highway. "Are we going to your *mother's* house?"

"No."

He made an even more disapproving sound as she kept driving. "*My* mother's?" Shayne was low contact with his parents. Grams was the only family he spoke to.

"Of course not."

When Marley parked in front of a large redbrick house in a subdivision filled with large redbrick houses, Shayne was clearly very confused. Marley was surprised she remembered where Nikhil's family's house was. She'd been here only once to study for a chemistry test. But Shayne had never been here, as far as Marley knew.

"The VIP lives in a Markham McMansion?" His eyes suddenly went huge, and he slapped Marley on the arm. "*Holy. Shit.* I only know of one Toronto celebrity who would have a connection with this neighborhood. *Nicky Shamdasani*...Marley, you've been styling the *Bronze fucking Shadow*."

She'd forgotten that Shayne used to call Nikhil Nicky, but she had suspected Shayne knew the Bronze Shadow was Nikhil. Shayne followed celebrity gossip, so Marley had no doubt he'd seen pictures. He probably hadn't mentioned it to Marley because of her and Nikhil's complicated past.

Marley unbuckled her belt. "All right...this is just you and me visiting an old friend, okay? And I didn't tell you I'm styling him; you figured it out on your own. Got it?"

Shayne nodded and made a gesture zipping up his lips and throwing away the key.

An older South Asian man in jeans answered the door after she knocked. Marley vaguely remembered him—Nikhil's father. He had Nikhil's eyes. Eyes that looked suspicious right now.

"Yes?"

"Is Nikhil here?" Marley asked. "I'm Mar— Mahreen Kamal. A friend of his."

Nikhil's father hesitated...rightly. He'd probably been warned never to let anyone know that Nikhil lived here.

"We went to high school together. I'm Shayne." Shayne put his hand out to shake. "This house's exterior is perfection. Did you do the landscaping yourself?"

Nikhil's father still looked suspicious. "I'm working with Nikhil, too," Marley added. "I'm his wardrobe stylist. I need to speak to him about...clothes."

Nikhil's dad finally smiled. "Ah yes, come, come. Nikhil just got home." He urged them into the house. The entryway of the house was vast, with white ceramic tile flooring and a glass chandelier high on the ceiling. In front of them was a curving staircase covered with pink broadloom carpet with an oak banister. It all reminded Marley of her own parents' house, which was only about five minutes from here.

"Nikhil always takes a shower when he comes home," Nikhil's dad said. He was clearly a chatty man. "He gets so sweaty when he's training! Have you seen the gym he works in? State of the art! No expense spared! Come, I'll pour some chai. You can call me Sunhil Uncle. So, you went to the art school with Nikhil? I didn't want him to go there. He should have been an engineer, like me, instead of this acting business. Do you live near here? Mahreen, do we know your family? Where are your parents from?"

"Kenya and Tanzania," Marley said.

"Wonderful. Have you eaten? We have friends from Tanzania. Come. I have fresh bhindi and rotli." Marley glanced back at Shayne behind her. He looked a little like a deer caught in the headlights. Which, fair—he didn't have as much experience with this brand of Indian hospitality. Marley's own parents were nowhere near this warm to Marley's friends. Especially her non-Indian friends.

They found themselves sitting at the breakfast bar in the

kitchen, warm chai in front of them, and a plate of Peek Freans cookies between them. It had taken a fair amount of effort to convince Nikhil's father that they had eaten enough shawarma and didn't need any bhindi or rotli. After about five minutes, a teenage girl came into the kitchen. Her eyes narrowed when she saw Marley and Shayne.

"Who are you two?" she asked. She was in a sweatshirt and jeans, and her long dark hair was in a ponytail.

"This is Mahreen and Shayne," Sunhil Uncle said. "They are friends of Nikhil's from high school. This is Nikhil's sister, Nalini. She didn't go to the arts school like him. Nalini is going to be a *doctor*."

Nalini's eyes went wide, staring at Marley. "You…you're Marley, aren't you?"

Marley frowned, nodding. Had Nikhil told his sister about her?

"Does Nikhil know you're here?"

Marley shook her head. At that, Nalini disappeared before anyone could say another word.

"She's very close to her brother," Sunhil Uncle said. "How do you like that chai? It's a new brand they had in Patel Brothers, but I'm not sure it's as good as Wagh Bakri. Do you like Wagh Bakri? Maybe I should make a new pot. Shayne, do you drink a lot of chai? Where is your family from? Nikhil's mother and I traveled to Tanzania years ago. We used to have the wanderlust then. She's not feeling well, but maybe you can come another time for her to meet you! She loves meeting the children's friends!"

Coming here was a mistake. This was supposed to be a professional relationship and now she was sitting in his parents' kitchen talking about chai and scaring the crap out of his sister. Nikhil was going to be furious with her.

Which...fine. Because she was furious with him. A few moments later, while Shayne was telling Sunhil Uncle all about his grandmother coming from Jamaica half a century ago, Nikhil himself burst into the kitchen. His hair was wet. He was wearing gray sweatpants with some charity-run shirt. And he looked...annoyed. Good.

CHAPTER NINE

Nikhil

Nikhil didn't believe his sister, Nalini, when she banged on the basement bathroom door yelling that his hookup from last night was now having chai and cookies in the kitchen with Dad and some man in a neon Hawaiian shirt, but it seemed too cruel a prank, even for Nalini. So he got out of the shower as fast as he could and threw on some clothes. He couldn't imagine why Marley would be here. Something to do with her store? Did she need the shirt from the junket back?

Or maybe she wanted to talk about the mind-boggling, amazing sex they'd had the night before. Or about the torturous fact that it would never happen again. That she hadn't even wanted his phone number.

She'd been distracting him all day...Every time his mind stilled, all he could think about was *her*. Her hands all over him. Her mouth on him. The memory of her body locked with his. Her scent. The feel of her skin under his fingers. He'd been completely useless in training today.

But he'd fully planned to honor their agreement. Friends with a single, one-time *benefit*.

What if she wanted to change that agreement?

When he got upstairs, sure enough, Marley was sitting on

one of the tall stools in the kitchen, drinking chai with Dad and…was that…

"Nicky Shamdasani," Shayne said, shaking his head. "The glow-up of the century. Look at you—you're a *vision*. Wow."

That comment made Nalini snort and his dad literally beam.

"Nikhil," Dad said, "Shayne said he would give me his grandmother's jerk chicken recipe! We can make it for a barbecue in the summer! Dadima loves Jamaican food!"

Nikhil stared at Marley. She was wearing loose cream dress pants and a black blouse that had a large bow at the neck. And her hair that had been piled on top of her head with his hair tie while he was inside her was now down in waves cascading around her shoulders. Shoulders that he'd tasted last night. He took a step away, mostly so he could resist touching her. It was clear that wasn't why she was here.

Nikhil finally found his voice. "Hi, Shayne. Great to see you again. What are you two doing here?"

Marley's gorgeous mouth was in a straight line. Was she angry? "I need to speak to you."

Nikhil frowned. "Okay. Um…yeah. We can do that. Let's go to the den. It's private."

Marley nodded. She was definitely mad. He looked at his dad and sister watching intently, clearly desperate to find out what this beautiful woman needed to talk to him about so urgently at nine o'clock at night. But he wasn't going to let them find out. He motioned Marley and Shayne toward the other part of the house. "Nalini, don't listen at the door."

Nalini pouted, but Nikhil knew she would obey him. Probably. Hopefully.

"Take your chai," Dad said as Shayne and Marley stood.

"Do you want me to warm up some dhokla, too? I have ladoos…or do you want some kulfi?"

Nikhil exhaled. "No, we're good."

Nikhil's heart was racing as he closed the door to the den/office. It was a smallish room, with a desk on one side and a small sitting area on the other. No one ever used the room—technically Dad was supposed to work from home here, but his father was way too social to want to be alone.

Actually, now that he thought about it, he was surprised Arjun didn't want to rent out this space as well as the basement. Marley sat next to Shayne on the old leather couch and put her cup and saucer on the coffee table. Nikhil sat across from them on an armchair.

"Cozy," Shayne said. Shayne looked exactly like he had in high school and was even dressed similarly—very stylish, very bright colors. The only thing different was less acne. And he had a mustache now.

Sitting in his childhood home with these two was messing with Nikhil. His past and present were colliding.

Marley's forehead furrowed. She was quite clearly upset. He had every intention of fixing whatever he had done to put that expression on her face. Even though she hadn't told him what was going on, he *did* know she was going through shit right now. And he hated the thought that he might have made her life harder.

"Your dad said your mother's not feeling well," Shayne said. "I hope it's nothing too serious?"

He shook his head. "Yeah, she's fine." Mom wasn't fine, but he wasn't getting into the whole story now. "So…what's going on?"

"You know why I'm here," Marley said. "I can't believe… after everything. I thought we were *friends*."

Nikhil frowned. "We *are* friends."

Marley snorted. "Friends respect each other's personal lives." She looked away, then quickly looked back at Nikhil. "It was a mistake to be open with you last night. I mean…you got what you wanted, right?"

Yeah, he got what he wanted. They both did. But what happened last night wasn't about wanting each other physically, or a release, or anything like that. What they'd both wanted was a chance, just for one night, to reconnect with the world like it had been before it had fallen apart. He understood that completely but didn't know if he should say it now.

Marley was still looking at him with complete disappointment. She might even have tears forming.

"Holy shit," Shayne said suddenly, looking back and forth between them. "You weren't at Ruby's last night. You two had *sex*. Marley, you kept the fact that you're not only *styling* a movie star from me, but also that you're *banging* one."

Marley turned sharply to her friend. "Shayne!"

Shayne would have none of it. "*Marley*! We're *best friends*! We're supposed to tell each other everything! I know you two did the dirty tango back in high school, but again? This is huge! Do you know how famous this man is? And you, Nicky." Shayne looked at Nikhil, disappointment in his eyes. "You never seemed like the cheating type. Aren't you *dating* America's literal sweetheart? And you're *sleeping* with your stylist?"

Marley's eyes went as wide as her chai saucer. "You're *dating* someone?"

Nikhil had no idea who or what Shayne was talking about. "No! Who do you think I'm dating?"

Shayne pulled out his phone. "I saw it on TMZ, like, yesterday. You're dating Serena Vox."

"You told me you barely knew Serena Vox!" Marley said. "You lied to me, sabotaged my job, and…"

Nikhil put his hands up in surrender. This was going too far. Even if Nalini wasn't listening at the door, he had no doubt his whole family was hearing this. Even Mom all the way upstairs. "Can we back up a bit…I have no idea what's going on."

"Yeah, me neither," Shayne said. "Are you sleeping with both my best friend and my only ever female crush? Because if so…*damn*."

Nikhil frowned, then looked at Marley. "Shayne should really sign an NDA." Marley looked like she was going to growl at him, so Nikhil decided to drop it. "Okay," he said, "one at a time. *Where* did you see that I'm dating Serena?"

"TMZ." Shayne held his phone in front of Nikhil. Nikhil took it, and sure enough, it was a picture of him and Serena in LA weeks ago when they'd met with the publicity team there. He was saying something in the picture, and Serena was holding on to his arm, laughing. They didn't necessarily look like a couple in the shot, but they did look close. Could this be what the publicists meant when they said it was time to release the pictures? He skimmed the article. It wasn't confirmation, but rather speculation that Serena was already dating her new co-star in the next Ironis film.

"It's for publicity," Nikhil said. "They released pictures of us to improve my image."

Marley frowned. "It says that you're dating."

He shook his head. "We're not. It's just celebrity gossip…I can't really control that. Honestly, I barely know her."

Marley's expression was…cold. "It doesn't matter anyway," she said. "Last night was a one-night thing. It meant nothing."

That statement felt like a stab in his chest, but he tried not to let that show on his face. Friends with a benefit...one night only. He had agreed to that. But it *had* meant something. To him, at least. "Okay, why do you think I'm trying to sabotage your job?"

Marley sighed. Then she told Nikhil about a meeting she'd had with her boss who told her that he'd insisted the studio contract her for six months as his exclusive stylist.

"What? I didn't do that!"

"Do you have any idea what your team does on your behalf?" Shayne asked, disappointed.

"I'm just telling you what my boss told me," Marley said. "Apparently you and the studio were so happy with my styling for Comicon and the junket that you insisted I keep working with you. They want me to go on a press tour with you, select all your looks, and coordinate with the store to get alterations and bespoke pieces made."

"Bespoke?"

"Custom made for you," Shayne clarified.

Nikhil cringed. He wasn't at all surprised that the studio had made this deal without asking him. It was true that they—he and the studio—were all happy with Marley's work. And he clearly needed a stylist. But they should have consulted him before asking for Marley.

"Jacqueline asked me to cancel my leave of absence," Marley said. "She pretty much implied that I'd never move to personal shopping if I didn't."

"Fuck," Nikhil said.

"If y'all are looking to do that again, I can make myself scarce," Shayne said. Marley glared at him.

"I can't style you, Nikhil," she said.

"No, of course not," Nikhil said quickly. "I'll call Lydia and tell—"

"You don't get it." Marley sighed. "This is the opportunity of my career. If I don't take it, I can kiss the personal shopping job I want goodbye."

Shit. He knew she wanted that. "But can't you...can you put off your leave? I mean, it's only six weeks until the film starts shooting, and I won't need a stylist then."

Marley shook her head, then looked out the window. "I'm having surgery on Tuesday, Nikhil. Major surgery. I can't put it off."

"Oh shit," Nikhil said. "Are you okay? What can I do to help? I can tell the studio you're having surgery...They'll understand."

Marley turned back to him and gave him a glare. "I don't want to tell them. I don't want to tell anyone."

"You can tell Nicky, though," Shayne said. "He's a friend."

Nikhil frowned. Clearly there was more to this than a simple surgery. Was she sick? Ugh. He wanted to do something, but he didn't know what. "How can I help? Can I get you books? Or...I can probably get screener copies of movies from the studio."

Marley snorted. And he noticed that she had tears forming. She looked straight at him. "I'm having a mastectomy, Nikhil." He blinked at that. Before he could open his mouth to ask more, she clarified. "I'm fine. It's prophylactic. I have a cancer-causing genetic mutation. This is so I *won't* get breast cancer."

Oh no. He thought back to grade twelve...to all those conversations they'd had when her aunt was going through breast cancer treatment. "Oh, Marley." He wanted to hug her. She wouldn't want that, though. He didn't know how to help her. "Do you need food? I can still make coq au vin. Or comfort food is better, right? My daal is amazing."

Shayne snorted. "You think lentils will solve this problem?"

Marley ignored his daal offer. "If I don't take the surgery date, it could be months or longer before another spot opens for me. I'll be in recovery when you go on that press tour. But this is exactly the kind of thing my boss holds a grudge for. She knows it's technically elective surgery."

"Can't you explain all this to her? There must be a way," Nikhil said.

"That's why we're here," Shayne said, looking at Marley, annoyed. "Not to *yell* at your client, or friend, or lover...or whatever you two are." Shayne looked at Nikhil. "We need to find a solution to this situation."

Shayne was right. Nikhil wasn't going to let Marley lose this opportunity to advance her career, and he wasn't going to let her put her health at risk, either. And now that the option had been presented to him, he wasn't going to let anyone other than Marley style him for the next six months.

Nikhil was a goddamn movie star. He was supposed to be able to have it all.

"Do you have to actually be with me to pick clothes for me? Like, in person?" Nikhil asked.

Marley nodded. "Yes. Personal stylists usually go to the client."

"Well, why can't I come to you, instead? While you're recovering. We can have the stuff from the store delivered. You won't have to lift a finger. Just sit back and tell me what looks good on me. Could you handle that?"

Marley shook her head. "I suppose in theory. But Shayne's

going to Paris on Tuesday, so I'm moving in with my mom and dad."

"So? Isn't that better? They live near here, don't they?"

Marley shook her head again. "If you come over there, it will light up on WhatsApp all over the East Coast. And the West Coast. There is no NDA strong enough for my mom and dad. Bad enough that I have to go there to recover at all. My parents and I have a...complicated relationship." Marley looked down at her fingers.

Clearly her parents' house wasn't the best place for Marley to be when she was vulnerable. Why was Shayne leaving his best friend right when she needed him?

"I told you, Marley," Shayne said. "You don't have to go there. Stay at home and Reena will come see you every day. You said only the first week or so will be really bad. You'll be so much more comfortable at home, and Nikhil can come to you in the city for styling. Or you can FaceTime."

Marley shook her head. "But Reena can't spend the night. She starts work at three a.m. every day." She exhaled. "The nurse said I shouldn't be alone overnight at least for the first week."

Nikhil could see how scared she was even though she didn't say it. Which was totally valid...He couldn't imagine what she was going through. Major surgery and a huge change to her body, and no one there to support her.

"I'll stay with you at night," Nikhil said.

She stared at him for a long time, barely moving. He couldn't read her expression. Finally, she snarled. Like an honest-to-goodness snarl, which somehow still looked beautiful on her. "We discussed this, Nikhil. Last night was a one-time thing."

Shit. He'd screwed up again. She thought he wanted to sleep with her. "No, no, Marley, I—"

"Do I need to leave you alone to have a lovers' tiff?" Shayne asked.

"We're not lovers," Marley said.

"No, but we *are* friends," Nikhil said quickly. "Look, I know it's not ideal, but this could work for both of us. I can stay with you while Shayne is gone. I'm at rehearsals all day…but I can be there to help you evenings and overnight. Lydia's been on my back to get out of my parents' house, anyway, because she says she can't secure this neighborhood from paparazzi. I could hide at your place for a few weeks. It's close to the studio. And I'd be there for you to style me." He could come back here to check in on Mom and Nalini every few days. It would be fine.

Shayne nodded. "Our neighborhood would be secure. Most of our neighbors are eighty-plus-year-old Eastern Europeans. I doubt they're keeping up with Ironis movie gossip."

Marley shook her head. "You can't take care of me, Nikhil! You're an actor!"

"And a fashion photographer is a better nurse?" Shayne deadpanned.

Marley glared at them both, shaking her head.

Nikhil exhaled. "Marley, I know you're a private person." He sighed. "Forget about all this stylist stuff—I'll tell Lydia I'll work with someone else until you are recovered, but no one other than you after that, so there's no way your boss will be mad. But let me help you. I took care of my mother after her back surgery—I'm not squeamish. I can do this for a few weeks."

"It's not a bad idea," Shayne said. "He can move into Gram's quilting room. It's better than going to your parents'."

Marley continued to stare at him. But then something happened in her eyes. A softening. And then a tiny nod. "Okay. Let's try. Call Lydia, see if she can convince Reid's to let me style you from home. I can probably do everything but travel with you. I can get a colleague to bring clothes from the store."

Nikhil exhaled. There. He'd fixed it. He was going to help her. And she would be helping him, too. This was perfect.

CHAPTER TEN

Marley

Marley was completely, 100 percent positive that this harebrained idea to have Nikhil move in and nurse her through her surgery recovery was beyond ridiculous, but she and Shayne stayed at Nikhil's family's house to hammer out a recovery/personal styling plan for the next hour. The excellent chai and dhokla helped. Nikhil then called Lydia and told her that he'd spoken to Marley and that due to a medical leave, she wasn't able to travel with him, but she could still style him from her home in Toronto. He asked Lydia to call Reid's and insist that they let Marley work with him while she was away from the store. Of course, Nikhil didn't tell Lydia what the medical leave was for, or that he would be *living* with Marley for a few weeks.

Nikhil also asked Lydia to send a quick NDA for Shayne, since he said Marley's roommate might be there when he went to see Marley. He didn't mention that Shayne already knew everything he needed the NDA for.

The next day, once Jacqueline was in, Marley went straight into her office expecting to have to fight to get the store manager to agree to the plan. But Jacqueline had already heard from Lydia and was on board. Marley walked out of Jacqueline's office shaking her head in disbelief. The studio must have thrown even more money or promises for future business at Reid's.

After work, Marley made the long drive to Markham for the second time in two days, this time for dinner with her parents. She hadn't told them yet that she wasn't coming back to their place after surgery the next day. When it came to her parents, Marley tended to withhold personal information as long as possible, mostly so she could put off the judgmental comments. And the oversharing.

"What do you mean you're not staying here anymore? Shayne's not going to Paris?" her mom said after Marley told them. Mom then looked at Dad. "Oh, Amin, you should call Rozmin. Now we can go to her party on the weekend."

Marley sighed as she scooped some keema with her rotli. They were in the formal dining room, which was where they ate dinner whenever Marley visited. She had no idea if her parents ate in the kitchen when she wasn't here…or if they even ate together.

Overall, Marley had an okay relationship with her parents. Mostly. Her biggest issue with them had always been that they were simultaneously very closed off about their lives while also oversharing personal details with others as some sort of social currency. Like, for example, they didn't tell anyone when Marley came out as bisexual, but they blasted in the extended-family chat group that Marley was going to study fashion merchandising in community college instead of going to university like they wanted her to. Also, when Mom was first diagnosed with breast cancer, Dad insisted that no one in the family be told about it. But then when they found out about the BRCA mutation, suddenly they started telling everyone and even posted any article they could find about Angelina

Jolie's mastectomy on WhatsApp. And they told everyone that Marley was a carrier of the mutation, too.

Marley didn't tell them much about her life anymore, because she didn't want the whole world to know everything, but also because she knew she wouldn't get a whole lot of support anyway. They weren't quite narcissistic but were definitely more concerned about their own lives and how things affected them than about what their daughter was going through.

Marley often wondered if Mom resented that Marley had learned about her mutation early enough to *prevent* getting breast cancer. Or if Mom felt guilty that her daughter had to go through all this because of a gene she'd passed on to her. Or...who knew? Talking about hard stuff wasn't something the Kamal family did.

"No, Shayne's still going to Paris," Marley said. "But another friend will be in town for a few weeks and offered to stay with me. This way I won't have to have Ruby come feed McQueen every day."

Dad looked skeptical. "Who is this friend? Where does she live?"

"He lives in LA."

Mom dropped the rotli in her hand. "*He*! You're having a *man* take care of you after surgery? You're having *breast* surgery. What will people say?"

Marley raised one brow. "Shayne's a man...You didn't have an issue with him taking care of me after surgery."

"Shayne is gay!" Dad said. He paused. "Is this man gay?"

Marley shook her head. "No, but did you forget that I'm bisexual? By your logic, it would be a scandal for someone of any gender to live with me." It was exhausting to have to remind her parents about her sexuality so often. It wasn't that they necessarily didn't accept her—more like it wasn't important information to keep at the front of their mind.

Mom's lips were pursed. Marley got that they were old-fashioned and grew up in a different time and place. But did they really think that only someone who had breasts (or who had once had breasts) could take care of someone after a mastectomy?

"I'll be way more comfortable in my own home with McQueen than here," Marley said. "And I won't be a burden on you. I know you guys are busy, too. If you're able to, you can drive me to my follow-up appointments with the surgeon."

Mom waved her hand. "Yes, of course." She frowned, maybe realizing she could keep her busy social life if she didn't have to take care of her daughter. "I bought you chocolates for after surgery. And I can cook for you, too. Tell me what you want to eat…I can make lasagna? Or do you want biryani? Last week I made paella for the first time, but your father didn't like it at all. Fifty dollars in seafood, right down the drain. But I invited the neighbors over…Did you know Sherry next door is getting a divorce? She'll sell her house, I think. She always waters my plants when we go away. I don't know what I'll do then."

Marley sighed. She wasn't surprised Mom changed the subject to herself.

"You didn't tell me your friend's name," Dad said after a while. "How do you know him?"

Marley frowned. She didn't think this through. Her parents didn't really keep up with Hollywood news, but they did keep up with anything having to do with Indians. Marley had no doubt that news that an Indian-Canadian actor had scored such a massive role in a blockbuster movie would have reached them.

"Devin."

"What?"

She sighed. "His name's Devin. I've known him since college. He lives in…California."

"He works in tech?" Dad asked.

Marley nodded. It wasn't really a lie…The Ironis movies had a ton of computer effects.

Dad smiled. "I'm sure you'll be in good hands, beti. I was afraid he'd be one of your artist friends."

An actor was an artist, but Marley agreed Nikhil had very good hands. She was sure they were better hands to be in than her parents'.

Finally, it was the day of her surgery. And Marley was scared. Actually, she was freaking terrified. She woke at dawn, since they needed to be at the hospital at seven. The plan was for Shayne to drive Marley downtown. His flight to France wasn't until late that night, so he would stay until she woke after surgery. The doctor anticipated that as long as everything went well, Marley would most likely be going home the same day, so Shayne should be able to bring her home and make sure she was settled before heading to the airport.

Marley was silent on the drive downtown. This was her first surgery ever, and she was a complete ball of nerves. It wasn't just fear about the aftereffects (although that was terrifying). She was also worried about being away from the store for so long, about how she was going to style Nikhil without being able to pick things herself, and of course, she was worried that she'd made a huge mistake by inviting him to stay with her.

But worrying about all of that was useless now. She pushed all her negative thoughts out of her mind and listened to the calming music Shayne had put on for the drive.

When they got to the hospital, Marley was checked in and given a robe and gown to change into, then hooked up to an IV. Finally, Dr. Abernathy came in and talked a bit about the procedure. He then stood in front of her and used a Sharpie to mark strange lines all over her naked chest.

"You'll be lying down when we operate, so I'm marking how your breasts naturally fall so we can try to replicate the size and shape with the implant."

Marley nodded. This was yet another indignity her poor boobs had to endure before they were removed. She balled her fists.

After Dr. Abernathy was done with her, she was led to a large waiting area while they prepared the operating room. Shayne was already there, sitting alone near a window. Marley wheeled her IV over and sat next to him.

"How you hanging in there, kiddo?" Shayne asked. He seemed nervous, too, but was clearly trying to be calm for Marley.

"Okay…" Marley tapped her foot rapidly on the tiled floor.

Shayne smiled. He had a magazine in his hand. "See this?" He pointed to a fashion spread. He must have brought the magazine with him because she doubted the hospital would have a new fashion magazine in the waiting room. "This was that House of Bhatt photo shoot I did a few months ago. Remember?"

Marley nodded. "Sounded fun."

He tapped the picture the magazine was open to. "This jacket would look amazeballs on you. Want me to ask Nilusha

Bhatt for a sample? We're going to meet up in Paris in a few days."

Marley nodded again. She was a bobblehead doll today.

"I'm also thinking about getting a tattoo while I'm there. Tramp stamps are apparently coming back in. Should I get the word *masterpiece* and an arrow pointing at my ass?"

"Sure. Sounds like a great time."

Shayne put down his magazine. "Marley, are you even listening to me?"

Marley frowned, blinking. "Um…yes?"

"Okay, pop quiz, then. What am I thinking of tattooing above my butt?"

Marley was horrified. "What? Nothing! You are *not* getting *anything* tattooed above your butt! We had a deal that we both have veto power over any permanent body modification. And tramp stamps are eternally off-limits!"

Shayne crossed his arms and glared at Marley. "*I know.* I said it to see if you were listening. Apparently, you weren't."

Marley sighed. "I'm sorry."

Shayne put his hand on Marley's knee. "Marley, you can admit that you're freaking out."

She didn't say anything.

Shayne handed her a white postcard. "I grabbed this while you were changing."

Marley took it. It was advertising some charity that did makeovers on cancer patients. Marley was pretty sure the nurse gave her the same one at pre-op.

"You should do this," Shayne said. "They'll help you with what to wear after the surgery."

"I'm literally in the helping-others-with-what-to-wear industry. I'll figure it out."

"Well then, maybe you can volunteer with them. They'll have people you can talk to who have been through it."

"I don't need anyone to talk to. I have you."

"I'm going to France."

"You're coming home. Until then, I'll have Reena."

"Yeah, and your movie star boy toy. But maybe it would be better to talk to someone who understands what you've been through?"

Marley didn't say anything. She looked down at the floor. Why was hospital flooring so...dull? What color was this... white? Blue? Gray?

In less than an hour, the body that she'd had her entire life would be changed. She had no idea what was going to happen. Something could go wrong; she could come out with botched breasts or chronic pain. Or when they opened her up, they could find out that they were too late and that cancer was already there.

Talking to anyone about all of it wouldn't change a thing. The only thing she could do was be here. Have her mastectomy. And she was doing that. "Shayne," she said softly, looking up at him. "Do you approve of this body modification?"

He smiled, then squeezed her non-IV hand for a moment. "Completely. You're doing the right thing, Marley."

She looked down, willing away the tears that were forming in her eyes.

"Reena is dropping off freezer meals today," Shayne said after a few moments of silence. "Your movie star can manage a microwave, right? Or is he too *bougie* for kitchen conveniences now?"

"Nikhil was in cooking class with us in grade eleven, remember?"

Shayne laughed. "Is he going to cook for you again? I mean,

since you two are reliving all your experiences from high school together."

Marley snorted.

Shayne flipped to the next page of the magazine. "Hey, you never told me: How was reliving prom night, anyway? Was the superhero…*super*?"

Marley shrugged—talking about sexual encounters was normal for Marley and Shayne. But this one felt too…sacred to talk about. Even though she and Nikhil were just friends. Probably because it was her boobs' last time.

"You two going to keep up with the prom-night reenactments while I'm gone?" Shayne asked.

She rolled her eyes. "I'll be recovering from surgery. I'll barely be able to move and will have drains coming out of my body. I will not be having sex."

"Okay then—after you are recovered. Are you two going to be…a thing?"

There was a hesitation in Shayne's voice. Marley couldn't tell if Shayne approved or disapproved of Marley and Nikhil as a couple. Not that they would ever be that.

Marley shook her head. "You're the one who always said to stay away from actors."

"Yeah, and it didn't stop you before, or now. I think you might actually have feelings for *that* actor."

Marley shook her head. "It was a one-night casual thing. That's it."

Shayne exhaled. "Well then, I'm glad you hooked up with him one more time. I mean, it's totally *iconic* that your last time before your mastectomy was with a *literal* superhero. I hope he fucking *worshiped* your boobs. I hope they had the best last meal in existence."

Marley nodded, feeling herself blush. "Yes—yes they did."

"Mahreen Kamal?" a nurse said. Marley closed her eyes a moment. It was time.

Shayne's hand was suddenly on hers again. "You got this."

Marley hugged him, and he kissed her cheek. "Love you," Shayne said in her ear. "I'll be here the whole time."

"Love you, too, Shayne."

With a deep breath, Marley stood and went through the doors to the surgical unit.

After a nurse took her vitals and she had a consult with the anesthesiologist, Marley was given the choice of either walking or being wheeled into the operating room. She chose to walk, pushing her IV cart in front of her. The room was bigger and had more people and equipment in it than she had expected. It seemed chaotic. As a nurse helped her get on the table, each person in the room introduced themselves to her and told her their role. Everyone sounded friendly. Unstressed. Dr. Abernathy was the last to greet her, right after the general surgeon he would be working with.

He smiled his warm, calming smile. "Everything okay, Marley?"

It meant something that the doctor remembered that she preferred the name Marley. "Everyone here seems nice."

"Best team in the world," Dr. Abernathy said. "We'll take good care of you. Here, lie down."

She lay back. The anesthesiologist came close and did something with her IV. "Your nails are so perfectly shaped," she said. "Do you get them done professionally?"

"Yes," Marley said. She was getting sleepy. "They told me I couldn't have polish today."

"Yeah, it interferes with one of the machines. With your

undertones, you can probably wear bright colors. What shades do you prefer?"

"I have to wear nudes for work," Marley mumbled. "Nikhil would like me in colors, though. I should do that for him."

And everything went dark.

CHAPTER ELEVEN

Nikhil

Nikhil was exhausted, and his day wasn't anywhere close to being done yet. The lead stunt coordinator, Caroline, showed up for the first time today, and she and his trainer Reggie spent the whole day watching him like a hawk to make sure his strength training was up to snuff before she started teaching him the fight sequences. He was pretty sure he failed their inspection because his mind clearly wasn't in the game today. Honestly, he was lucky he didn't injure himself.

But at around three o'clock, he breathed a giant sigh of relief when a text from Shayne came, saying that Marley was out of surgery and in recovery and that everything had gone well. The doctor said she'd likely be able to go home tonight. Thank goodness.

On his way out of the gym, he got a call from Esther. He got into his car to answer. Or rather, his mom's car. He'd been using it since he got to town because she never went anywhere.

"Babycakes, did you get the promotion schedule I emailed you? I got them to agree to Canadian outlets instead of New York, so you won't have to travel as much. You will have to go to LA, though. Lydia will be taking care of all your travel arrangements."

"Oh. Okay." He hadn't seen Lydia today...or even heard from her, which was unusual.

"I'm making them go through me first for everything now. Same rule for you: no more demands without checking with me first—I mean it. Something is fishy...I don't like how they're spinning you and Serena."

"Do you think the studio is behind those rumors that we're dating?"

"I wouldn't put it past them. They denied it...but if it smells like a porcupine, it usually is a porcupine. You smile and nod when the studio asks you to do something. Let me be the one to push back. I smoothed over this last one, but you're on thin ice."

"What are you talking about? What last one?"

"You insisting that you'll only work with that shopgirl stylist, even though she has no availability to actually work."

That was barely a demand at all. It was blatantly unfair. Other emerging stars could do anything—be complete divas, go all asshole-method-actor and treat everyone like shit, and even get bottle service at a different club each night—and they would be called the next It Boy. They didn't need to be warned to behave. "Marley is having *surgery*. That's why she's not available." Well, she had surgery. Thank God it went fine.

"Yeah, and there are plenty of other pretty girls who can make your hot body look even more smoking. Even ones you haven't scared off yet. I agree that one's a miracle worker. I saw the video. But this is your *career* on the line. You're going to need to be accommodating. Everything is dependent on these next six weeks before filming. Don't let your infatuation with this shopgirl get in the way of making your dreams come true."

"I'm not infatuated with Marley. She's an old friend."

"Sure thing, babycakes. I want to be on the receiving end of that expression one day. I'm not surprised that lip-licking video went viral."

Wait…what? "What lip-licking video?"

Esther sighed. "I know I warned you not to search yourself on socials, but you actually listened to me? Do more of that eye fucking on the press tour and the people will love you. Anyway, I must bolt…I've got a meeting at the Chateau Marmont. Ta-ta, babycakes!" Esther disconnected the call.

Nikhil stared at his phone. Had he gone viral? He held his breath before searching his name on social media.

Welp. There it was. The top post, with tens of thousands of likes and shares, was a clip from one of the interviews he'd done at the junket. When he'd been losing his cool and suddenly had an unexpected glimpse of some spectacular cleavage.

Had he really licked his lips while looking at Marley's breasts? Ugh. Had Marley seen this? That was doubtful, since she'd been in surgery all morning. He read the top comments.

> My Kingdom for a man that looks at me the way
> Nik Sharma looks at whatever is to the right of
> the camera!

> This! This is my BRONZE SHADOW!!!

> Bronze hottie, you mean.

> MY BODY IS READY

Nikhil sighed as he put his phone away. He really, really needed to stop lusting after his old prom date.

He started his car, glad he only had the fifteen-minute drive to Marley's house instead of the hour drive to his parents'. When he got there, he parked on the street, let himself in with the key she'd given him on Sunday, and rolled his suitcase into what would be his home for the next two weeks. He paused in moderate shock the moment he was inside.

Marley *had* told him it was Shayne's grandmother's house, but this wasn't what he expected. Well, he wasn't really sure what he expected, but not this. The exterior of the house was old white siding, and he expected the interior, since it was Marley and Shayne's, to be sleek, stylish, and perfectly staged like a magazine spread. Instead, it was…funky. Like 1970s funky, with some '80s flair, too. The house was small, so he could see most of the main floor from the entryway, including the orangey-yellow sofa and the huge number of plants in colorful ceramic pots, and hanging from the ceiling. On the hardwood floor was a multicolored shag rug with interlocking concentric circles that would probably look amazing if he were stoned. And a round wicker coffee table. Everything was kind of warm and cozy…It looked curated, not simply left behind. Well, everything was cool except a hideous brown fake-suede recliner next to the sofa in the living room.

There was a cat on the recliner—a long-haired beige thing that barely looked up when Nikhil came in. That must be McQueen. Marley had mentioned him that night at the hotel.

"Hello, cat," Nikhil said.

At that, McQueen hopped off the recliner and rubbed

against his leg. Nikhil leaned down to pet its head. It was softer than he expected.

There was a knock at the door. Good—the groceries he'd ordered earlier were here. After bringing the bags inside, he put the food and kitchenware on the kitchen counter, then explored the cupboards. The kitchen was simple—it looked like it had been redone ten to fifteen years ago, and it was mostly stocked, but he was glad he'd added a food processor and Instant Pot to the food order.

Nikhil put away the groceries and started cooking. When he told his father he was going to take care of Marley after surgery, Dad had given him a list of foods with healing properties to help her get her strength back. A mung bean daal with extra ginger, turmeric, and cumin seeds was at the top of the list. He opened the bagged beans and rinsed some in a colander, then put them in a bowl of water to soak while he diced an onion.

He probably didn't need to cook—Shayne had assured him that Marley's friends and family would be bringing her meals daily. But he didn't feel right to just sit on the sofa waiting for Marley to get home. He needed to be doing *something*. And he needed to think—which had always been best done while cooking.

Esther's comment earlier about him being too demanding wouldn't leave his head. All he did was insist that the studio accommodate his chosen stylist while she had major surgery. The fact that he couldn't get that chosen stylist out of his head was beside the point. The fact that he'd slept with her was even more beside the point. He wanted to work with Marley because she was damn good at her job, and she respected him. And he wanted to help her make her career dreams come true.

Nikhil closed his eyes and took a breath. Being here, taking care of someone—this would be good for him. He needed to feel useful. He needed to focus on something other than work.

He texted his sister while the daal was cooking. Nalini said Mom was having a good day and had even had dinner with them. He exhaled. Then she told him about this app her biology class was using that had 3D renderings of the human body. She asked if he'd taken his iPad because she couldn't find hers.

A car pulled into the driveway then, and Nikhil immediately went outside, taking care to make sure the cat didn't follow him. Shayne got out of the driver's side as Nikhil walked around to the passenger side. "Is she okay? Should I carry her?" Nikhil asked, seeing Marley through the window. Her eyes were hooded, and her head was leaning on the seat. There was a pillow across her chest under the seat belt.

"I can walk," Marley said. She didn't raise her head or move.

"She was nauseous on the drive," Shayne said. "I had to lower her window."

Nikhil opened her door and put his arm out to help her. She was in sweatpants and an oversized hoodie. Her hair was piled on top of her head, and she wasn't wearing any makeup. Her face was twisted in pain as she reached to undo her seat belt. Nikhil's heart clenched at seeing her like this. He leaned over and got the seat belt for her. She grabbed his arm to help herself up.

"Perfect," Shayne said. "You and your biceps get her. I'll get her bag."

"How is she doing? Is she okay?" Nikhil asked Shayne.

"I hurt like hell, and I feel like I'm going to throw up, but I'm not dead. You can ask me," Marley said, scowling.

"She's a little crabby," Shayne said, closing the trunk. He walked toward the door carrying a pale-pink duffel bag.

Marley didn't even look at Shayne. "Let's see how crabby you'd be after major surgery and rush-hour traffic," she said. Then she winced again.

Nikhil put his arm around her waist, trying to take all her weight as she slowly walked into the house. Thank goodness she wasn't resisting his help. She even put both her hands on his as she kicked off her shoes. McQueen meowed at her in greeting.

Nikhil had expected…hoped…that seeing Marley like this was all he'd need to squelch this infatuation of his. And yes, she really wasn't looking her best. Her normal icy-warm eyes were currently red and puffy. Her flawless skin was blotchy. Her silky hair was a mess and actually looked a bit greasy. And she smelled vaguely like a hospital—of antiseptic and sweat.

But she was still the most beautiful person in the world to him.

Well, crap. Maybe this was more than a mere infatuation.

"Her painkillers have worn off," Shayne said. "Marl, you want to be downstairs or in your room? I'll get your meds once you're settled."

"Upstairs," she said, but then she looked at the flight of stairs in front of her and winced. "Every step hurts."

"I can carry you," Nikhil offered again. When she just stared at him blankly, he reassured her. "I had to pick up a body double today to get ready for when the Bronze Shadow pulls the Silver Siren from a train hatch."

Marley still stared at him with no expression.

"Hey, himbo," Shayne said. "You stay here. I'll get her into bed." Shayne guided her upstairs. The cat followed close behind them.

Nikhil *wanted* to help, but he was only getting in the way.

He went back to the kitchen. He needed to make the tadka, the tempered spices for the daal, anyway.

He was swirling spices and dried chilies in a small pot of ghee when Shayne came back downstairs.

"That smells like heaven."

"She's okay?" Nikhil asked.

Shayne crossed his arms. "That's the third time you've asked that. Are you too neurotic to take care of her?"

Nikhil cringed. Maybe he needed to ease up a bit. "She looked like she was in so much pain."

Shayne nodded. "She is. The painkillers will kick in soon. She's a lot stronger than she looks." He headed to the living room. "Traffic was brutal. I need to head to the airport in a half hour. Let me show you her medication chart."

Marley had been prescribed a cocktail of painkillers, anti-inflammatories, and antibiotics to prevent infection. Shayne showed Nikhil each bottle and marked on the chart when she would need each one. Then he showed Nikhil the drain chart. "She should be able to empty her drains on her own, but she may need help rinsing the bulbs out after measuring the output. You're not squeamish, are you? It's kind of gross."

Nikhil patted his midsection. "Stomach of lead. Will she need help in the...bathroom?"

Shayne snorted. "Probably not. She's quite mobile, just slow. She's not allowed a full shower until her drains are out. Her cousin will be here in the morning to help her clean and change." Shayne handed him a handwritten note with a bunch of phone numbers. "That's her cousin Reena's number, plus my grandmother's, Marley's other cousin Ruby, and Marley's mother. Call people in that order if there is an emergency."

Nikhil nodded, frowning. Why wasn't Marley's mother higher on the list?

"I'll have my phone on me the whole time, so text me whenever." He handed Nikhil another printed piece of paper. "Here are her post-surgery instructions." He then handed Nikhil more stapled pieces of paper, these ones with even more writing. "Here is everything you need to know to take care of McQueen. He gets wet food at dinner, and the automatic dispenser gives him dry food in the morning. The last two pages are the instructions for the plants. They're all named—you can find the names on the bottom of each pot. Make sure you turn Baryshnikov every day."

Nikhil nodded. This was a lot of information. He hoped he wouldn't screw up. Shayne then gave Nikhil a tour of the house, including the basement laundry room and the room upstairs that Nikhil would be staying in. Marley's room was next to Nikhil's, but the door was mostly closed. Shayne checked his watch when they got back downstairs. "I gotta go." He looked at Nikhil. "You sure you got this?"

Nikhil nodded. "Yes. I'll take good care of her."

Shayne pointed upstairs. "I love that girl more than life itself. Take care of her, Superman."

"I'm the Bronze Shadow."

Shayne squeezed Nikhil's bicep, nodding. "Yes—yes you are."

"I'll take care of her. And the cat. And plants."

After Shayne took his bags and left, Nikhil opened a can of cat food, which made the cat run down the stairs and rub against his legs, meowing. He spooned some food into McQueen's bowl. Should he check on Marley now? See if she wanted any food? She was probably resting, maybe even sleeping now that she had drugs in her again.

He might as well settle in. Unpack his own things. He took his bag up the stairs to his room. Shayne's grandmother's quilting room was small, but there was an empty dresser to put some things in. The furniture, like all the furniture in the house, was straight out of the seventies, and the walls were covered with floral wallpaper. In the rest of the house, Marley and Shayne had clearly added some touches so the decor looked fresh and intentional, but here it just looked old. And cluttered. The closet was filled with plastic bins of fabric, there was a sewing table with two sewing machines on it, and an ironing board was against the wall. The bed was a narrow twin, which was, of course, covered with a multicolored patchwork quilt.

As he was putting his clothes into the empty dresser, he heard a feeble "Hello?" from the room next to his. Marley's room. He rushed over.

"I'm here. You okay?"

She was on her back on what looked like a dozen pillows. She even had two brightly patterned ones wedged under her arms.

"I can't reach the TV remote." She nodded toward the bedside table on the far side of her bed.

Nikhil smiled. He fetched the remote and handed it to her. Marley's bedroom was bright, with cream walls, a pale wood-framed bed, and a long wood bench at the end of it. Wispy floor-length cream curtains lined one wall, and the flooring was blond wood. It was clearly all new. "I thought you were sleeping."

"The painkillers make me a little wired."

"How's the pain?"

"Better now." She was very stiff, but her face looked more relaxed than before.

"You hungry? I can bring you some moong daal. My dad insisted that you need ginger and turmeric…for their healing properties."

Marley blinked, looking at him. "Yeah, that sounds perfect."

Nikhil nodded, then went downstairs and ladled some of the daal into a bowl. He cut up a lemon and squeezed it into the bowl and then sprinkled some cilantro leaves on top. He found a tray in the kitchen and placed the bowl, a napkin, and a spoon on it. He brought it upstairs and set it on the bed. "Shayne bought sandwich stuff, too, so let me know if you're hungry again. We weren't sure what you'd want to eat."

She took a spoonful of daal. "This is delicious," she said. "Thank your father for me."

"Okay, but I made it."

She looked up at him. "You made this?"

"Yeah, when I got here. I bought you an Instant Pot."

"You cook."

"I told you I cook, didn't I?"

She shrugged, then winced from shrugging.

"Here, I'll let you eat. Holler again if you need me. And if I don't hear you, text me." He made sure her phone was within reach.

She frowned. "You're leaving?"

"Yeah…unless…you want company?"

She looked…sad. Or maybe in pain? But she didn't say anything. He looked around the room. The bedroom had only one chair, a wicker thing near the dresser that held the TV, but there was a stack of clothes and sheets on it.

"Stay," she said softly. "I'll put on a cooking show."

He sat next to her on the bed. It was soft, and the bedding was lush and silky. Posh. Like Marley herself.

They watched a baking reality show while she ate. She only managed to get through half the bowl before she said she was full. He took the dishes downstairs, and then came back. Her head was lying against the pillow, and her eyes were closed. She was resting.

"You're staying, right?" she whispered.

Without saying anything, he slid in next to her on the bed.

"Thanks, Nikhil," she whispered. "I'm glad you're here."

"Me too, Mahreen."

CHAPTER TWELVE

Marley

In an upright position, with more pillows than an IKEA store, Marley was somehow, miraculously, able to get some sleep. But she woke at five a.m. in a world of pain. Like…So. Much. Pain. Her meds had clearly worn off. She needed to check her drains and get more pills, but the mere thought of getting up felt like a form of torture. She took deep breaths and tried not to feel sorry for herself. Maybe breathing exercises could take the edge off so she could get up.

Breathing exercises didn't do shit. She clutched the side of her duvet as she choked back a sob. McQueen opened one eye, then closed it again. Marley felt so alone. She was usually fine being single, but right now she kind of *hated* being unpartnered. Shayne was right—"cat lady" was not a relationship status. If a person were here next to her, they could help her. They could distract her from the pain. They could get her pills and sit with her until they kicked in and—

"Marley, are you okay?" Nikhil was at her door. He must have heard her cry. Mortifying.

"Just…need painkillers." Her voice was shaky. "And I have to empty my drains." And she needed to pee, but she didn't say that out loud.

Nikhil sprung into action and checked the medication chart. He handed her two of the good pills and a glass of water. She swallowed them. Even doing that hurt. She lay her head back on her pillow, eyes clenched shut.

"You should have called for me," Nikhil said.

Marley wasn't in the mood for talking. For explaining that she hated being a burden and hated that the only person with her was someone she barely knew. That it was so scary to be facing this alone. That she'd made a huge, irreversible mistake in having surgery, and she regretted it so much right now. It wasn't even a sure thing that she would have gotten cancer. She didn't say that her chest felt so tight and foreign…like someone was pulling a vise around her.

And she didn't say that she'd never felt more alone in her life. Couldn't say all that. She felt the tears flow freely on her face.

The bed shifted. When she opened her eyes, Nikhil was sitting next to her in the exact spot he'd been in while they watched that terrible baking reality show. "Once the painkillers kick in, I'll help you with the other stuff."

"You don't have to…I'm okay. Thanks for the pills, but I can—"

"Marley, I am literally here to help you at night. That's my job."

She nodded. He was right. She hated putting him out like this.

It was still dark out, but the barest bit of light had started coming through her sheer curtains. Marley focused on the rising sun and on her breathing, and miraculously, the pain eased. Well, not miraculously. Pharmaceutically.

"How did you sleep?" she asked softly.

He chuckled. "Surprisingly well. That's a comfy mattress."

"Grams always bought the best. That's why we kept all her stuff."

"I figured your house would be all modern and trendy."

"I like the aesthetic."

"I like it, too. It's soothing. Pills helping?"

She nodded. "I need to empty my drains."

After Nikhil helped her with her drains and she went to the bathroom, she shuffled her way back to bed. "You can go back to bed now...I should be okay."

He nodded. Now the sun was almost completely up, and Marley could see that he was wearing plaid flannel pants and a gray T-shirt. He looked so...normal. Not like a movie star or a superhero. Just her friend who was helping her.

"Thanks," Marley said.

"Of course," he said. "Your cousin will be here in a few hours, right? I can stay if you need me to."

"Yeah, she'll be here by nine. I'll be okay."

He nodded. "Okay...I'm right next door if you need me."

Marley had no trouble falling asleep after Nikhil left. Because it didn't feel like he'd left. He was right here...in the next room. She wasn't alone.

Marley woke when she heard a noise that sounded like a shriek from downstairs. It was probably McQueen looking for his breakfast. Marley checked the time—eight o'clock. Her last dose of painkillers was still in effect. She propped herself up in bed, cringing with the pain of the movement, when her door suddenly swung open, and Nikhil burst in. He was wearing athletic joggers and a black T-shirt stretched over his muscles.

"What's wrong?" Marley asked. His eyes were wider than sunflowers.

"Your cousin…She's here."

Marley sat up. *Crap.* She'd had no idea Reena would come early. She probably saw Nikhil and recognized him. "It's okay," Marley reassured him. "She's cool. She won't say anything if you ask her not to. But you can get an NDA for her if you think it's necessary. You may as well get one for her husband, too, but I trust them."

He blinked, looking at Marley. "Your cousin is…*Reena Remtulla*."

Marley frowned. "Yeah…so? Although I think her legal name is still Manji…You need legal names for NDAs, right?" Marley's had said Mahreen, not Marley.

He shook his head vigorously, then threw his hand in the air. "Marley! Reena Remtulla is my favorite YouTuber! I freaking love her cooking videos! That daal last night was her recipe! My dad and I have been watching her for years!"

"Yeah," Marley said. "Shayne and I help her with her videos."

His eyes somehow looked wider. "Holy shit, that's why your kitchen looked familiar. She filmed an episode here! The pineapple cake! I can't believe I was cooking in the same kitchen as Reena Remtulla!"

Marley raised a brow. Then winced because somehow that hurt. Was this superstar celebrity…starstruck by her cousin Reena?

"Marley!" Reena was in her doorway now. She was in a

sweatshirt and jeans, and her eyes were as wide as Nikhil's. "Are you fucking serious right now that your mystery friend is the *Bronze Shadow*?" She raised a brow at Nikhil. "You *are* Nik Sharma, aren't you?"

He nodded, too starstruck to speak.

"Holy shit." Reena looked back at Marley. "Nadim is going to *flip his lid*. He's been obsessed with the guy since Comicon!"

"You swear more than you do on YouTube," Nikhil said.

Marley closed her eyes and put her head back on her pillow.

"Marley, are you okay?" Nikhil said. "How's your pain? You shouldn't need painkillers yet. It's only been three hours since your last dose."

Marley did not open her eyes. "No, I'm fine. I'm deliberately not looking at the two of you because then I'll laugh at how hilarious you are, and it hurts to laugh."

"I'm not hilarious," Nikhil said.

"You're literally a comedian, aren't you?" Reena asked.

"I have your cookbook," Nikhil responded. "Can you sign it? Wait—it's in LA. Can you sign my dad's copy?"

Marley opened her eyes and shook her head. "Nikhil, shouldn't you be at the gym?"

"Yeah." He looked at Reena. "Do I need to show you her meds? There's a chart."

"I think I can handle it. Hey, did you know you went viral yesterday for—"

"Bye, Marley," Nikhil said, interrupting Reena. "Call me if you need anything! Nice to meet you, Reena." He mock saluted Marley, then rushed out of the room.

Reena looked at Marley, one brow raised. "You, dear cousin, have a lot to tell me."

Marley nodded as she slowly turned so she could get out

of bed. "Yeah, but first, can you help me change out of these sweats?"

While Reena helped Marley empty her drains and change into clean sweatpants and one of the mastectomy shirts Ruby had given her, Marley gave Reena a short version of how Nikhil ended up here, leaving out the whole wild-sex-in-a-hotel part—both back when they were eighteen and last week.

"But why didn't you tell me?" Reena said after they'd made their way downstairs. Marley sat on the hideous recliner while Reena made some tea and toast.

"I signed an NDA. I couldn't. I didn't even tell Shayne until Sunday."

Reena made a dismissive noise. "Still. You know I'm good for secrets. My sister—don't tell *her* anything. But..." Reena put the tea and a thick slice of sourdough toast on the table near the recliner. "I can't even believe it. You know Nadim was there at Comicon when they announced his casting? He texted me immediately about the Brown Bronze Shadow." She shook her head, sitting on the sofa next to the recliner. McQueen immediately meowed and sat next to Reena, who started stroking the top of his head. "What's he like?"

"I don't know him that well. We were friends in high school, but people change."

Reena stared at Marley for several seconds. Then shook her head again. "The guy is *literally* living in your house taking care of you after you had major surgery. You know I adore you like a sister, but it's frustrating how you keep everyone, even your closest friends, at arm's length."

"Do you mean I'm keeping him at arm's length or you?"

Reena snorted. "Both. Some people are an open book. You are not one of those people. Which is fine. I love you the way you are. But...I really don't believe that you would let someone you claim to *barely know* take care of you after *surgery*."

Marley blinked wordlessly, then took a bite of her toast. It was one of Reena's breads from her bakery: a sunflower flax sourdough. Reena had smeared it with a chunky guacamole, also from her bakery. Reena was not only a gifted baker and cook, but one of the few people who noticed when Marley was pushing people away.

Though she was hardly keeping Nikhil at arm's length. She'd opened up more to him than she had to almost anyone else in her life. She'd freaking had a casual hookup with the guy...which was so out of character for Marley that Reena would either give her a standing ovation or take her temperature if she knew about it.

But no, Marley couldn't tell Reena that she'd had sex with Nikhil. Sharing it with others meant it wouldn't be just *hers* anymore. Which was preposterous. Just because it was the last time her real boobs got any loving didn't mean the sex was anything more. At the thought of her boobs, Marley felt a sharp pain in her chest. She winced.

"Painkillers are probably wearing off. Here—let me check your chart," Reena said, picking up the clipboard. "Wow, your superhero is thorough. Still don't really understand why he's here, but at least he seems to be a genuine help right now."

Marley took the pills Reena handed her and swallowed them. And that was the bottom line. No matter how complicated Marley's feelings were, and no matter how much she and Nikhil had made this arrangement each for their own selfish reasons, at the end of the day, Nikhil was helping her. A lot. And that was because she was letting him. And letting someone into her life was something that Marley usually found difficult.

But it had been so easy to make Nikhil part of her life again, and that was a huge surprise to her. She wondered what would have happened if they'd been mature enough to talk to each other after prom. They could have had ten years of friendship. Or maybe more than friendship. But the past didn't matter. She was glad to have her friend back now.

CHAPTER THIRTEEN

Nikhil

After he finished rehearsals, Nikhil called his father from his car. It had been a brutal day, and every muscle in his body was sore. He was supposed to have dinner with his parents tonight, but he just wanted to go back to Marley's house. He needed to know that she was okay. Maybe he should pick up some takeout first.

"But I made so much daal makhani!" his dad protested.

Dad's daal makhani sounded amazing right now. Would it be strange for him to send a driver to his parents' to get some home-cooked food?

"Next time. I'm wiped. I'm working on learning my stunts now, and they're pushing me extra hard."

"Nikhil, you said this wouldn't be a dangerous—"

"I'll have a stunt double for anything remotely dangerous, but I'll be doing the less-risky stuff myself. The coordinator is teaching me to do it safely."

"I wish you would have picked an acting movie instead of an action movie. Dev Patel got to play David Copperfield! You should be like that. *Slumdog Millionaire* was so good!"

Nikhil sighed as he started his car. Damn that Dev Patel for setting an unattainable standard that every parent of every desi actor reminded their children of weekly.

"I'll tell my agent to call Danny Boyle."

"Okay. And maybe when you come next time, you can bring your girlfriend, too! You said she was from Nairobi. Does she know—"

"Her *mother* is from Kenya. I don't know where. But I told you she's not my girlfriend. Just a friend."

"My friend Salim is from Kenya. His son's wedding was so expensive! They even imported the *bride* from India. Did I tell you my friend Ashwin's son started online dating? He's a dentist, so it's no wonder he needed an arranged marriage. He would ask the girls if they were single, and they couldn't respond because their mouths were open."

Nikhil shook his head. He loved his father and always found it amazing that one small man could encompass just about every Indian stereotype—both male and female. But maybe Dad had to be all the things because Mom couldn't be anything.

"How's Mom?" he asked.

"Oh, she's fine. Resting. Nalini tired her out…They were watching that cooking show with the Bangladeshi woman. But Nalini talked through the whole thing, so your mother had to watch it a second time. Nalini has been so hyper lately! She needs to let your mother rest. Can you talk to her, Nikhil?"

"Yeah, of course." He frowned. He knew his sister had been spending more time with his mother since Nikhil wasn't there.

"I talked to your brother today. Did he tell you he's taking college courses online? He's thinking of doing an MBA! Speaking of online dating, he wants to try that when he gets home. I think settling down is exactly what he needs to get back on track, but I don't know about this online shaadi idea.

Maybe you can help him meet girls? He's going to be able to come home for visits soon. Is your friend—"

Nikhil *needed* to change the subject. Now. "Dad, you *know* I don't want to talk about Arjun." Not if he could help it, at least. Thank goodness he was staying at Marley's now—the last thing he'd want was to see his brother if he came home for the weekend.

"Your mother will be sorry you won't be here for dinner... She loves having dinner with you kids. You'll come on the weekend? I can save some daal."

Nikhil sighed. There was almost zero probability that Mom would even come downstairs, let alone sit at the dining table if he came home for dinner.

"I may have to be in LA. Don't worry about the daal. I'll make some myself."

"Good idea. Yours is better than mine anyway."

"I need to get going. Love you, Dad."

"Oh wait, Nalini is here...She says you're trendy." Dad paused, and Nikhil could hear his sister in the background but couldn't make out what she was saying. "Nalini, what are you doing licking your lips like that? What does that mean? Nikhil, I don't understand this one. Boys are so much simpler than this girl." The call disconnected. Nikhil assumed his father hung up by mistake.

Nikhil sighed. Maybe he *should* go home for dinner. He'd been glad the movie was filming in Canada because he'd thought being closer to them meant he could ensure his parents didn't get sucked into his brother's bullshit again, but he wasn't sure that plan was working. It seemed his father hadn't heard anything about Arjun's idea of renting out the basement, at least. But now that Nikhil had temporarily moved out, maybe his parents would be more susceptible to their first-born's manipulation.

The very thought of introducing Marley to Arjun, though… *ugh*.

Before leaving the parking lot, Nikhil checked, and yes, the lip-licking video was still trending. Nikhil tossed his phone on the passenger seat. He wanted to escape all this at Marley's cozy little house.

Reena's car wasn't there when Nikhil got to Marley's, and the house was quiet when he let himself in. Neither Marley nor McQueen were in the living room. She was probably resting upstairs. Nikhil resisted the urge to check on her.

He felt weird eating the food from Marley's fridge, so he ordered some tacos for himself and some sopa de lima for Marley in case she woke up hungry. He flipped on the TV and put on some cooking videos on YouTube while he waited for his dinner.

McQueen came downstairs meowing right after the food arrived. Nikhil leaned down to pet him.

"Hey, dude, how's your mommy feeling? Maybe if she's resting, you'll watch YouTube with me. Or…why are you looking at me like I stole your salmon?"

"The you-stole-my-salmon stare is hunger," a feeble voice from the top of the stairs said. Marley was awake. Without really thinking about it, Nikhil rushed up to help her down the stairs. She waved him off.

"I can walk," she said, her face showing her irritation. Nikhil wanted to ask her if she needed painkillers, but he also assumed she wouldn't appreciate being asked why she was grumpy. So instead, he opened the fridge to get the can of McQueen's food. Marley had made it down the stairs by the time he filled the cat's bowl. She looked...exhausted. Her coloring was pale. She was wincing with almost every movement. Her hair was piled on top of her head. It had clearly been a rough day.

"How are you feeling?" he asked as he helped her into the recliner. He fit her pillows under her arms.

"Like someone cut me open and shoved boulders under my skin that are way too big for my body." She winced again, then looked up at Nikhil with her big eyes. "Pain's bad. Reena left an hour ago, and I tried to sleep but couldn't get comfortable."

Nikhil checked the medication log. It had only been two hours since her last painkiller so she couldn't have more. Maybe he could distract her with good food.

"I ordered Mexican. Ever had sopa de lima? It's lime-and-chicken soup."

Marley looked at him again with that same heartbreakingly pained expression. Ugh. He wished there was more he could do. "I have," she said. "In Cancún."

He opened the bag of food and poured the soup from the cardboard container into one of the brown bowls from the kitchen. It wasn't piping hot anymore, so he warmed it in the microwave, then sprinkled fried tortilla strips and chopped cilantro over it. He put it on the tray table in front of Marley before plating his own tacos.

"Mmm," he heard her say while he was still in the kitchen.

"Good?" he asked. He brought his food to sit near her in the living room.

"It's amazing. Where did this come from?"

"Armadillos." He told her about the article he'd read about the new place nearby making authentic Yucatán food.

She looked at him with one brow raised. "You really are a foodie, aren't you?"

He shrugged before taking a bite of his taco. It was perfect. Tender shredded chicken cooked with citrus and chilies and topped with tangy red onions and bright herbs. "This is amazing," he said. "I'll be ordering this a lot while I'm here."

Marley smiled, taking another spoonful of soup. "I could eat this every day." She looked better already—that was the magic of chicken soup. Maybe more chicken soups would help her. He could make Chinese egg drop or even chicken pho for her.

"I thought you were going to watch YouTube," she said.

"I was going to watch YouTube with your cat."

"But not me? I can glare at you like McQueen."

He laughed. "Nah, your cat has mastered the glare like no other. It's so perfect that he's named after Steve McQueen." He gave the cat a stern McQueen look.

Marley snorted. "He's not named after Steve McQueen. He's named after Alexander McQueen. The fashion designer?"

Nikhil frowned. That made sense. He picked up the TV remote. "What's your poison?"

She frowned. "Huh?"

"What do you watch on YouTube when you don't want to think? You into game streamers? Productivity gurus? PressTube?"

"PressTube?"

"This guy crushes random household stuff in his hydraulic press. It's very satisfying to watch Lego bricks extrude like pasta."

Marley laughed. Not chuckled. Not giggled. Full on laughed. And didn't wince with pain. Nikhil felt the satisfaction of that laugh deep inside.

"So what's your vice? Don't make me look at your YouTube history…"

She shook her head. "Nothing too exciting. There are a few fashion stylists I follow…just to keep up with trends and such."

"What do you watch that has nothing to do with your work? Just to satisfy the deep, primitive part of your brain? Like, my sister loves *The Bachelor* for some reason."

"I like *The Bachelor*, too. But mostly…nail-art compilations."

He chuckled. "Nail-art compilations?"

"Yeah. People painting art on their nails to soothing music."

He chuckled. "Do you watch it because you're not allowed colors on your nails for work?" It seemed like a silly rule. He wondered if her black, white, and gray clothing color scheme was also something the store dictated.

She shrugged. "I don't mind the nude polish. I just find the videos relaxing. You watch cooking videos, right?" she asked.

He nodded. "If you weren't here, I'd be watching your cousin's newest. She posted one today."

"Why can't you watch it with me here?"

He shrugged. "I'm sure you don't want to watch me fanboy your family."

"Shayne and I have been helping Reena with her videos for years now. Started back when she entered this contest, the—"

"*Home-Cooking Showdown*. Yeah, I saw it. She and her husband were only engaged then, right?"

Marley snorted. "Sort of. Put it on."

While they watched the video of Reena making paneer rolls, Nikhil got as much dirt on Reena as he could from Marley. Which didn't turn out to be that much dirt at all. In fact, Nikhil wondered if she'd signed an NDA with her cousin, too.

After that clip was done, they watched some nail-art compilations, which were weirdly both compelling and relaxing. Nikhil was completely chill by the time he was done eating, and Marley looked almost as comfortable as him. Until her phone buzzed. She glanced at it.

"My mother," she said.

"Do you want me to leave to give you some privacy?" McQueen was currently sitting on Nikhil's lap, kneading his sweater. Nikhil wondered if the cat learned to knead like that from Reena.

Marley shook her head. "Nah. It's fine." She accepted the call. Nikhil tried not to listen. Marley didn't say much, anyway. Just that she was fine, had plenty to eat, and was recovering well. And she thanked her mom for something.

Marley disconnected the call. And then winced in pain. A lot of pain. The cat jumped from Nikhil to sit near his owner.

"You okay?" Nikhil asked.

"I think it's time for my painkiller," she said.

"I'll get it." When Nikhil handed her the two small pills, he saw that she had tears in her eyes again. A lot. She attempted a smile. "Thank you."

"It's no problem. That's why I'm here."

She quickly swallowed the pills, then cringed as she shifted to find a comfortable position. "I don't think I fully grasped what a mess I'd be…Thanks for putting up with all this." She blinked away another tear.

He said nothing and sat down on the sofa close to her. The cat jumped back onto Nikhil's lap and started to burrow into the large pocket of his hoodie.

"You can stop him, but he likes to hang out in pockets," Marley said.

Nikhil laughed, shifting so McQueen could climb inside his pocket. He'd never had a cat before, and this one was kinda funny.

"Are you close with your parents?" Marley asked after a while.

"I suppose. You met Dad. He's a typical desi parent. He was so stressed because he made daal makhani and I wasn't coming to eat it."

"I love daal makhani. It's unusual that he's the cook in your family. Does your mother cook?"

"She loves to cook, but she doesn't do much lately." He rubbed the cat's head sticking out of his pocket.

"My parents are more...distant," Marley said. "Like, it seems like they don't care to get to know me. Right before the surgery, Mom gave me chocolates and made a big deal about them being my favorite, but they were caramels. I hate caramel—it gets stuck in my teeth. I always ate the fruit fillings and left the caramels when I was a kid. I wonder if Mom resents that I could have surgery to prevent getting sick like she did."

Nikhil had no idea what to say to that. He couldn't imagine what her family was going through, and he didn't want to say the wrong thing.

"I've always been independent," Marley said. "So maybe she doesn't think I need her now."

"Do you need her?" Nikhil said.

She shrugged, then took a spoonful of soup. It must be cold by now. Nikhil wondered if he should warm it up again.

"My parents think I'm a bum who would never amount to anything," he said.

She turned to him. "Do they know you're the Bronze Shadow?"

"That's a recent development. But before that, I didn't get a lot of roles. Random tech guy, or shopkeeper, and always the comic relief. I even had to put on a fake Indian accent a few times. When the roles dried up, I relied on my side hustles."

"What side hustles?"

He chuckled. "All of them. I drove for Uber, waited tables, was an extra on film sets. I worked so many catering jobs that I can make eight dozen turkey sandwiches in half an hour. Still, I couldn't have afforded LA rent without a roommate." He ran his hand through his hair. "My parents think that because Riz Ahmed and Dev Patel make movies, then there must be plenty of roles for Brown guys, so I must not be trying hard enough. And my brother...he's always planted the idea in their head that I was a waste of space. Even now, when he's..." His voice trailed. He didn't tend to tell people what was going on in his family. Families like Nikhil's didn't air their dirty laundry.

"Even when your brother's what?"

Nikhil ran his hand over his face. He should tell her. He was living with her now; she would probably find out about his family drama. And Marley was honest with him about her situation. "My brother's in prison."

Marley's eyes went wide. "What? Why? Is he okay?"

Nikhil nodded. "It's a minimum-security place a couple of hours from here. White-collar crime. He scammed some people in a real estate deal...I don't know all the details—I don't want to know. Anyway, my parents refinanced the house to pay for Arjun's defense. The house was paid off by then. I tried to convince them not to do it—I mean, I didn't know if my brother was guilty or innocent, but he's always been a little shady, you know? More concerned with the acquisition of wealth than how it was acquired."

"Wow. He was found guilty, then?"

Nikhil nodded. "He'll be there for a while, and my parents had an enormous new mortgage to show for it. When I got the Bronze Shadow, I paid off that mortgage."

"Holy shit," Marley said. "And they still *talk* to your brother?"

"Of course they do." Nikhil knew he sounded bitter. "He's always been the golden son. The businessman with the BMW and designer suits. Not the family-fuckup actor that no one's heard of. But now the tables are turned, and I'm successful and he's in prison and I think no one knows what to do with that. Anyway, I wanted to be close to home for a bit to make sure Mom and Nalini are okay."

"What's the matter with your mother and sister?" Marley asked.

Nikhil didn't answer. He didn't know if he should. Marley had her own family drama—she didn't need his, too.

"Never mind. I don't mean to intrude," Marley said.

"No, it's fine. Mom's always been a bit…moody. But I'm pretty sure she's got full-on depression now. She's barely left her room since Arjun was sentenced. But we can't convince her to get help." He sighed.

"I'm sorry. It's probably hard…her oldest kid in prison. What's going on with your sister? Is she okay?"

He smiled. "Yeah, Nalini is great. She's the smartest one of us. She's on a scholarship for university and wants to go to med school after this. She has ADHD, though, and she needs someone to…you know, look out for her. Keep her on track." He chuckled. "We used to call her the Phone Annihilator because she lost or broke her phone every few months. She's been better lately, though. And she's so resilient. She could take care of the rest of us."

"You dote on your sister."

"She's the baby. We all do. But I want them *all* to be okay. Mom seems to be detaching herself from the world even more." He sighed. "Why did I think the fuckup son could help, anyway?"

"Of course you're helping! You paid off their mortgage! And now you're here helping me! You're the furthest thing from a fuckup I've ever met. You're..." Her voice trailed off.

"I'm what?"

"You're an amazing friend. And...you're literally a superstar. You're going to be huge."

He didn't really believe that. He was on his way to being *infamous* instead of famous. He scrubbed his hand over his face. He really didn't want to talk about his family right now. "I got the schedule for my promos. It's not that bad...I'll need outfits for some talk-show appearances in LA next week. And probably some social stuff while I'm there."

"I should be okay to pull together some looks online tomorrow."

He nodded. "No rush. We have time. And, Marley?"

"Hmm?"

"Thanks for listening, too. You're also an amazing friend."

She smiled. Nikhil was growing very, very addicted to that smile.

CHAPTER FOURTEEN

Marley

The next morning was a little easier for Marley. Nikhil left before she woke up, but he put out a little saucer with two of her good painkillers (since opening the bottles herself hurt) and a glass of water on her nightstand. Marley stayed in bed with McQueen until the painkillers kicked in.

She eventually got up, emptied her drains, and went downstairs. Nikhil had left her breakfast out near her recliner—a thermos of tea and some fruit and granola. She smiled to herself as she sat and poured the tea. It was a little over-brewed, but it was better than the pain of making it herself. When Nikhil came home at the end of the day, they ate the kheema and bread Reena had left when she'd visited that afternoon, then watched reality TV until Nikhil finally helped her go to bed.

On Friday morning, her mother took Marley back to the hospital for her first post-op appointment. Dr. Abernathy said Marley was doing well, but her drains would probably need to stay in for another week. Marley was exhausted when her mother dropped her back home, so she took a nap. In the afternoon, she started feeling restless. She wasn't used to doing… nothing, so she picked up her iPad and started scrolling the stock on Reid's website to get clothes for Nikhil's trip. But the painkillers were jumbling her mind, and Marley couldn't keep track of what he needed. She spent fifteen minutes on a site detailing the hottest new offerings in menswear before realizing the article was three years old. By then she needed to use the bathroom, which of course took forever.

She was going to fail. Maybe she couldn't do this job. Jacqueline was going to be pissed. Marley would be working on the selling floor forever. Abused by customers. Treated like crap with no autonomy.

Marley closed her eyes. She was spiraling. She checked the time in Paris: six p.m. Shayne knew how to stop her brain. She opened a FaceTime call.

"Marley, darling, how are you? Paris is *amazing*."

Marley could feel her tension easing the moment she saw her best friend's face on the screen. He seemed to be outside, but the light was dim and hazy. The sun was setting. "Shayne... I'm useless. Nikhil's trip to LA is soon, and I can't focus online for more than thirty seconds."

"How far into this doom tunnel are you, babe? Did you already imagine Jacqueline firing you?"

Marley didn't say anything.

"Can't you have Nicky to help you?" Shayne asked. "Hey, how's that going, by the way? Is he walking around topless? I need to know how to imagine my house right now. He's got a six-pack, right?"

"Shayne."

"You know you got this. I have to go—a delicious, young design assistant wants to show me a Paris night market. Au revoir, ma chérie!" The call disconnected.

She rolled her eyes. Shayne did have a point, though. Nikhil said he'd help her. She texted him and asked him if they could look at clothes together later, and he immediately wrote back that he'd be happy to. Just like she knew he would.

At around five, there was a knock on the door. Had Nikhil forgotten his keys? Marley wasn't expecting Reena, or even Ruby, to drop by today. She was nervous—she wasn't exactly presentable for guests. She pulled a robe over her mastectomy shirt and answered the door.

She was shocked at who she saw there.

"Oh! You're Nikhil's sister!" Marley said, narrowing her eyes. "Nalini, right?"

Nalini grinned. She was a pretty girl, with a round face framed by shoulder-length straight hair parted in the middle. She was wearing a brightly patterned sweater in a style that Marley's father had worn in the nineties, and boot-cut jeans that were completely frayed at the bottom. Marley wondered if Nikhil's poor fashion sense was a family trait.

"Yeah, that's me! Marley, right? Nikhil said I could use his iPad. I have this massive bio assignment and I can't find mine. Ooh, you have a cat!"

McQueen stepped into the doorway and rubbed up against Nalini's shins, so she reached down to pet his head. "Oh my god, *so cute*. I want a cat, but my mom's allergic. But I mean, allergy shots exist, right? Where's Nikhil?"

Marley tightened the robe around her. "He…he's not home from rehearsals yet."

"Shoot. Lemme text him." Nalini pulled her phone out of her pocket and started typing on it.

Marley didn't want to be rude and leave Nikhil's sister outside, so she took a step back and motioned her into the house. McQueen followed. After sending her text, Nalini looked at Marley.

"You're supposed to be recovering from surgery, aren't you? Go, sit." She looked back at her phone. "Nikhil said he'd be home soon. Is it okay if I wait on your porch? Or, he said his iPad is on the dresser in the quilting room. I can't believe you put my brother in a *quilting* room. Hey, do you need help with anything? I volunteer at a rehabilitation hospital...not because I'm, like, a saint or something. I'm applying to med school next year and it looks good on applications. Why aren't you sitting down?"

This girl was...a lot. "Um, I'm okay. You can wait in here if you want..."

Nalini shook her head. "No, you're not okay! You had major surgery!" She kicked off her shoes. "Lemme help."

Marley had no choice but to let this girl gently guide her back to the recliner. Nalini immediately sat on the sofa, and McQueen, who was delighted there was another person to lavish him with love, jumped on her lap.

"You should get this cat registered as a therapy cat," Nalini said, stroking McQueen's head. "There's a cat that comes into the rehab hospital. The patients love him. He's so chill. Believe it or not, the cat's name is Mayhem. Can you imagine a therapy cat named Mayhem? They should have changed it to *Don't Worry, You'll Be Fine. Do Your Physio.*"

Marley snorted a laugh. "That's not a great cat name, though."

"What's this guy's name?"

"McQueen."

"Ah! Like the race car from that Disney movie?"

Marley shook her head. "No, like Alexander McQueen. The fashion designer?"

"Of course. *Duh.* You're Nikhil's stylist—makes sense you're into fashion. Our family isn't exactly known for our fashion sense. Anyway, you seem to be helping Nikhil. I saw a TikTok calling him a *snack*, and I was like, *Ew*. That's my *brother*. But no way anyone would say that the way he dressed before. I'm not much better, though." She looked down at her sweater. "This was Nikhil's. I don't know how I ended up with it. But I *hate* clothes shopping."

"I can take you one day," Marley offered. Nalini reminded her of Nikhil, except chattier. "I mean, you can wear whatever you want, but I take people who don't like shopping out all the time."

Nalini smiled, tilting her head. "Like, you can be my stylist, too! You know, I've never met any of Nikhil's girlfriends before. This is really cool."

"Oh, your brother and I aren't—"

"I know." She waved her hand. "You're friends, hookups, whatever. Still. With him all the way in California, I kind of wondered what kind of friends he had. I was afraid everyone he hung out with was, like…a douche or an influencer or something. But I like you." She sighed. "I wish he lived closer. He's really the best brother."

Considering Nalini's other brother was a criminal, it wasn't a high bar for Nikhil. But Marley knew that Nalini was right—he absolutely was the best big brother.

Marley was an only child, and even though she was always surrounded by cousins, she missed having a sibling bond. She felt kind of bad for Nalini, though. She had one brother in jail, and the other one was living all the way in LA. She smiled at her. "Do you want to stay for dinner? Nikhil mentioned you liked *The Bachelor*. I think a new episode dropped today."

"Oh my god, *yes*. Let's watch. I'm dying to know what Cassidy whispered into Marcus's ear last week."

That night, Nalini and Nikhil both helped Marley go over Reid's stock. They kept her brain on track, even though both their instincts on what to wear were horrendously wrong—Nikhil could not wear an animal-print bomber jacket to a talk show. They made a list of things they thought would work and sent it to Ruby, who said she'd bring the clothes the following evening.

Shayne was right. Marley could do this. Just not alone.

Ruby came over Saturday night after her shift with four huge Reid's bags full of clothes. "Am I going to finally find out who the VIP is?" she asked as she took off her shoes. "The NDA they made me sign told me absolutely nothing. Why do you still look so fabulous after a mastectomy? You're unreal, Marley."

Marley was still on her recliner. She was having a better day painwise but was still taking it easy. She didn't feel fabulous at all.

"Shut up, Ruby. I look like crap."

"You look like gilded crap. I looked like a coughed-up hairball for a month after my surgery." She bent to scratch McQueen's head at that statement.

Ruby brought the garment bags into the living room. "So… the dude is, like, here?"

Marley nodded. "Upstairs." Ruby didn't know Nikhil was *living* here…and Marley wasn't sure if she wanted her to know that. Would the NDA cover something that the studio itself didn't even know?

"Is it Tom Hardy? I think these would be his size."

"Don't you think Tom Hardy would be an old hand at dressing for press tours by now?"

"So it *is* Harry Styles."

At that, Nikhil came down the stairs dancing and singing "Watermelon Sugar." Marley rolled her eyes and Ruby laughed. Then froze. Then turned to Marley.

"Shut. Up. *The Bronze Shadow* was just using Shayne's grandma's pink toilet? This guy has been trending all week. People are saying he's going to be a *major* style icon."

Nikhil preened. "Are you surprised that Mahreen Kamal can create a fashion icon?"

Ruby's eyes narrowed. "Wait—*Mahreen*…How well do you two know each other?"

"Take out the clothes," Marley said. "Let's see them on him."

Ruby gave Marley a suspicious look but then unzipped the garment bag.

"What do you think about those wide pants with the blue silk?" Marley asked. She was on her recliner, eyeing the latest outfit Nikhil was wearing. The blue silk shirt was supposed to be with the blue velvet pants, but the look ended up feeling a bit too "Christmas party" for her.

"Ooh, yes—try that," Ruby said.

Nikhil saluted and headed upstairs to try on the new combination. Marley asked Ruby how things at the store had been while she'd been gone.

"Oh, you know, the same. You're lucky to get away from that place for a while. I am so ready to get out of there. Eight months until I leave."

"Are you serious about leaving Toronto again?"

Ruby nodded. "Leaving *Canada*. I have some details to work out...but yeah, it's time to go. I'm twenty-seven, and my prospects are worse than Charlotte Lucas's. I'm already a burden on my family."

Marley snorted. "You're thirty-two, Ruby." And she had no immediate family to be a burden on. Ruby's mother, Maryam Aunty, passed away when Ruby was twenty, and Ruby hadn't spoken to her father since he left her mother.

"Twenty-seven-year-old spinster at heart." Ruby sighed. "I need to find myself an English husband before I'm thirty-five. Not everyone has hot actors hanging around their house." She turned toward the stairs. "Oh wow—that's most definitely *the one*."

Marley looked at Nikhil, and *wow* was right. The slightly shiny black wide-legged pants were amazing with the drapey navy shirt.

"You look hot," Ruby said.

Nikhil put on his sultry face. The same one from the infamous lip-licking video. Marley felt herself flush...She had to turn away. This was exactly the devastating, sexy look the studio wanted to see. Nikhil *was* going to be a style icon.

Once they had a handful of outfits, including a few casual ensembles for him to be seen around town in, Ruby left, promising to get the clothes to Fernando in the morning so he could rush the alterations. Marley couldn't miss the flirty wave Ruby gave Nikhil when she left, and she didn't blame her cousin.

Nikhil was...well, *hot* today. More than that. Charming. Sexy. Charismatic. He was so different from the slack-jawed ball of self-doubt and existential angst he'd been when he first came into Reid's. No wonder Ruby and everyone else, it seemed, couldn't take their eyes off the man.

And if Marley was honest, she should add herself to the list of Nikhil's fans around the world. She'd grown quite attached to him in the few days he'd been here.

They'd watched cooking shows again last night. Just watching, joking around, and not getting into anything heavy. She knew he was going through a lot and his family situation was a mess, and maybe that's why he seemed so comfortable here. And for Marley, things were so much easier when Nikhil was next to her.

But also…whenever she was comfortably hanging out with him, memories of their night at that downtown hotel invaded her head. It had been incredible. The feel of his hands on her body was imprinted on her forever. On her back. On her breasts. She'd never again feel someone's hands on her breasts like that. Nikhil would always be the last one. *Ugh.* Marley needed to stop thinking about it if she wanted this attraction to go away. No. Not attraction. More like…*fascination.*

Of course, she was usually smart enough not to move someone who looked tasty enough to lick into her house. Marley thought that having major surgery would have knocked her libido down, but apparently, Nikhil Shamdasani was too potent these days for mere pain to hold back.

But in the state she was in, a physical attraction was pretty much useless. Not to mention…

He. Was. Her. Client.

He might have felt like a roommate, or a friend, or whatever right now, but he was her client first—and mixing business and pleasure was always a monumental mistake.

Nikhil sat on the sofa heavily. He was wearing gray sweatpants and one of his old T-shirts. His hair was loose, falling in soft waves just to his shoulders. Marley thought he looked even better than he did in the designer clothes he'd been in minutes ago.

She was in trouble.

"That was exhausting. I need a drink," he said. He pushed his hair behind his ears. "I can't find any of my hair ties."

"Check under the fridge. McQueen steals them." She winced with a twinge of pain.

Nikhil looked at her concerned. "It's not time for painkillers yet. You okay?"

Marley nodded. "Probably did too much today." The sharp pain went through her again. She was only on Tylenol today—the nurse had warned her not to take more of the heavy painkillers than she needed so she wouldn't get dependent on them.

"I was in agony every day when I first started training with Reggie," Nikhil said. "He wouldn't let me take painkillers, because he's a cruel, sadistic bastard. I quickly discovered that the best way to distract myself is to feel pleasure in another part of my body."

His talking about pleasure wasn't really helping her inability to get sex with the man out of her head. She narrowed her eyes. "Is this story going to end up in one of those *Cosmo* celebrity-sex confession pieces?"

He laughed. "Miss Mahreen Kamal, get your mind out of the gutter. Not *that* kind of pleasure." He shuddered. "Thinking about sex and Reggie...no."

Another wave of pain, this one sharper than the last, went through her. Marley closed her eyes and put her head back. She started counting under her breath.

"What's wrong?"

"I'm fine," she managed to say.

"I don't think you are. Is it the same pain?"

Yes, it was the same pain. The same goddamn pain, all day. Her face twisted. It was all too much. A few hours of work and she couldn't even think straight. She hated her stupid defective gene with a passion. It just wasn't fair.

What would be happening in Marley's life if she'd inherited her father's working gene instead of her mother's broken one? Would she be doing these fittings with Nikhil in the store instead of in her living room? Would Erin be so impressed that she would insist that Marley transfer full-time to personal shopping?

What would her life be like if none of the women in it had this mutation?

A hand was suddenly on her face, wiping her tears. She sighed. She'd had no idea she was even crying again. She was worried that having a massive crush on a client was unprofessional—well, bursting into tears every thirty seconds with him couldn't be good, either. Apparently, all her emotional regulation had been in her breasts.

The hand that was on her cheeks moved to her forearms, stroking and rubbing them softly. "Can I show you how Reggie helped me?"

Marley chuckled, still not opening her eyes. She wasn't sure she wanted to know the pain-relieving methods of a sadistic physical trainer. But she trusted Nikhil. She nodded.

After guiding her up from the recliner to the sofa, he crouched on the floor in front of her and took one of her hands in his.

The light strokes on her hand turned into a full-on massage. He pulled on her fingers. Rubbed the soft tissue between them. This massage was…intense. Not sensual but focused. He seemed to be trying to hit specific pressure points. The touch of his hands on hers was making all the muscles in her body relax. The pain wasn't exactly leaving—he wasn't that good—but this was helping. A lot.

He talked while he massaged. "I once dated someone who was into healing touch. She took this woo-woo stuff way too far, but the constant back rubs were nice." He moved on to Marley's forearm.

"This is heaven."

He told her about this sports massage guy that Reggie had brought in for him early into training.

"They don't do anything like that for me anymore," he said. "The honeymoon period is over. Now it's just abuse with no cycle of love bombing."

When he reached the part of her arm where the sleeve of her shirt started, he paused. To be honest, it would feel pretty good to have his hands on her upper arms and shoulders right now. She wasn't really a prude, and he'd seen her completely naked only a week ago.

"Um…it's not pretty," she said. The last time he'd seen her bra it was a lace La Perla. Now it was an enormous, tight white surgical bra with a long row of hooks up the front and wide straps. Plus, there were still drain tubes coming out of her armpits.

He chuckled softly. "Okay, but you're Marley Kamal—I'm not sure it's possible for you to be not pretty. I don't care what it looks like. I want you to feel better."

She sighed. She also wanted to feel better than she did right now. She let him undo the buttons down the front of her mastectomy shirt, then the snaps on the sleeves. It was slightly… humiliating. She chuckled nervously.

"I wish more women would wear tear-away clothes," he said. "So convenient! Would recommend!"

He didn't say anything as he continued the massage, probably realizing that Marley wasn't really listening. She was feeling too...good. Relaxed. After working her shoulders and her neck, he finally leaned her head forward to massage her scalp. Marley said a silent thank-you that Reena had washed her hair in the sink the day before, because this was *heaven*. It reminded her of when her mother used to rub coconut oil into her scalp as a kid, a soothing ritual that made her feel protected and loved.

After a while, Marley felt him lean down and kiss her forehead. He smelled like that soap he used, plus...like him. "You're falling asleep. Want me to help you upstairs?"

She nodded. She didn't want him to stop touching her, but she wanted to sleep, too. He helped her up the stairs, and even helped her empty her drain bulbs. After fluffing up her pillows, Marley got into bed while Nikhil filled her water glass and took two painkillers out for her to take in the morning.

"Thank you," she said once she was settled on her nest of pillows. Nikhil pulled up her white duvet to cover her.

He smiled. "Anytime. Good night, Marley." He flicked off the light in her room as he left.

Marley fell asleep almost immediately, and had easily the best night's sleep since her surgery.

CHAPTER FIFTEEN

Nikhil

Nikhil was sweaty and completely out of breath on Tuesday after rehearsal. Every muscle in his body was hurting. If this pain was anywhere close to what Marley was dealing with, he totally understood why she kept erupting into tears since her surgery.

Reggie and Caroline had increased his training yet again. And they'd had the dietician come see him in the gym today. He was now officially only allowed to eat what she told him to eat. No more takeout with Marley. No more of his own cooking. He hadn't even had the chance to make Marley daal makhani yet.

This was the price he had to pay for the role, he supposed. He was still in the gym changing when his phone buzzed with a call—Lydia. He braced himself before answering—he was totally not in the mood for her.

"Meeting at the studio in ten. Kaelyn's office" was all she said when he answered.

"Ten minutes?"

"That's what I said."

"How do you even know I can make it to the studio in ten? I could be across town. Or at home."

He could get to the studio in ten minutes from Marley's place—if traffic was accommodating. But Lydia thought he lived in Markham with his parents, not in the spare room of the stylist she'd hired for him.

"Seriously, Nik, I know where you are *all the time*. You just finished up training with Reggie, so you should be at the gym either toweling off, or maybe even blow-drying those shiny locks of yours. The gym is literally across the street from the studio—you could be here in three minutes if you wanted to. Giving you ten is being generous. Now, put some pants on and get here." She disconnected the call.

Nikhil looked down at his bare legs and sighed. If Lydia's purpose was to prevent actors from getting a big head, she was *excellent* at her job.

In eight and a half minutes, Nikhil was walking into Kaelyn's office. Lydia; the other publicist, Carmen; and an executive were there.

"Nice, Nik," Lydia said, looking at her watch. "Sit." She pointed to the empty seat next to hers. She was smiling, weirdly.

Kaelyn was also smiling. Did that mean he wasn't in trouble? "We wanted to all talk together about what you can expect when you're in LA next week. We need to do some more publicity damage control."

More damage control? He'd thought things were better since that lip-licking video. He was being called a sex symbol and style icon now, wasn't he? "I think I need to get my agent on the phone."

Lydia looked a little irritated for a split second, then dialed a number on the phone on the desk. Esther answered it. "Esther, Lydia here. You're on speakerphone. I'm with Nik, along with Kaelyn, Carmen, and Harlan Green."

"Nicky, darling," Esther drawled. "How's my superstar doing?"

"Great," Nikhil said. Even though he wasn't. "Not sure why they called me to the principal's office, though."

"Let's cut to the chase," Harlan said. "We have concerns about Nik's reputation."

Nikhil frowned. "I thought fans liked me now."

Harlan nodded. "There is a definite contingent of fans who love you. More than we expected, actually. But at the same time, your detractors are becoming more vocal that you are not *their* Simon DeSouza. Maybe because your fans are so outspoken. You must have seen it on social media."

"I've been ordered to stay off social media," Nikhil said.

"I monitor the accounts for him," Lydia said. She looked at Nikhil. "TL;DR, your haters hate that you have so many lovers."

"And that's why you're sending him to Los Angeles," Esther said through the phone. "We've discussed this to death."

Harlan nodded. "Yes, but the executive team in LA are breathing down our necks to do even *more* to fix this publicity problem. All they're seeing is that damn hashtag to boycott *Ironis 3*."

Nikhil cringed. He had no idea there was a hashtag.

"The studio promised it would not cave to racist pressure," Esther said.

Carmen shook her head. "It's not *racism*. It's because Nik is an outsider and doesn't have the right personality for the role. There is even a whole campaign to get him replaced with Riz Ahmed."

So, his haters didn't hate him because he was Brown but because he was inexperienced and unlikable.

"He's an actor!" Esther said. "They do get that he'll be *acting* in the movie, don't they?"

"Of course," Lydia said.

"The pictures we leaked of him and Serena did well, so what we're proposing—"

"Releasing those pictures without warning was beyond the pale," Esther interrupted. "You knew the tabloids would assume they were in a relationship."

Nikhil really didn't want this to turn into an argument. "So what do you want me to do?"

Carmen smiled. "We're proposing we make it official while you're there. You're from Toronto, and Serena lives in LA. Makes sense that she would show you around, right? Hold hands in Long Beach or on Rodeo Drive. We're even thinking a trip to Disneyland. Nothing is better for your image than being seen with your girlfriend at the happiest place on earth."

"Serena is not my girlfriend, and I've lived in LA for years."

"We've spun you as a Toronto native," Kaelyn said.

"Is Serena Vox on board with this fake relationship?" Esther asked.

"Yes," Carmen said. "We've been on the line with her agent today. She's willing to sign a standard relationship contract... ending after the film wraps principal photography. This will be great for the movie. People will want to see the chemistry between the leads if they were in a relationship during shooting."

"Fake relationship," Nikhil said. "You said standard relationship contract, but it would be fake, right?"

"Of course," Harlan said. "We do this all the time."

A relationship, fake or not, with Serena Vox was the fantasy of pretty much every heterosexual—or hell, bisexual—man on this continent. But...what about his parents? Would they be told the truth? Would this make Mom happy? Would she start analyzing what color sari Serena should wear for the wedding? Would Nalini think Serena Vox was going to be her bhabhi?

And what about Marley? There was nothing going on between Nikhil and his stylist. There likely never would be anything between them. But it was also true that Nikhil was in so deep with her that he couldn't think straight when he was around her. And he was around her all the time since they were living together.

A relationship with someone else wasn't cheating on Marley, because he wasn't in a relationship with Marley. A fake relationship with someone else was even less like cheating. But it still felt so wrong to him.

"Do I have to say yes to this, Esther?"

"Of course not," Esther said. "We can talk privately, but I will say that I'm not a fan of these relationship contracts, especially for the lower-profile partner. It's true that it would be great publicity for the movie, but if things go upside down, your reputation will take a bigger hit than hers. Don't worry, though—I'll negotiate the terms of this and any agreement on your behalf. I'll make sure it's worth your while. But it's your decision."

"Then no," Nikhil said. "I am not interested in a relationship, real or fake, with Serena Vox." It was too complicated. With his family, with Marley—hell, with *himself*. "I'll act in your film and do everything I can to promote it, but my personal life is not up for negotiation."

Harlan looked at him for several long seconds. "Okay. If that's what you want. Would you at least be open to some more pictures with Serena in LA...not as a couple but just friends? I think that would be useful, too."

FARAH HERON

"Sure, that's fine." Maybe he and Serena could actually *be* friends. It would certainly make this whole movie easier.

But Nikhil could not be in a relationship with her, even if it was fake. Not when he was *obsessed* with someone else.

That night when Nikhil got home, Marley was in her normal spot on the recliner talking on the phone. He waved to her, and she nodded but didn't stop talking. Well, not really talking. More like…nodding and saying yes a lot. Must be her mom. He went upstairs to his room to change.

After he pulled on some sweats, his phone buzzed.

Marley: Sorry. I'm off the phone. You can come down now.

When Nikhil went back downstairs, Marley looked sad. He almost asked her how she was feeling, but he realized that that was almost the only thing he ever asked her.

He sat next to her on the sofa and turned to smile at her. "Dinner?"

She nodded. "I wish I could go out. There's this pasta place on College…or…I dunno." Her eyes glazed over a bit. "Spanish tapas. Maybe a tasting menu. Hell, at this point I'd be happy with Swiss Chalet."

"We can get takeout?" He loved Swiss Chalet, a chain of rotisserie-chicken restaurants that reminded him of his childhood. He couldn't eat it now—but he would order it for her if it would pull her out of this funk.

"No. Takeout isn't the same. I want to be sitting in an

uncomfortable restaurant chair. Having a cocktail, then maybe a nice glass of wine. I want to lean over my table and take a bite from my date's plate."

Nikhil wanted to be the date. He narrowed his eyes playfully. "Oh, you're one of those, are you?"

"One of what?"

"A food stealer."

She chuckled. And didn't wince with pain. Progress.

"Was that your mother on the phone?"

Marley nodded. "She's taking me to the hospital in a couple of days. Hopefully I'll get the drains out."

"That's good news. What would you be wearing?" he asked.

"To get my drains out? I assume I'll be topless."

"No, at this hypothetical dinner date. At the Italian place, or the tasting menu somewhere. Not Swiss Chalet."

She smiled again. "My green dress."

"What's that look like?"

"It's…slinky. Sexy. Not bodycon but perfectly fitted. It's completely backless."

Nikhil had never really thought of a woman's back as a particularly attractive body part, but that night in the King Street hotel, he'd run his fingers over the impossibly smooth skin of Marley's back, and it was very sexy. Everything about Marley was sexy. He wanted to see her in this green dress.

"I have no idea if it will fit me after I'm healed."

Nikhil frowned. "Why? Because you'll have been vegging on a recliner for weeks?"

"No. I won't be the same size as I used to be."

Shit. Of course. She'd told him that the doctor was going to replace her natural breasts with silicone ones, but he'd never wondered if her new breasts would look the same as the old ones. She'd been living in those oversized shirts and hoodies zipped all the way up since surgery, so he hadn't really noticed if she looked any different. Even that day he'd given her a massage, he'd seen her in her bra, but it was so huge and she was so swollen that he couldn't really see anything. And besides, all he'd noticed was that she was in pain that day.

"Are they...Have you...I mean, are you a different size?"

Marley's mouth was a straight line. "I don't know," she said. "I haven't looked at them."

Nikhil didn't say anything. What would it be like to have your body change like that when you didn't want it to? A body that she'd been happy with. That others had loved, too. He reached over and put his hand on top of hers.

"I looked away at my last exam," she said. "My doctor said everything looked good, though. I have a lot of swelling..."

He squeezed her hand. She wasn't looking at him, but he could see that her eyes were welling with tears again.

Honestly, if Nikhil could take all this pain—physical and emotional—from her, he would. It put things into perspective...Here he was, being all woe-is-me because some fanboys didn't think he was the right actor to play a part in a movie, and Marley was facing a problem infinitely more real.

"You don't have to look at your body yet," he said. "Take your time healing...mentally and physically."

She nodded.

"Are you...scared you'll be different?"

They were still holding hands. She wasn't moving, though. Not running her fingers over his. Not squeezing at all. Just holding.

"Not *will be* different," she said. "I *am* different. I mean, I won't look the same. I have no sensation anymore there. They removed my nipples. And..." She looked down. "Mine were sensitive."

Nikhil squeezed tighter. He remembered. She'd squirmed and panted when he'd had his mouth on them. It was so unfair that she'd never feel that again.

What the hell did he know about supporting Marley through this? This was one of the hardest things she'd ever been through. She should have her mother here, or her best friend. Or hell, any friend.

Not a self-important actor with an identity crisis. He was Nikhil Shamdasani—class clown. The pawn of the Ironis franchise. He was of no use to Marley.

After neither of them said anything or moved for a few minutes, Marley looked up at him. "Enough pity party. Tell me about your day."

"I had a meeting with the studio publicists today. Apparently, my haters are getting louder. Execs are freaking out that hashtag 'boycott *Ironis 3*' is trending."

She cringed. "I don't get it at all. Is your job at risk?"

He shook his head. "Doubt it. At least I hope not."

"I don't understand why people are talking about *boycotting*? Is it because you're..."

"Brown? Inexperienced? Unlikable? Who knows?"

"You *are* likable. I like you."

He smiled. She was holding his hand, and she said she liked him. Who cared if no one else liked him? Marley did. "They want to do all these publicity stunts, but I'm not interested."

"But this is the biggest role of your career! You might have to."

He shook his head. "Not sure it would make a difference. I'm positive the execs regret hiring me. People are analyzing those interviews I did and are saying I'm off-putting. And maybe they're right. I love acting, and I am *so* looking forward to shooting the movie, but right now I'd much rather be here with my friend who has real problems instead of gallivanting through Los Angeles with people who don't actually want me there."

Marley's hand tightened around his, and he couldn't stop thinking about it. About how turned on he'd been when he'd massaged it the other day. About how perfectly formed it was. About how Marley's capable hands were two of the most beautiful things in the world. All he wanted to do was hold on to her and try to give her the strength she thought she was lacking. Even though she was the strongest person he knew.

"They can recast me after this film," he said. "Or just not feature the Bronze Shadow in the next Ironis movies. I don't care. But I'll at least get this movie."

"You just wait until shooting starts. Everyone will fall in love with you."

Nikhil shrugged. "There is nothing I can do right now but wait and see."

They continued to hold hands like that for several long moments.

Finally, Nikhil couldn't go another second without telling her. "Marley?"

"Hmm?"

"You don't need to worry. You'll still be beautiful. I mean, your face, of course, but…Can I tell you something that's probably totally inappropriate?"

"Okay…"

He exhaled, then looked at her. God, she was stunning. "You have the *sexiest* body. Your legs. Your shoulders. Your back…

I've never thought a back was hot until I saw yours. I think that your new breasts will be fine, but even if they aren't…I think there will be enough sexy still in you to make up for it. By a mile."

Marley smiled small. Then squeezed his hand. "You're sweet."

"I mean it. You're beautiful. You always will be."

"I'll just have frozen pizza for dinner. And then I want to eat popcorn and watch reality cooking shows with you."

Popcorn was the only approved snack on the list from the nutritionist. "That sounds perfect. No butter."

CHAPTER SIXTEEN

Nikhil

Nikhil was in LA for about an hour and a half when he remembered why he'd been glad to be out of California for a while. Everything was so *big* here. And sprawling. And he could never tell if people were being real with him.

And it was damn hot.

He went straight to his best friend and former roommate Tyler's house after getting out of the busy airport late Sunday night. Tyler was now a series regular on a medical show, and he insisted that Nikhil stay with him instead of a Hollywood hotel while he was in town. Nikhil had agreed since he wasn't sure he'd have much time to see Tyler otherwise. Plus, Tyler had a husband now who was even nicer than Tyler, and Nikhil wanted to see him, too. He got in too late to hang out much, though.

In the morning, a car took Nikhil to his first talk show appearance—a daytime show hosted by a former pop star. The interview went fine. The bubbly host seemed genuinely kind and positive, and Nikhil couldn't imagine anyone thinking he was grumpy when talking to her. She didn't ask about those pictures with Serena but did mention the lip-licking video. She even presented him with a wrapped gift, which ended up being a multipack of lip balms from her celebrity skin-care line.

He was taken to tape another talk show afterward that

would air late at night. Then he was brought to a hotel for a press junket.

It was about the same as the Canadian junket a couple of weeks ago, except this time he was joined by Serena for the interviews. He had a few seconds with her in the room before the reporters came through.

Serena Vox was, of course, stunningly beautiful. In person, she seemed both bigger and smaller than she was onscreen. Taller but thinner. And she looked older. Or rather, her in-person mannerisms were more mature than her typical screen presence. She had a round face; sparkling brown eyes; pale, milky skin; and shiny dark-brown hair. He'd always found Serena a little cold in person. Not in the same way that Marley seemed cold, though. Marley was just…reserved. She held her emotions close to her. Although lately she cried at the drop of a hat, but that wasn't normal.

Serena's coldness seemed more…targeted. Like he was always left wondering if he'd offended her. But when a camera was on her, her smile changed instantly to the warmest girl-next-door glow.

After a publicist gave them a briefing on what kind of questions to expect and what was off-limits, someone came to retouch their hair and makeup. Finally, they were ready for the first interview. It was all straightforward—clearly, Serena would be doing all the heavy lifting as most of the questions were for her. Nikhil was the sidekick, which was fine.

Serena was a pro. Nikhil didn't need media training; he just needed to watch her navigate a busy junket. She answered every question like it was the first time she'd heard it. She laughed, she grinned, she patted Nikhil's arm. She even flirted a bit. But only when the camera was rolling.

"Did you have any input on the casting for the Bronze Shadow?" asked Chrissy Snyder, a popular entertainment reporter.

Serena turned to Nikhil and put her hands on his arm briefly. "None at all! I leave casting to the pros, but I couldn't be happier with their choice. One read with him, and I knew... there is no other possible Simon DeSouza. Wait until you see him in the Bronze Shadow costume!"

There was no way that Serena had seen him in the final costume since *he* hadn't even seen it, but okay.

"Nik, what about you? How does it feel to step into a role that is so beloved? Do you think you can do the Shadow justice?"

"I'm certainly going to try my best." Nikhil gave his practiced smolder to the camera. "This role is a dream come true for me. I used to spend my allowance on a new Ironis comic each week." That wasn't true, but he'd been coached to say it. He turned to Serena. "I have it easy since I'm stepping into an existing franchise. Serena and the Ironis team have already done the heavy lifting. I'm the new kid. I hear the Ironis cast have the best hazing rituals!"

Serena laughed. "No comment on that one!"

The next interview went as well as the first. Light teasing. Friendly. But the third was from some sci-fi fan site, and Nikhil could tell immediately that the interviewer wasn't going to play as nice as the others.

It started when he directed the questions at Nikhil instead of Serena. And after the softball ones, he asked how Nikhil felt about stepping into a role that was favored to go to an experienced actor. Then the guy cut him off before he was two words into an answer. "Have any actors sent you steaming poop in the mail? This was the *coveted* role of the year."

Nikhil frowned. How was he supposed to answer that? "Of course not. I've had nothing but well-wishes from colleagues."

Serena flashed a charming smile. "I wouldn't let anyone do something like that to anyone in the Ironis family. Nik earned this role fair and square."

"Did he, though?" the man asked. "May I ask, Nik, are you at all worried about viewers connecting with you in this role when they've been picturing someone different as the Bronze Shadow?"

"You mean someone white?" Nikhil asked, even though he knew he shouldn't.

Kaelyn, who had flown in from Toronto with him, shut it down immediately. "You've been warned," she said, pointing at the interviewer.

"Okay, I'll rephrase," the guy said. He smiled at Nikhil. "Are you going to bring this"—he waved his hand at Nikhil's blue silk shirt and wide pants—"flair to the role? People are expecting to see the Simon DeSouza from the comic books. Are they going to see an ethnic Harry Styles instead?"

Kaelyn looked at Nikhil. "Don't answer that." She pointed at the interviewer. "That's your final warning. I'll see that your outlet loses press privileges at any Ironis event for life."

Thankfully, the guy behaved after that. Sort of. He asked about Nikhil's experience in action roles and about his training, but there was a clear subtext that he didn't think Nikhil could hack it. Nikhil frowned through the whole thing. The next interview was as rough as that one. Or maybe the interview wasn't as bad, but Nikhil's mood had soured so much that he felt like it was.

"Why would how I dress make *her* look bad?" Nikhil asked after the interviewer questioned Serena if she thought Nikhil's style was upstaging her.

When someone asked him about how important it was for him to represent his community to all the young children who wanted to look like the Bronze Shadow, Nikhil shook his head. "I don't know. I'm only one person and can't be expected to represent all South Asian actors. Do you expect Serena to be the voice of all white brunettes?"

"Okay, let's take five," Kaelyn said, waving away the next interviewer. She handed Nikhil and Serena bottles of water. "There are four more after this one. Can I get you anything?"

He exhaled. "Honestly, I'd kill for a whiskey."

Kaelyn nodded. "Yeah, I can make that happen."

She started to walk away, when Serena called after her, "Make that two."

Nikhil knew he was bombing the interviews. He was annoyed. He wasn't able to brush off all this crap and put on the fake charm. It was probably pointless, anyway. No matter how charming he was, no matter how hard he worked, he would never be good enough for people who thought he was just here for the studio to fulfill some agenda.

And maybe those fanboys were right. He wasn't here because he was really the best person for the job.

"Those sci-fi guys are the worst," Nikhil said to Serena.

She shrugged. "All part of the job. Spandex is thin—you're going to need to build up a thick skin under it if you want to get anywhere."

She picked up her phone and stayed on it until Kaelyn was back with two shot glasses of golden whiskey neat. Nikhil sniffed his. Smelled like a good single malt. Which reminded him of Marley and that night in the hotel. He wished she were here.

"Cheers," he said. Serena wasn't looking at him, though.

Nikhil sighed and downed his drink. The whiskey was not the magic bullet to make it all better, but it did help a little.

Before they started up again, Kaelyn informed Nikhil that he had a meeting at the LA studio office the next day after his talk show appearance to go over this junket. And that Esther would be there as his representative.

When the next interviewer asked Serena if she was going to attempt to get her figure down to what it was in the first movie, Nikhil almost snarled at him. Serena gave him a disarming smile, but it didn't help.

He needed Marley. Marley with her full lips and thick hair. Marley to smile at him, tell him he was doing great, and fix the scarf around his neck. Marley was the only one who could fix Nikhil's grump lately. Serena's stylist was here. He wished his were, too.

But so long as Marley was his stylist, she would never actually be his.

It made him even grumpier, which wasn't great when he was a little tipsy. He probably shouldn't have had that whiskey before lunch.

He was really starting to hate LA.

"I can't believe you did shots with Serena Vox in a press junket," Tyler said, shaking his head. "Oh, how the lowly hath risen."

He was sitting near the pool in his friend Tyler's backyard with a beer in his hand, watching Tyler's film-editor husband, Angelo, barbecue sausages at the other end of the yard. Angelo's son, Felix, was splashing in the pool. It was a very domestic tableau…night and day from the party-kid lifestyle Tyler and Nikhil had lived for years in downtown LA.

"Shut up, *Emmy nominee*," Nikhil said. Tyler had been nominated for a supporting role on his show last year but lost. Nikhil hadn't forgiven Tyler for taking his husband to the award ceremony instead of Nikhil.

Tyler chuckled. "We've both come a long way, haven't we?"

Nikhil shook his head. "*You've* come a long way. I'm still on the road. And somehow, I don't think I'll be reaching the destination."

Tyler scoffed. "Nah, man, your screen tests were *fire*. Everything will be fine when the movie is out. Fans need to see you to love you. This pre-production promo is ridiculous. Their caving to the masses…that never works."

"But when the masses are this angry…"

"They'll get over it. Things are *changing* in this industry. Look at me, a gay Mexican who got an Emmy nod for a storyline that had nothing to do with homophobia or illegal immigration. Progress is here—it's just taking baby steps, that's all."

Nikhil shrugged, then took a long gulp from his beer bottle. He wiped his mouth on his sleeve. "Maybe. Or whatever. I just…" He looked at his friend. "I don't know, Ty. Do I even *want* this life anymore? I thought I did. Hell, I worked my ass off for years to get here. We both did. But you…you *fit* here. With your hot industry husband and Hollywood Hills home. I just…" He sighed. It was brutal. All his dreams had come true, and now he didn't even know if he wanted them anymore. "The last few weeks I've felt more grounded than ever in Toronto—but only when I'm not in rehearsals."

Tyler raised a brow. "At your parents' house?"

Nikhil exhaled. "No. I've been staying…somewhere else."

"Ah. I knew that gossip about you and Serena Vox wasn't true. Can I assume there is a *person* behind this keeping-you-grounded situation in Toronto?"

"Yeah." He sighed, looking out at the breathtaking view at sunset. "I've been staying with my friend Marley. She's…great. But we're just friends."

"Seriously, Nik? I can see right through you. You in love with her?"

Well, there was an interesting question. Nikhil was infatuated…fascinated, preoccupied, crushing hard…but *in love* with Marley?

"How long have I known you?" Tyler asked. "You can be honest with me."

Nikhil huffed a laugh. He'd known Tyler since two days after showing up in LA a decade ago. "I've known Marley longer. She was my high school prom date."

Tyler loudly put his bottle down on the table between them. "Get out of town, Nik…This is *Mahreen*? The love of your life?"

Nikhil made a face. "How do you know about Mahreen?"

"Because you *told* me all about her, you dumbass! Years ago, not long after I met you. We were drunk or stoned or who knows what, and you told me all about the *pinnacle of female excellence*, as you called it. You said it was impossible for anyone to be as perfect as Mahreen and that you'd never forgive yourself for screwing things up with her."

Nikhil chuckled. Now he remembered. He really had it bad for her back then. He almost didn't move to LA after what happened on prom night, even though that had been his plan forever. He had fantasies of flying back to Toronto and showing up at her house with a truckload of flowers and apologizing for it all. "I was pathetic."

"Sounds like you still are. And that answers my question. Yeah, you're in love with her."

"How do you know?"

"Because the easiest person in the world to fall in love with is the one you used to be in love with. What is it about this girl, anyway?"

Nikhil looked out into the distance. "I don't even know. She's just...different. She's gorgeous and very...posh. And she's, like...reserved. Private. But deep inside, if you can get past that shell, she's different. She's the sweetest person ever and also really...passionate. She's always been like that. And she...she sees me."

"Like your family doesn't."

Nikhil nodded. It was such a cliché. He left Toronto all those years ago because he'd never be Arjun, and he was tired of his parents' criticisms about it. Even at school, everyone said he was an idiot for wanting to be a comedian or an actor instead of doing something normal with his life. No one ever took him seriously.

Only Mahreen. She genuinely laughed at his jokes. Told him he was talented. And she opened up to him like she rarely did for anyone else.

"It always felt like no one noticed me back then," Nikhil said. "At home or at school. But Mahreen did. And it felt like she liked what she saw. It still feels like that."

Tyler smiled. "You need to be honest with her this time, Nik. Don't let her be the one who gets away. Again."

"Nah, she wouldn't want that. Gonna keep it unrequited again."

"She let you move in with her. You don't think she's interested?"

Nikhil shook his head. "It's not like you and Angelo, Ty. Marley's not in the industry. And she's going through stuff right now…It's arguably an even worse time for her to be in a relationship than me. Who'd want this? Paparazzi following me. Gossip columns saying I'm dating Serena Vox. Nerds hating me."

"I mean, I checked your hashtag. A lot of nerds *want* you, too." Tyler shook his head. "I can't understand why."

"Asshole," Nikhil said. "Why are we friends, Ty?"

Tyler chuckled. "Because we're the *same*, my man. Hopeless romantics. Hollywood glamour, the love of the craft, art, entertainment. And we have an almost irrational drive to succeed. But we're also a different kind of romantic, too. We're… idealists. We want the dream but on our terms." He took a sip of his beer. "Let me tell you something I've learned in the last year. The dream *is* possible, but it's a fuck ton more complicated and way more work than we realized. And…it's so much better…like, monumentally better. But you need boundaries to keep the bullshit out." He looked over at Angelo. "And I think you need a partner to remind you that you aren't the hot shit that everyone says you are…or the steaming shit. The only grounded people in Hollywood are the ones without yes-men or sycophants."

"You're on a family show, Tyler."

"Yeah, that's why I swear so much off set. It sounds like there is more to your situation with her than you can say right now. I'm not going to pry, but…you *do* realize movie stars live in Toronto, right? Not only is there a healthy industry there—I mean, your own blockbuster is filming there—but also? Film shoots are what—a few months at a time? If coming home to this girl makes you feel anywhere close to how I feel coming home to Angelo, then trust me: it's worth it."

Nikhil looked over at Angelo, who had jumped into the pool to play tag with Felix. Nikhil didn't know if he wanted *this*—a house in the suburbs, kids—but he had to admit this was the most peace he'd seen in LA. It was as cozy as Marley's house in Toronto. And it all looked so great on his friend.

Maybe Tyler was right. Maybe peace like this was worth fighting for. "Anyway, we work together. I can't be with her—she's my stylist."

Tyler shrugged. "So? Get another stylist. They're a dime a dozen."

"No, not ones like Marley, they aren't."

Nikhil video called Marley after dinner to see how she was doing. She didn't turn her camera on, though—she probably thought she looked tired. Or maybe she'd been crying again.

"Hey, Hollywood," she said when she saw Nikhil. He could hear the smile in her voice. He had no idea why he ever thought Marley didn't smile. "How were your events today? Wow, look at that view behind you. Where are you?"

He moved the camera so she could see the expanse of the Hollywood hills. "My buddy Tyler's backyard. I'm staying with him instead of a hotel...so much friendlier." Tyler was standing to go inside. "Here, Marley, say hi to Tyler. You'd like him...he calls me out on my BS." He held the phone out to Tyler.

"Ah, lovely Marley," Tyler said. "A pleasure to meet you.

Whenever you're in LA, you're also welcome to stay here…
with or without this sad sack. I'm going in. Have a wonderful
night."

Once Tyler was inside, Marley let out a squeal that Nikhil
didn't know she was capable of making. "Nikhil, that was *Tyler
Castillo* from *Vegas Hope*! You didn't tell me you were friends
with Tyler Castillo!"

"I told you about Ty, didn't I? We were roommates for years.
Great guy. Real smart-ass. How's your pain level been today?"

"No, we're going to talk about *your* life. You're in a TV
star's house in Hollywood! It's infinitely more interesting than
my life right now. You don't want to hear about me scratching
McQueen's ear for an hour. Or about the glassblowing reality
show I binged. How was that daytime talk show? Was the host
as nice as she seems on TV?"

"Nicer. And she smells like apples."

Marley smiled. "Not surprised. And the junket went well,
too?"

"Yeah, it was great," he lied. The junket was terrible. He
didn't want to worry her by telling her how awful it was.
"You've been resting today, right? Reena's there?"

"Yes, and she knows not to let me do anything. Your sister
came over to watch *The Bachelor* with me, too. She brought
aloo parathas your dad made."

He smiled. He'd thank Nalini for that later. "And your
mother is taking you to the hospital for your appointment
Wednesday?"

Marley nodded. "Yes. Drain output was low again today, so
I'm hoping they can come out."

"Crossing my fingers for you. I'll be there that evening."

"Okay. Enjoy Tinseltown and see you then!"

"Wait, Marley—turn on your camera. I want to see you."

Seconds later her face filled the screen. She didn't look tired, or sad. She looked beautiful.

"There you are," he said softly. "You…sleep well, okay? I'll see you in two days." He didn't disconnect the call, though. Neither did she. They stared at each other for several moments. Finally, Nikhil said, "I wish you had been with me today. These junkets are better with you."

"I wish I could have been with you, too," she said. "Maybe one day we can hang out in LA together."

That was the first time she'd ever hinted that this—whatever this was between them—would continue past her recovery. He smiled widely. "I would love that."

"Good night," she finally said.

"Good night," he responded.

She disconnected the call.

And Nikhil realized that Tyler was right. He was so in love with this woman. *Again.*

Nikhil had another talk show interview the next morning, which went fine. He suspected that Kaelyn gave them an earful about off-limit questions. After the talk show, he was whisked away for a lunch with Serena on the patio of a restaurant frequented by paparazzi. Serena spent most of the meal on her phone. At least the stuffed-pasta dish Nikhil had ordered was tasty. Reggie and the nutritionist were miles away—Nikhil deserved a treat. Finally, a car came to take him to the studio offices for a meeting with the LA publicity team. The sterile conference room he was led to was empty, but not for long.

"Darling! Ah, it's such a delight to see you in person!" Esther came into the room with her arms wide.

He hugged Esther and kissed both of her cheeks. "Sorry to bring all this chaos to you."

She patted his cheek. "Nonsense, my boy. And you need to drop those Canadian habits if you're going to get anywhere. No apologizing. And don't you worry—I'm going to fix everything."

Nikhil didn't really have the chance to say much, because four people came into the room then—two men and two women—but the only one he knew was Kaelyn. She introduced Nikhil and Esther to the others. There was Veronica, who was in publicity like Kaelyn, but more senior. And the two men were studio executives—Nikhil recognized their names but hadn't interacted with them yet.

After they all sat, the taller man, Stuart, got right to business. "We need to talk to you about your poor media skills. We understand the junket didn't go well."

Nikhil felt like he was being sent to the principal's office again. He opened his mouth to speak, when Esther put her hand out to stop him.

"No," Esther said. "We need to talk to *you* about how the studio isn't supporting my client. How can you send him into the den of alt-right wolves like that? Seriously? The *Sci-Fi Sentinel*? We all knew the fanboys weren't going to love this casting, so why are you putting their spokesperson in front of him?"

"The *Sci-Fi Sentinel* has been one of the Ironis franchise's biggest supporters," Kaelyn said.

"The problem wasn't just yesterday," the other executive said. Nikhil didn't remember his name. "Can we discuss how many handlers he's gone through? Plus stylists and trainers. He

even saw three different dentists! Your client is clearly struggling. He also knew what he was in for when he took this
role—he said he could handle it."

"I haven't fired anyone in weeks," Nikhil said. Not since
Marley came on board. Esther put her hand on his arm to shut
him up.

"Let him handle the job he was hired to do!" Esther said.
"He's an actor, not a PR person."

Stuart shook his head. "There are four weeks until shooting. And if we leave things how they are now, the movie will be
a flop even before the first frame is printed."

Esther put her hands on the table. "Yes, and it will be
because you ghouls aren't letting him be himself! *Fix that
tooth, build that muscle. Don't eat that bread. Don't wear that!*
None of this was in his contract, you know. I get the training
boot camp—but the rest of this? Press junkets and appearances
and all those pictures with Serena? We've been accommodating because we want the movie to succeed, too, but my client's
mental health comes first. Always."

"Does he need a therapist?" Veronica asked. "We have
one—"

Esther shook her head. "What he needs is to control his
own life. You have him stressed to the gills. Look, you know
what's bad PR? Even worse than racist fanboys calling him a
diversity hire? Progressive fans calling you out for harassing
and putting way too much pressure on your only POC cast
member."

The executives stared at Esther. Nikhil knew exactly what
Esther's threat here was: if they didn't lay off, then a few anon-
ymous tips and social media posts could go out about how the
studio had been treating Nikhil. Right now, the racists were

talking about boycotting the film. If progressive fans got wind that they were putting an unfair amount of pressure on the only marginalized main cast member, that would add more fuel to the already-burning fire.

Nikhil actually had the upper hand here. He had a lot of fans on his side. One more video of him licking his lips and he could have even more. They could turn this whole movie into an even bigger shit show.

"What are you suggesting?" Stuart said. "Who's his handler? Let's get her on the line."

Esther shook her head. "No. I want the team gone. No more handler."

"Yes!" Nikhil loved that idea. No more Lydia sounded like a dream.

"He has to have a handler!" Stuart said.

Esther crossed her arms in front of herself. "No, he doesn't."

The other executive nodded. "Okay. He'll have to manage his own schedule, though."

"I'll get him a personal assistant," Esther said. "I want everyone Lydia hired gone, too. No more media trainer, dentists, even the dietician. He'll still go to training and rehearsals, but that's it. Cancel the rest of this pre-production promo. No more talk show hosts or press junkets until release, as is stated in his contract. And stop with the fake-girlfriend stuff. No more leaks to the gossip pages about him. He'll lay low… Everyone will forget he exists until closer to release."

Nikhil nodded. He loved all this. He loved Esther.

"Stylist, too," Esther added. "He can pick his own damn clothes instead of working with that store."

Nikhil's head shot to Esther. *Marley* was his stylist. She was the only good thing that had happened to him in all this. She was his savior, the one who was grounding him every night. He couldn't do this without Marley.

The execs only nodded. Clearly, they were terrified of Esther.

"Nik is a professional and an absolute doll if you let him be himself. I promise I won't let him slack off on his diet, and he won't look like a couch bum. He'll do a better job of what is required in his contract for post-promotion with his mental health intact. Do we have a deal?"

It was clear that Esther *wasn't* trying to make a deal here—she was telling them how things would work from now on. And they had no choice but to agree.

Stuart sighed. "Fine. We're canceling Lydia and everyone she hired." He pointed to Nikhil. "You're on your own—but you'd better keep up or this contract will be considered breached. And lie low."

"Excellent." Esther stood. "Now, I've got to make sure my client gets some rest before his early flight tomorrow. Good afternoon."

But Nikhil couldn't rest after that meeting. His mind was racing too fast. How the hell was he going to tell Marley about this? He'd pretty much just lost the studio's contract with Reid's. Marley needed the client. Her promotion to personal shopping was riding on it. Maybe he could tell Esther that he wanted to keep Marley and the store only.

Marley was the only one on his team who was *actually* on his team. She was his lifeline through all this chaos. He wanted her with him. And she needed him, too.

But he didn't have to lose her. Not being her client anymore didn't mean he couldn't still be her friend. In fact...without a working relationship, maybe they could have another kind of relationship. But Nikhil didn't want that…not if it meant Marley would lose her dream job as a personal shopper.

Tyler had said that having it all was a lot harder than they thought it would be. And yep, Nikhil couldn't see a way out of this one.

CHAPTER SEVENTEEN

Marley

Wonderfully, spectacularly amazingly, Dr. Abernathy agreed Marley's drains were ready to come out when she saw him on Wednesday. Even better news was that he said she could finally take a proper shower under running water. After the drains were removed, the doctor rebandaged her and left her alone to dress. There was a large mirror in the room—which made sense since it was a plastic surgeon's office—so Marley stood in front of it. Most of her bandaging was gone now. Only thin strips of tape on her incisions remained. For the first time since her surgery, Marley intentionally looked at her new body.

It had only been two weeks since her surgery, and she was still bruised. Not quite black and blue, but a sickly yellow that was kind of hard to see under her brown skin. And she was definitely swollen—especially under her arms. Her new breasts were round, tight, and high. Also, totally uneven. And without nipples, her chest looked like a Barbie doll's.

But…she looked *human*. She still looked like *her*. Her skin was still smooth brown. Her stomach was still soft with an innie belly button. Her legs in her black leggings were still long. She wanted to turn around and look at her back to see if it really *was* sexy like Nikhil had said it was.

She maybe looked a little weird, but she knew her skin would get used to the implants and heal. And also? Her chest was just one part of her body. The rest of her was still her.

On the drive home, Marley tuned her mother out. Mom was just talking about herself anyway. About how the traffic on the highway might make her late for her volunteer shift cooking meals for seniors at the prayer hall. About how her father started playing pickleball, so Mom had to do laundry more often. About anything except how Marley was healing.

But Mom *did* take her to the doctor today. And being at the hospital had to be hard for her after her own surgery and cancer treatment. Maybe Marley shouldn't expect her mother to be anything but who she always was.

The first thing Marley did when she walked into her house— after scratching McQueen's ears—was take a shower. And it was as glorious as she'd expected. Even if she couldn't shave her legs or shampoo her hair (which was fine—Reena had washed her hair yesterday), it was amazing to have water running over her whole body. Afterward, since no drains meant she didn't need the mastectomy shirts anymore, she took out the designer loungewear she'd bought from Reid's the day after she'd finally been given a surgery date two months ago. The outfit—loose pants, a slinky shirt, and matching robe—was a vibrant cranberry-red color and made of the softest imaginable fabric. She vividly remembered the day she bought it—she hated that she needed to have the surgery, and she had no idea how she would feel about her body after, so she bought this exorbitantly expensive and fabulous loungewear, deciding she could at least dress well while going through it all.

Even though she'd been worried then, she had to admit that she'd *underestimated* how monumentally craptastic she'd feel, both mentally and physically, after surgery. It had honestly been brutal. She'd been in more pain than expected, been more emotional than she expected, and felt sorry for herself a lot more than she ever had.

But now Marley was almost feeling human again. She was still quite sore and she could barely raise her arms, but every day was easier than the one before it. There was most definitely a light at the end of the tunnel. She'd even looked at her new breasts today and didn't hate what she saw.

She was going to be okay.

Even in her job—she'd had some hard moments styling Nikhil while she was hurting, but she managed to get him off to LA with enough clothes to look fresh, stylish, and approachable for his events. She'd looked at some of the LA press he'd done, and he was being called a style icon thanks to Marley's work. She had no doubt that Jacqueline was going to be so impressed that Marley would get the permanent personal shopping role.

Everything was falling into place. And she couldn't wait for Nikhil to come home so she could tell him how well her doctor's appointment went. She made herself comfortable on her recliner and put on the glassblowing reality show.

Nikhil walked in her door at seven. Marley grinned when he came into the living room rolling his suitcase behind him. He wasn't wearing any of the Nik Sharma outfits she'd picked out for him but was in his own Nikhil clothes—oversized, worn jeans that looked incredibly soft, and a yellow cable-knit sweater that reminded her of a cozy hug. With his hair back with frizz escaping the elastic instead of blow-dried smooth, he seemed more like he did when they first met in the store a few weeks ago. Marley realized that she liked this Nikhil best. He let go of his bags smiling.

"Does that outfit mean you got your drains out?" he asked before even saying hello.

She nodded proudly. "No more foreign bodies in my body! Except, you know, the implants themselves. Fifty percent fewer foreign bodies in my body!"

His grin was huge. "So amazing. How do you feel?"

"I feel good…like I can move again. I've been given the go-ahead to start some exercises to get some range of motion back."

"So great."

"Reena left some biryani yesterday if you're hungry. I want to hear all about your trip."

He nodded, still smiling, but Marley detected something in the smile. Maybe LA wasn't as great as he'd hoped. He'd seemed like he was in a good mood when she talked to him the other day at his friend's house.

"Yeah, I'm never going to turn down Reena's food. I bought you some things from the airport. Let me show you; then we can eat."

He'd bought her *a lot* of things at the airport, which was a little unexpected but very sweet: a box of See's chocolates, a navy blue Los Angeles hoodie, a slightly terrifying LA Rams stuffie, and a bottle of her favorite Hermès fragrance. Had he noticed that the one on her dresser was almost empty?

"Nikhil, you didn't have to get me all this."

He shrugged. "It's just duty-free—I had time to kill in the airport."

"Still." She picked up the box of chocolates. "They're all

fruit fillings!" Marley didn't wait—she ripped the plastic off the box and opened it right away. Oh, yum. She loved fruit and chocolate.

"Okay, I'll take a quick shower, then get dinner warmed up."

"Take your time," Marley said, picking out a raspberry-cream milk chocolate. "I have my appetizer."

They ate together at the dining table, but Nikhil seemed… quiet. She'd expected him to be his normal chatty self. But he was clearly preoccupied with something. Marley had to keep the conversation going.

"I heard from Shayne," she said. "Apparently, Philip is already talking about bringing him along to Milan Fashion Week later this year."

"Do you know when he'll be coming home? You'll want me out of your hair then. Or…" He looked down at McQueen, who was lounging near Marley's feet. "Or…you seem to be doing well. Maybe you want your privacy now?"

Marley put down her spoon and looked at him. Technically, yes, she was doing well. She hadn't really needed him in the middle of the night for a while now. He'd been gone for the last three days, and she hadn't needed him at all, actually.

But she'd *wanted* him. She hadn't expected she would miss him quite so much while he was in LA. But it wasn't Nikhil her caregiver she'd missed—it was Nikhil her *friend* she was missing.

Or…more than a friend? She knew they'd been inching past their boundary for a while. Hand rubs, wiping tears, and massages. And she knew this little crush she'd developed was completely inappropriate. She'd been so emotional for these last weeks...and he was here. Here for her in a way that no one else was. The thought of him moving out of her house now was terrifying. And it was equally terrifying to be needing someone this much.

"I know shooting starts in four weeks," she said slowly, "and you'll be working long hours then, but before that, you can stay...only if you want to. I mean, I'm past the worst part of recovery, and I don't think I need someone every night anymore. But if you don't feel like moving? I'm closer to your rehearsals than your parents...and I assume you'll need clothes for the rest of your press. Totally your call. But Gram's room is there, and I don't know when Shayne is coming back..." She couldn't read his expression.

His face finally fell. He glanced away, toward the living room. There was definitely something he wasn't telling Marley. "Nikhil, what's wrong?"

He sighed as he looked back at her. "I was going to wait until you heard it from your store, but yeah—something happened in LA yesterday."

Marley squeezed her fist. What could have happened that had anything to do with her? Maybe...the studio hated the clothes she picked?

Nikhil ran his hand through his hair. "It's...the junket. I didn't tell you the other night, but it didn't go so well. Worse than the Toronto one, actually. There was this sci-fi outlet that was terrible to me and Serena. And...I kind of lost it on the interviewer. It screwed up my whole day...I couldn't get my mojo back." He exhaled. "I wish you had been with me like at the Toronto one."

Ugh. Poor Nikhil. He didn't have to say—she had a good

idea what kinds of things this sci-fi platform said to him. "Why do they keep putting you in these situations? Your publicist should have stopped them. This isn't your fault—it's theirs."

He nodded. "Yes. That's exactly what Esther, my agent, said. She ripped the studio execs a new one in the meeting yesterday. She said none of this pre-production promo was in my contract, and all the pressure they're putting on me was affecting my mental health. She shut it all down."

"Good agent."

He nodded. "Esther's the best. And she's right. The fanboys accepting me or not isn't on me at all. The *studio* hired me. They should deal with the fallout—not me. But the studio is making it seem like my messy hair, my unstylish clothes, or me not being pleasant when I get microaggression after microaggression is going to make this movie flop."

It was blatantly unfair. Marley could name countless hot, young actors who could get away with being eccentric, or surly, or whatever. And no one ever said the movie was a failure because of them, did they?

And it *was* affecting his mental health. Marley knew him well enough that when he closed off like that…when he seemed grumpy, it was because his anxiety was spiking. His confidence was going to complete hell. That wasn't really him.

She didn't know how to tell him that he was enough just the way he was. Without the team telling him what to be, and what to wear, or how to dress. Anyone who didn't see that the real Nikhil Shamdasani was a million times better than Nik Sharma was so incredibly wrong.

"I'm glad your agent has your back."

Nikhil took a deep breath. "She fired them. All of them. Starting with Lydia. No more pre-production promotion. No more press tour or handlers, media trainers, or anything until the normal publicity cycle at release. She said it was either that or she would make sure the media knew exactly how much pressure the studio was putting on the only POC main cast member."

Marley exhaled. "Wow."

He nodded. He didn't look relieved, though. "You were on that list. You're not my stylist anymore. The studio won't be working with Reid's."

Marley blinked. Shit. That was...not good. This job was supposed to be her ticket straight to personal shopping.

Nikhil sighed, then stood up. "Let me clean up dinner, then let's sit in the living room so you can be comfortable."

Marley agreed. But after he put away their empty dishes, Marley didn't go back to her recliner and instead sat on the sofa to be closer to him. She was so damn tired of that recliner.

He turned to look at her once they were both sitting. "Hiring you to style me was the best thing they did for me. You're the only one on that team who knows me...who *listens* to me. Esther is right—the whole team trying to make me into this perfect movie star was messing me up. You saw...I was a basket case when we met. I can't let the studio make these demands on me. But I can keep you as my personal stylist...just not through the studio."

Marley shook her head. While a movie star was a great client for Reid's to get in personal shopping, a *movie studio* was a much, much bigger prize. Jacqueline had been hoping to get connected with the costuming department. She was hoping they'd send more stars Reid's way. Marley agreed getting rid of the handlers was good for Nikhil, but it meant Marley was back to square one with her goal of getting that personal shopper role. "Jacqueline's going to be so mad."

"Marley, I am so, so sorry. I'll tell them I still want to work with you. Or make them give you a reference or tell them to bring you another client instead."

She shrugged. Or she at least tried to shrug. She may have been having a better day pain- and mobilitywise, but she wasn't quite there yet. "It's fine. I don't even know if one client was going to get me that job, anyway. And I still have a month before I go back to work. When I get back, I'll find another way to wow Jacqueline. Your mental health is more important. This is very good for you, Nikhil. You didn't *want* all those people turning you into someone you're not. You *hated* it."

He didn't say anything for several long moments. Just looked at her. Finally, he whispered, "Yeah, but I *wanted* you."

Marley smiled. It was funny—she'd known him for years. Hell, she'd had sex with the man twice (well, actually more than twice, but on two nights), but she didn't really feel like she *knew* Nikhil until they'd lived together for the last two weeks. He was incredibly caring and considerate. He was loyal to his family and determined to stand by them while they were in crisis, even though he didn't know if he was helping. He was a great cook but couldn't make a decent cup of tea if his life depended on it. He'd tried to make her ginger tea several times, and he always forgot to put the heat down after adding the milk, which caused it to boil over and make a mess. But he always cleaned the mess without complaining. He was distractable but also capable of hyperfocus. And he was scared. His whole life was changing, and he was terrified that at the end of the transformation, he wouldn't recognize himself.

Marley remembered looking in the mirror at the plastic surgeon's office today. She'd been afraid that she wouldn't recognize herself. That the trauma her body had been through would make it feel like a different person was looking back at her. And yes, she *was* different. Her breasts weren't really hers anymore. She no longer had nipples. But she was still *her*. Just a new her. Marley had no idea if this acceptance...this *peace* she'd made with her body would have happened without Nikhil here supporting her for the last two weeks. But she knew that she had to support him through his transformation, too. If not in a professional capacity, then definitely in a personal one.

She took his hand in hers. "You *have* me. I'm not going anywhere, Nikhil. Partially because I can't walk very fast right now, but mostly because I *want* to help you. I meant it—stay here until the shooting starts. I'll pick your clothes, give you moral support, whatever you need. Stay even after shooting starts if you need to. No strings attached."

He didn't say anything for a while. She had no idea what he was thinking. Was she making this weird? Maybe she shouldn't have held his hand. He finally spoke. "But...I feel like I've screwed everything up for you. If you help me now, it will be for no reason."

"Did you forget *you're* the one helping *me* here? I wouldn't have gotten through the last two weeks without you."

If he wasn't a client, the strict professional boundary wasn't needed anymore. But maybe she should keep the boundary up. No matter how attracted to him she was, it was probably a bad idea to act on it. Physically, because she could barely move right now, but also—a relationship with a *literal movie star* would be hell for a private person like Marley. And

Nikhil was going through a lot, too. They were both leaning on the other while dealing with the hardest thing they'd ever gone through.

Maybe these feelings weren't real. Florence Nightingale effect—that was it.

They stared at each other for some time like that, with his hand in hers. Neither of them would admit what they were thinking...what they were feeling. But the elephant sitting in the middle of the room was a little too conspicuous.

Marley bit her lip. "I suppose there could be a *benefit* to us not having a professional relationship anymore."

Nikhil exhaled. "Okay. Yeah, that's what I was thinking."

"I...um...really?"

He chuckled, looking down at their connected hands. "Uh, yeah. I have definitely thought about the fact that if I wasn't your client, and if you weren't in a boatload of pain, then us being in the same house alone for two weeks could have gone very differently."

"I...I am in a lot of pain, but I'm getting better." She smiled. "And...I may have a crush on the movie star living in my house."

Nikhil smiled widely, and it was so...breathtaking. He made her feel so warm and tingly that she wondered if maybe *crush* wasn't a strong enough word. It was how she felt when they were kids, and she saw how hard he worked to keep her mind off her aunt's illness in chemistry. When she realized that there was no one in the school as sweet as Nikhil Shamdasani. She wasn't mad about him ghosting her back then anymore. They were literally kids, and he needed to get out of his parents' house to become the person he was now. And she'd ghosted him, too. And now they may have another chance.

"Well, I've had a crush on you since grade-eleven cooking class," he said.

Marley smiled. "You didn't see me for almost a decade."

He chuckled, looking down. "That doesn't mean I didn't have a crush. Hell, the first thing I did when I found you in that magazine was figure out how to see you again."

Marley raised a brow. "You mean asking me to be your stylist was just because you had the hots for me?"

He faced her, shaking his head. "No. It was because I needed someone on my team who actually...*liked* me. Knew me. Wouldn't treat me like trouble, or a goofball, or a basket case. And you always had the best fashion sense. Having the hots for you maybe had some influence, though." He turned his hand so he could lightly run his fingers over her palm.

Marley blinked. If it was true, and he'd never lost the feelings he'd caught when they were teenagers, then his feelings now weren't just because of his mental state or because they were together at such a heavy time for them both. She looked at their hands. His were broad and somehow muscular. What exactly was Reggie making him do in boot camp every day that his *hands* were getting buff? And hers was long and pale. Because she'd barely left the house in weeks. Because her body was healing.

"Nikhil, this...this is incredibly bad timing for you and me to start something."

His free hand started moving, trailing up her arm. "If you mean because I can't maul you...that's fine with me. I'll maul you later." His smile was huge.

She shook her head. "No, it's because...later, when I'm healthy and can actually move again, you'll be filming your incredibly intense movie. Then you'll go back to LA and eventually be whisked away for a worldwide publicity tour. You'll be a movie star. You can do so much better than just a shopgirl."

He frowned. "You are Mahreen Kamal—the most gorgeous, the classiest, the hottest girl in our high school. There is no better out there. Believe me. I've looked."

"I'm…complicated." In so many ways. She was a private person, and she couldn't live his public life. Plus…there was the other thing. The big, bad thing that she hadn't ever talked to him about.

Even after having this surgery and reducing her breast cancer risk, her body *would* fail her one day. This defective gene also gave her a high risk for ovarian cancer, so she was planning on having her ovaries removed within a decade, and that would cause other issues for her body. Surgical menopause could affect her heart, her bones, even her appearance. She had no idea if she wanted to, or if she even *should*, have kids before that. And of course, she could develop cancer before that surgery. And she had other increased cancer risks that couldn't be reduced. It was her fate, and she had to live with it. But it was too much to expect someone else to deal with it, too.

Marley was complicated. She wasn't exactly a catch.

"My body…"

"Is beautiful."

She shook her head. "But it's not *working*. I could still get sick. I—"

"And I could fall off that building when I film the rooftop fight scene. Life *is* risk. All we can do is manage it the best we can. You had the surgery to manage your risk."

"But managing risks has its own costs. And there are risks I can't do anything about."

"Marley, I'd never run away because of your health."

Of course he wouldn't. He wasn't a monster…He was the sweetest man in the world. But how well did she know him, really? Maryam Aunty presumably *thought* she knew her husband, the husband who ran for the hills the first night that his wife couldn't make him chai while she was sick from chemo.

She didn't know how to tell Nikhil all this. How to make him see that she wasn't the person he saw in front of him. The idealized Mahreen he'd held on a pedestal for the last decade didn't exist. The real Marley came with way, way too much baggage.

"Marley," he said. "Wouldn't dealing with all of life's uncertainty and bad shit be easier with someone?"

It certainly had been easier having Nikhil with her for the last two weeks. His fingers were lightly playing on her arm, and it was making her feel warm and giving her chills at the same time.

"Tell me to stop and I will," he whispered.

She couldn't. She knew it was wrong and totally not fair to him…but she couldn't stop him. This felt way too good. Nikhil suddenly shifted closer and leaned into her neck. "I'm not going to do anything but kiss your neck and your cheek. Tell me when to stop."

Marley closed her eyes and let her head fall back. Soon, soft lips were on her neck. Grazing. Leaving soft kisses. The same lips had sucked, bit, and kissed with ferocious passion a few weeks ago but now were gentler and infinitely more emotional, yet just as arousing.

She sighed.

He kept kissing while he talked. "I'm not expecting anything here. Believe me. I know how complicated this is. And maybe you're right—the timing is terrible. But I just want to be close to you. No promises. Just together now. Do you want that?"

She looked at him. His eyes were so sweet and kind. Marley leaned forward, taking matters into her own hands, and kissed his lips. Gently. No promises, nothing more. They could figure out the other stuff later. Now just closeness.

She pulled back and nodded. "I want to be close to you, too."

CHAPTER EIGHTEEN

Nikhil

Nikhil slept in Marley's bed that night. Not wrapped around her, but near her. Being close meant he didn't have to worry about her having a painful sleep or that she'd wake up looking for her painkillers before he had the chance to leave them out for her. Most of all, being near meant he could be sure she was still feeling all the things she said she was feeling last night.

She did seem to sleep soundly. When the sun came through her gauzy curtains, rousing him from sleep, Marley was in the same position she'd been in when he closed his eyes. He watched her for a while, feeling like he'd finally earned the right to do this. That night at the hotel, they'd also slept in the same bed. But it hadn't felt anywhere near as intimate as this.

Last night had been amazing. Never in his wildest dreams would he have expected that Marley would be the first to confess to having caught feelings for him. He still couldn't believe it. She *wanted* him. Not just for sex, not just as a friend. Mahreen Kamal had always been the ideal for him but completely unattainable. Getting through that thick wall that Marley kept up around her feelings? He never imagined it was possible.

But this Marley wasn't the same Mahreen he'd loved in school. She was wiser, a hell of a lot stronger, and she was... sweeter. The way she'd bashfully turn away when he'd flirt with her. The way she cried about everything. The way she cared so much about his mental health and fully supported Esther firing all his handlers, even if it meant she'd lose the promotion that she'd wanted for so long. He loved how she picked tea based on her mood, how she talked to her cat like he was a person, and how she knew exactly what clothes would make anyone look, and feel, the absolute best they could.

But was a relationship with Marley, or anyone, even possible right now?

He wished they could stay in the bubble they'd created here in this little 1970s house. Without Marley being in pain, of course. But also...now that Esther had put her foot down and reduced his pre-production promo, he was finally looking forward to shooting the movie. He'd been working so hard learning lines, getting to know the character—plus, of course, he'd put his body through the wringer to get ready physically.

This was his first major movie. The script was amazing. And *acting*...not the fame or the promo or anything else but acting...this was his reason for being here. Things had been rough for him lately, but that didn't mean he didn't *want* the life that he'd built. Even if it came with losing his privacy, and dealing with unrealistic expectations, and people telling him what to do and who to be...it was worth it because he was getting to make *movies*.

He was a romantic, like Tyler said. He wanted it all. A partner to come home to, to eat meals with, to watch TV after work with. And at the end of a long day, he wanted to wrap himself around the person in his bed. And it wasn't fair to expect Marley to be that person. Not when he'd chosen the most public life imaginable. She was Marley. The most perfect but also the most private person he knew.

She started to stir a bit. Her long lashes fluttered against her cheeks, and her lips pursed sweetly before relaxing. She was so beautiful. No one came this close to perfection. No one ever had.

She opened her eyes. After a moment of disorientation, she turned and saw him looking at her. "Good. You're still here."

He leaned forward and kissed her briefly on the lips. He was never going to take these kisses for granted. Because he knew they wouldn't last. "Nowhere else I want to be. Can I get you painkillers? I should have gotten up to make your tea."

"Were you just…staring at me?"

Busted. He nodded.

She chuckled. "It's fine. The pain's not that bad. I feel like a whole different person since getting the drains out. You going to the gym today?"

He shook his head. "Nope. I'm supposed to rest after LA."

She smiled. "Nice."

"I'll get your toast and tea started. You need help getting up?"

She smiled softly. There wasn't a hint of regret or apprehension in her expression. Remarkable. "I don't think I deserve you, Nikhil."

He leaned down and kissed her forehead. Because right now, at least, he could. "Come down when you're ready."

He went downstairs and made some tea and toast. When she came down and sat at the dining table, he smiled at her. "Peanut butter or marmalade?"

"Marmalade."

"Okay." He brought the jar of orange-ginger marmalade that Marley had gotten from her cousin's bakery to the table and sat. It was clear they needed to talk. Last night they were tired and emotional, and even if neither of them seemed to regret anything, they should make sure they were both on the same page. Being seen in public was probably out of the question—right now, at least, while there was this media frenzy about him. There was no way he'd subject her to that. And sex was also out of the question. Of course, there was more to a relationship than sex and meals together. There was companionship. Caring about each other.

Buttering each other's toast. Literally, not figuratively.

"We should probably talk," she said.

He chuckled while spreading marmalade on her toast. "Yeah. I was just thinking the same thing. Dating is impossible, right?" He was also wondering about sex, but he didn't need her knowing that he was thinking with his little brain right now.

"Yeah…" Her voice trailed off.

He slid her plate of toast to her. "But…that's what you'd want? To date?"

She shrugged. Which was amazing because a week ago she couldn't shrug without wincing in pain. "I mean," she said, "I didn't want this to happen. I wanted to, you know, help you. Be your friend. I knew we had this…chemistry, but I thought I could get over it. Probably would have worked better if you hadn't moved in with me. Or if you…" Marley took a bite of toast and finished chewing, staring at him the whole time. Finally, she finished her sentence. "Or if you weren't the kindest, most thoughtful person ever."

He smiled. Yup…he was the luckiest man in the world.

She sighed. "I've known you a long time, Nikhil, so I'll be honest with you—I am not...relationship material. I'm a bit of a wreck."

"You're not saying the I-can't-be-in-a-relationship-because-I-might-get-sick thing again, are you?"

She sighed. "It's kind of an important thing. But...also I'm *terrified* of getting into a relationship right now. I'm super emotional. I'm already too dependent on you. But I don't think I can ignore this thing between us, either. I'm kind of...well... I mean, it's rare for me to like someone like this."

He raised a brow.

She clarified. "I mean, I'm not really a casual kind of person. Even with friends. I don't warm up to people easily. My feelings have to be all or nothing."

"Um, Marley. We've had casual sex twice."

She looked down. "You're the only person I've ever done that with."

Nikhil exhaled. Forget *world*—he was the luckiest person in the *universe*.

"I'm not usually attracted to someone unless I'm really into them," she continued. "Emotionally, I mean. And I rarely get that emotionally attached to people." She looked down. "I'm standoffish. My ex Celeste said I was an android or something when she broke up with me. And I'd thought we were solid."

Nikhil shook his head. "Your ex is wrong. You have a ton of feelings. You cried during an Amazon commercial."

"Yeah...well...this Marley"—she pointed at herself—"this isn't the normal Marley."

"I've known you a long time. You're still you. And I don't know if you noticed, but I'm also going through shit now."

"And that's why this might not be real! Neither of us are in a *normal* place in our lives. We're both messed up, and we've both become each other's crutches. This isn't real life, Nikhil."

He wanted to argue. To tell her that this was as real as it was going to get for him. That he'd been in love with her for a decade, and his feelings would be there no matter when they came back into each other's lives.

But he didn't say that, because a part of him thought she could be right. "So, the timing is bad, both because I'm about to start filming a blockbuster and you're recovering from major surgery…and you're afraid that our feelings are just because we're leaning on each other so much right now. But also…the feelings are rare and too strong to ignore, right?"

She nodded. "That's about it."

He exhaled. He had no idea what the solution to this puzzle was, but he was sure there was one. There had to be. "Okay, I have an idea." He reached over the table to hold her hand. Her warm, ridiculously soft fingers fit so perfectly in his own. "There *is* something here between us. And yeah, it could be because of all the crap we're both going through, but so what if it is? That doesn't make the feelings fake. Why don't we pretend circumstances are more…normal while we test this out?"

"Pretend? Like, play house?"

"Yeah—just keep doing what we're doing now. What we did last night. No commitment beyond that. No promises. Call it a trial run. A screen test. If this were TV, we'd be doing the pilot."

"And I assume no taking it public."

He swallowed. As much as he wanted to scream from the rafters that he finally had Mahreen Kamal, he knew he couldn't. "Yeah."

"And after filming?"

"You'll be back at work. And I'll be…freer, timewise. We can reassess what we want." And they could also have sex again. And he could cook for her, and take her to restaurants, and hug her.

They were still holding hands. Marley was thinking hard about this. He wished she would agree to give them a try enthusiastically and without reservation, but he also liked that she wasn't the impulsive type.

She finally smiled one of her small Marley smiles. "Okay. A screen test. Should we shake on it?"

Nikhil pushed his chair out and stood. "How about a kiss instead?" He walked over to her, leaned down, and kissed her. A little longer than their kiss last night. He wanted to put his hand around the back of her neck and pull her close, but he resisted that urge. He did dip his tongue into her mouth so she knew how much he wanted her.

It was perfect. Nikhil was happy to wait for more if they could have this now. She was still smiling when he pulled away from the kiss. He didn't think he'd ever seen Marley smile so much.

"So what happens now?" she asked.

"We could watch TV," he suggested. "Ever seen the special-effects makeup reality show?"

She frowned. "That's it? You just want to watch TV?"

He nodded. "I want to watch TV with *you*."

When Nikhil got to the gym Friday morning, Caroline started working with him on the choreography for one of the early fights in the movie. It seemed easy enough. Reggie stepped in with anything that was tricky. But even if it was pretty simple, it was exhausting to have to do the sequence so many times in a row. Nikhil collapsed onto the bench at the side of the room when Caroline said they were done for the day. She sat near him, handing Nikhil a bottle of water.

"You did better than I expected."

Nikhil took a long sip, then wiped his mouth with his arm. He had no idea where Caroline had acquired these low expectations of him—probably from Serena. Caroline was Serena's longtime stunt double in addition to being the stunt coordinator for this movie.

"Did you think I was a clumsy buffoon incapable of learning complex sequences?" Nikhil had sounded bitter there. And honestly, he *was* bitter. He'd been working his ass off, and he still didn't feel like anyone had any confidence in him.

Caroline shook her head. "This is your first action movie, and you move like you've been doing this for years. You're a natural."

He blinked. Well. "You might be the only one in this whole operation who thinks I'll be able to do this film."

Caroline laughed, a throaty, almost sensual laugh. She was wearing black leggings and a huge hoodie, which was how she normally dressed at the gym. Caroline was about the same size and coloring as Serena, which made sense. But while Serena had a wholesome, girl-next-door vibe, Caroline looked more no-nonsense and world-weary. Like she'd seen a lot, and it would take only two beers to spill the best stories about the industry.

"Serena thinks you'll be great, too. She's looking forward to rehearsing with you."

Nikhil raised a brow. Serena had barely said two words to

him when they'd had that forced paparazzi bait meal together in LA.

Caroline must have seen the skepticism on his face, because her expression softened. "Maybe it's not my place to say anything, but Serena *is* sorry about how things are going down for you. She's worked her ass off to get this far, and you have to see how hard it is for her to see these negative comments for the franchise. Even if she knows it's racist and not right."

It seemed that Serena was closer to her stunt double than he'd realized. He wondered if Caroline knew that he'd rejected the studio's plan for him to have a fake relationship with Serena. Probably not. That was supposed to be top secret. But Caroline probably also signed the mother of all NDAs.

It was no wonder he had so much trouble trusting anyone in this industry. So many people were contractually obligated not to tell the truth.

He stood. "Well, I need to shower. Same sequence tomorrow?" The studio was having him come in on the weekend to make up for the time he was in LA. Even though they *sent* him to LA.

Caroline nodded. "Yeah. I think one more day and you'll have it down."

After his shower, Nikhil was alone in the small changing room in the gym when Kaelyn called to tell him that she'd set up an interview with *The Confab* for him on Wednesday.

"I thought I wasn't going to do any more pre-production press."

"No, we talked about this weeks ago. *The Confab* has offered an at-home interview. We love the idea…It could really humanize you. I know you're living with your parents…That's totally fine. It will add to your charm—you could even give a tour of your childhood bedroom."

There was no way in hell he'd let camera people into his house. "You were there in LA, Kaelyn. My agent told you I'm not doing any more press until release."

The line was silent for several long seconds.

"Look, I need to head home," Nikhil said. "Send any requests through my agent, please." He disconnected. Esther said he was being too Canadian polite—well, he was happy to put his manners behind him.

When the phone immediately rang again, he assumed it was Kaelyn again, annoyed at him for hanging up on her. But it wasn't.

"Hey, little brother. I hear you have a girlfriend now."

Fuck. "Arjun, how did you get my phone number?"

"We're *brothers*. Why don't you want to talk to me?"

"Because you're a criminal."

Arjun didn't acknowledge that comment. "I heard online that you're dating a movie star in Los Angeles, *and* I heard from Dad that you moved in with your girlfriend in Toronto. You've never been a player—which is it?"

Clearly his brother was keeping tabs on celebrity gossip from prison. "Why do you care? And don't say it's because we're brothers, because you certainly didn't care about my life until I got this role."

Arjun sighed. "I've got a lot of time on my hands in here. Been rethinking my life, you know? You and I should be closer. It stings that Hollywood gossip pages know more about my own brother than I do."

Was Arjun being genuine? He *did* have a lot of time to think. Maybe he was actually remorseful for how he'd treated

Nikhil for years. Or maybe this was just because he wanted something.

"If you want money, you can forget about it."

"Nikhil, don't be like that," Arjun said. "I'm trying to make amends here. I know you've got this gorgeous new life now, but don't be a dick to your brother just because you're famous."

"I don't trust you, Arjun. It's going to take a lot more than one phone call to change that."

Nikhil's brother didn't say anything.

"Look, I'm busy right now," Nikhil said. "Don't call me again." He disconnected the call, which he knew would piss his brother off. But he didn't care much. Maybe Nikhil should change his phone number again.

Nikhil wasn't going to let himself worry about Kaelyn or Arjun or anyone else. He was going home to Marley. Who he'd slept next to for the last two nights. Who he was fully able to kiss pretty much whenever he wanted to.

Things were amazing right now. The best they'd been for him in…well, ever. Arjun was right about one thing: Nikhil's life had never been so gorgeous.

CHAPTER NINETEEN

Marley

Marley spent the next few days in a ball of nerves, expecting to hear from the store about losing the studio as a client. She didn't know for sure if they would call—she *was* technically on sick leave. Maybe Jacqueline would save her dressing down for a couple of weeks from now after she was back at work.

But despite being more anxious and on edge than ever, Marley also felt like a new person. It was strange how much getting those drains out seemed to have flipped a switch in her body. Her pain was less. Her mobility was better. And she seemed more like herself. She'd started the exercises the nurse had shown her to get her range of motion back, and she could already feel some improvement. She hadn't even burst into tears in the last few days.

But she was pretty sure that most of her exponential improvement was not because of getting her drains out, but because of Nikhil. Pretending to be in a healthy, normal relationship with him was…amazing. He'd slept in her bed every night since he got back from LA. Marley could touch that glorious body of his whenever she wanted to. He gave her another shoulder and neck rub, and even cooked her favorite meal from scratch on the weekend—a Thai curry soup called khao soi that was total comfort food. She'd stopped using the recliner, since cozying up to him on the sofa was even more comfortable. He also kissed her a lot. On her neck, her cheeks, her forehead. Her lips…but always very chaste and brief. Clearly, he was letting her take the lead on what she was ready for physically.

Marley's mind and body weren't in the same place, though. In fact, her mind didn't want any of this *chaste* business. She wanted him…in every way. That night at the hotel replayed through her mind so many times. She wanted to turn off the world like she had done then and feel nothing but Nikhil inside her. Wanting someone like this was so strange for Marley. She liked sex fine, but she didn't ever remember craving someone this much. Needing to be close to them, wanting to be in physical contact with every part of their body.

But her body…she was *terrified* her body wasn't ready. Not only because she was still weak and sore, but also, she didn't look the same as she used to. Didn't feel the same. True, Marley had been able to look at herself at the doctor's on Wednesday without screaming or crying, but no one else had seen her new breasts (except for what felt like every doctor, nurse, and medical student in the city).

Her breasts weren't symmetrical. They were still kind of yellow with bruising. And she had no nipples—just a scar where her areola should be. The silicone implants were sitting high and tight in her chest. She knew her skin would loosen and the implants would drop as her body got used to them—a process the nurse hilariously called "drop and fluff"—but now they looked wrong and plastic and…not real. Not to mention her skin. She also had no sensation at all from about two inches below her collarbones to an inch below her breasts. Marley had no idea when she'd feel physically and emotionally ready for sex again.

On Monday, after Nikhil had left for the gym for training and rehearsals, she finally heard from someone at Reid's. But surprisingly, it was Erin and not Jacqueline who called her.

"Marley, my dear, how are you feeling?"

"I'm fine. Recovering well."

"Excellent. You and I need to have a little chat. Preferably in person. Can you come to the store?"

Marley cringed. She didn't want to step foot into Reid's like this. People would talk. Tova would take one look at her and know she'd had breast surgery. When Marley didn't answer right away, maybe Erin realized what Marley was thinking. "Or we could do coffee somewhere. I have a gap in clients at three."

"Coffee sounds great."

Erin named a cafe that was thankfully not very close to the store, then disconnected the call. She'd sounded curt and short with Marley, but that didn't necessarily mean this was bad news. Why was Erin the one to contact her, though? Erin wasn't Marley's direct supervisor—Jacqueline was.

Marley was super nervous, so she took extra time to shower and dress carefully in her most comfortable semiprofessional outfit for the meeting. She chose a pair of loose black trousers that were perfectly on trend yet still felt like a pair of sweatpants, along with a crisp white T-shirt and a bulky cardigan over it. When buttoned up, the sweater camouflaged her swollen and stiff chest.

She took an Uber to the cafe. Erin was already there, sitting at a small table near the back, when she got in.

"Hi, Erin. You look fabulous," Marley said. And she did—in the standard unofficial Reid's uniform of black and white. She had on shiny black leggings and a black turtleneck with a white oversized blazer over it.

"Likewise. Here, sit." Erin pointed to the seat across from her—an ornate high-backed padded armchair in a rich teal velvet. Marley wondered if Erin had picked this cafe—and this table—for Marley's comfort. Doubtful.

A server came by then, and Marley ordered an orange cardamom oolong tea and pear scone.

Erin got straight to the point. "There was a bit of drama in the store on Friday about you."

Marley's shoulders fell. So they *had* heard from the studio. *Drama* sounded ominous. She lifted her brows questioningly, hoping her nerves weren't showing.

"Jacqueline heard from Lydia at that movie studio. They've cancelled the contract with Reid's. Were you aware they were unhappy? I know you and Nik Sharma were friends…Did you have a falling-out?"

Marley exhaled. No, they'd had about the furthest thing from a falling-out. They'd had a *falling in*. "Um…no. Nik and I are fine. They fired his whole team. Not just me."

Erin nodded. "Hollywood is so fickle. Well, they did warn us that he was a spoiled diva. May I ask what happened?"

"He didn't have an issue with me or the store specifically. His agent insisted he didn't need people hired by the studio, and he could hire his own team." Of course, Marley wasn't going to tell anyone the truth—that the studio was treating him like crap. And of course, she wasn't going to say that she and Nikhil were together now. Sort of.

"That aligns with what they told Jacqueline, that they had no complaints at all about Reid's, but the studio was going in a different direction with the talent. Doesn't help you much. Jacqueline wasn't pleased."

Marley cringed. "Yes. I expected to hear from her."

"I convinced her to let me get your side of the story first." Erin took a sip of her latte, then smiled. "Look, Marley, I'll be real with you. I need help in the personal shopping suite. I can barely keep up with my regular clients, and we have no opportunity to grow the business this way. I've been wanting *you* to join me in personal shopping for a while."

What? "Really?"

"You're the best consultant in the store. But Jacqueline has been resistant to promote you."

Marley frowned. She wished she understood why Jacqueline didn't like her.

"She's concerned you don't have the *personality* for personal shopping," Erin continued. "You have a different selling style than I do—you're more detached with your clients. But you still sell, so your style clearly works. Jacqueline wants someone who fits in more with the clientele…who can be one of them. You aren't that."

No, because Marley didn't grow up in Forest Hill, her father didn't have a country club membership, and she went to a public school. And she was Brown.

"This studio contract was a huge break for you," Erin added. "I couldn't have planned the timing better myself. A client Jacqueline would literally kill for, and he *asked* for you. Only you. Jacqueline and I made a deal—if it went well, then in June, she would move you to personal shopping full-time."

Marley exhaled. That was only two months away.

"But now…" Erin said.

"I've lost that opportunity."

Erin shook her head. "No. Not necessarily. Here." She pulled out her phone and opened a picture. It was of Marley and Nikhil at the press junket in Toronto. Marley remembered this moment—he'd been between interviews and was feeling the pressure after Lydia told him off for something. Marley was straightening his collar in the picture, but she was also telling him that he was doing fine. That he was nailing these interviews, and everyone was going to love him. The intimacy between them was clear as day in the picture, and this was taken even before anything had happened between them.

"I'm gathering you two are pretty close."

Did Erin know that she and Nikhil were more than friends? That was a problem. It was wildly inappropriate to hop into bed with a client, or hell, a former client. "Yeah, we were good friends in high school, and we're friends again."

Erin raised one brow. "We'd hoped that the studio would bring more clients our way than the one actor. They made promises of connecting us with the costume department. And now we've lost that opportunity. But...I wonder. He's also close to Serena Vox, right? We can't discount the possible benefit this could still have."

She was having trouble following Erin. "What are you saying?"

"I'm saying I've convinced Jacqueline to hire you as a personal shopper. Now. I want you in the shopping suite when you come back from your leave, while your *close personal friend* is filming here in the city. Maybe you can even get an invite on the set. Maybe gossip columnists will mention you."

Marley blinked. She had the job...*now*?

Erin slid a paper in front of Marley. Marley took it and skimmed. It was an offer of employment as a full-time personal shopper at Reid's, reporting directly to Erin. Marley's compensation would increase, she would be able to hire her own full-time assistant, and she'd have her own office. Marley exhaled.

This was everything she wanted.

"You have two weeks before you start, of course," Erin said. "And it looks like you're recovering well. I suggest you use the rest of your leave to your advantage. Half of this job is networking. I suspect you'll be able to bring some of your more loyal current customers to personal shopping, but you'll need a lot more to fill your schedule. Let's see how many superstars you can bring thanks to your...*friendship*."

Marley didn't care how she filled the client list. She'd schmooze and suck up and do whatever was necessary. She didn't care that she was getting the job because of *who* she knew instead of her abilities. She didn't even care that she was getting this job because everyone thought Nikhil was close to Serena Vox even though Marley knew they barely spoke.

She was getting the job. She nodded vigorously. "Yes. Yes, I can do that. Thank you for standing up for me, Erin. I...honestly, I'm shocked. And honored."

"Don't make me regret it. Now, can you stick around a bit? I'd love to go over my strategic planning for the shopping suite for the next year."

Marley had all the time in the world if that was what Erin wanted. She was buzzing...*She was a personal shopper.* She was feeling great.

Despite the amazingness of that meeting with Erin, being out of the house was exhausting. But worth it. She couldn't wait to tell Nikhil about her new job, but she didn't want to bother him in the gym. She'd wait until he got home.

When she tried to unlock her front door, she was surprised to see it already unlocked. Maybe Nikhil was home early. But the moment Marley stepped into the house, a cheeky voice called out.

"*Finally.* You're supposed to be *recovering* from surgery, and instead you're out gallivanting all around town!"

"Shayne!" He was standing with his hands on his hips in an annoyed gesture, but Marley could see in his eyes that he was actually delighted to see her up and around. Without even taking off her shoes, she rushed to him, wanting to throw her arms around her best friend and hug the stuffing out of him. But even the thought of hugging someone made her wince with pain, so she grabbed his upper arms and squeezed. "When did you get here? Tell me everything…How was Paris? I thought you were coming at the end of the week! Oh my god, is something wrong? Did something happen?"

"Slow down, girl! You look amazing. Changed to an earlier flight because I got a new shoot up north this week. I've been here five minutes. C'mon…let's sit."

Marley kicked off her shoes and sat in the recliner, so happy to see Shayne. "I can't believe you were going to surprise me in this state. I could have…I don't know. Fallen on my ass and opened my incisions or something."

He raised one brow as he sat on the sofa. "I was hoping I could get you to actually talk to me…and I thought weakening your defenses with a surprise might do it."

"Talk about what?"

"Talk about why the movie star living in my grandmother's sewing room is major gossip fodder and I don't know any of it! What the hell is going on, girl? I signed his damn NDA. I saw more dirt that he's dating *Serena Vox*?" He paused and looked around the room. "Is he here? Is that the superhero's Tesla parked on the road?"

Marley frowned. "He's at rehearsals. And he drives a Civic."

Shayne recoiled at the car model.

Marley laughed. "I'll explain it all later. First, I have to tell you where I just was. I had a meeting with Erin...who officially offered me a full-time personal shopper position, starting when I get back from leave!"

Shayne stood from the sofa. "Marl!" He knelt at her feet and put his hands on her thighs. "Are you serious? Tell me everything. Wait, we should celebrate. You're not drinking, right? Tea? I brought you a fancy French white tea."

Marley nodded. While Shayne brewed the tea, she told him all about her meeting with Erin. He was as thrilled as she was. It felt so good to have her best friend back.

"I can't believe Erin went to bat for you with Jacqueline. Seems the barracuda is really a kitten."

"I wouldn't go that far. I only got the job because now I'm close to a movie star."

"I don't really understand how all this happened, though. Why did Nikhil fire you in the first place?"

Marley shook her head. "He didn't. His agent fired that Lydia woman—his handler. And I was technically working for her, not him. He's free to hire me himself now, not that he needs a stylist until the film starts publicity in a year, though."

"Well, if you're not working with him now, and I'm home, I guess we don't need him anymore. The guy can move out."

Marley blinked. She didn't want Nikhil to move out, of course. But she wasn't sure if she should be telling Shayne about their relationship upgrade. They really did need to keep it all on the down-low for a while…maybe even permanently. "Um…do you have any issue with him staying a few more weeks until the movie starts filming?"

Shayne frowned. "I don't, but, Marley, don't you? You didn't want him here at all. You said he was practically a stranger, and I know you don't like people all up in your business."

Marley didn't say anything. She blinked back at Shayne.

"Holy shit. He's not a stranger anymore. He's not banging Lily Lavender; he's banging you!"

"Um…remember my surgery? I'm not banging anyone."

He nodded. "Okay then, are you going to be banging him when you're better?"

Marley sighed. "What I am about to tell you is covered by the NDA. It stays here. In this room. Okay?"

Shayne crossed his heart in a leftover gesture from when he was Catholic. "Swear. What's the dirt?"

"He's not with Serena. They barely know each other. But he and I are…together."

Shayne exhaled. "Phew. I go to France for three weeks and my BFF is caught in the biggest Hollywood scandal all year. Tell me everything, bestie."

"I did! That's everything!"

"I don't believe you."

She rolled her eyes. "Tell me about Paris."

Shayne clapped his hands together. "It was fabulous, Marley, really…like, *exceedingly* amazing. I met everyone. Like, I literally showed a picture of McQueen to the creative director of Alexander McQueen. I even met important Toronto people.

Oh, and get this: I met this fashion influencer who's having this big party here in the city this week, and she wants me to be the head photographer. You can come, too. You can make tons of contacts with big names."

Marley frowned. "I…I really don't think I'm up for a party…" Yeah, she was doing a lot better, but not *that* much better.

"Nonsense. You look fabulous. By then you'll be even better."

Marley shrugged noncommittally. "So, what happened with that guy…the one you were about to have dinner with when I called you freaking out?"

"Ah…Gabriel…such a Paris cliché. All style and no substance. I saw him a few times, but I doubt he's feeling any lovelorn heartbreak about me leaving." Shayne shrugged. "And of course, I have no interest in long distance."

Marley would normally agree with Shayne. But she also just started a relationship with someone who lived on the other side of the continent. Maybe he'd be here for a while, but Nikhil *lived* in LA and would be going back one day. What the hell was she doing?

"Anyway, enough about my non–love life. What is going on between you and the Bronze Shadow? How did that even happen? This is the biggest spill of tea since the American Revolution."

Marley gave Shayne a warning glare. "NDA, Shayne. Seriously…this is not tea. This needs to stay private."

Shayne raised one brow. "I know, girl. This tea is all for me only. Exclusivity is hot. Without leaving the house and without sex, what have you been doing?"

Marley exhaled. A lot—that was what. She and Nikhil were…

caring about each other. Supporting each other. Watching TV, talking about their day, leaning on each other, and most of all, being the partner they both needed right now. But it was incredibly hard to explain this weird dynamic. "Just hanging out. We're not really in a relationship, just trying things on for size. You don't mind that he's staying here, do you? The studio is putting him up in an apartment when they start filming. It's only about three more weeks."

Shayne shrugged. "Nah, I don't mind. Go nuts…and enjoy your *not a relationship* while you can have it."

Marley smiled. She spent the rest of the afternoon drinking delicious tea and catching up with her best friend.

CHAPTER TWENTY

Nikhil

On Tuesday, Nikhil had an early rehearsal with Reggie and Caroline. When he walked in, they were at the far side of the room. Caroline had her back to Nikhil and was wearing a workout tank.

But then Caroline turned around, and Nikhil almost dropped his bottle of water. It wasn't Caroline. It was Serena Vox. They looked exactly alike from the back—which made sense because Caroline was Serena's stunt double.

Reggie grinned and waved him over. "Come, Nik! Look who's here!"

Nikhil took a deep breath before heading over to see them. Serena had a friendly smile. Fake, he assumed.

"Serena! When did you get in from LA?" She may not be fond of him, but he could pretend to be friends, too.

"Yesterday. Shall we get to it?" She glanced over to one of the changing room doors where Caroline had just come out wearing her normal hoodie. Then Serena reached out to hug Nikhil. He stiffened. Odd. Why was she being like this when there were no paparazzi around? Maybe he'd misjudged her and she didn't actually dislike him?

Nikhil didn't know what he was expecting when they started rehearsing, but Serena was nothing but professional. As the day went on, she grew friendlier and even made some small talk with Nikhil. He was so relieved that Serena had finally warmed up to him. Their rehearsals were physically brutal—it was way better to have a co-star who seemed to enjoy working with him.

The next two days were a blur of long and grueling rehearsals and the coziest imaginable nights with Marley. Even though Shayne was back from France, he'd gone up north for a shoot for a few days, so Nikhil and Marley were still alone every night. Tyler was on to something—having someone warm to come home to did make the work so much better. Things between Nikhil and Marley felt as close to perfection as he could imagine, even with her recovering from surgery and him putting his body through the most intense physical demands of his life. Yes, she was still Mahreen, the epitome of perfection in his mind since high school, but the actual person, Marley, wasn't the Mahreen he'd put on a pedestal in high school. Marley was sweet and funny and thoughtful, and she fit into her skin better than the girl he knew back then. She seemed...softer. Approachable instead of aspirational. She was willing to be vulnerable, and she was incredibly caring.

Nikhil realized that he hadn't been in love with her in high school. Not really. He hadn't known her well enough. He'd been in love with her perceived perfection. But now? The veil had lifted. He knew her better than he ever had. And he was completely, *stupidly* in love with her. She was all he could think of—all he could focus on. All he wanted all day was to crawl under the crisp white bedding in her serene room and feel her warmth next to him. To smell her floral citrus scent. He wanted to look into those eyes, see past her cool perfection straight through to her warm core.

He felt like a different person thanks to her. He was at peace. He didn't care about his haters or his fans. He didn't worry about his family, his career, or anything. His mind didn't swirl with not knowing whether the next step he took was solid ground or quicksand. She was his rock and his soft place to fall. She was everything.

He'd spent at least ten minutes looking at the soft skin behind her ear one morning while she was sleeping. He'd replayed that night on King Street over and over until he was aching hard, frustrated at the heavenly torture of sleeping next to her every night. He wanted her. In every conceivable way. Physically, emotionally—everything. And even though he knew that it was probably incredibly stupid to have let himself fall so deeply because he was in for a world of hurt when it all inevitably fell apart, he couldn't make himself pull back. The past week with her was more than worth whatever would happen after.

On Friday after he'd been training with Serena for a few days, Nikhil came home to find Marley sitting alone reading on the sofa with McQueen on her lap. She seemed to be engrossed in a book and didn't notice him coming in. Nikhil watched her for a few seconds, not wanting to disturb her. Her hair was a little damp—clearly, she'd washed it today. Her face was clean, and she was in sweatpants and one of Nikhil's T-shirts. It did something to him to see her wearing his 5K Disney fun-run shirt. It was the most…comfortable and domestic scene ever. The evening sun lighting her face. The fluffy cat on her lap. The house plants. The yellow sofa. And the most beautiful woman in the world, who wearing his shirt.

"You going to keep staring at me like a creeper or come in?" she said, not even looking up from her book.

He chuckled. "Busted."

She looked up at him, a small smile on her face. "What were you thinking, anyway?"

"That this is the nicest view to come home to. Is Shayne back yet?" He sat next to her.

She shook her head. "He came home, then went out again. Some influencer's party." She started scratching McQueen's neck, which made the cat roll onto his back in pure bliss. Nikhil detected something in Marley's voice there...a touch of resentment about Shayne. He'd gotten pretty good at reading her moods.

"I'm craving pizza," Nikhil said. "I heard about a place that has a cauliflower crust that Reggie won't yell at me for eating."

Marley smiled. "Get me a mushroom-and-spinach. On bread...not cauliflower."

He nodded, then ordered two pizzas from the app on his phone—the mushroom-and-spinach one for Marley, and a red-pepper-and-spicy-salami-on-cauliflower for him. Reggie would be pissed about the salami, but Nikhil needed a break from boiled chicken and protein powder.

After the pizza came and they'd been eating for a bit, Marley mentioned something about the party Shayne was at tonight. Nikhil detected a slight annoyance.

"What's this party about, anyway?"

"Oh, it's some influencer thing. He tried to get me to go with him, but there is no way I'm ready for that."

"You don't think he should have gone without you?"

Marley shook her head. "Nah, it's fine. It's...I'm being silly. Now that I've had my surgery, I hoped things would be more like they used to be with him. I need to give it time. He *just* got home from France."

"How did things used to be?"

She shrugged as she finished chewing her bite. "We were always super tight. I know I've had a lot of crap to deal with... but since my mom's cancer diagnosis, it's kind of felt more... distant. I mean, he supports me, and I know he loves me, but..."

"You're drifting apart a bit."

"Yeah, exactly." She exhaled. "I'm asking too much from him, I think. Shayne's...well, he's not, like, self-absorbed or anything, but he can be in his own head a lot. Especially when something big is going on in his life. That's why..." She hesitated. Like she wasn't sure if she should say something.

"That's why what?"

"It's okay. I'm being selfish."

He shook his head. "No, you're not. You do get that I *want* you to tell me what you're thinking, right? Tell me about all your shit. I'll listen...always."

She smiled, and it seemed a bit wistful. "You always have. In fact...you're the reason why I notice when people aren't fully here for me."

His brows knitted together. "Huh?"

She sighed. "Back in high school, when my aunt was sick, Shayne was pretty wrapped up in his own problems at home. And I mean, they were *real* problems. His parents were terrible. But he didn't even realize how sick Maryam Aunty was. Every conversation turned into being about him. But you always listened when I wanted to talk."

He nodded. He'd listened because she'd seemed like she needed it. "I wanted to help you."

"You asked me how she was doing almost every day. I could tell you about how much it hurt seeing her like that, about how much I missed the way she used to be." Her voice cracked. "About how scared I was that she would never get better. No one else let me say those things without giving me their... stuff...back."

"I didn't do anything special. I just listened." Most of the time he felt like he didn't know what to say.

"That was enough. That was more than enough. Relationships are supposed to be give-and-take...but you've never made it feel like a...I don't know. A transaction." She smiled sweetly at Nikhil. "Maybe I'm too complicated. I don't *want* to be unloading my crap on everyone all the time. There's only so much..."

He shook his head. "I'll take it, Marley. All your crap. Always. I'm all in. Even if this 'playing house' doesn't work out, I'll still be your friend." He hesitated. "I won't do what I did before. I was scared and I..." His voice trailed off.

She smiled. "I know. I forgive you. It was a long time ago."

He exhaled. He didn't deserve this. "And I've been unloading my crap on you, too. This has been give-and-take."

She looked at him for a while. Then smiled. "It doesn't feel like it, does it?"

He understood exactly what she meant. Helping each other just felt...right. Not like either of them was doing it because they had to.

After he'd cleaned up the dishes, they sat on the sofa to watch TV, but after an hour or so of flipping through shows and not settling on anything, Nikhil could tell that she still wasn't quite herself. He wished he could look inside her brain to know why. Was she sad about drifting apart from Shayne?

Or worse—was she feeling unlovable? Too complicated for anyone to want to be there for her? Nikhil wanted to tell her that she *was* lovable. That he'd fallen so hard for her that he couldn't think straight.

But this was supposed to be a fling. Just temporary. Casual. Admitting his feelings would scare her away.

But if he couldn't tell her how incredible she was, maybe he could show her. "Hey, since you don't seem to be in the mood to watch anything, do you want to turn in early? I can give you a back rub or something."

She tilted her head. "Just a back rub?"

"Whatever will make you feel better."

She chuckled, looking down. "What I want to do and what I *can* do might not be on the same page."

Oh wow. He knew he wanted her—a lot—in the week since they'd been together, but…she'd been feeling the same thing? He smiled. "Do you think there's any overlap there?"

She shrugged. "Maybe. I'm nervous."

"We'll do whatever you feel comfortable doing. But I think you deserve to feel good right now."

She nodded, then slowly lifted herself off the sofa. She held out her hand. "Let's go upstairs, Nikhil."

CHAPTER TWENTY-ONE

Marley

Marley had been wanting to take things a little further with Nikhil physically for a few days now, but she'd had no idea how to ask for it. The last time she'd seen her doctor, he had said that she was still healing well, and she should continue her exercises to increase her range of motion, and that slow and low-impact sexual activity was fine, too (which was a weird conversation, and Marley was sure she had turned as red as a tomato). He said not to do anything intense and, of course, to stay away from her incisions and implants for now. But Marley had been too scared to do anything.

But now…the fear didn't feel like something that should hold her back anymore. Even if she and Nikhil were only *pretending* they were normal people having a normal relationship, it felt real to Marley. She still wanted him. So much so that she couldn't think straight. And she knew there was no person in the world who would make sure she was comfortable more than Nikhil.

When they got to the room, the first thing he did was take off his shirt. Which…wow.

"Look at you…You're a god." She stood in front of him and ran her hands over his firm chest muscles.

"What will you think of me when I'm not on a daily training regime anymore?" he said.

She smiled, running her hands over his sides. "Good question. The first time I saw this chest"—she let her fingers skim his nipples, relishing in the shiver it sent through him—"it didn't look like this. But I liked it just as much as I do now. I don't think I'll care what your body looks like later, as long as it's yours." Marley didn't have any physical preferences, other than a tendency to be drawn to the biggest smile in the room.

His mouth slowly transformed into a sultry grin. That. His smile was her favorite thing about Nikhil. And it always would be.

He dipped his head briefly and kissed her. She knew he was holding back…being careful…but it didn't feel like he was. It felt like he *wanted* to go as slow as honey. His hands barely skimmed her sides as they kissed slowly, tongues sweeping through each other's mouths like they had all the time in the world. Which they did. She wanted it to go on forever.

Eventually she settled herself onto the bed, propped up on pillows and on top of her duvet.

"You comfortable?" he asked.

She smiled. "Extremely. Come here."

He slid next to her. "What do you want? What can I touch?"

"Everything. My chest is obviously off-limits, and go slow and easy, but you can touch whatever you want."

His eyes were so warm, and kind, and so, so sexy. "Let me worship you, then."

He helped her get out of her sweatpants and T-shirt, leaving her in nothing but simple cotton underwear and her tight surgical bra, then held up the bottle of healing vitamin oil that she'd been rubbing on her incisions.

"Can I use this on you?" he asked.

"Yes, absolutely." She smiled.

He knelt next to her, rubbing some oil on his hands, and began massaging her all over. He started with her fingers and made his way up her arms, stroking and rubbing and pulling on her skin. It was as heavenly as the last time he'd massaged her arms. Marley put some music on through her phone, a light lo-fi beat.

After working on both arms to her shoulders, he asked if he could massage her legs. She nodded. He started with her ankles.

"That feels amazing," she said. Her mind was all floaty and soft. All those feelings of inadequacy she had had over dinner were long gone. She felt comfortable, desirable, and valued. She was eternally grateful to Nikhil for giving her this now, when she needed it.

"You have amazing skin."

She chuckled. She was due for a leg wax—it had been weeks since she'd been to the salon. "I spend a small fortune on skin care, so I should." He kneaded her calf. "Mmm…Why does that feel so good?"

He moved on to her next leg.

He stopped when he got to her thighs. She was still wearing underwear, and he asked with his eyes how far he could go.

"Nothing is off-limits except my chest, Nikhil. Make me feel good."

He grinned, then leaned down to slowly kiss, lick, and tease the skin of her stomach and sides. She closed her eyes, letting all her senses take in everything—the soft music, the lavender-and-citrus scent of the vitamin oil, and most of all, the feel of Nikhil on her body. His tongue. His hands. His hair brushing against her skin. She'd been with this man twice before this, but neither time had felt anything like this experience. He *was* worshiping her.

"You're so beautiful," he murmured. "This feels like a dream. Tell me it's real, Marley."

"This is real, Nikhil." This was so real that it should scare the hell out of her, but she only wanted to sink into the sensations deeper.

He licked and nibbled her side below her rib cage, and she swore it felt as good as if he were on her actual breasts. Her nerves were firing into overdrive and she was squirming, seeking release. Who knew her sides were an erogenous zone?

"Nikhil…" she moaned. "More…"

He took his lips off her, and she shivered with the loss of his warmth. "Give me half a minute to wash the oil off my hands."

Marley took a mental check on her body while he was out of the room. She still felt no pain, tightness, or discomfort. Actually, this was the most comfortable she'd felt since her surgery.

When he was back, he returned to her side. "Tell me immediately if it's too much and you need to stop. Okay?"

She nodded, then lifted her body so he could pull down her peach cotton underwear.

Achingly slowly and gently, Nikhil made her feel better than she'd ever felt in her life. Using his hands and his mouth, he teased, licked, sucked, and stroked, bringing her to a slow orgasm unlike any other. It was gentle, but no less intense. Her toes curled, but she never left the dreamy, floaty feeling. She called out his name at the peak, fully aware that Nikhil was the one giving her this.

Her Nikhil. The man who'd somehow become her everything in the last few weeks. Who'd come back into her life at the worst time possible and been the best person to get her through it. Nikhil, her friend, her companion. Her love.

She'd fallen in love. And maybe it was a mistake, and maybe she should be putting the brakes on this because she knew she needed him too much, and they had no idea what either of their lives would be like in a few weeks, but right now, at this moment, she was in love.

And it felt so, so good.

He smiled at her like he'd conquered an army as her breathing slowed back to normal. "How was that?"

She smiled in return. "Amazing. Better than amazing. Thank you."

He leaned down and kissed her briefly on the lips. "No, Mahreen, thank *you*."

CHAPTER TWENTY-TWO

Nikhil

Nikhil rode the high of getting physical with Marley all weekend. They hadn't had sex again since Marley wanted to take it easy, but they somehow felt even closer. Even more affectionate with each other. Even more…intimate. Marley's hand would reach for his whenever they were close, and Nikhil found himself kissing her soft neck whenever he had the chance. Even Shayne noticed it, accusing them of eye-fucking at the dinner table. Nikhil was surer than ever that he'd never been in love quite like this. And he knew that somehow, he had to make this relationship last. This was too perfect, too precious, to walk away from. There had to be a way, somehow, to keep Marley.

But first she needed to focus on her recovery and her new job. And he had to focus on being ready for this movie. But later, maybe when he finally moved out of this house for filming, they were going to have a long talk.

On Monday, Nikhil was in the gym training with Reggie and Serena. Caroline wasn't there for some reason, but no one mentioned why. Serena and Nikhil were going over one of the trickier fight sequences, and they couldn't seem to manage a complete run-through of the three-minute segment without Serena stopping them, claiming Nikhil was doing something wrong.

"That was fine! I did it exactly how I did it last time," Nikhil said, wiping the sweat off his brow.

"You need to take three steps after you parry," Serena said. "That was five. You looked like you were tap dancing or something."

Nikhil shook his head. What difference did it make how many steps he took? He looked at Reggie. "Why are my steps precisely tracked but Serena is allowed to improvise after she punches the guy? She's done it different each time!"

Serena picked up a towel and wiped the back of her neck. "I have more leeway because I've done this many, many times. Plus, I've studied mixed martial arts for years. You're what—a comedian?"

Nikhil exhaled. So much for the camaraderie he thought they'd developed last week. It almost felt like Serena silently, or this time not so silently, was hoping the movie would bomb because of him. Which didn't make an ounce of sense. This was *her* movie. Nikhil was her co-star for this one, but the sequels could easily happen without him.

Reggie put his hand on Nikhil's shoulder. "You got this, man. I have total faith in you." He looked at Serena. "I'll work with him a bit longer. You'll see—this guy's going to rock it. He's a beast. We got this, right, Nik?"

Nikhil nodded at Reggie. At least someone thought he was capable of this role.

Halfway through their next run, his phone rang. There were only three people he had his phone programmed to audibly ring for—Marley, Nalini, and his mother. He glanced at his smartwatch—it was Marley. Something had to be wrong.

"I need to get that," he said, heading to the side of the room where his phone was.

"You can take the call later," Reggie said. "We need to stay on track if you want to master this."

He shook his head. "It'll just be a second."

Nikhil wasn't about to ignore a call from Marley, even if her timing was bad. He answered.

"Nikhil, can you talk? Something's wrong."

"Are you okay?" Something was wrong. He turned so the others wouldn't hear. "Are you in pain?"

"Yes." She inhaled sharply. "Lots of pain, and there is some new swelling on my left side. It's warm to the touch. I called the doctor, and he said it could be an infection. He said I should come right away. To his office, though—he's not at the hospital today. Shayne's not answering his phone...and my mom is busy. I can call Reena or an Uber...but I thought maybe if you were done—"

"I'm on my way," Nikhil said. "Give me fifteen minutes to get home."

"Are you sure? If you're busy—"

"Marley, I told you. I'm all in. Be there soon."

"Thank you. I'm scared, Nikhil."

"I know. I'll be there before you know it. Stay strong."

"Okay. See you soon."

Nikhil disconnected the call and walked toward the others. "It's an emergency. I need to get my friend to the doctor right away."

Serena frowned. "Can't they call an Uber or something? Or an ambulance? That's what they're for."

"We're almost done, anyway. I'm sorry—I'm going." He headed toward the changing room. He wouldn't have time for a shower...maybe just a reapplication of deodorant.

"You're going to have to figure out your priorities if you

want a future," Serena said. Nikhil ignored her. Actually, he considered calling Esther. This was exactly what she'd been talking about—their expectations of him were unfair. He'd been here in training and rehearsals for weeks. Serena waltzed in four weeks later and now claimed he's not committed?

But he didn't have time for that. He needed to get to Marley. Now. He left without saying another word to the others. He'd never heard Marley sound so scared. So alone. He was supposed to be with her.

Marley was standing on the porch waiting for him in a matching sweat suit when he got there. Her eyes looked puffy. Like she'd been crying.

"Do you think I screwed something up? Maybe I've been too active," she said the moment he climbed the porch stairs.

He gave her a little side hug, then a quick kiss on the lips. "Let's see what the doctor says."

She nodded, leaning into him for a moment.

On the drive downtown, she was mostly silent. He didn't know what to say. His instinct was to say everything was going to be okay, but he didn't know if that was true.

"According to Google," she said suddenly, "this could either be an infection, a hematoma, or a seroma. Or, I suppose, a broken implant."

"You suppose?"

"Google said that was unlikely."

He knew she shouldn't be relying on a Google diagnosis, but the last thing he was going to do now was mansplain her breast pain.

"It started in the middle of the night," she continued. "I couldn't sleep because of the pain."

"Why didn't you wake me?" he asked. He hated the thought of her worrying and hurting next to him while he was sleeping.

She shrugged. "I thought it would pass. When it got worse, I called my mom and she started telling me all about these botched boob jobs she saw on this reality show...Then she said she couldn't take me to the doctor because she had book club."

Nikhil exhaled. "I'm glad you called me."

She nodded. He knew what they were both thinking. Soon he wouldn't be able to drop everything and come help her. He couldn't be there for her the way a partner should be there. And after the movie was done, he would be back in LA. And maybe on another film set for months at a time.

He had a terrible job to be there for someone.

When they got to the building, Nikhil parked and put on a beanie and a face mask. He was getting recognized pretty often when he went out lately. Not that he expected anyone would bother him in a doctor's office, but he needed to be careful. Marley was also wearing a mask—hers so she wouldn't catch anything.

The waiting room for the plastic surgeon was mostly empty. Nikhil was glad that the doctor wasn't in the hospital today, because he doubted the hospital would be anywhere near as deserted as this. The office was fancy with leather couches and black light fixtures. This was a plastic surgeon in high demand—of course his office would look posh and...*expensive*.

After Marley checked in, they sat in the empty corner of the room on a plush leather sofa. Marley was still quiet.

Nikhil wanted to find a way to make her talk like she had in the car, but he didn't know how to do it. Maybe if they talked about him, instead of her.

"Serena was pissed I left. She said I need to figure out my priorities."

Marley looked up at him, eyebrows raised. "Wow. After you've been rehearsing for weeks and she showed up, what—a week ago?"

Nikhil nodded. "That's exactly what I thought."

"Why does she have it in for you?"

"I don't know. I'd thought she finally liked me, but I guess not. She's so hot and cold." He shrugged. "I'm giving my all for this role, and if that's not enough, there's nothing I can do to change that. The director will have my back."

Marley nodded. "Maybe you shouldn't have left early today."

He shook his head. "No. You needed me, so I'm here. It's already killing me that you were up worrying all night and didn't tell me...I was right there."

"You can't always be there for me, Nikhil."

"I'm damn well going to try."

"I can't...I *shouldn't* need you this much." She bit her lip, her forehead tense with worry.

He looked into her eyes. What did that mean? She didn't *want* to need him? Was she pulling away? She seemed to be doing both...leaning on him for support, while putting up emotional walls at the same time. It was so Marley—a contradiction in every way.

"Look at me, Marley," he said. Their eyes locked for several long moments. Nikhil pulled down his mask and tried his hardest to plead with her without speaking. *Don't push me away. I love you. I'll be here for you. No matter what.*

He saw the moment she seemed to understand him. Her

eyes softened and she pulled her mask down before leaning toward him. He kissed her, lingering a moment to take in her soft citrus scent.

His lips were still on hers when the nurse called out.

"Ms. Kamal, the doctor will see you now."

"You got this, Marley," he whispered. "I'll be right here."

She nodded, then followed the nurse to the examination room.

Nikhil put his mask back on and picked up his phone to read the Ironis script. He needed to be beyond ready for shooting. He couldn't control what Serena, the publicists, or the studio executives thought of him. All Nikhil could control was how prepared he was. And he was going to be absolutely flawless.

CHAPTER TWENTY-THREE

Marley

So it's not an infection?" Marley asked. She was in that position that she'd grown used to—standing in front of Dr. Abernathy while he was on his desk chair, his face inches from her naked breasts.

He shook his head. "No, I don't think so. Maybe a bit of inflammation. And a seroma here." He pointed to the alarming little swelling near her left incision. "I'll prescribe a gentle antibiotic to be safe. The seroma is harmless. It's a fluid buildup since your drains were removed. It may absorb into your body, or it may require draining." He rolled back a few inches to look at her whole chest. "I like what I am seeing on this side, though," he said, waving his hand over her right breast. "The incision is healing well. Are you planning to get nipple tattoos or nipple reconstruction?"

Marley shrugged. These were questions she knew she needed to think about eventually.

"I recommend waiting a year before surgical nipple reconstruction and six months for tattoos. Sarah Kagen is the best medical tattooist in the city. If you're interested, you should make the appointment with her now, as she books at least six months out." He paused and smiled. "You can get dressed now. Make a follow-up appointment to see me next week. Keep wearing your tightest compression bra until then." He handed her the script for the antibiotics.

Marley nodded, then exhaled heavily after he left the room. Thank God. She was fine. Dr. Abernathy didn't seem worried, so she felt a lot better.

Nikhil was reading his phone with his hat pulled down and his mask on when Marley walked out.

She didn't disturb him right away. Even with his mask on, she could see that he was tense. Was all this fair, what Marley was doing to him? One thing she'd learned about Nikhil in these last weeks was that he took on too much of other people's...stuff. He seemed aloof with a devil-may-care attitude sometimes, but he cared deeply about what was happening to those around him. This minor emergency only added to the enormous stress he was dealing with. Maybe Marley was being selfish for leaning on him so much. The last thing Nikhil needed was complications in his life. And Marley was one giant complication.

But she was in love with him. And she would put money on his feelings being just as deep, even though neither had admitted it yet. Marley wondered if she should walk away and let him focus on making his dreams come true. Let him be a movie star, let him date movie stars, and let him create all the beautiful, healthy movie-star babies he wanted.

Yet Nikhil Shamdasani had somehow become the most important person in Marley's life. And even though these enormous feelings might fizzle once they weren't living in the same house anymore, she didn't know how to walk away now.

Something out of the corner of Marley's eye caught her attention: a woman...maybe in her early twenties. She was masked, so Marley couldn't make out all her features, but she was white, with a golden tan and honey-brown hair with blond highlights. And she was staring at Nikhil while holding up a phone.

Shit. He was being recognized. Had that woman been there when they first walked in? Marley didn't remember. They needed to get the hell out of this office. Marley quickly went to the receptionist and made an appointment to see Dr. Abernathy at the hospital the following week, then waved at Nikhil. He was on his feet and followed her as she rushed out straight into an elevator. There was someone else getting on with them, so Marley didn't speak. She shook her head when Nikhil started to say something.

"How long was that woman staring at you?" Marley said when they were finally out of the building and walking toward the car. The street was busy with downtown workers leaving their offices.

"What woman?"

"Sitting on the other side of the waiting room. I don't remember if she was there when we arrived. I think she may have recognized you."

"Doubt it. What did the doctor say? Do you need help with your seat belt?"

Marley got into the car. "I got it." She carefully fastened her seat belt, cringing when the twinge of pain hit as her body turned. She leaned back into the seat, closing her eyes. "He said it's probably not an infection but gave me a prescription for antibiotics just in case. And there is a seroma—a fluid buildup at the incision. He said it might resolve on its own, or he'll have to drain it."

He started the car and drove toward the exit. "Ugh. I'm sorry, Marley."

She looked at him. "Don't be sorry. It's not serious. He didn't seem that concerned." She sighed as Nikhil paid the parking fee. "I probably overreacted. I...I'm sorry I made you leave work."

He shook his head as he wove through the downtown traffic. "Marley, it's no problem. It's your body—of course you're worried."

"I know...I don't want you to have to deal with me and my shit when you have enough of your own."

"I told you I want to deal with your shit. I love your shit. It smells like—"

"Nikhil, be serious!"

"I am being serious! Look, you're not the only one bringing baggage to this relationship—I may not be physically leaning on you in the same way, but there is no way I would have gotten through the last month without you. You *want* to support me, right?"

She did. She wanted him to be healthy and happy, and she would do anything she could to make his dreams come true. "Of course."

"So we keep doing that. Supporting each other. I'm not here out of obligation any more than you are."

Marley wasn't so sure. She was, of course, relieved that the horror stories Mom had told her this morning weren't happening to her, but at the same time, this little scare felt like a test to her. Or an omen.

Could this relationship *really* weather the enormous storms that could come for them?

When they got home, Nikhil helped her in the house and back into the recliner. "Do you want food?" he asked. "There's some pasta left from yesterday."

Marley nodded. She didn't have much of an appetite, but she figured she might as well eat something.

They ate quietly, neither of them saying much. Marley didn't know if he was distracted because of her health or his issues at the rehearsals. After the pasta, Marley sat back in her recliner and put on a nail-art video. Nikhil brewed her some ginger tea (he was getting better at it—he rarely had boilovers now), and they watched YouTube together.

When they went to bed that night, Marley still felt out of sorts. The pain had eased since she'd taken the good painkillers. But all she could think about was what would have happened if Nikhil hadn't been able to come help her today.

Marley was an independent person who'd never in her life wanted to commit to someone. But now she wanted to be with Nikhil. To watch bad reality shows with him, order pizza, and watch him cook. She wanted to sit on the sofa for hours with him and the cat and just…exist together. But she also wanted to go to restaurants, take him shopping, and travel with him. She hadn't felt like this for another person in a long time. Actually, ever.

But right now, she wondered if her love was enough to weather a complicated relationship like this one. When the next crisis hit, they'd both realize that nothing could be as simple as it should be with the two of them.

Marley found Nikhil's hand under the covers. He turned and wrapped his arms around her waist and kissed her long and slow. Eventually they lay side by side, holding hands, and Marley tried to knock the unease out of her mind. But all she could think about was that woman with the honey hair staring at Nikhil in the doctor's office.

❦

Marley woke to the sound of her bedroom door opening. It was Shayne, and he looked furious. Even though they'd lived together for a while, he never barged into Marley's room without knocking.

"Shayne…what's wrong?" she said, trying to get up. She cringed as she felt a sharp pain on her incision.

Shayne shook his head. "Why are you still sleeping? I thought you and Nikhil would be in crisis mode!"

Marley frowned and checked the time. It was ten thirty a.m. "Crisis mode? Why? I told you yesterday—the doctor said I was fine."

Shayne sat on Marley's bed. "Marl, I'm not talking about your doctor's appointment. I'm talking about the security breach on Nik Sharma that happened literally, like, twenty minutes ago."

"What breach?"

"I just sent you a post," he said, pointing to her phone.

Heart pounding, Marley picked up her phone from the nightstand and found the social media post in a text from Shayne. It was from one of those less-respected celebrity gossip sites. But…their gossip was usually true.

The post had several pictures, clearly taken yesterday at Dr. Abernathy's office: Marley and Nikhil talking in the waiting room, Marley and Nikhil staring into each other's eyes. Nikhil kissing Marley.

"Oh my god," she said. She felt sick. Someone took a picture of them inside her doctor's office? Clearly it was that woman staring at him. Marley hated people right now. The text under the post said,

> Hot dirt on the Ironis movie franchise's newest It
> Boy—check the link in our bio for all the juicy
> details.

Marley wanted to throw up. She needed to tell Nikhil about this.

"Open the article," Shayne said.

She reluctantly opened the link, which took her to a full article on the gossip page.

"The Bronze Shadow's Secret Love Nest" was the headline. And the article went into a lot of detail about Nik Sharma's torrid affair with his wardrobe stylist. There were more pictures, including some taken on the porch of Marley's house when he picked her up yesterday. And other pictures of Nikhil coming and going from the house.

"I saw that black Tesla parked on the street so many times," Shayne said. "I thought Mrs. Costello across the street was having an affair, but now I think it was a photographer."

"How did they get our address?" Marley's voice shook. "Does Nikhil know about this?"

"Keep reading," Shayne said.

> We received an anonymous tip that Nik Sharma has been cavorting with his stylist, Marley Kamal, for some time. A source from her employer confirmed that Marley is a stylist at Reid's Department Store, and she was contracted to style Nik Sharma for all his pre- and post-production appearances. Another tipster confirms that these pictures were taken in a plastic surgery office after the stylist had some complications from the breast enlargement surgery Nik paid for.
>
> The timing of this scoop is certainly unfortunate for Nik. Not two hours ago, his co-star in *Ironis 3*, Serena Vox, finally confirmed rumors that

the two have been in a relationship for months. Serena and Nik were expected to be a major Hollywood power couple.

"Fuck," Marley said.

"My sentiments exactly," Shayne said. "I can't believe a bloody paparazzi was outside my house. Vultures. They are a stain on my profession."

"Why does it say Serena confirmed their relationship?" Marley asked.

"Look at her Instagram," Shayne said.

Marley opened the app and searched for Serena's account. Her most recent post was from early this morning. The caption was simple, just two sentences: *Monumentally happy to have this guy in my life for the last few months. They say you shouldn't mix business and pleasure, but I've got a good feeling about this one.* The picture was clearly taken in Los Angeles. Nikhil was laughing at something Serena was saying. His superhero arms were on full display, and Serena was as gorgeous and radiant as ever in a simple gray tank with her wavy hair down. In another shot, Serena looked fresh, a little flushed, and her eyes were downcast in a shy, pleased expression while Nikhil was gazing at her...and yeah. If Marley didn't know the man so well, it would look like he was looking at her with affection. Like he was about to kiss her.

But he wasn't. That wasn't the look he gave Marley every day. His eyes were always so intense before he kissed Marley.

"Why is she saying this?" Marley said, her voice cracking.

"Is it possible this is true? Maybe he *is* dating Serena and you."

Marley shook her head. "He's not. I trust him." There wasn't a doubt in her mind. A sharp pain under her breast reminded Marley that this was a terrible time for a crisis.

"Well then, honey," Shayne said, giving her a sympathetic look, "someone's sabotaging y'all. You need to talk to him."

Marley nodded, then exhaled. "Painkillers first, please."

Shayne helped her get her pills. "I have to be downtown for a shoot in an hour. You okay, or you need me to cancel? If you'd like, I could do some naked gardening in case we're still being watched. Fucking paparazzi." He shook his head with disgust.

Marley tried to smile. "You go to work. I'm going to call Nikhil." She had to believe that Nikhil hadn't seen this—or he would have called her. She picked up her phone. He answered on the first ring.

"Nikhil, can you talk? Are you alone?"

"Yeah, I'm in the changing room. What's wrong?" he asked. He sounded out of breath.

Marley blinked away a tear. "Shayne sent me…Did you see the piece in *Pop Hollywood*?"

"What? No. What piece? We've been practicing a fight scene all morning."

Marley sent him the link to the article. How could she have taken him out in public now, when he was being watched like a hawk? This was her fault.

"Fuck," Nikhil said.

"I'm sorry," Marley said. "I should never have called you yesterday. I could have taken an Uber to the doctor—"

"Marley, *no*. This is what I was talking about. If my girl-friend needs me to take her to the doctor after surgery, then I want to be able to do that. I *need* to be able to do that. Other-wise, what's the point of any of this?"

Marley frowned. "Girlfriend?"

He sighed. "Whatever. I should probably call Esther." He paused. "Shit. She's been calling me all morning. I wonder if Serena and Caroline have seen this."

"There's more, Nikhil. Did you see Serena's Instagram post?"

"What? No...let me check." He paused, clearly looking up his co-star's Instagram. "What the hell? Honestly, there is nothing going on between me and Serena."

"I know. Why is she lying?"

"I have no idea. They wanted me to agree to a fake relationship with her a while ago, but I said no. I don't know what game she's playing."

"Can you put your own Instagram post up saying you're not together?"

"They'll ruin me if I go against Serena." He paused. "They *own* me, Marley. If I want to work in this industry, they fucking own me. I have to work three times as hard, put up with three times the bullshit, and still...they own me. Fuck. I need to talk to Esther. I'll get those pics of you taken down. They can't violate your privacy like that."

"Okay. Let me know how it goes."

"Yeah. I'll call you."

An hour later, Marley's painkillers had kicked in, so she showered and changed. The piece was still up on the gossip site, and she hadn't heard from Nikhil. She assumed he was in crisis mode with his team, and she didn't want to bother him.

Marley's phone rang. Unknown number. She cringed. Maybe someone she knew had seen the damn article.

"Hello?" Marley said when she accepted the call.

"Marley, this is Jacqueline Richards."

Shit. "Oh, hi, Jacqueline. What can I do for you?"

"We've gotten word about this social media situation. We'll need to see you in the store this afternoon to discuss it."

"Oh, yes, of course, but if you are talking about the post with Nik Sharma, he is going to get it taken down. And there is nothing—"

"One o'clock work for you, Marley? My office. We can send a car if you'd like."

Marley exhaled. "Yes, one works. I don't need a ride."

"Excellent. See you then." Jacqueline disconnected the call. Marley stared at her phone for several seconds. Clearly someone from the store—maybe Tova—spoke to the so-called reporter about Marley.

Marley felt her stomach drop. She had no doubt in her mind—she'd lost the personal shopping job. She hadn't done anything wrong—Nikhil wasn't her client when anything happened between them, both that first time at the King Street hotel, and again now.

And Nikhil and Serena weren't together. Nikhil hadn't bought Marley fake boobs, either. Marley had had a mastectomy, not a boob job.

But she'd still lost the personal shopping role. She knew it without a doubt.

CHAPTER TWENTY-FOUR

Nikhil

The first thing Nikhil wanted to do after reading that blasted gossip article was quit this damn movie and move to New Zealand where he was pretty sure everyone still thought he was dead. The second thing he wanted to do was go home and kneel in front of Marley and beg for her forgiveness for bringing this chaos into her life.

Instead, he called his agent.

"Esther, they're not allowed to take pictures in a doctor's office, are they?" he said the moment she accepted the call. He was still on a bench in the men's changing room at the gym. No one had come to get him, so he assumed everyone out there had checked their messages and was now doing their own damage control.

"Absolutely not. I've already put a call into the lawyer the agency has on retainer. I'll get this pulled by the end of the day, babycakes."

That wasn't really much help at this point. "Everyone has already seen it," he said.

"It's the best I can do. One question, Nik," Esther asked. "How much of this is true?"

"Esther, you know I'm not dating Serena. You were there when I said no to the fake dating contract."

"But are you dating the stylist?"

He didn't say anything. He didn't know if confirming it now could make things worse for Marley, and he didn't want to take that risk.

"We'll figure this out, babycakes," Esther said. "What worries me is this little gossip piece has made a fool out of the darling of the franchise."

"Serena."

"You got it. I have no idea why she posted those pictures this morning, but your gossip piece going up right after? It's a publicity nightmare. No doubt the gossip site was holding this information for the perfect moment. And the studio will be more focused on salvaging her reputation than yours."

"Am I going to lose my job, Esther?"

"Not if I have anything to say about it. The lawyer's on the other line. I'll be in touch. Stay near your phone and keep your nose clean."

"Will do. Thanks, Esther." He disconnected the call.

Nikhil sat on the bench for several long minutes before getting up. He didn't want to go out there and face Serena. She was probably furious that her lie on Instagram post had failed spectacularly. But he couldn't hide forever. He stood, wiped the sweat from his forehead, tossed his towel into the laundry hamper, and headed back to the rehearsal space.

Serena was on a bench on the side of the gym with her head in her hands when he got there. Caroline was beside her with her arm on her shoulders. Reggie was on his phone on the other side of the room. As soon as Serena saw him, she stood. "All right, let's finish this," she said, getting into fight position next to Nikhil. Reggie put his phone down and he and Caroline stood across from them, standing in for the enemies.

Nikhil frowned. No one was even going to mention the PR crisis? Fine. He could work. He picked up his practice sword and lifted it over his head.

But after they'd done a few run-throughs, it was clear Serena was taking out the whole mess on him. She was even more critical of his work than she'd been yesterday. Claiming he was missing his marks when he wasn't. Claiming he didn't know the choreography when he did. Caroline even stood up for him when Serena was taking it too far.

This was ridiculous. Why was Nikhil still here working his ass off when Serena would never accept him? He shook his head at her. "Are you trying to make me quit or something? I mean, you could just leave it to the studio to fire me for *daring* to associate with another woman instead of bullying me like this."

Serena blinked at him. "I have no idea what you're talking about."

He put his hands up in the air. "That's the problem... neither do I! I don't have a clue why you're out to get me! Is it because you've seen the gossip piece in *Pop Hollywood* today? Are you actually upset that I can't count my steps? Are you mad that the fans hate me? That I ruined our fake relationship that I'd never agreed to anyway? Or that vulture photographers followed me into my friend's *doctor's appointment*?"

He knew he shouldn't be saying this in front of Reggie and Caroline. Nikhil had no doubt they both knew that the relationship Serena posted about this morning on her Instagram didn't exist. After all, anyone spending any time with Nikhil and Serena would know they weren't together.

Reggie turned to Caroline. "We should disappear. I think these two need to clear the air before someone gets hurt."

"No," Serena said. "Don't go anywhere. There is no air to clear." She glared at Nikhil, pointing at his face. "I *fought* for you. They wanted to go in a different route with casting, thought we needed a bigger name…but after our chemistry read, I *only* wanted you. But clearly that was a mistake because you don't have the experience to be in the public eye. I never let personal drama get in the way of the job we're here to do, and you need to learn that, too."

He gritted his teeth. "Are you seriously implying I'm not working hard enough? I've been busting my butt every fucking day. While you and the studio say I don't dress well enough, that my tooth is too broken, that I can't fight for shit. I've been a complete professional. If you wanted *me* for the role, why won't you let me be me?"

"I never said that you weren't professional."

He shook his head with frustration. "No. You never say anything! But you certainly have a lot to say about me on your Instagram. I don't broadcast my personal life, or let it get in the way of my job!"

She raised an eyebrow. "Excuse me? Yesterday you ran out of practice because your girlfriend's boob job was hurting!"

Nikhil had enough of this. He threw the wooden practice sword to the floor. "Screw this role. It isn't worth it. And Marley didn't have a fucking *boob job*. She had a double mastectomy!" Shit. He shouldn't have said that. He exhaled. "Not that there's anything wrong with boob jobs. But…she's going through a lot, and I was trying to support her. And your little Instagram stunt this morning has added to her stress."

Serena didn't say anything. Just stared at him, blinking. She glanced at Caroline, then back at Nikhil. He had no idea what she was thinking. What any of them were thinking. He sighed. "I shouldn't be telling Marley's secrets. I'd appreciate if you'd all keep that to yourselves."

"Of course," Reggie said quickly. He sounded sincere, at least.

Caroline stepped forward. "I think we need to cool off a bit. I'm calling this rehearsal. Go home. See you tomorrow."

Serena was still staring at Nikhil. "Yeah," she finally said. She headed to the bench and picked up her warm-up hoodie.

"You too, Nik," Reggie said. "Take a rest day. Be back tomorrow."

Nikhil shrugged. "Fine." He grabbed his towel and headed toward the showers.

"Wait, Nik," Caroline said. He turned back to look at her.

She hesitated a moment. "Don't worry—I'll keep your friend's personal information to myself. So will Serena. Please trust us here."

Weirdly, he did trust Caroline. "Thanks," Nikhil said.

"And…" Caroline added, "I hope your friend is okay."

He nodded. "Yeah, she'll be fine, I hope. Thanks for your concern."

Caroline nodded but didn't say anything else, so Nikhil walked straight into the showers. He was so, so close to never coming back here again.

By the time he was at his car, he had a text from Esther. The publicity team was meeting now to discuss options. She said she'd call him when they were done.

He'd been driving for about ten minutes when his phone rang. Why wouldn't people just leave him alone? He answered it on the car's speakerphone. It was his sister, who, as a plugged-in nineteen-year-old, had probably already seen the gossip about her older brother on TikTok.

"I can't believe you cheated on a movie star," Nalini said.

Nikhil sighed. "I can't cheat on someone I'm not dating."

"Are you saying Lily Lavender *lied*?" There was mischief in his sister's voice.

"Nalini, stop. I could use some sensitivity here...Someone took our picture at Marley's doctor's office. It's a huge invasion of her...of *both* of our privacies. You want to be a doctor—you should know how wrong that was."

"Yeah, it's very wrong." She sounded sincere now. "Did photographers follow you from work?"

"Maybe. But the gym location is kept a secret. Somehow someone got Marley's address, though. Very few people know I'm living there."

"Have you had any other leaks of personal information?"

"No. Other than Arjun somehow getting my new unlisted number. Mom probably gave that to him, though."

There was silence on the other end. Finally, Nalini said, "Shit. I think I know what happened."

"What?" He was at Marley's house by then, so he pulled up in front of it. He didn't get out of the car, though.

"A couple of weeks ago, Arjun came home for a bit. They called it day parole," Nalini said.

"No one told me that!" Then he remembered his father had mentioned it a while ago, but Nikhil had said he didn't want to hear about Arjun.

"It was while you were in California. Dad told us not to tell you, because you didn't want to see Arjun. I didn't want to see him, either, but Mom insisted I stay. I couldn't find my phone while he was here. I found it in the den after Arjun left, and I swear I hadn't been in there all day."

"Shit. And my phone number was on your phone."

"Yeah, and Marley's address from when you gave it to me to pick up your iPad. I've been using Mom's old phone since my last one broke, and the lockscreen is disabled. Do you think Arjun would have told someone where Marley lives?"

Nikhil remembered that call from Arjun last week. It was a few days after Nikhil had come back from LA, so it would have been right after Arjun had the day parole. And Arjun was asking questions about Marley. He even knew Nikhil was living with her. "I have no doubt our brother would have given information to the gossip pages for money."

"I'm sorry, Nikhil. This is my fault."

Nikhil exhaled. Nalini's ADHD had always made her scatterbrained and disorganized. He couldn't believe that their brother would exploit that.

"Say something, bhaiya," she said softly. "Are you okay?"

Nikhil's heart tugged at Nalini using the term she used to call him when she was a kid. "Yeah, choti behen, it's okay. It's not your fault—it's Arjun's."

"Is Marley mad?" Nalini asked.

"Yeah. I'm about to go talk to her."

"Tell her I'm sorry. I really like her. She always manages to find something nice to say about those *Bachelor* girls. No one should be that nice."

Marley *was* that nice. "I have to go, Nalini. I'm waiting to hear what the studio says, and what the fallout from all this will be. Don't tell Mom and Dad about this."

"I got you. And I'm sorry again."

"Thanks, Nalini." He disconnected the call.

CHAPTER TWENTY-FIVE

Marley

Marley took an Uber to the store for her two o'clock meeting. She had no idea what was going to happen, but she was ready for anything. She even put on her work clothes for the first time since surgery—one of her looser blouses and an oversized blazer that hid her surgical bra well. Heels too.

On the drive there, she went over all the possible things that could happen in this meeting. She figured best-case scenario would be Erin doing some damage control. Maybe talk to her about being careful not to be seen with a client going forward in her role as a personal shopper. Worst-case scenario would be Marley getting demoted back to sales consultant, which would be...*ugh*. Marley didn't want to even think about that possibility.

When Marley was led into the small meeting room in the back of the store, her stomach dropped. It wasn't Jacqueline and Erin waiting for her.

It was Jacqueline and Olivia, the store's HR representative. This could be worse than the worst case. Marley cringed as she sat down.

"Marley, thank you for coming on such short notice," Jacqueline said. "I regret to inform you that your employment with Reid's is being terminated effective immediately. This letter outlines the compensation you are being offered if you sign this release." Marley froze as Jacqueline placed an envelope in front of her. She was being...*fired*? For being followed by photographers into a doctor's office? That was medical discrimination, wasn't it? "May I ask why I'm being let go?" Marley was impressed with herself that she kept her voice steady.

Jacqueline nodded. "Breach of contract. You violated the terms of this NDA." She placed the Reid's personal shopper NDA that Marley had signed on top of the envelope. "You publicly disclosed the personal information of a personal shopping client and allowed yourself to be photographed with him. In recognition for your years of service, however, we are offering a generous compensation package. Please sign on page three."

Somehow with blurry eyes, Marley opened the envelope and skimmed the termination letter. Basically, they were offering a few weeks' termination pay above the statutory minimum for the number of years she'd worked at the store, but in return she had to sign away the right to sue for wrongful dismissal, or for more money. Marley looked up at Jacqueline.

"I can't believe you're *firing* me. I didn't disclose anything about Nik. Do you think *I* went to the gossip pages telling them where to find him? We were followed!"

Jacqueline briefly looked at the HR rep, who appeared terrified, then back at Marley. "Mahreen, Reid's reputation is paramount to our success. Our customers can go anywhere...They can buy the same products we sell at countless retailers online. Not to mention most of them travel extensively. They come to Reid's because of the level of service we offer, and because this store is aspirational. They want to be seen and be served by our team. The reputation of our sales staff means *everything*."

Marley still didn't understand. And why was Jacqueline

calling her Mahreen now? "And because I was in a plastic surgery office, I'm not aspirational anymore?"

Jacqueline snorted. "Hardly. Most of our customers have probably been in that very office. The issue lies with you becoming involved with someone already in a relationship. We cannot have someone infamous in the tabloids serving customers. Not to mention, you're in a relationship with a client."

"*Was* a client," Marley said. "His agent fired me as his stylist, remember?"

"Were you fired so he could start a relationship with you?"

No, she was fired because Nikhil was being suffocated by people telling him what to wear, how to act, and who to be. But there was no use telling Jacqueline that. There was no point doing anything. Jacqueline wasn't going to change her mind. Marley didn't have this job anymore. But she still did have her dignity, and she wasn't going to lose that.

She looked down at the paper again. It said she had three days to sign. That was enough time to find a lawyer to tell her if this termination was fair. She refolded it and slipped it, along with the signed NDA, into the envelope.

"I will get back to you on this," Marley said, standing.

The HR rep managed to look even more terrified. Which made Marley think she probably had a case against Reid's here. But something else passed over Jacqueline's face. A touch of compassion, maybe? Marley hadn't realized Jacqueline was capable of that. "I wish we didn't have to do this, but my hands are tied. If it had been anyone other than Serena Vox, maybe we would have been able to make this work."

"What does Serena Vox have to do with it?"

"You are the Angelina Jolie in this situation…and our customer base will always relate more to Jennifer Aniston."

Marley chuckled at that. Angelina Jolie famously had this exact broken gene, and she'd had a mastectomy, too.

Marley shook Jacqueline's hand before she left. She knew better than to burn bridges on her way out. "And please, I would be more than willing to give you a personal recommendation for your next role," Jacqueline said. She almost sounded human.

"Be sure to return the letter in three days," the HR representative said as Marley left the room. A member of store security was waiting outside the door, ready to escort Marley out of the building, as was routine for all terminations.

Marley walked out of the store where she'd worked for years with her head high. In fact, it wasn't until she was alone in the Uber that the tears started falling again.

She'd been *fired*. She had not just lost the personal shopper job or been demoted to sales associate, but had been full-on fired. She'd never been fired from a job in her life. After six years, Marley was no longer an employee of Reid's Department Store.

When she walked into the house a half hour after losing her job, Nikhil was sitting on the sofa with McQueen. He looked as terrible as she felt.

"Marley," he said, standing. "Where were you? I've been texting you." She checked her phone, and yes, he'd been looking for her for half an hour. She hadn't noticed her phone buzzing. Probably because she'd been crying.

Marley sat heavily on her recliner. "I got called into an emergency meeting at work."

"Fuck," Nikhil said. He sat back down on the sofa close to Marley. "You should have waited for me. I could have taken you."

Marley frowned. "Being seen together is how we got into this mess in the first place."

He recoiled a bit. Marley sighed. This wasn't his fault. She shouldn't be taking it out on him.

"I was fired, Nikhil," she said, her voice cracking as the words came out.

His eyes widened with surprise. "You lost the personal shopping role?"

Marley shook her head, then looked away. She still couldn't believe this was happening to her. "No...they fired me from Reid's completely. For violating the NDA. They offered me a small payout and had me escorted out of the store."

"What? They can't do that! You didn't do anything wrong!"

Marley shook her head. "Didn't I, though? I mean, I slept with a client." She didn't mean to sound so bitter. "My name and the store's name were printed on that gossip site. Everyone thinks I'm a home-wrecker. I was very careless."

Nikhil shook his head. He looked furious...rightfully so. But fury wasn't going to help.

"Nikhil, I've worked my ass off for years there. I have loyal clients and was about to move to personal shopping, too."

"Fuck. I'm going to kill Arjun."

Marley turned sharply to him. "What does your brother have to do with this?"

Nikhil exhaled. "I think he sold your address to the paparazzi. He came home for a day while I was in LA and went through my sister's phone. He got my phone number and your address. Nalini feels terrible—she said to tell you she's sorry."

Marley sighed, still looking at Nikhil. She didn't blame Nalini. She *did* blame Arjun...but if he hadn't found her address, she had no doubt someone else would have talked eventually. Hell, someone from the store also talked to the press. "If it hadn't been this leak, it would have been another one," she said. "I worked so hard, and now I have nothing."

"And you think I haven't been working hard? Marley, we've both been violated here!"

"I know!" Marley shook her head. "That's my point! We're a disaster! We can't do this! It's impossible to just *play house*. To pretend to be partners. Because as soon as we act like a normal couple, someone sells us out. This life isn't normal!"

Nikhil stood, then knelt at her feet. His eyes were so sad it was hard to look at them. "This hasn't been *pretending*, Marley. And you know it." He took her hands in his.

Nikhil's beautiful face had come to mean everything to her. But she couldn't do this. Her heart was breaking into a million pieces, and she couldn't lean on him to put her back together this time. He was right—it had never been pretending. But they'd never really been partners, either.

Marley was way too private to have a partner. She always had been. And even if she could manage to really let someone in, he was literally a public figure. He couldn't be that someone.

"All this chaos will pass," he said after they'd been staring at each other for several seconds. "I'll hire some PR people. We can ride it out, then go public with our relationship. And I can help you find a better job. We'll get through this."

She looked down so she wouldn't see his face as she removed her hands from his. She folded them in her lap.

He was silent for a while. Finally, he spoke softly. "Don't

pull away from me, Marley. Don't you want to weather the storm together?"

"No." She shook her head. She finally looked at him, feeling the tears running down her cheeks. She didn't wipe them. "Because even if we get through this storm, another will come." When she saw the glassiness in Nikhil's eyes, she almost threw her arms around his neck. She didn't want to be causing him pain. But it would only hurt more if she let this go on longer. "I can't do it. I can't live in your life. I can't be in the spotlight like that."

He blinked. "You can't or you don't want to."

"I don't know," she whispered. "Both."

He shook his head, eyes pleading. "Marley, you said before that what we have is rare. It's worth fighting for. It's worth seeing if it can last, isn't it?"

Marley was tired of fighting. Fighting with Jacqueline to prove she deserved to be at Reid's. Fighting people like Tova who wanted her success without the work.

Fighting this damn genetic mutation so she wouldn't get sick. For a while when she was recovering, she felt like she didn't have to fight anymore. She could let Nikhil support her and take some of her burden. But it was never going to last. They couldn't be what the other needed.

He looked at her, blinking, until he finally got up off the floor. "That's it then, I guess. There isn't a reason for me to be here anymore. You fulfilled your end of the bargain, and I've done my part. Even if it all ended up a mess, we don't need each other anymore. Give me fifteen minutes to get my stuff together, then I'll be out of your hair."

Marley didn't look at him as he walked up the stairs. Or when he came back down ten minutes later with the suitcase he had come with a few short weeks ago. She did look when he was at the door, though. He was so…gorgeous. No, more than that. He took her breath away. He was everything she'd needed for the last month.

But she couldn't live in his world, and she couldn't subject him to hers.

"I'm sorry," she said softly. He stayed in the doorway of the living room, not coming closer. Only a few nights ago she'd been sure she'd never been as close to another person in her life.

"Goodbye, Mahreen. I wish things could have been different, but I always said I would do whatever you needed me to do. Even walk away."

She didn't *want* him to walk away, but yes, that was what she needed.

She nodded softly. "Goodbye, Nikhil."

He nodded back. Then turned and walked out the door.

At that moment, McQueen jumped onto her lap. Marley hugged her cat close and cried into his soft fur.

CHAPTER TWENTY-SIX

Nikhil

Nikhil drove straight to his parents' house when he left Marley's. He thought about going to a hotel to save himself from explaining why he suddenly needed a place to stay, but the last thing he needed was to be seen in public again.

When he got to the house, his father was too engrossed in a new Bollywood movie to pay much attention to him. And Mom, of course, was resting upstairs. Nikhil gave some excuse for being there, made a plate of leftovers from the fridge, and took it downstairs to eat. Nalini joined him after a few minutes, but she seemed to understand that he didn't want to talk about himself at all right now. She started telling him how her university classes were going and how she was starting to research medical schools.

"Pick whatever school you want. I'll pay," Nikhil said.

Nalini raised a brow. "I'll get scholarships and can take some loans. I mean, doctors make enough money to pay them back. Plus, you don't know—"

"I don't know if I'll get another role like the Shadow—I know." And he'd already used a bunch of the money to pay off this damn house. He sighed. Was it possible this cheating scandal, or not-cheating scandal, was going to affect his future earning potential?

His phone buzzed with a call then. He checked the screen—it was Esther.

"My agent," he said.

Nalini stood. "I'll go. You do your damage control."

"They want to see you at eleven tomorrow," Esther said the moment he answered. "At the studio's Toronto office."

"Did they sound angry when you talked to them?"

"They're not pleased. As expected, the biggest issue here is that the timing made Serena look bad. They need her to seem invincible like the character, not like a spurned woman."

He exhaled. "God, I wish I didn't have to face them alone."

"Honey, if I could, I'd be on a plane to Toronto in the next hour. Don't say a word in that meeting until you have me on speakerphone."

"I know. You think they're going to fire me from the movie?"

She huffed. "For taking your friend to the doctor's office? Of course not. Remember, Nicky boy—you did nothing wrong here. Privacy breeches like this happen all the time. All they'll do is tell you how they plan to spin the whole thing. Maybe they'll have a statement for you to post somewhere saying the girl is just an old friend."

"I don't get it. I already said I wasn't interested in a fake relationship with Serena. Why the hell did she post that?"

"Good question," Esther said, sounding more than annoyed. "Believe me—I tried to get an answer to that. They kept talking in circles whenever I asked. But us exposing her lies now makes the movie look bad, and we don't want that any more than they do."

"Can they *force* me to be in a fake relationship with her?" It would mean the end of him and Marley. Not that he and

Marley weren't over already anyway. She didn't want all his celebrity baggage. He closed his eyes, feeling a sharp pain behind them.

"Of course not. Like I said in LA, none of this nonsense is in your contract. You call the shots on your life, Nicky. But… remember what else isn't in your contract…"

He opened his eyes. "A sequel."

"You got it, babycakes. Serena Vox is the star of the Ironis movies. You want a place in the playground, you're going to have to play by her rules. To some degree."

"But it wouldn't affect my prospects in other roles, would it?"

"This industry is a fickle bitch. It wouldn't be the end of your entire career, though. I could get you streaming episodic work right away. Especially now that you're a style god."

As the sidekick. The funny friend. The co-worker.

Not the lover. Not the leading man.

"All right, Esther. Let's hear what they say tomorrow."

"You got this, Nicky. And remember: don't say a word till you have me on the phone."

CHAPTER TWENTY-SEVEN

Marley

Marley thought long and hard and decided she would stay here on this recliner with her cat on her lap for the rest of her life. Doing anything else—showering, her exercises, or God forbid, leaving the house again—was out of the question. Not when she couldn't even see her damn surgeon without someone snapping a picture of her. Thankfully, there was a glass of water nearby because she had no doubt that she would have otherwise passed out from dehydration with how many tears she'd shed.

She'd cried a lot in the last month. Probably more than she ever had in her life...or at least since that year when Maryam Aunty passed. But today was the hardest—asking Nikhil to leave hurt more than the surgery.

How had she let herself fall in love with an *actor*? A person whose goal had always been to be famous? But...she hadn't. She hadn't fallen in love with an actor, a movie star, or with a client—she had fallen in love with *Nikhil*. Sweet, caring Nikhil, who'd once been an amazing friend when she'd needed him when they were teenagers, and who now had come into her life exactly when she needed him again. She had no idea how she was going to survive without him.

But she had to. She couldn't be herself...couldn't live her

life, with a partner in the public eye. She would always be afraid of being watched. Be worried that everyone knew her private business. She wanted to be in the background making people look their best…not be with a star.

Shayne walked in the door after Marley had been feeling sorry for herself on the recliner for a few hours.

He stared at her with his hands on his hips in the living room archway. "Marley, girl, you look like hell."

This was Shayne, so she knew the critique came from a place of love. "Shayne, never go to fucking France when I'm getting surgery again. Look at the mess I've made."

He shook his head and sat on the sofa next to her. McQueen looked up, wondering if he should go greet his daddy, but finally decided that Mommy needed him more. "Do you really think I'm capable of stopping you from making mistakes?" Shayne asked. "You know we're both useless there. I'm a chaos king. I would have pushed you to make an even bigger mess." He tilted his head, concerned. "I take it you guys broke up?"

She nodded.

"Fuck. I'm sorry. You were really into the beefcake, weren't you?"

Marley snorted loudly in response.

Shayne raised a brow. "Mar, do I have to call Reena? Resurrect our old Brie, bread, and wine nights?"

Marley nodded again. Back when Reena, Marley, and Shayne all lived in the same building, they used to eat piles of bread and cheese with cheap wine whenever they had relationship woes. Of the three, Marley's love life had always been the least dramatic. But clearly, she'd outshone the others now.

Shayne pulled out his phone. "I'm on it. And, girl, change. Why are you in your work clothes?"

Marley looked down at her fancy blouse, now with added snot stains. She finally got out of the recliner. "I'll explain when Reena gets here. Tell her to bring the brioche."

"This seems bad. I'll ask for sticky buns, too."

Forty minutes later, Marley, Shayne, Reena, and Reena's husband, Nadim, were in her living room. Marley's hair was wet from the shower she decided to take, and she was on the sofa instead of the blasted recliner. Maybe she should burn that chair in a giant bonfire.

Marley had already told Reena, Nadim, and Shayne everything that had happened today, starting from waking up to find herself in a Hollywood gossip site to getting fired from her job, to breaking up with Nikhil. Marley still couldn't believe it—she'd lost everything: her privacy, her career, and Nikhil in one huge, unexpected tsunami.

"So, that's it? He moved out?" Reena asked. She had brought her brioche rolls, her signature country sourdough, and sticky buns from her bakery, along with some various cheeses, jams and chutneys, and some tea. She also brought her husband, Nadim, but Marley didn't mind. Nadim's enthusiasm about literally anything in the world was kind of comforting tonight. He'd always reminded Marley of a golden retriever, in a good way.

Marley started unrolling a sticky cinnamon roll. "Yeah. I asked him to go. I assume he's gone back to his parents'." She cringed. Hopefully his brother won't be home on another day pass anytime soon.

"We should have invited him to our place," Nadim said. Nadim was low-key obsessed with the Ironis movies, so Marley wasn't surprised he'd welcome an Ironis star into his home, even if it was an ex of his wife's cousin. And Marley wouldn't have had an issue with it...What happened wasn't Nikhil's fault; maybe Nikhil needed a friend here.

Was he even Marley's ex? They were a couple for barely two weeks. They'd never gone out in public together—except to her doctor. Marley closed her eyes, hoping she wouldn't start crying again, then took a long sip of her oolong.

"We'd need to keep him away from the bakery," Reena said. "My sister saw me grabbing all this and knew immediately someone had a breakup." Reena's sister, Saira, who worked with Reena, wasn't known for discretion. That would be another person they would have had to be careful around if Marley and Nikhil had stayed together. "I told her Shayne was the heartbroken one."

Shayne blinked. "Excuse me? I do not *heartbreak*."

Reena sliced some more bread. "You heartbreak *worse* than all of us. You literally ruined my green fleece because you were crying so hard when Anderson left you."

Shayne frowned. "We're not supposed to say his name."

Marley hadn't told Shayne that she'd bumped into Anderson a few weeks ago. Because...well, Shayne would spiral. She sighed. "I didn't think I heartbroke, either." She didn't remember ever feeling so...*sad* after a breakup.

"You don't," Shayne said. "At least not normally. When you and Celeste broke up, you shrugged, then put an extra sugar cube in your tea to let loose."

Marley glared at him, then filled her mouth with a bite of sticky bun.

"Yeah, you've always been the most *together* of the three of us," Reena said. "Lord knows y'all have been there for me through way too much relationship drama." She patted her husband on the knee. "But here's Marley, always upstaging me without even trying."

"I'm not upstaging you..." She wasn't intentionally upstaging anyone, at least.

Reena tilted her head. "Seriously, Marley? You've outdrama-ed the rest of us now. I read about you in BuzzFeed."

Marley cringed. "I still can't believe we were *followed*. And that someone took a picture of me in the doctor's office."

Shayne nodded. "Celebrity photographers have no shame. The money is good, but I couldn't imagine being desperate enough to do that."

"This is why I can't be with him. It's only going to get worse. He's a paparazzi magnet. I'm a private person—I can't live like that."

Nadim shook his head. "It's not his fault, though. Put the blame firmly where it's due—on the ghouls who follow him around."

Marley nodded. "I know it's not his fault. It's Serena's rabid fans, the racist industry, and his incredibly demanding publicity team. And of course, people like his own brother who are willing to sell him out for some money. He's a victim, but that doesn't make all these issues go away, does it? I've lost my *job* because of this mess. It's not worth it."

"What are you going to do about Reid's?" Shayne asked. "Are you going to sign the termination letter?"

Marley shrugged. "I don't know yet. I'll do some research tomorrow. Maybe find an employment lawyer." She did not want to deal with this now, but she had to. She sighed, then stuffed more sticky roll into her mouth. Reena added cardamom to hers, which was why they were Marley's favorite. "Thanks for bringing this, Ree. Fuck, I'd love a drink...Let's promise to meet up here with bottles of rosé in two months when I'm healed."

Reena shrugged. "I'll need to wait longer...seven months. More if I breastfeed."

Marley blinked, looking at her cousin.

"Um...Reena...is there a...baby in your future?" Shayne asked.

Reena grinned ear to ear. "We were going to wait until I passed the first trimester, but..."

Nadim grinned proudly.

Shayne got up and tackled Reena with an enormous hug. Marley wanted to do the same, but hugging was still hard.

"Reena! You're going to be a mom! I'm so, so happy for you!" Marley said. Reena and Nadim deserved happiness more than anyone. She was so glad at least one of them was lucky in love.

"And you two are going to be the most fabulous aunty and uncle around," Nadim said.

Shayne grinned. "You bet I am. I'm ready. I'm taking your maternity photos. And your baby pictures. Versace is making strollers now, you know."

Reena and Nadim gave them more details about her pregnancy and about how excited they were. "I can't even believe it," Reena said. "Not long ago, I was a chronically unemployed and single hot mess, and now look at me. Married, running my own business, and now having a baby."

"Couldn't have happened to a better person," Marley said. "And who would have thought that I'd take over your hot-mess status."

"Marley, you're not a hot mess," Nadim said. "You're just going through some stuff." Marley shrugged. That was an understatement. She couldn't think of anything that wasn't a mess in her life right now. She'd fallen in love with completely the wrong man. She'd lost not only the promotion she'd been working for years to get, but also her previous role as sales consultant. She wasn't sure she wanted kids, but with her genes, she probably shouldn't have them anyway, which might be an issue if she wanted a long-term relationship.

Oh, and also? She had no nipples.

She would probably be single forever and get sick alone, thanks to this mutation. Which was for the best—why would she want to subject someone else to her fate?

Shayne looked at Marley, head tilted. "Question, Marl. I've known you forever, and I've never seen you fall for someone like this. Is this because he helped you while you're healing? Or because he's a hot movie star now? Or is this real?"

Marley closed her eyes. It was hard to say for sure. They didn't live in a vacuum, and all the shit in their lives right now was influencing everything. Including their feelings.

But at the end of the day, it wasn't his fame, or his body, or even how good he was at helping her recover from surgery that she fell in love with. She fell in love with the man who loved to Netflix and chill as much as her. Who she could talk to for hours about their families, or food, or where they wanted to travel. Who would laugh at himself every time the chai boiled over, then clean it up. And who managed to make her smile exactly when she needed it. The Nikhil she fell in love with was the one she'd known years ago. Not the movie star, but her old friend. "I don't know. It feels real. I love him. But I can't be with a celebrity. It's not me."

"I get it." Shayne slunk down into the sofa. "Welcome to the falling-in-love-with-the-wrong-man club."

CHAPTER TWENTY-EIGHT

Nikhil

Nikhil barely got any sleep that night. Not because there was anything wrong with the futon in his parents' basement, but because it turned out that he was addicted to sleeping with Marley next to him. And withdrawal was a bitch. He headed upstairs early, figuring he could go sit in a cafe or something to clear his head before driving into the city for the meeting at eleven. But when he got to the main floor of his parents' house, he saw that his mother was in the kitchen. Cooking. He didn't remember the last time he'd seen his mother out of bed before noon.

"Do you want a fresh paratha?" she asked.

He blinked. His mother used to always bribe him with a fresh paratha with extra butter if he agreed to cook them while she rolled them out. But it had been years since he saw her making parathas. Making anything, really. Both his parents loved to cook, and rotlis and parathas were always something his mother made when he was growing up. But when Mom's mental health took a hit when Arjun was criminally charged, Dad took over all the cooking.

Nikhil slipped on a blue apron and picked up the spatula next to the stove. A pale-brown paratha was ballooned on the tawa. He flipped it over and pressed on the bubble.

"Are you going to your rehearsal?"

He nodded. He hadn't told either of his parents exactly why he'd moved his things back to the house yesterday. Only Nalini knew. "Where's Dad?"

"Still sleeping. I told him I'd make your breakfast today."

"You didn't have to."

Mom shrugged. He watched her for a few seconds, trying and failing to gauge her mood by her eyes. Maybe if he was home more, he'd be able to read her better. "It's been a long time since I made parathas," she said. "Nalini said she wanted me to teach her to make them, and I didn't know if I remembered how." She chuckled, but the laugh didn't reach her eyes. This paratha-making wasn't thanks to a sudden clearing of her depression. "There is no way Nalini would stay still long enough for this, though."

"It's great to see you cooking again," Nikhil said. Maybe he shouldn't have said that. He didn't want to make her feel bad.

"It's nice to have you home again. At least for now..." Her voice trailed off.

The paratha he was roasting was ready, so he flipped it onto the plate near the stove, and his mother put a new one on the tawa.

They cooked silently for a while like that. Nikhil could feel the giant elephant in the room—neither had mentioned that she was rarely *here* anymore. Rarely functioning. Was this a good time to suggest she get some help? That it was long past time for her to tell her doctor that she wasn't doing well, and that her family was in crisis?

"I heard from your brother last night," she said after the silence became almost unbearable.

"Mom," he said. She knew he didn't want to talk about

Arjun. After his brother sold him out like that, he was positive he never wanted a relationship with his brother again.

"It's okay, beta. I know he told that reporter where your friend's house was. What he did wasn't right. I told him he can't come back here again since he doesn't respect his family."

Nikhil's eyes widened. Mom *knew* what Arjun had done? That was the first time he remembered Mom ever admitting that Arjun was wrong. Nikhil had always assumed that his mother was incapable of seeing any flaw in her golden first-born son. Mom started rolling out another paratha. "I always wished you boys could be closer."

Arjun and Nikhil *should* have been close. They were only a year apart in age. But they were so different—Arjun was the kid who read all the get-rich-quick books in the library and was convinced he'd be a millionaire before he was twenty-five. He'd convinced the whole family, too—the golden boy was going to make them all so proud. Nikhil was...well, his head was always so high in the clouds that no one on earth noticed he was up there. He sometimes wondered if his dream of being an actor was so people would notice he existed, because it never felt like his parents did.

"It's not going to happen, Mom. After what he did to Marley, I never want to see him again."

Mom nodded, then looked down at the ball of dough she was rolling out. He still couldn't read her expression. "I always thought Arjun was the easy one," she said. "He was a straight-A student. You? You got a fake ID to sneak into comedy clubs."

Nikhil chuckled. He'd been determined to make it big as a stand-up comedian back then. He had no idea how anyone in those clubs didn't figure out that he was only sixteen.

"You had big dreams. You were so young when you left home. But I knew you'd be okay."

He'd barely turned nineteen when he moved to Los Angeles. It was unheard of for an Indian teen to skip university and run off to be an actor instead of staying and taking care of his family. But he hadn't needed to be the perfect Indian son, because they already had one of those.

Even when he finally got his big break, he *still* wasn't the golden son. His success wasn't enough to brighten the cloud over the household from Arjun's downfall.

"Your friend," Mom said after a few more moments. "Is she okay? Or are you not…friends anymore?" Mom slapped a new paratha on the tawa.

"She'll be okay. But…yeah, I guess we're not…friends anymore."

"And you're okay with that?"

He nodded. "Yeah, it's fine." He was doing it, too—saying he was fine when he wasn't. Just like his mother did. Just like Marley did.

Mom rolled out the next flatbread. Nikhil realized he wanted the opposite of what pretty much any second-generation Indian kid wanted…he *wanted* Mom to intrude. To get all up in his business and find out what really happened with Marley. He wanted her to be the kind of mom who just *knew* when her youngest son was heartbroken. He wanted her to say time would heal this pain. And he wanted to be able to tell his mother that he'd lost the person he'd first fallen in love with when he was that dreaming teenager.

But he couldn't unload his troubles on his mother. She had enough of her own to deal with.

"Every time I saw your prom picture on the wall downstairs, I wondered what happened to that girl," Mom said suddenly.

Wait...Mom *knew* that Marley was *Mahreen*? Did she know back then how bad he had it for her? Did Mom know that he almost threw away all his dreams for her?

Or that he was seriously thinking about throwing them all away for her again?

"Beta, do you remember that when you were a boy, you told me you were going to win an Oscar and an Emmy? But not a Grammy because you couldn't sing."

He frowned. He didn't remember that.

"But you sang in *The Last Time He Cried*. I thought you were good. Maybe you can get an EGOT."

Nikhil laughed. "You watched that?" There was a terrible karaoke scene in the movie.

"Of course. I watch all your movies. That one's my favorite. I always wanted to watch it with you. Maybe...while you're here, we can do that? Watch together?"

Nikhil smiled. "Yeah. We should."

He didn't remember the last time he'd watched a movie with his mother. Her timing wasn't random. Mom being here now, making parathas with Nikhil the day after he left the love of his life, was her way of supporting him. This was what she was capable of giving right now, and maybe it was enough.

Blinking away the tears welling in his eyes, Nikhil flipped a paratha on the stack, then got the butter from the counter.

"Should I make each of us one with butter and sugar?" he asked.

Mom nodded. "Yes. I think that's exactly what we need."

The boardroom at the Toronto studio office was sleek and modern, with walls lined with movie posters and a huge screen with the studio logo projected on it. And everyone Nikhil expected to be there was there. Lydia, Kaelyn, and Carmen. Plus the producer, Sasha Keller, and some studio execs. Weirdly, Serena wasn't there, though, which pissed him off. This concerned her, too. But then again, part of the reason he was here was probably because of their blowout fight yesterday. Serena was the superstar, and he was the nothing. So, he'd have to take the heat for what had happened. Before Nikhil said anything else, he told them he needed to get his agent tapped into the room.

"We have her and others waiting on video conference," Kaelyn said.

In seconds, the screen filled with faces. Two LA execs and Esther. Still no Serena or Serena's representation.

"Okay," one of the executives on the screen started, "before we get into damage control, be aware that legal is looking at Nik's contract right now to see where he has breached it."

"He hasn't," Esther said. "I would never have allowed my client to sign a contract that would disallow him from taking his friend to the doctor when she needed it."

"Of course not," the executive said. "But he does have a morality clause. Him buying boobs and hooking up with his stylist in a plastic surgery office kind of ruins that perception."

"I didn't hook up with her! I kissed her because she was upset. And she's not even my stylist anymore. Esther told you all—"

"Nik, darling," Esther interrupted. "Let me handle this."

"This is what I don't understand," Lydia said. "You and that girl hadn't seen each other for years before we hired her. How did that evolve to buying her new boobs weeks later? That surgeon's waiting list is years long. He's the best."

"My client's personal life is not up for debate here," Esther said. "He has not broken the morality clause by taking his friend to a doctor."

Nikhil wasn't going to betray Marley's privacy again and tell them that she had had a mastectomy, not a breast augmentation. Not that that should make any difference at all. She was entitled to do whatever she wanted to her body. And this was literally show business—why did they care if Marley had had plastic surgery?

"Okay," Sasha Keller said, motioning everyone to calm down. "It was just a kiss. And you didn't pay for her plastic surgery. But what we need to know is—are you *with* that girl? Will photographers see you together again?"

"He doesn't have to answer that," Esther said. "If you didn't want him to be photographed with anyone, then you should have put it in the contract. And you should have paid him more accordingly."

There was no answer to that. This is why he adored Esther—she had his back.

"Now," Esther said, "let's get back on track here. Our first question is why Serena Vox posted on her Instagram that she's dating Nik after he explicitly stated that he was not interested in an arrangement like that."

"We've spoken to Serena's team, and the post will be removed," Kaelyn said. "We have some suggestions for how to mitigate the damage from the *Pop Hollywood* piece."

"That still doesn't answer the question," Esther said almost to herself. "But let's hear your suggestions."

Kaelyn picked up her iPad and started reading. "Okay, first, would the stylist be willing to post on her Instagram about her breast surgery? She could imply it's something she's been wanting/planning for a long time and that it has nothing to do with Nik. She'll no doubt get comments and questions on the post—I can assign a publicity intern to moderate. We'll delete anything insensitive immediately. Any questions about Nik will be responded to, stating he is an old friend she'd recently reconnected with. This is all true, so anyone who knows Nik personally will be able to confirm. I even have his prom picture—we can use it if necessary."

"I am not asking Marley to do that. She's not even my stylist anymore. And where the hell did you get my prom picture?" Nikhil asked.

No one answered that question, unsurprisingly.

Kaelyn continued. "If the stylist won't post to her social media, we can arrange an interview with her where she can talk about turning Nik into a style icon, and she can deny they are anything other than friends. Then we'll book a talk show appearance for Serena and Nik together. To talk about the movie, of course, but they will slyly confirm together that the two of them *are* in a relationship. We're willing to use a Toronto-based outlet for this. We'll do this right before filming since we'll be locked tight after, and there shouldn't be any more leaks."

"Can this 'relationship' end before filming is done?" Esther asked.

"Of course. So long as Nik and Serena stay on good terms." Esther nodded. "Nik, this work for you?"

Nikhil blinked. Maybe he should just agree. Marley broke

up with him, so what difference did it make if he was in a fake relationship with Serena now?

When he hesitated, one of the LA executives on the screen spoke. "We are prepared to compensate you further for agreeing to this. And of course, the studio would be very grateful."

Nikhil sighed. He doubted the money they were willing to throw at him would be enough to make a difference. What was really at stake here was this *gratitude*. If he didn't agree, then he could kiss more Ironis movies goodbye.

He sighed. "Okay. I'll do the talk show, but Marley won't be involved. If anyone asks me, I'll say she's an old friend. I will not ask her to do any press for me, and she will not post anything about me or her medical information on her social media."

Kaelyn frowned. "This would be good for her reputation, too. Her connection to you could open doors for her as a stylist."

"And the studio could send business her way," Lydia added.

Nikhil shook his head. "No. I'll say whatever you want, but Marley stays out of this."

Lydia snorted. "She shouldn't be so precious about her boob job. Everyone has them. Tell her she'll get thousands more Instagram followers."

Nik glared at Lydia. "You are a very unpleasant person. Why are you here, anyway? Didn't we fire you?"

Lydia smiled. "That was your first mistake. If I were still your handler, I could have prevented this whole mess."

One of the executives put her hands out to silence them all. "Enough. Fine. The stylist stays out of it. If anyone asks you about her, you say she's just a friend, okay? You don't have to lie."

It was still a lie, though, wasn't it? They weren't *just friends*. Nikhil was in love with her. She'd been perfection in his eyes for years. Perfect and unattainable. But now, Marley was something beyond perfection. She was *real* but still unattainable. And this time it wasn't because she was out of his league. She was unattainable because of the life he had chosen for himself.

He nodded. "If you or any of your people go digging into Marley's personal, medical, or professional life, then I will be extremely open to all the gossip sites about Serena's little Instagram lie. I don't give a fuck about what my contract says. I am more than willing to blow all this up, including my career, to protect Marley's privacy."

Esther nodded. "It wouldn't even destroy his career," she said. "Not with me on his side. It would destroy your movie, though."

Everyone was silent for several moments. Nikhil was pretty sure Esther was bluffing there. Going after Serena *would* destroy his career. And his income. His ability to pay for Nalini's medical school. His ability to bail his parents out if Arjun did something stupid again.

But he knew it would be terrible for the movie, too. For Serena's reputation. And as the face behind the franchise, Serena was leaps and bounds more important to them than Nikhil.

Lydia looked at Nikhil. "You would really throw everything away for a girlfriend? Relationships between stars and civilians never work."

"She's not my girlfriend."

"Are we done here?" Esther asked. "I have a pool party in Bel Air tonight, so I must get waxed."

One of the executives looked at Nikhil. "You good with all this?"

He didn't have much of a choice. His career was in shambles. His co-star hated him. He was about to be sequestered with these people for three months or longer to film this movie.

And he'd lost Marley.

"I'm grand," he said. He was an actor. He could act like everything was okay, at least. He'd been doing it all his life.

When he got to the gym after leaving the studio, Serena and Caroline weren't there. He talked with Reggie a bit about the meeting and even asked if Reggie knew why Serena had put up that Instagram post. Reggie was sympathetic and kind, but he had no idea why Serena had lied.

"I guess it doesn't really matter," Nikhil said. "Can we repeat the sequence from yesterday a few more times?"

Nikhil worked with Reggie until he could have done the sequence with his eyes closed. He put everything he could into the job.

Because this was still living his dream. And the dream was all he had left.

CHAPTER TWENTY-NINE

Marley

Marley was still having a love-hate relationship with her ugly recliner. Most of the time, the sight of the beige ultrasuede monstrosity in her otherwise colorful living room made her cringe. But today, on the day after she lost both her job and Nikhil, the recliner felt like a gift from the heavens. All she needed was it, McQueen, and delivery apps. Which was good because that was pretty much all she had. She had no career. Her closest friends were busy living their own lives. She had no boobs.

And she didn't even have the man she loved.

This was her life now—she was going to stay here, cocooned on this comfortable chair, and avoid the world.

A sharp twinge of pain on her chest reminded her of the stupid fucking defective gene that had been the catalyst for everything falling apart. This defective DNA had been the cause of all the pain in her life.

Maryam Aunty's death. Her mother's illness. Marley's surgery. And the huge mess her life had become since the surgery.

Marley knew she had some decisions to make, but she had no idea what she should do. Accept the severance package Reid's offered? Speak to an employment lawyer? She didn't know how to even begin to find one. Her dad would know, but the last thing she wanted to do was call her parents now. Then she'd have to tell them that she'd lost her job because a movie star who was rumored to be dating a megapopular actress kissed Marley in a plastic surgery office, and her boss was concerned that customers would think Marley was too much of a home-wrecker to buy Armani and Elie Tahari from. There was no way Marley could make them understand that. Hell, she didn't understand it herself. Bad enough she'd have to explain it to a lawyer.

The sharp pain in her breast hit again, almost making her cry out. What the hell? This was a new pain—not like the one that had sent her to the doctor a few days ago. Should she call Dr. Abernathy again? But this pain passed as quickly as it hit.

She was still sitting there on the recliner a few hours later when someone knocked on her door, and McQueen growled. Shayne had left early in the morning for a shoot. And everyone else she knew was at work.

She slowly got out of the chair and made her way to the door. She was shocked at who she saw when she opened it.

"Ruby! What are you doing here? Shouldn't you be at the store?"

Ruby put her hands on her hips. "Are you nuts? Not when my cousin was *fired*…I had to walk out in solidarity."

Marley cringed. Ruby better not have quit her job. Marley's mother would kill Marley if Ruby did that. "Don't tell me—"

Ruby shook her head. "No. I thought about actually quitting, but I wanted to talk to you first. I told Jacqueline I ate bad shrimp and felt like throwing up. She waved me away."

Marley chuckled. Jacqueline had a well-known phobia of bodily fluids.

Marley motioned Ruby inside, then took her seat back in

the recliner. God bless the recliner. McQueen jumped onto Marley's lap.

Ruby sat on the sofa, hugging a chenille pillow in her arms. "Someone said you were fired for telling Jacqueline that her hair is stuck in 1993, but I doubt you would do that. Even though for sure you've thought it."

"Um, that's not at all what happened."

"So then what happened?"

Marley sighed. "Jacqueline claimed I violated the NDA because a celebrity photographer in a Tesla followed me and Nikhil to my plastic surgeon's office and took pictures of him kissing me."

Ruby's eyes went wide. "Your plastic surgeon *kissed* you?"

Marley cringed. "Ew. No. Nikhil kissed me."

That did not make Ruby's eyes go back to normal. "Marley, tell me everything. Celebrity clients are kissing you in public now?"

Marley sighed. "Okay. So can I assume you didn't see the celebrity gossip featuring me and Nik Sharma from yesterday?" Marley had checked, and the piece had finally been taken down. A little too late, though.

Ruby made a face. "I only read UK gossip."

Of course she did. Marley told Ruby everything. Well, almost everything, at least. She told her about her past with Nikhil, about prom, and about catching feelings when they were living together. She skipped some stuff...like their King Street hotel antics. But this was the most Marley had told anyone about how she felt about someone in...well, actually, the most she'd ever talked to someone about a relationship. Even Shayne.

Ruby, understandably, was surprised at it all. The normally cool and collected Marley had fallen so hard for someone that she was practically sobbing over a man. "This stupid surgery has made me emotional," Marley said, blowing snot from her nose. Which startled McQueen awake. He glared at Marley for daring to interrupt his sleep.

"Is it the surgery, or is it the relationship?"

Marley waved her hand. "The *surgery*. I don't get emotional over relationships. But I just had healthy boobs removed and lost my job, so I think I'm entitled to be in my feels." Maybe she shouldn't be unloading this on Ruby of all people. This was probably triggering for her.

Ruby nodded. "Not arguing that. Be in your feels. I know I was after my mastectomy. I don't really follow a ton of Hollywood gossip—unless Harry Styles is involved—but didn't I hear that Nik was dating Serena Vox?"

"Yes, but not really."

"That makes no sense."

"Show business makes no sense." Marley sighed. "Serena claimed they were in a relationship, but it was for publicity. And now the world thinks I broke up Serena and Nikhil and that he bought me boobs. She looks like a woman scorned. And he looks like a player."

Ruby shook her head. "Honestly, Marley, you're the least likely person who I imagined could fall into a Hollywood scandal."

Marley narrowed her eyes at Ruby. Why was everyone so surprised at this happening, or at how Marley was reacting? Once again, Marley was starting to wonder if she was maybe a little too private.

"I do think it's complete *bollocks* Jacqueline would let you go for this," Ruby continued. "You were violated; you didn't break the NDA."

"Just say 'bullshit,' Ruby. We're not in jolly old England. They can technically let me go for anything, as long as they pay me enough severance, and as long as it's not discrimination of a protected class. Dating a superstar's pretend boyfriend is not a protected class." Marley still couldn't believe this was her life now. Another tear started running down her face. She ignored it.

Ruby shook her head. "After everything you did for the store. Customers *came in* because of you! You managed to satisfy people like Angel Durand!" She winced. "Customers are going to be upset."

"I'm sure Tova will be thrilled to take them."

"Of that I have no doubt," Ruby sighed. "We all give our heart and soul for that store. We bend over backward to please the clients and management, and at the end of the day, this shows that they don't really care for us nearly as much as we care for them. All they care about are profits. Bottom line." She exhaled. "I'm glad I'm leaving Reid's. There is no reason to show loyalty to anyone."

"So, you really are leaving? I hope not because of me..."

Ruby shook her head. "Not just because of you, but yeah, I bought a plane ticket a few days ago. One-way...Toronto to London. I'm moving in January. After the Christmas rush at Reid's."

It made sense to wait until after the holidays—sales associates made huge commissions during the holiday season. And Ruby had always loved Christmas. Ruby had moved around a lot since her mother died. Vancouver, Ottawa, Montreal. But this was the first time she'd talked about leaving the country.

"Seriously?"

Ruby nodded. "*Seriously*. You know it was Mom's and my

dream to move there. I'm young, I'm single. It's time to make that dream happen. There's nothing for me here...except you. But now you're untethered, too. You should come with me."

Marley exhaled. Maryam Aunty and Ruby used to talk about one day leaving Canada to open an inn or a tea house in England. They used to watch real estate shows from the UK and daydream about buying a cottage there. Now Ruby was making it happen. It was tempting to go with her since Maryam Aunty couldn't. Marley could just leave everything and start over. But...that was *their* dream, not Marley's. Marley's dream had always been the same—being a personal shopper at Reid's.

"Maybe," Marley said. "I need to think about what I want to do next."

"You can do whatever you want. Other stores, like Holt Renfrew or even Saks, would jump to hire you. Or you could freelance. I'm sure that having a movie star boyfriend would open enough doors for you to have a bustling personal stylist business. You could work with Shayne and style photo shoots. You could even style Nik. If you guys manage to work it out."

Marley cringed. She wasn't sure she was cut out for the freelance life. She'd have to be...exposed, public...for that. And she definitely couldn't style Nikhil...even if they managed to stay friends. Dress him? Pick out clothes so the rest of the world could see the Nikhil that she saw—the incredible, kind, sexy person that she couldn't have? It was impossible. "I told you, he's not my boyfriend. I can't be with a movie star, Ruby. There is no privacy. Always living in a fishbowl. Not to mention he lives in LA. He's only here for his movie."

"Yeah, long distance sucks. But you're still going to be friends, aren't you?"

Marley shrugged. She had no idea.

"I get why a relationship is doomed, but you were friends before he was famous. And you didn't break up because of anything either of you did wrong. Why not stay friends? Famous people have nonfamous friends all the time."

"I've never stayed friends with someone I've dated."

Ruby frowned. "Why not?"

Maybe it was because real physical attraction wasn't a common thing for her—well, at least not as common as it seemed to be for others, so it was hard to move on from it? The thought of being only friends with Nikhil now seemed too painful. It felt like she would need time to process the end of the relationship before even thinking of being friends.

She'd grown so attached to Nikhil since he'd been back in her life. She'd fallen in love with him. But it had also been unbelievably amazing to have him back as a *friend* right when she needed him. Right when she was facing one of the hardest physical and emotional things she'd ever gone through. Ruby was right—neither of them had done anything wrong. There was no good reason not to try to keep the friendship, at least.

Marley felt that same twinge in her right breast again. She winced, her hand reaching for it.

"You okay?" Ruby asked.

The pain eased as quickly as it came. She breathed through it. "Yeah, fine."

"You don't look fine. Is this the thing you went to the doctor for?"

Marley shook her head. "No, that was the other boob. But it's okay. Better now."

Ruby raised one brow. "You do remember that I went

through all of this, like, a year ago, right? You never seem to want to talk to me about your surgery."

Of course she didn't want to talk to Ruby. Ruby had been through enough. More than enough. "I don't want to…trigger you."

Both Marley and Ruby had mothers diagnosed with breast cancer, but Marley's was still *alive*. Watching Maryam Aunty die was the hardest thing Marley had ever gone through, and it had to have been so much harder for Ruby, Maryam's own daughter. Marley couldn't unload her crap on Ruby.

"Marley, you're being silly. I'm right here. I *want* to be here for you. You and me—we're in this together, coz. You don't have to pretend to always be okay when you're clearly not."

Marley didn't say anything. What could she say? That she desperately wanted to talk to someone, but every time she tried, she got burned. Her mother would go on about botched surgeries, or someone would take pictures of her at the doctor.

Finally, Ruby sighed. "Marley, I get it. You're you. I can't force you to open up to me. We're family, and that makes it complicated. But there are support groups. I went to a BRCA one a few times in Montreal."

Marley exhaled, remembering the brochures the nurse had given her. "There's one in Toronto." A month ago, Marley had no interest in calling that peer support group. The very thought of talking to *strangers* about what she was going through seemed torturous. But now? More strangers knew things about her than ever. Hell, apparently BuzzFeed knew who she was. "Maybe I'll call them," she said, even though she wasn't sure she would. "And, Ruby, I'm sorry. I don't mean to push you away."

Ruby smiled. "I know. You don't know how to be anyone

but the person you are, Marl. It's fine. My mother used to say that you were a closed book, but you had the most amazing universe between your covers."

Marley smiled. "I miss your mother."

Ruby nodded. "Me too. She'd be so happy that I'm finally going to England. I want to visit the house they filmed *Pride and Prejudice* in for her."

Marley and Ruby then did something that they hadn't done since Ruby moved back to Toronto. They put on the 1995 *Pride and Prejudice* miniseries and spent the afternoon talking and reminiscing about Maryam Aunty. All of the good things, none of the bad. It was exactly what Marley needed.

After Ruby left, Marley sat on her chair with her cat, watching the sun go down. The house was quiet. She texted Shayne and asked when he'd be home, but he said his shoot was running late. He'd barely been home since getting back from France. She could call Reena, but her cousin was probably tired after baking so early while pregnant.

And that was it. Marley's entire support system. She'd been slowly drifting away from people for years, and now here she was. Alone. Just her and her cat. And she was the only person to blame for it. After years of telling everyone she was fine when she wasn't. Of making everyone think she was coping when she wasn't. For years, she'd told herself that she liked not having many friends, but now she needed someone, and there was no one here.

Not even Nikhil, who'd told her he'd be there for her always, no matter what happened. But could she blame him? She *asked* him to leave. She wasn't willing to be friends, so she was alone.

Marley was so fucking tired of being alone. But like Ruby

said, she had no idea how to be anyone other than the person she'd always been. A closed book.

Well, maybe in one area of her life she could change the way she dealt with things. She dug up the brochure for the BRCA support group. It was still in the Chloé bag she'd taken to her pre-op appointment. The picture on the pamphlet was of fiftysomething-year-old white women sitting around a table, smiling and talking. Clearly stock photography. She gave the information a skim. The group met in person on the third Thursday of every month in a private meeting room uptown.

Tomorrow was the third Thursday of the month. Was this a sign? There was an email address to get more information. Marley sent a quick note, explaining she wanted to talk to someone about the mastectomy she'd recently had.

It was long past time for Marley to *ask* for the support she needed.

CHAPTER THIRTY

Marley

In the morning, Marley had an email in her inbox from a woman named Jaime, the facilitator of the BRCA support group. It said that Marley would be welcome at the meeting tonight, but if she wasn't ready to talk to the whole group yet, Jaime would be happy to have a coffee with her alone before the group started.

Despite her previous determination to ask for help, everything in Marley wanted to say no. She didn't know a thing about this woman—why would she talk to her about everything she was going through? Marley had done fine bottling everything in for so long. She had McQueen. That was enough.

But *was* Marley doing fine? She was a mess, afraid of every pain, and terrified about what her future with this broken gene would be like. And this was just coffee with one person. Not a whole group. She wrote back, thanking Jaime and agreeing to meet.

The coffee shop Jaime suggested was in the north end of the city. Jaime had told her she'd be wearing a tan blazer with a black T-shirt, so Marley easily found her sitting alone in a booth in the back. Marley squared her shoulders and approached the woman. She was nervous but determined. "Hi, are you Jaime? I'm Marley."

Jaime smiled widely and stood to shake Marley's hand. She was East Asian and looked about Marley's age or maybe a bit younger. She was wearing loose pants with her tan blazer, and Marley thought the outfit looked fabulous on her. "Happy to meet you, Marley. Grab yourself a drink, then we can chat."

Marley smiled awkwardly. This woman seemed so friendly. "Okay…I'll get…tea."

After getting a matcha latte, Marley joined Jaime in the booth. "Thanks for agreeing to meet me."

"Not a problem. I come straight from work, so I usually hang out here alone before the group every month. Having someone to talk to is so much better than reading legal briefs." Marley must have looked confused, because Jaime explained. "I'm a lawyer."

Oh. Marley assumed that she was a social worker or therapist or something. But it made sense. It was a *peer* support group, not a professional support group. Marley had no idea what to say, so she settled on small talk. "Do you work nearby?"

Jaime nodded. "Not far. So, in your email you said you had a mastectomy. When was your surgery?"

"It'll be a month tomorrow."

"Wow, for only a month out, you look fabulous! I was still so stiff a month after surgery. What procedure did you have? I had tissue expanders. They were *hell*. Like bricks strapped to my chest."

Marley was taken aback. Jaime was so open. And seemed so…healthy and happy. Marley wasn't sure what she was expecting, but it wasn't this.

"The doctor called it one step?"

"Ah. Direct to implant. Lucky. I couldn't do that because, as my surgeon put it, I was too *ample*. How's recovery been? Any complications?"

Marley shrugged. "Some." She told Jaime about the seroma and possible infection. Jaime said something similar had happened to her, but the fluid absorbed easily into her body after a few weeks. Marley asked her about the new sharp pain on her right side.

"Oh my god, isn't it the worst? It's nerve regrowth. It's a good thing—it means you'll hopefully regain some sensation—but, man, I wish they'd told me about it. I was on the phone with my sister the first time it happened, and I screamed. She had a mastectomy a few years before me, so she could tell me what it was. Do you have sisters?"

Marley shook her head. "I'm an only child. I have a lot of cousins…One of them had a mastectomy. But we don't really talk about it."

"Ah. I'm sorry. I'd be lost without my sister…not just about this BRCA stuff, but in life."

"Is she in this group?"

Jaime shook her head. "She lives across the country. Which is why it's great to have this group. These people are like my stand-in sisters."

"Really?" Marley would not have thought people could get so close in a medical support group.

Jaime nodded. "I know it's weird—we meet once a month to talk about our boobs—but these ladies are *amazing*. You'll love them. If you decide to join us, that is."

"Is it just women?"

"Technically, we're open to anyone who has an increased

risk of breast or ovarian cancer because of a BRCA mutation or other genetic marker, and have, or once had, breasts and/or ovaries. It's a peer support group for people who are going through the same thing, you know?"

Marley nodded. That made sense. She asked some more questions about the group, like how many people were in it, and if any of them had ever had a cancer diagnosis or were like Marley and found out about the mutation before they got cancer. Jaime said all were welcome, but most regulars had not had cancer before. She said those who'd had cancer usually preferred formal groups for people who've had a cancer diagnosis. Jaime described this group like friends getting together more than anything else.

"You seem to be doing great. Are you going back to work soon?" Jaime asked.

Marley exhaled. Here was another thing that was hard to talk about. "I was supposed to. But change of plans."

Jaime nodded. "I ended up taking a whole two months off because I'm a wimp who can't take pain. And I don't even have a very physical job."

"What kind of law do you practice?"

"I work in a firm that specializes in employment and disability law."

Marley snorted at that. This meeting really was fate. "That's really funny, because I was about to look for an employment lawyer. I'm not heading back to work, because I was fired a few days ago."

"What? While you're on *sick* leave? They can't fire you because of a medical condition! That's against the Human Rights Code!"

"No, it wasn't because of my surgery. It's...complicated."

Jaime reached into her purse and pulled out a card. "Email me at work...I wouldn't consult with you myself because I'm more of a disability law specialist, but I can refer you to an amazing colleague." Marley took the card. "Where did you work?" Jaime asked.

"Reid's Department Store."

"Ugh. Good thing I already hate that place. Bunch of snobs."

Marley chuckled. Jaime was right. Reid's was a bunch of snobs.

"Hey, if you worked in fashion, you should come to the Still Glowing benefit next month! It's a charity I work with. We arrange makeovers for people who are affected by breast and ovarian cancer."

This was the charity that the nurse had told Marley about before her surgery. That seemed like so long ago now. "Nah, I'm good."

Jaime didn't pry when Marley declined, which Marley appreciated. Jaime seemed to have the perfect balance about what was okay to talk about and what would be intrusive. But she did ask a personal question next.

"Do you have a romantic partner?"

It was weird, that phrasing. *Do you have a romantic partner?* instead of *Are you in a relationship?* She *had* been in a relationship until recently. But not for very long. Nikhil hadn't been around long enough to be her partner.

But it felt like he was. Even before they were officially together, it felt like they were a team. They'd helped each other. Leaned on each other. Watched bad TV together, and even taken turns feeding the cat. It was a short relationship, but it was the most partner-like one Marley had ever had.

Marley looked up, eyes welling with tears. She huffed a laugh. "Sorry. I'm going through a lot right now. I've been an emotional wreck all month."

Jaime nodded sympathetically. "Recovering from major surgery alone is hard on the body but hard on the heart, too. I was a ball of tears for so long after my surgery. Losing your job, too. That's a lot for you to deal with alone."

Marley shook her head. "I wasn't alone. I…I had a relationship. Sort of. Until recently. Been a rough week."

Jaime exhaled. "Wow. That's *way* too much at once. I'm sorry you went through that. But it's a common time for relationships to end. Surgery is so stressful on relationships…and some people just can't support us like we need them to."

Marley shook her head. "No, he was *amazing* at supporting me. The best. We broke up for other reasons. It's complicated."

Jaime was silent a few moments, then smiled. "You know, I've been facilitating this group for a long time and have met so many people. Some have had cancer, some have had preventative surgery so they don't get cancer, like us, and some are struggling with the decision of what to do. Almost all have had the trauma of watching people in their family—people they *love*—get sick or die. You know what I've learned?"

"What?"

"Women are a hell of a lot stronger than we think we are. Sometimes our emotions get so big that it feels like we aren't coping, but really, we are. You can have huge feelings and still be doing fine. Women with BRCA mutations have usually been through so much before they even find out they have the mutation, so they're already strong. But even strong women need support. Someone who stands by you while you're emptying surgical drains is worth their weight in *gold*. Friend, partner,

sister—whatever. You don't know how many times I've heard
of partners leaving women because of a cancer diagnosis, or
because of this mutation. Friendships fading away. Family
members awkwardly pulling back. It's tough what we're going
through. A lot of people don't know how to support us."

Tough was an understatement. Maryam Aunty's husband
could be added to that statistic of people who walked away. But
not Nikhil. He didn't walk away because of Marley's mutation.

"I don't actually blame people who don't have the bandwidth for this," Jaime continued. "People have their own
issues, too. And friendships come and go. That's why this
group is a great place—we can talk to each other instead of
unloading on people that don't get it. But if you find someone
who steps up to the plate for you? *Solid gold.* My partner is
amazing. Couldn't have done this without him. We were only
dating when I had surgery, and we're engaged now."

Marley blinked. She was actually low-key jealous of Jaime.
Jaime had her sister, an amazing partner, and she had this
group that she said was her lifeline. But how much of Jaime's
support system was there because Jaime was open with them?
Because Jaime let them in?

But Marley *had* let Nikhil in. More than anyone else she
knew. He *was* worth more than gold. Platinum. "Can I ask,"
Marley said, "if you ever feel like you're, I don't know, burden-
ing your partner? I worry…I may need another breast surgery.
I'll probably get my ovaries out in a few years. Who knows
about having children? And even with these preventative surgeries, I can't completely remove my cancer risk. It's hard…I
don't know how I can let someone sign up to be with me for
this."

Jaime shook her head. "Life is unpredictable. No one knows

what can happen in the future. I assume there's a lot more to you than a defective gene. That's not *all* your partner is going to get from you."

"Yeah. I know. It's just…"

"I've always thought that at least with relationships, having a BRCA mutation has been a blessing for me."

How could Jaime think anything about this stupid gene was a good thing? "What? Why?"

"Because I can *see* someone's true colors. It's like…a short-cut to level up your relationships." Jaime suddenly looked at her watch. "I need to head to the support group. The meeting room is in the office building upstairs. Do you want to join me?"

Marley thought about it. She did want to. She wanted to talk to Jaime more, and to meet the people who were Jaime's lifeline. Even just listen to them. But…maybe next time. Marley needed to think now. And she was tired. She promised she'd come next month when she'd have more energy and said thank you to Jaime. She called an Uber to take her home.

Jaime's words didn't leave Marley's mind as she got into the car—namely, that she shouldn't let someone who'd stuck through all this chaos and uncertainty walk away.

Nikhil had been there for her in a way that no one else had. He had told her—many, many times—that he wanted to be there and support her. He said he was all in. They never talked about commitment, but he *showed her* he was committed. Yes, his life was a circus. Hers, too. But at the end of the day, he was more than willing to step into her circus to support her. And he was willing to let her into his chaos, too.

Was it fair to give him even more chaos in his life?

But maybe that wasn't her decision to make. Marley was

only now realizing that the reason she shut people, including Nikhil, out of her life was because she didn't want to burden them. She didn't want them to feel the way Marley felt when Maryam Aunty was sick. And with Nikhil, when her feelings for him got stronger, she became so scared of letting him into her life when she had no idea what the future would hold for her. Part of it was because she didn't want to be a burden on him, but also?

She was afraid he'd walk away. Like her uncle did. Marley didn't think she was a worthy enough partner for Nikhil. She had asked him to leave because she said she was too private for his public life, but a big part of ending it was because she thought she was too defective.

But Jaime was right. There was a hell of a lot more to Marley than this gene. Nikhil had been her friend long before she knew this BRCA mutation even existed. He'd been her rock, and if she let him, he'd continue to be her rock whenever she needed it. Even with his chaotic life, and even if they were apart for months while he was on a shoot, he'd be there for her. He'd be all in.

And Marley wanted that. She wanted someone all in—someone who supported her, brought her tea, helped her empty her drains, no matter how gross they were. Someone who she could talk to when she was scared. She was strong enough to face whatever came, and she was determined to get support—from people who understood. But also? Marley was worthy of having a partner love her.

She wanted to be all in for him, too. Help him with his wardrobe, of course, but also help him unwind after a long day, help him with his lines, be a sounding board when he needed to vent about his challenging job.

But was it even possible? At the end of the day, he was still a public figure. And as much as she'd learned in the last month that maybe she was a bit too *private*, it was one thing to speak to a support group and a whole other thing to date a movie star.

But...if she wanted to be *more* than just her defective gene, then maybe she had to see him as *more* than just his job. The movie star was him professionally. She wanted him personally.

"Excuse me," she called out to the Uber driver. "Can I change the destination for this trip?"

"You have to do it on the app," the driver called back.

Marley opened the app and input an address in Markham. Seconds later, the driver wordlessly changed course.

It was a long trip, so she started rehearsing what she would say to him. She had no idea if he would even want to see her, but Marley needed to tell Nikhil how she felt.

CHAPTER THIRTY-ONE

Nikhil

Nikhil was in the basement watching cooking videos when his sister came down the stairs.

"Nikhil, *someone* is here for you," she said in a singsong voice.

Shit. The paparazzi had found him. He hopped to his feet. "You can't admit to anyone I'm here! Is it a photographer?" He'd been parking in the garage in case any of those vultures knew his car, but he wouldn't put it past someone to follow him from the gym. Hell, a Serena superfan could have tracked him down.

Nalini's eyes went wide from his reaction. "It's okay. It's not a photographer; it's Marley."

Holy crap—that was worse. Well, not really *worse*, but more...surprising. What was she doing here? The last time Marley had come to this house it was to yell at him after Lydia had hired the store for all his styling. Was she here to yell at him again?

He'd almost called her or texted her so many times in the last couple days, but she had asked him to leave. She'd said she needed him out of her life, and he would always do what she needed.

"Why is she here? Is she okay?"

Nalini shrugged. "I dunno. I came down from my room and she was talking to Mom about saris or something in the living room. Dad's making her a plate of food."

His *mother* was talking to Marley?

This was bad. He rushed past Nalini and saw Marley at the top of the basement stairs with a plate in one hand and a mug in the other. His breath hitched. She looked beautiful. Her hair was loose around her shoulders, and she was wearing slim white pants with a pale-blue button-up shirt tucked into them. And minimal makeup, which was still more than he'd seen on her in weeks. He immediately rushed to meet her so he could take the plate and mug from her hands. The mug was full of his father's steaming chai, and the plate was filled with pakoras and samosas.

"Your parents insisted," she said as he took the plate.

"Of course they did," Nikhil said. "My father is incapable of not feeding someone who comes into the house."

He took the plate to the coffee table quickly and was back at Marley's side to see if she needed any help with the basement stairs. She waved him off, claiming she was fine. He still fussed—he'd taken care of her for weeks, so it was a habit now. And the last time he saw her they'd just come from the doctor for a possible infection. Should she be out of the house this late? She was usually getting ready for bed around this time.

"Hi, Nalini," Marley said. "You didn't come watch *Bachelor* this week. I've been saving the episode."

"Oh. I..." Nalini glanced at Nikhil. Looked like his sister wasn't sure if she should still be hanging out with Marley. Which was silly.

"You can still watch TV with her," Nikhil said. "Later, though. Can you...I mean, can you let us talk now?"

Nalini nodded. "Yeah. I'll keep Mom and Dad out."

"Thanks," Nikhil said. Nalini rushed up the basement stairs, and he heard the door close.

Marley sat on the sofa near where he'd put her plate. He couldn't believe she was here. She looked beautiful, but there was something in her face...red eyes and pale skin under her makeup. The anger he'd seen in her a couple days ago was gone. Now she looked sad. There was nothing Nikhil wanted more than to wrap his arms around her and tell her that it would all be okay.

He sat on the love seat across from her. "How did you get here?"

"Uber," she said. She took a sip of her chai, then smiled while looking around the room. "We studied together down here for a chemistry exam once. Do you remember?"

Of course he remembered. They sat on that very sofa. She'd smelled like vanilla back then. "I'm surprised *you* remember."

She nodded. "You were wearing a blue Roots sweatshirt. We ate sour cream and onion chips and drank root beer."

Huh. She remembered more than he did.

"Marley, why are you here?"

She sighed, leaning back on the sofa. "I thought...we should talk. I had a really crappy couple of days since I last saw you."

He snorted. "Yeah, my week hasn't been the best, either." That was the understatement of the century.

She looked at him, her otherworldly large eyes sympathetic. "What happened at the studio?"

He exhaled. "They're doing damage control. Don't worry—I made them promise to leave you out of any plans."

She nodded. "Thanks." She took a bite out of one of his famous onion pakoras, like everything was fine and normal here.

"Of course, Marley. I feel terrible. You lost your *job* because of me."

She shook her head. "No. I lost my job because of the intrusive photographer who took pictures of us while we were at my doctor."

"And because my brother sold us out." He winced. "I...I should never have come into your life. I've been like a wrecking ball, destroying everything."

She took another bite of pakora. "These are really good. Did your mother or father make them? Or are they store-bought?"

"I made them."

Her eyes widened. "Shut. Up. You *made* these? Why didn't you ever make me pakoras?"

He shrugged. "I would have if you'd asked. I'm not allowed to eat them, though. Nalini begged me to make some when I got home from the gym today. She's studying for a biology exam, and she said she needed fried food to concentrate. The samosas are store-bought."

Marley chuckled. Then looked up at him. "I don't know why I ever let you walk away."

What? She didn't *let* him walk away; she *asked* him to walk away. "Huh?"

Marley put down the pakora in her hand and wiped her mouth. "Here's the thing, Nikhil. *Yes*, you did plow through my life like a wrecking ball. But...I think all the things you destroyed were things I needed to get rid of anyway."

He raised a brow. He was not following.

"You know where I came from tonight?" she asked.

He shook his head.

"A BRCA peer support group. I didn't actually go to the group, but I had coffee with the facilitator before it. I talked about my surgery, about this weird new pain I'm having, about how scared I am about my future. About my health."

Marley talked to a stranger? *Amazing.* "What new pain?" he asked.

"It's normal—apparently nerve regrowth. I think that it's some sort of metaphor…because I do feel like I've been growing new feelings lately. That's cheesy, right?"

"I love cheese."

She chuckled. "Jaime—that's the facilitator—she was cool. It was weird to hear her talk about her health and her surgery openly. But she was so accepting of her body and her ongoing risks. She has all these people that she leans on when she needs them, and she supports others when they need her. I think…" Marley paused. "I *know* I've been scared to open up to people because I'm afraid of being a burden."

"You're *not* a burden."

Her face scrunched in annoyance. "This is hard to say. Let me finish."

He smiled. "Sorry. Yes, go ahead."

"But now I'm realizing it's not just about being a burden. I'm *terrified* of commitment. The fact is, even with all these preventative measures, I could still get sick. And I will need more surgery. I thought I was too defective to be in a relationship."

Nikhil shook his head. "That's ridiculous."

She smiled. "Yeah. Because I am a whole entire person, not just a broken gene."

He chuckled. "Isn't that what I've been telling you for weeks? That Jaime person sounds like a miracle worker."

"I needed to hear it from someone who's gone through this. Do you remember when my Maryam Aunty was sick when we were in high school?"

He nodded. Marley had been hurting so much back then. It was heartbreaking. He remembered a day in chemistry when he looked over at her and saw she was crying while taking a test. That day he decided he would make her smile at least once a day. "Yeah."

"She was put into hospice right after prom. She died before graduation."

That, he didn't know. "Fuck, Marley. I am so sorry I wasn't there for you. I was such an idiot back then. I should have talked to you."

She shook her head. "No. I mean, I didn't tell you why I left school. The past is the past. You had to go to LA, and I didn't want to talk about it, anyway. That's not why I'm saying this now. I'm telling you this because my aunt's husband left her when she was diagnosed with breast cancer. That's why she lived with us when she was going through treatment."

Nikhil's fist clenched. "Asshole."

Marley nodded. "It's pretty common. Jaime said not everyone has the bandwidth to be a caregiver, but Jaime's more generous than me. I agree with you—he was an asshole. My aunt was a *lot* like me. She was very stylish. Loved clothes. She used to take Ruby and me to luxury department stores to look at the fashions all the time. Everyone used to say that I should have been Maryam's daughter. She was also very reserved. Some people called her cold...especially compared to my mother, who can be a little in your face." Marley sighed. "When my uncle abandoned her, I wondered if I was capable of making someone love me enough to stay if I got sick."

Nikhil wanted to laugh. He was *obsessed* with Marley at the same time she was wondering if anyone could love her. He should have told her then. "I think your uncle deserting her was an uncle problem, not an aunt problem."

Marley nodded. "Jaime said that when it came to relationships, she saw her BRCA mutation as sort of a blessing because it helped her weed out the duds. She's engaged. Her fiancé was there with her through her surgeries. He was just her boyfriend then."

"I would never, ever walk away from someone I love because they were sick."

She nodded. "I know you wouldn't. It's not in you. You told me so many times—not just with words but with your actions—that you would stand by me. You *did* stand by me. You said you were all in and I should have believed you. I'm sorry, Nikhil."

He couldn't stand being so far from her anymore. He got up and sat next to her on the sofa, and she immediately rested her head on his shoulder. He leaned down and inhaled deeply that citrusy floral scent. Weeks ago, he'd thought her perfume was so posh. That it added to the unattainableness of her. But now it was the opposite. Now it was comforting and…home. He kissed her soft hair.

He had no idea what any of what she said meant for them. Even if she'd realized that he would never walk away because her health made things difficult, there *was* a reason *she* should walk away from him. A bigger and completely reasonable reason.

His life. His career.

"I can't make any promises about my future, either," he said. "Things have been rough for me lately, but, Marley, I *love* my job. This is it for me. Acting is what I want to do."

She nodded. "It's what you're supposed to do. I *want* you to make your dreams—all of them—come true."

"But…" How could she commit to someone who could very well be completely unavailable to her in the future? This career meant travel. Being away for months at a time. Long hours on sets. Not to mention, even if she wanted to start being more open about her life, there was open and then there was *dating a celebrity*. Her head was still on his shoulder, and if he leaned down a bit, he could kiss her lips. He wanted to. He wanted to bury his face in her and forget about everything else.

But he wanted to keep making movies, too. He wanted it all…the busy, intense, fulfilling work, and he wanted to come home to Marley's soft smile at the end of the day.

She finally spoke. "I admire what you do. Your drive and persistence. And I wouldn't walk away from someone I love because their life turns into a media circus through no fault of their own."

Wait. What did she say?

She sat up to take a sip of her chai. "This is so good. Did you make this, too?"

He snorted. "You know I can't make decent tea. That's my dad's famous karak chai. You spend any time with this family you'll learn all our specialties. My sister has a way with macaroni and cheese. The boxed stuff."

She smiled. "I met your mother. I guess Nalini told her that I offered to take her shopping, so your mother asked if she could come, too."

"Mom's been *trying* lately," Nikhil said. "I think Arjun selling your address to photographers was a bit of a wake-up call for her. She said she won't let Arjun into the house again, and

Dad even called Arjun's parole officer and told them what he did while on day parole."

"Oh wow," Marley said.

"Mom's even cooking again. We watched your cousin's new video together. And she made an appointment to talk to her doctor about her mood. I think she realized that mourning one kid was making her miss out on the other two. I hope, at least. You don't have to take her shopping, though."

Marley shrugged. "I don't mind. I want to get to know your family. I want to be all in, too." She smiled, then glanced over to the photo wall. "Is that our prom picture on your wall?"

He chuckled. He'd consciously prevented himself from looking at that picture too much in the last couple days. Too painful. "My folks are all about the family pictures."

"Are there embarrassing ones of you up there?"

"Lots. And more in the albums on that shelf. Stick around and you can learn all my secrets."

Marley turned to look at him. "I *want* to stick around. I can't promise anything, Nikhil. But…maybe all this chaos would be easier to manage together?"

He didn't say anything. He didn't have to. He put his hand around the back of her neck and pulled her in for a kiss.

And when their lips touched, the little sigh of relief that escaped her was everything. He told her he couldn't know what his future would be like, but he made a silent promise with himself then that he would *always* be there for this woman. Through whatever should come her way, or his way, he would be present for her to lean on. He loved her, and he wanted to be hers forever.

He'd gone ten years without her in his life. And yeah, every-thing hadn't been rosy in those ten years, but he'd been *mostly* happy. He had friends. A few relationships here and there. But he hadn't had this…this all-consuming comfort. This feeling that there was nowhere in the world he was supposed to be but next to this person.

The kiss was short but so sweet. When he pulled back, he kept her close, pressing a soft kiss on her forehead. And then, because he couldn't not say it anymore, he told her. "I love you, Mahreen. Thanks for coming back."

"I love you, too, Nikhil. Thank you for finding me six weeks ago."

He had so much more he wanted to say. They needed to figure out how they were going to make this work. Maybe she could come to LA. Work in a boutique there. Or they could try long distance. He was still in town for a few months. He wouldn't have a ton of free time once filming started, but they could figure it out. And he wanted to help her with her job issue. Brainstorm ideas for what she could do now. Did she want to stay in retail? Take some time to reassess her options?

He also wanted to tell her how miserable he'd been for the last couple days without her. He missed her. He missed McQueen. He missed her '70s throwback house and missed all the plants everywhere. He even missed the scent of her oolong tea. But he didn't say any of that. They could talk later.

Because all that mattered now was that she was here. In his arms. He'd wanted her since the day he met her when they were fifteen. And now he was going to stay hers forever.

"Nikhil," Nalini called down from the stairs. "Dad wants to know if you all are staying, and if you want jalebi gathiya."

Marley chuckled.

Nikhil looked at her. "Are we staying?"

"Maybe…or…do you want to come back home with me?"

He grinned. "Yes. That's exactly what I want."

After packing up a few things, including some jalebi and gathiya that Dad insisted they take, Nikhil drove Marley back to her house. They were both exhausted. He told her he loved her again as they got into bed. And she said she loved him, too.

Nikhil had never been happier in his life. And he was determined—this time he wasn't going to lose her. He'd looked for a decade for someone even half as perfect as her; that person didn't exist. Marley was the only one for him.

He fell asleep as the big spoon to her little spoon.

Nikhil called Reggie in the morning to say he wasn't coming in. It was his prerogative—this was the first day he'd called in since he started training/rehearsals. And right now, there was nothing he wanted to do more than stay in bed with Marley for as long as possible. He and Marley finally headed downstairs past noon. After Nikhil made Marley some tea and toast, they sat on the sofa and talked about everything that had happened in the last few days. Marley told him more about her meeting at Reid's on Tuesday. He became angrier at his brother the more he heard. She'd lost her *job* because of this...not just the personal shopping role she'd wanted for so long, but her entire employment at the store she'd worked at for years. Nikhil offered to have the studio call Reid's and say they would never work with the store, ever, for doing this, but Marley insisted he let her deal with it.

"Lucky break that you happen to randomly meet someone who works in employment law," he said.

Marley nodded. "Yeah. I'll call Jaime's office on Monday.

And I guess I need to start looking for a job, too. I have no idea what I want to do now. The thought of moving up the ladder from the bottom in another luxury department store seems so daunting."

"Is that your only option? Luxury department stores?"

"I suppose I could try smaller boutiques. I imagine with my experience it wouldn't be hard to get into a store in Yorkville."

"But…maybe this is an opportunity to make a change. What's your fantasy job?"

Marley shrugged. "It's always been to be a personal shopper. Even before I started at Reid's, that was the end goal. I love building relationships with clients, and I love helping put together outfits for specific situations. I want to do what Erin does. That's my fantasy job."

He hated the idea of her putting all that effort into working for someone else. "What about freelancing? A personal stylist?"

She snorted. "That's exactly what Ruby suggested."

"Is it something you'd want?"

She was quiet for a few moments, thinking about the possibility. It was clear she was scared. "You don't have to make the decision now," Nikhil said quickly. Maybe now wasn't the right time to be thinking about the long-term future. She was still healing after surgery. It had barely been four weeks. Actually…it had been a month today.

She nodded, then curled her legs up under her. It was a gesture he hadn't seen her do before. He couldn't believe how much she'd already healed, and he knew she would just keep getting better.

"Are you sure you're okay with me going along with the studio's plans? I'm going to be confirming I'm dating Serena. We'll be seen—and photographed together," Nikhil said. If he'd known he'd be back with Marley, he wouldn't have agreed to it.

"Yeah. It's only until after the movie's done, right? It's probably a good idea for us to lie low for a while anyway. It would be better for my job search."

Nikhil sighed. He didn't want to lie low...He wanted to scream from the rooftops that Mahreen Kamal loved him. "Things would have been so different if I hadn't gone looking for you that day I had my tooth fixed," he said. "You'd still have a job."

Marley smiled small. "Yeah, but I'd rather have you."

At that, McQueen jumped onto his lap and burrowed into his hoodie, climbing into the pocket like he used to.

They continued to sit in the living room talking. They speculated as to why Serena posted that damn Instagram post. They talked about Reena's pregnancy, and about Shayne being away so much. They talked about Nalini's med school plans. They avoided talking about one specific topic, though: what would happen in a few months when his filming was done and he'd be heading back to LA. They had time, and Nikhil wanted to see how the next few weeks went before making any decisions. And the last thing he wanted to do was make Marley feel pressured into doing anything that wasn't exactly what she wanted.

At around five, the door of the house opened, and Shayne came in loudly. He had a few large totes hanging over his arms and was carrying a large foil tray.

He frowned at Nikhil. "Oh. *You're* here. For the party, I guess. OMG...Are you two a *thing* again?" Shayne's shoulders slumped. "Damn it—I lost my bet with Reena."

Marley raised a confused brow. "What party? And you guys bet on whether or not we'd get back together?"

Shayne shook his head. "No. We bet on *when* you'd be getting back together. We knew it was a sure thing. I thought you'd wait until at least the movie started shooting, but Reena said it would be sooner. You owe me twenty bucks."

Nikhil snort-laughed. "Do you need help with that stuff?"

Shayne glanced down at the cat head poking out of Nikhil's hoodie. "Nah, I got it. You sit with the cat. Marley, why are you in sweats? The party is in…like…half an hour. Do you still fit into that vintage zebra-print wrap dress?" He took the foil tray and the tote bags to the kitchen. "Grams made jerk chicken *and* curry chicken. And rice and peas. I wanted oxtail, but she said I was being spoiled. Do you guys think I'm spoiled?"

"Yes," Marley said without hesitating. "Now, what party are you talking about? Why did Grams make so much food?"

Shayne shook his head, looking at the tray of food. "Because she is *incapable* of making a small amount. I told her it was only five of us…" He looked at Nikhil. "Well, now that the superhero is back in the picture, *six*, but I swear, she hears the word *party* and assumes minimum a dozen. We'll be eating jerk for the rest of our lives."

"Shayne! What *party*?"

He put his hands on his hips. "Your silicone celebration! We planned it during your ta-ta-to-your-tatas party!"

Nikhil raised a brow at that.

Shayne was still talking animatedly. "Don't tell me you forgot, girl. We said we'd all meet here a month after your surgery to celebrate your new…what did you call them? Foobs! Fake boobs! This is your foobiversary party! Grams has been

cooking all morning! Reena and Nadim will be here soon!
Ruby, too!"

Marley winced. "Oh. Right. Forgot about that."

As if on cue, there was a knock at the door. Shayne put his
hands up in the air. "Now they're here early, and I haven't had
the chance to put up the decorations yet. I bought *so many* nipple pasties!" He headed to the door.

While Shayne answered the door, Nikhil considered exactly
how Shayne was planning to decorate with nipple pasties. He
was pulled out of his train of thought when Shayne squealed
and slammed the door shut. He rushed back to the living room,
looking as if he'd seen a ghost.

"What is it?" Marley asked.

"Um." Shayne looked at Nikhil. "I assume this has something to do with you. Can you tell me why *Lily Lavender* is on
my grandmother's front porch?"

Nikhil's head shot toward the door. "*Serena* is here?" What
the hell? How did she even know where Nikhil was? Unless…
She'd better not be here to harass Marley. He glanced at Marley, who looked like a deer caught in the headlights.

Shayne shook his head. "I can't believe this. Do you know
how many posters of her I had on my bedroom wall right
upstairs?" He fanned his face. "This is a lot. Now I'm all
flushed."

Nikhil got up quickly from his seat and went to the door.
And yes. Serena was there. Caroline was with her.

"What are you two doing here?" Nikhil asked. "How did
you know where to find me?"

"Reggie knows everything," Caroline said.

Of course he did.

It looked like they'd come from the gym, since both

Caroline and Serena were in their athletic wear, and Caroline's hair was damp. Serena tilted her head, looking curiously at Nikhil. "Is there a cat in your pocket?"

He absently started rubbing McQueen's head, who was peeking out to see who was visiting. "Yes. Why are you here?"

Caroline smiled. She looked…well, uncomfortable, yes, but also like she was here to extend an olive branch and fix things between all of them. "We missed you in rehearsals today," Caroline said. "Can we talk a moment? We won't take too much of your time. Maybe…inside?" She glanced at the road behind her.

Nikhil understood Caroline's point. The last thing they all needed was to be seen. He supposed he had no choice but to let Serena and Caroline into Marley's house.

"Take your shoes off," Nikhil said as Serena and Caroline crowded into the small entranceway of the house. "We can talk in the…" Marley and Shayne were in the living room. He could take them to his room—actually, the sewing room. It wasn't his anymore.

Shayne was still standing with a shocked expression in the middle of the living room. "I…uh. You…water?"

Nikhil frowned. "I think he's offering you a glass of water. This is Shayne. He lives here. And Marley"—he gestured to Marley, who was still sitting on the sofa—"my…friend."

Marley looked less starstruck about Serena Vox being in her living room. She looked unamused. Which made sense because this superstar had caused a lot of grief for her recently. But Marley still had manners, so she started to stand to greet the guests.

"No, please don't get up," Serena said, smiling and approaching Marley to shake her hand. "It's so great to finally meet you. I'll be honest—more than one person has told me that I need to hire the stylist who turned Nik Sharma into a style icon in only a few weeks. Is that your cat in Nik's sweater? It's adorable!"

Marley narrowed her eyes. Nikhil didn't blame her. He didn't trust Serena, either. Why was she being so...pleasant?

At that moment there was a brief knock at the door, quickly followed by the sound of Reena and her husband talking as they came into the house. Nikhil cringed. The fact that they walked right into the living room where Shayne, Nikhil, Serena, and Caroline were all still standing was awkward enough, but the way they were dressed...

Wait. *What* were they wearing?

Both Nadim and Reena were wearing large white T-shirts. And both had what looked like huge beach balls stuffed under them at the stomach. Marley had mentioned that Reena was expecting, but this was a strange way to announce it. That's when Nikhil fully registered that there were triangles of red fabric covering a portion of each ball-stuffed shirt. And with the two of them standing side by side, it was clear they were dressed as breasts wearing a skimpy red bra. Reena and Nadim were staring at Serena Vox, mouths agape.

Nadim was the first to be able to speak. "You're..." he stammered.

Shayne was a little more acclimatized to the A-list celebrity in the room and could speak. "She's Lily Lavender."

Marley snorted a laugh. "Reena, why are you dressed like that?"

"Um, your party?" Reena said. "Surprise?"

Caroline shook her head, laughing. "I'm Caroline, the stunt coordinator for the Ironis movies. And this is Serena. I *love* that costume. Can I steal the concept for a breast cancer fund-raiser I'm doing next month?"

Reena awkwardly pushed a big multicolored ball out from under her shirt, letting it drop to the floor, which made McQueen jump out of Nikhil's hoodie and chase it. "Um... nice to meet you," Reena said. "I'm Reena. This is my husband, Nadim."

Nadim was still staring at Serena. Nikhil knew he needed to do something now before someone here fainted. Or embarrassed themselves further. There was another knock at the door then.

"That'll be Ruby," Shayne said.

It was time to get Serena and Caroline out of here. "Okay, you wanted to talk? We can go upstairs. Oh, and don't worry about these guys. They've all signed the studio NDAs."

Caroline nodded. "Yeah, upstairs works."

Nikhil looked over at Marley. He wished he could bring her along. He was not looking forward to this conversation.

Marley gave him a reassuring nod. "I'll be here. We'll set up the party. You go ahead."

He smiled at her.

Upstairs, they crowded into the sewing room, Nikhil and Caroline perched on the bed and Serena on the rolling chair at the sewing table.

"Sorry it's tight," Nikhil said. "It's a small house."

Caroline shook her head. "No worries. Clearly our timing wasn't great."

He shrugged.

"I wanted to call you," Serena said. "But Reggie and Caroline thought we should speak face-to-face. And without publicists or agents."

He didn't want to deal with publicists, either.

Caroline glanced at Serena before turning to Nikhil. "We… wanted to explain."

Serena nodded. "And I owe you an apology. Reggie told me that you thought *I wrote* that Instagram post about us."

Nikhil frowned. "It was your account."

Serena shook her head. "I haven't logged into my own socials in years. The studio's been managing them while I'm filming this movie. I know they wanted to make it seem like you and I were dating, and I told them sure, whatever, if you're game for it. But when you said no, I thought that was that. But then…" She glanced at Caroline and sighed. "I'm going to trust you here, because I think we would work better as allies than enemies. Don't make me regret it, though."

Nikhil raised one brow. "You know I'm bound by an NDA, too."

"Yeah, but we'd rather you kept our confidence because you *want* to, not because you have to," Caroline said.

"Of course," Nikhil agreed. "You have my word." He still trusted Caroline.

Serena took a big breath. "You're not the only one who's been recently followed by photographers. Last weekend I was followed by a photographer who got pictures that the studio was not happy about. They were able to buy the pictures and kill the story, but there may be more out there. I'm…I'm in a relationship that doesn't match their script for who the lead of the Ironis franchise should be with."

Serena was the *star* of this film. She was a huge celebrity, and they weren't even letting *her* be herself?

Nikhil suddenly looked at Caroline. It all made sense now. Serena was dating *Caroline*. Her stunt double. And a publicist had put up that post to deflect the fact that she was in a same-sex relationship. He couldn't believe the studio would do that.

But this was the same studio that was overly concerned about the fans not being happy that the Bronze Shadow was an Indian man.

"How long have you two been together?" Nikhil asked. The more he thought about it, the stranger this was. He liked Caroline, but Serena had never been a pleasant person to him.

"A while. A year," Caroline said.

He smiled at Caroline. It would be kind of weird to date your literal *double*, wouldn't it? Was this a Hollywood narcissist thing? Clearly, there was a lot more to these two than what he saw in their daily training.

"So why didn't you come clean when you realized the publicists lied on your Instagram?"

Serena shook her head. "I didn't know they lied. I mean, I knew you and I weren't really together. When they called me in to yell at me about the pictures of me and Caro, they said that you'd finally agreed to a publicity relationship and they were going to post it on my socials. That's why I was so angry with you that day...I thought you went and kissed your girlfriend in public *after* agreeing to date me. I thought you set out to humiliate me on purpose."

"Fake date," he said.

Serena nodded. "But then Reggie told me today that you *never* agreed to the fake relationship and didn't know that post on my social was going up. That's when we realized that we needed to apologize. To you and Marley."

"Mostly to Marley," Nikhil said. "She didn't choose this life. We were *followed* into her doctor's office."

Caroline frowned. "I can't stand celebrity photographers. Or this studio's publicity team."

Nikhil had to agree with Caroline there. "So, they told you I'd agreed to fake date you before that post went up? Why?" He'd been quite clear that his personal life was off-limits.

Serena shrugged. "I guess they thought if my Instagram confirmed we were in a relationship, you'd have no choice but to go along with it. But then the *Pop Hollywood* piece went up with the worst possible timing."

"Who's *they*, anyway?" he asked. "Specifically who told you I'd agreed to the fake relationship?"

"Your handler, Lydia," Caroline said.

"Of course it was Lydia. She's not even my handler anymore. My agent fired her while I was in Los Angeles."

Serena shook her head. "This is my shocked face. And they know she's to blame, but they want to keep it pinned on us."

"On me," Nikhil said. "You're Serena Vox. I'm the disposable pawn." He paused. "Okay, so this tells me why you were mad at me the other day—but why've you been so hot and cold for weeks? You always seemed like you didn't want me around."

Serena exhaled low, then shook her head again. "Yeah, I know I haven't been very welcoming. Look, it takes me a while to warm up to people—especially to new people I have to work closely with. I've been burned too many times. People want or expect more from me than…Anyway, I just like to keep my distance. Keep things professional with people I work with."

"Except Caroline, apparently," Nikhil deadpanned, which made Caroline snort a laugh.

Serena rolled her eyes. "Caro pointed out I should be nicer to you because this racism shit was clearly affecting you. It's not right what they're saying about you. And I'm sorry I was so cold."

Nikhil kind of saw her point. She'd been a star almost her whole life—many people had probably taken advantage of her, sold her out, or expected something from her that she didn't want to give. He'd only been famous a few weeks and his own brother sold him out to the paparazzi.

"I almost wonder if Lydia knew you were dating your stylist, and she did all this to turn the movie into a media frenzy," Caroline said. "More drama, more attention."

"I hate this industry sometimes," Serena said. "Things like this happen all the time." She looked at Caroline. "Any ideas on how to fix it?"

Caroline pulled out her phone. "Let me call a freelance PR firm. They can brainstorm with us."

Nikhil put his hand up. "No. No more publicists. Let's go downstairs and brainstorm with Marley and her friends."

Serena raised a brow. "Are any of them in PR?"

Nikhil shook his head. "No. They're an out-of-work fashion stylist, a fashion photographer, a baker, and a real estate developer. Oh, and a lingerie salesperson."

Caroline snorted. "What, no candlestick maker?"

"The fact that they're *not* in the industry is a good thing," Nikhil said. "Marley's the one who's been violated the most here. She deserves to have her support system involved."

Serena sighed. "You're probably right."

Nikhil stood. "You two like Jamaican food?"

CHAPTER THIRTY-TWO

Marley

Six weeks ago, if someone had told Marley that she would be sitting at her dining table celebrating her mastectomy with her boyfriend, Shayne, Ruby, Reena, Nadim, and *Serena Vox* and Serena's stunt double, Marley would have asked exactly what the hallucinogenic substance was that caused such a bizarre prediction. And if someone told her that *Nikhil Shamdasani* was the boyfriend in question, and that he and Marley were now madly in love, Marley would have requested to have some of that drug, too.

It was amazing how different things were now. Back when Nikhil first reappeared in her life, Marley still thought he was the fuckboy who'd ghosted her after prom. But now she saw things differently. She'd pushed him away back then, too. And now they've both grown up. They were finally ready to be *partners*. She knew it would be hard with the complicated baggage they brought to the relationship, but it would be so, so, worth it.

The movie star and her stunt double being here for her celebration certainly was a head-scratcher, though.

After Serena made sure everyone's NDAs were up-to-date, they all sat at the dining table that Shayne had decorated with a sequined nipple pasty on each plate. He'd clearly raided the bachelor aisle of the party store, too, because there were paper boob straws in everyone's glass, and the napkins were covered with illustrations of bras. You would think that the Hollywood star showing up at the house would have made him reconsider decorating like this, but Shayne insisted that even Serena Vox couldn't stop him from celebrating Marley's foobiversary.

Nikhil made sure Marley's plate was full before taking any food for himself. Marley chuckled. "I'm fine." She looked at the others at the table. "He dotes."

"It's adorable," Caroline said.

Marley liked Caroline already. She was honest and down-to-earth. Serena less so, but it was clear the two were close.

"This house is really cool," Caroline said. "It's...peaceful. It's lovely, isn't it, Serena?"

"Yeah, it's nice," Serena said.

"We call it geriatric-core," Shayne said. "Coastal-Caribbean Grandma."

"My grandmother lives in Palm Beach...Add a few more palms, and this place would be a dead ringer for hers," Caroline said.

After they all had food on their plates, Serena took a breath. "Thanks for letting us crash your party." She looked at Marley. "I wanted to apologize to you specifically for that whole Instagram mess." She then explained the story she'd shared with Nikhil upstairs.

"Wow," Marley said. "Why the hell would Lydia do that? They're sabotaging their own movie!"

Serena shook her head. "No, they're not. Relationship drama between the stars sells tickets."

Caroline nodded. "And it's a great way to deflect attention from the information they *don't* want people to talk about."

"What information?" Shayne asked. "What are they trying to suppress?"

Serena looked over to Caroline, a question in her eyes.

"You don't have to tell them anything you don't want to," Nikhil said before Serena answered the question.

Serena sighed, then looked at Marley. "You trust these people?"

Marley looked around at her closest friends at the table. "With my life. They're the best."

Serena smiled. "Okay then. I'll trust them, too. Caroline and I were photographed in a…compromising position over the weekend."

Marley raised a brow.

"We were kissing," Caroline clarified. "We've been dating for a year, and the studio doesn't want Serena to go public with it. Not until the film premiere, at least."

Holy shit. That explained it. But why did the studio care so much? This wasn't the 1950s.

Shayne grinned. "OMG. I can't believe I know what would be the *biggest gossip* of the year if it got out."

"You cannot say anything," Serena said quickly.

"Are you kidding?" Shayne shook his head. "I'm *thrilled* that I can't say anything. I know something about Lily Lavender that very few people know. *Exclusivity* is hot."

Marley rolled her eyes at Shayne. "Look, I get it. I've dated women, too." That seemed to surprise Caroline and Serena. But Marley kept going. "And of course, you know the risk to your own careers better than we do. But Nikhil's career is just starting. You can't let them throw him under the bus to save yourself. Not to mention me. I lost my *job* because of this."

Serena recoiled. "You *lost* your job?"

Marley nodded. "They claim I violated the NDA, even though I didn't. I suspect they think a sales consultant who ruined Serena Vox's relationship would hurt business. Reid's is anti-home-wrecker."

Serena cringed. "Ugh. I can have the studio call them." She picked up her phone. "Let me—"

"No." Marley shook her head. She sighed. "Reid's was toxic. The fact that they would let me go for this is proof." Marley sighed. "I don't know what I'm supposed to do now."

Serena shrugged. "Go freelance. Make it known that you were the one who created this one"—she pointed to Nikhil—"and you'll have a line of clients waiting for you. Seriously."

Marley shook her head. "Wouldn't I have the same problem? I'm your home-wrecker. No one would want to work with me."

"Not if they came out," Shayne said. "Of course, that's your decision, though."

Serena shook her head. "I can't. Not now. I promised the studio."

Marley agreed and didn't think that Serena should come out, either. "But the fact of it is, as long as you're single, me and Nikhil are villains," Marley said.

"Tell your publicity people to find you another fake relationship?" Shayne suggested.

"I'll do it," Nadim offered. "I'm a great fake boyfriend."

Reena slapped him on the arm. "I'm *literally* pregnant with your child."

Nadim kissed his wife on the cheek. "I know, Ree. We could probably pay for the kid's college with a Hollywood fake-relationship contract."

Serena snorted. "You guys are funny. I really don't want to lie again."

"God, I hate this whole publicity mess," Nikhil said. "We should ignore what they all say and just go to the media and tell them we're only friends."

"Why couldn't you?" Reena asked.

Serena shook her head. "Because all movie promo goes through the publicity team. It's in our contract."

"What if it's not movie promo?" Caroline suggested. She frowned, forehead wrinkled in thought. "I have an idea…" She looked at Marley. "Maybe you could style *me*. I'm doing a benefit next month for the Still Glowing Foundation. They do makeovers for women who've had cancer surgery. Maybe we can pitch a TV segment where you style me after my mastectomy?"

Marley nearly dropped her fork. "You've had a mastectomy?"

Caroline nodded. "I had breast cancer a few years ago. I hope I'm not prying…but Nik mentioned that you are recovering from a mastectomy, too." She looked around at Shayne's decorations. "And I mean, clearly y'all are celebrating your surgery."

Nikhil cringed. "I'm sorry. It slipped out."

Marley smiled at Nikhil. "It's fine. Totally." But this idea of Caroline's…Could Marley do it? Even if she didn't mention her own mastectomy to the media, this was still more *public* than she was used to being.

But admitting she had a mastectomy would address the gossip that Nikhil bought her a boob job, too. And best of all, it would bring attention to this charity—the same one that Jaime worked with. "Maybe," Marley said slowly. "If we find media we can *trust*…maybe I would do it."

Nikhil looked surprised she agreed.

"I don't know many people here," Serena said. "Do you have any media contacts who wouldn't sell us out and tell the studio publicists that we came to them?"

Marley grinned, nodding. "*Confab*."

Shayne shook his head. "No."

Reena's eyes went wide. "Holy shit, *yes*."

Shayne pointed at Reena, glaring. "*You* are not helping."

Nikhil looked at Nadim. "What are they talking about?"

Nadim shrugged. "I only understand about half their conversations."

"*The Confab*…" Caroline said slowly. "Isn't that a talk show out here? Like *The View*?"

Marley nodded. "One of the hosts would do *absolutely anything* if a certain person at this table asked."

Shayne continued his glare. "He would *not*."

"I remember!" Nikhil said. "The guy we saw at the press junket."

Shayne's head whipped to Marley. "*You saw him?* And you didn't tell me?"

Serena frowned. "Who are you all talking about, anyway?"

"Shayne's ex," Reena explained. "We don't say his name."

"I didn't tell you because I knew you'd freak out," Marley said to Shayne. "Which is what you're doing now."

"I am not freaking out. And we're not going there, Marley. No way, no how. He's off-limits."

Serena was on her phone. "Anderson Lin?"

"Don't say it!" Reena said.

Shayne waved his hand. "It's fine. She's America's sweetheart. She gets amnesty."

"We're in Canada," Nadim clarified.

Marley looked back at Shayne. "C'mon, Shayne. You *know* he'd do this." She paused for a moment. "And I trust him."

Marley was tired of keeping it all in. It was time to tell her own story.

Shayne exhaled. "Okay, fine. I'll call him. But only because it's for you, Marl."

They spent the rest of Marley's foobiversary party planning their own little PR stunt.

Later, after everyone had left, Marley cornered Shayne in the kitchen while he was putting away the leftovers. He'd called Anderson, and although Marley didn't hear the conversation, Shayne said Anderson was completely on board and would speak to his producers in the morning.

"Thanks for doing that, Shayne."

Shayne only shrugged as he spooned rice and peas into a large container.

"You don't have to come with me when we do the segment."

"I know."

Marley paused. "Shayne, are we okay? I mean, you get why I didn't tell you I saw Anderson, right?"

"Yeah." He still didn't look at Marley.

"Then…" She sighed. "Why don't we talk anymore?"

Shayne put the spoon down and looked at Marley. "We're talking now, aren't we?"

"Yeah, but it feels like we're…surface level. For a while, actually. We don't go deep anymore. I don't even know why Anderson dumped you."

Shayne looked at Marley for several long moments. Then shook his head. "Actually, I ghosted him." He exhaled. "I'm not proud of it."

Marley's eyes widened. "What? Why?"

"Honestly?" he said. "I was scared. He was getting the job on *The Confab*, and amazing things were happening, and I was scared we would just…fizzle. I thought I wouldn't be as important to him anymore."

Marley tilted her head. It was just like Shayne, actually. He talked the talk, but he had an insecurity deep inside. A part of him was always afraid that he cared more about someone than they cared in return.

"I wish you'd told me that then," she said.

"You had your own problems, Marl. Ones I had no idea how to help you through."

Marley shifted so she could bump hips with him. She wanted to hug him but wasn't ready yet. "You *have* helped me, Shayne. Look at this whole party! You're my best friend. Don't keep me out of your life. You're never going to be a burden on me. I know I've been in my own head for a while. I'm sorry if I haven't been there for you."

He smiled. "Seriously, Marley? You've been through a lot. And look at you, getting through it all with a new superhero boyfriend now, too. Talk about thriving."

"I couldn't have done it without you, Shayne. Seriously. I love you."

"Love you, too, girl. And I *am* coming to the studio when you go on Anderson's show. He insisted…but I want to, anyway."

Marley frowned. "You sure?"

He nodded. "Yeah, I'm sure. It's time. I need to tell him the truth. My best friend taught me to do the hard thing even if it's scary. Now go upstairs. *Superman* is in your bed, for God's sake. Why are you here with me?"

Marley grinned, kissed Shayne on the shoulder, and headed up the stairs where Nikhil was waiting for her. She'd never in her life felt more loved.

Three days later, Marley and Caroline were sitting under the bright lights at *The Confab* studio being interviewed by Anderson Lin. Marley's hands were shaking and her heart was racing, but being in front of the camera wasn't nearly as terrifying as she'd expected. It helped that Anderson was the one interviewing them—she'd always liked him.

They'd already finished filming the first segment, where Marley demonstrated on Caroline how she could style her clothes to minimize the appearance of her single mastectomy.

"So do you use those tricks in your day-to-day life?" he asked Caroline.

"Not daily, no. I'm a stunt coordinator, so I have a pretty physical job. Scarves and cowl-necks aren't practical. I resort to baggy hoodies. But yeah, when I go out and want to look less lopsided, I'll wear things like this. Or use a prosthetic."

"Marley, how did you get involved with Still Glowing?"

Marley smiled but steeled herself inside. "I myself had a mastectomy last month. I'm a BRCA1 mutation carrier, which is a genetic mutation that puts me at a high risk for breast cancer. Caroline told me about the foundation and the amazing work they're doing to help women be confident and stylish after changes to their body. I'm a fashion stylist, so I love the idea of helping women who are struggling with similar body issues as me. Making people *feel* fabulous by *looking* fabulous has been my passion, and my job, for years."

Anderson smiled. "Yes, I think the whole world has been admiring your talent for that in the last few weeks, even if they didn't realize that it was *your work* they were admiring. Which, of course, ties into how you and Caroline know each other. Do you want to reveal to the viewers who introduced you two?"

Marley nodded. This question was, of course, planned. "Yes. Why don't we bring him out?"

Anderson grinned at the camera. "Here's a big surprise for you all. Marley and Caroline's mutual friend and the star of *Ironis 3*, Nik Sharma!"

Nikhil came out then, and of course, the studio audience went wild. They had no idea he'd be there. Nikhil smiled, waving to the crowd, and sat on the sofa next to Marley.

"Nik, wow—the crowd loves you!" Anderson said.

Nikhil chuckled. "Still getting used to all this. But we're not here to talk about me, are we?" He grinned at Marley.

"You two are old friends, right?"

"We've known each other a long, long time," Marley said. "We were even prom dates."

"So," Anderson said. "With Nik in Toronto shooting the Ironis movie, can I assume he's been helping you recover after your surgery last month?"

Marley nodded, looking at Nikhil. "I don't know what I would have done without him."

Nikhil smiled back at her. "Same goes for her." He ran his hand over the deep-midnight-blue jacket with a Nehru collar he was wearing.

"Okay, you two are too cute. Are you sure you're just old friends?"

Marley laughed and said, "No comment," just as Nikhil

took Marley's hand in his, indirectly confirming their relationship status.

"Now," Anderson said, "I don't *always* believe celebrity gossip, but there was some buzz going around about you being in a relationship with your co-star."

Nikhil smiled. "Anderson, you should know not to believe everything you read online. Serena and I are friends. Great friends. She's been so amazing helping me get used to action movies."

Anderson looked at Marley. "You've met Serena Vox, too?"

Marley grinned. "Yes. In fact, the four of us recently had this huge meal together...My friend's grandmother makes the best jerk chicken in the world."

Anderson's eyes widened, knowing exactly who Marley was talking about. "I would love to have been there for that."

"Hopefully next time, Anderson," Marley said.

Anderson looked straight at the camera then. "You can catch Nik Sharma, along with Serena Vox, in *Ironis 3*, coming to theaters sometime next year, right?"

"As soon as we film it!" Nikhil said.

Anderson laughed. "And I think you can find Marley wherever Nik is. There's more information about the Still Glowing Foundation and their fundraising gala next month on The-Confab.com. After the break, picnic cocktails!"

Someone yelled, "Cut," and Marley could finally exhale. Nikhil leaned in and kissed her cheek. "You were amazing."

"Do you think that worked?" Marley asked Nikhil.

He nodded. "No doubt. You made everyone fall in love with you," Nikhil whispered in Marley's ear. "I love you so much."

Marley smiled, leaning her head against his. "I love you, too."

EPILOGUE

Marley

Nik, who are you wearing?"
     "Nik, over here—show us your smolder!"
   "Nik, what's coming next for you?"
   It had been seven months since Marley started dating a real-life movie star, and this was her first red-carpet experience. It was, well, overwhelming. She was so glad Nikhil insisted that she didn't need to walk the carpet *with* him. The camera flashes, photographers, and yelling fans were…intense. Intrusive. And Nikhil wasn't even in this movie—he and Marley were only here to support Serena and her new holiday rom-com.

   Marley was instead walking with Caroline a few paces behind the actual stars. But even if this was a lot, and Marley had no interest in a public profession like her boyfriend's, Marley *loved* watching Nikhil work a red carpet, or any press event, actually. He was a natural. Preening for the camera. Laughing. Even flirting a bit. The camera *loved* him, and the fans *loved* him.

   And it all made Marley love him even more.

   Dating an actor had meant a lot of new experiences for Marley. They'd had to duck into shops to avoid photographers while shopping in Los Angeles, she'd randomly seen her own name in TMZ more than once, and pretty much every person Marley had ever known had contacted her at some point to try to get access to Nik Sharma. But also, she'd hung out with celebrities, had the phone number of an actor from her favorite medical drama in her contacts, and she and Nikhil had even been invited to exclusive fashion shows, since his reputation as a style icon was still going strong. Overall, the positives way outdid the negatives. And of course, Nikhil himself was the biggest positive of all.

Once past the chaos of the red carpet, Marley walked into the theater and immediately saw Nikhil waiting for her in the entrance. He grinned and came right for her. Marley smiled as he kissed her cheek lightly, knowing not to smudge her makeup. They hadn't seen each other since she arrived in LA that afternoon—she'd had appointments at several boutiques to pick up clothes for her Toronto clients, and he had a meeting with his agent.

"You made it," he said. "That dress is gorgeous."

She was wearing a dress she'd had for a while, a slim, green cocktail-length dress with a lacy overlay that was completely backless. It was handy that her silicone breasts meant she could go braless now. Her hair was curled lightly and pulled to the side, and she had tall nude heels on. "We're going to sit together, right?" he asked.

Marley chuckled. "I hope so. I came all the way from Toronto for this—if you weren't going to sit with me, then I would have just watched from my living room with McQueen."

He laughed, putting his hand on her lower back to guide her in. Once they were seated in the theater, the charismatic, schmoozing Nik Sharma was gone, and it was just her Nikhil. Her attentive, doting, little-bit-goofy boyfriend.

He poked a finger through the gauzy lace of her dress. He was always very tactile with her. Especially with her clothes. "How did your shopping trip go?" he asked.

"Pretty good. I may have to do a little more shopping while I'm here, but then I'm all yours for the rest of the week."

He grinned at that and leaned in to bury his nose into her neck.

Marley's personal styling business had been doing very well since it launched six months ago. And to her relief, it was doing well without any promotion or advertising from her. She didn't have to hustle on social media or put herself out there more than she was comfortable doing. And she still had more clients than she knew what to do with. Many were her customers from Reid's who were happy to come to Marley wherever she was, and their word of mouth was enough to sustain her business. That plus Serena's and Caroline's referrals, too. Despite her busy client list, she still found the time to volunteer with the Still Glowing Foundation as a stylist. And she did her best to attend the monthly BRCA peer support group with Jaime. The women in the group had become such an important support system for her.

And of course, Marley was spending a ton of time with Reena and her new baby son.

Marley had never been busier...and adding a long-distance relationship to the mix wasn't ideal. But she wouldn't change anything for the world, because she'd also never been happier than in the eight months since her mastectomy.

She'd been to LA several times to see Nikhil, and he came to Toronto whenever he could. His family was doing better—his mother was finally on antidepressants, which seemed to be working, and Nalini was in her second year of her biology degree and was still determined to go to med school. Arjun was still in prison—he'd been denied parole thanks to him selling information to the paparazzi, so they had some time before they had to figure out how to avoid him.

Nikhil had been to tons of auditions and had been working steadily since he filmed the Ironis movie. In January, he was starting principal photography on a limited streaming series for Netflix that would be shooting in Toronto. It would be the longest stretch of time that they'd be in the same city since *Ironis 3* filmed six months ago, and Marley couldn't wait.

"When do you have to go back to Toronto?" he asked. He was leaning in close so he wouldn't have to speak loudly, and it felt like they were alone in this busy theater.

"Friday. On Saturday, Shayne and I are throwing Ruby a goodbye/birthday party."

"Is she leaving already?"

"No, not until January, but she'll be too busy at Reid's for a party in December. You know, this will be the first Christmas in ten years that I won't be working retail…I'm not sure I'll know what to do with myself."

He leaned in and kissed her neck. "I have an idea…What if I came home with you and we spent December together?"

Marley looked up at him. "Can you do that? I thought you had a guest spot on that cop show."

He grinned. "Esther got me out of that. She had some news for me today. I've been officially offered *Ironis 4*. They want me and Serena in it together again. My role will be bigger this time."

"Nikhil! That's amazing!" Marley threw her arms around him. This was exactly what they were hoping for. He'd never set out to be an action star, and he'd taken the Bronze Shadow role mostly for the money. After the pre-production hell he went through, he'd thought he wouldn't want to go anywhere near the franchise again. But he ended up *loving* filming the superhero movie with Serena. His director was amazing, and he and Serena actually became close friends. Best of all, while he was filming in Toronto, he came back to Marley's little house every night for all the cozy comfort either of them could want.

Marley was delighted that they would do it all again.

"So, I'll have to be in Toronto for the Netflix series for a few months, then *Ironis 4* rehearsals and shooting...I was thinking maybe it's time for me to get my own place in Toronto."

Marley tilted her head. "You could. Or...you could always move back into the quilting room. Shayne will probably be moving in with Anderson soon." Shockingly, Marley's chronically-afraid-of-commitment best friend had settled happily into a committed relationship with his talk-show-host boyfriend.

Nikhil raised a brow. "The quilting room?"

Marley shrugged, grinning. "Yeah. But actually...that's where your sister sleeps when she doesn't want to drive back to Markham after a late class. Wouldn't want to kick Nalini out. How would you feel about sharing my room?"

Nikhil grinned huge. "That's what I was hoping you'd say. There is nowhere else I'd want to be. Just you and me."

"And McQueen."

"Yes, and McQueen." He kissed her. "I love you, Mahreen."

"Love you, too, Nikhil. Now shhh...Watch the movie."

She squeezed his hand, and he squeezed hers right back.

RECIPES

Nikhil's Green Moong Daal (Mung Bean Curry)

This is Indian comfort food at its best—green mung beans simmered in onions, tomatoes, and spices. It's super simple, and the beans do not need to be soaked if made in an electric pressure cooker like an Instant Pot. Enjoy as a soup along with a side of rice, or over rice as part of your Indian meal.

Servings: 4

INGREDIENTS

1 c. whole green mung beans (green moong daal), rinsed
1 tbsp. ghee or oil
1 tsp. cumin seeds (jeera)
1 green chili pepper, chopped (optional)
1 tsp. grated ginger or paste
1 tsp. minced garlic or paste
1 c. onion, diced

1 c. tomato, chopped

¼ tsp. ground turmeric (haldi powder)

1 tsp. coriander powder (dhaniya powder)

½ tsp. red Kashmiri chili powder (mirchi powder) or cayenne pepper

½ tsp. garam masala

1 tsp. salt

3 c. water

1 tbsp. lime juice

Cilantro for garnish

Slivered fresh ginger for garnish

INSTRUCTIONS

1. Start the Instant Pot in sauté mode and heat oil or ghee in it. Add cumin seeds and green chili and sauté for 30 seconds.

2. Add onions, ginger, and garlic. Sauté for 3 minutes or until onions are soft.

3. Add chopped tomato, turmeric, coriander powder, Kashmiri chili powder, garam masala, and salt. Stir. Cook until the tomato is mushy.

4. Add lentils and water. Stir well. Press Cancel and close the Instant Pot lid with vent in sealing position.

5. Press Manual or Pressure Cook mode for 15 minutes. When the Instant Pot beeps, let the pressure release naturally for 10 minutes, then release the rest of the pressure.

6. Open the lid and add lime juice and cilantro. Top with ginger and more cilantro in a bowl.

Marley's Ginger Chai

Servings: 2

INGREDIENTS
2 c. water
2 tsp. black tea powder or black tea leaves
2 to 3 tsp. ginger, grated
½ c. low-fat milk
2 tsp. sugar, honey, or other sweetener (optional)

INSTRUCTIONS
1. Add water to a medium saucepan on medium-high heat.
2. Add tea and ginger and bring it to a full boil. Reduce heat immediately, and simmer for 3 minutes.
3. Add milk and bring the tea to a full boil again on medium-high heat. Reduce temperature again and boil gently for 3 minutes. Watch pot carefully and stir to prevent a boilover!
4. Add sugar or sweetener of choice. Strain into two mugs and enjoy hot.

AUTHOR'S NOTE

About a decade ago, my entire life was turned sideways and upside down when I found out I was a carrier of the BRCA1 genetic mutation. I was told that I had a 90 percent lifetime risk of developing breast cancer and a 40 percent chance of ovarian cancer. To say that discovering I had this broken gene rocked me to my core would be a huge understatement. I was married with two young kids at the time and had recently started grad school to retrain as a therapist. I had always been the healthiest in my family, and I took it for granted that I would stay that way. And like many carriers of the BRCA1 gene mutation, I had recently seen family members struggle through cancer diagnoses and treatment.

I was faced with incredibly difficult decisions. Should I have a prophylactic mastectomy? If I do, should I get breast reconstruction or stay flat? Would silicone implants or reconstruction with my own tissue be better? When should I have my ovaries removed? What would happen if I got sick while my kids were young? It was a very difficult time for me, and I confess I did not cope well. Eventually, I found two things that helped me enormously. First, I found a peer support group: a group of women that met monthly who were in the same place I was—struggling to decide how to deal with this difficult diagnosis. Or they had been through it already and could tell me what to expect with my choices.

And the second thing that helped me was I started reading romance novels. I'd been a romance reader back when I was a teenager, but as an adult I moved to literary or general fiction with the odd thriller here and there. But romance—*joyful,* optimistic happily ever afters—became a lifeline for me at this time. I inhaled these books. I read them both to escape my problems and to help me process how important love, family, and joy were for me.

I eventually ended up taking over as facilitator of that peer support group after I had my own surgeries, and I ran it monthly for years. I met the most amazing people and was constantly inspired by the strength and the bravery that these women would discover deep within themselves.

And after reading so many romance novels, I eventually started writing my own.

When I told my BRCA friends I'd started writing, the one question I was asked repeatedly was if I would be writing *my story.* Was I planning to write about BRCA mutation carriers? And my answer was always no. I wanted to write *romance.* Funny and fluffy books about young women whose entire worlds were turned upside down by falling in love. A BRCA story might be okay for women's fiction or literary work, but *romance* was my happy place. And I wasn't ready to connect the hardest thing I had ever gone through with that joy.

But now, finally, I am ready. *Just Playing House* is my seventh published romance novel and the first time I've written a character with a BRCA mutation. Marley isn't me—and her story isn't mine. But we have a lot in common. This book is a capital *R* Romance, with a great big, fluffy happily ever after and the sweetest cinnamon-roll hero who loves to cook and just happens to also be a sexy movie star. And they fall in love *while* she's recovering from her mastectomy.

I wrote this book for the hundreds of women I've met with this mutation. Women with partners who stuck by them, and women whose partners left them. Women who found love *after* having a mastectomy or a cancer diagnosis. Woman who lost family members to cancer, and who helped their mothers, sisters, and aunts deal with this mutation. Women who found out that they could do so much more than they thought they could.

And it's for me a decade ago, when I didn't know how to associate this gene with joy.

If you are concerned about your own cancer risk or are struggling to find support coping with a BRCA mutation, I urge you to seek out peer support.

For more information about hereditary cancer risks and to find a support group in the USA, visit FORCE (https://www.facingourrisk.org/). For Canadians, visit the Canadian Cancer Society (https://cancer.ca/). Outside of Canada and the USA, google *BRCA Support*, plus the region you are located in to find support resources. Also, two Facebook groups, the BRCA Sisterhood and the BRCA Sisterhood Canada, are fantastic resources filled with hundreds of members who want to help others.

ACKNOWLEDGMENTS

I'll never not be grateful to the universe that I get to live out my dreams and have another book in the world with my name on the cover. Even though this is my seventh release, the joy of writing acknowledgments never gets old.

In addition to the universe, I'd especially like to thank Leah Hultenschmidt, my editor at Forever. Her support, patience, kindness, and her unreal skill of knowing exactly what I am trying to do better than I even know are unmatched. And thank you to the other Forever team members that I've had the privilege of working with: Sabrina Flemming, Sam Brody, Estelle Hallick, Luria Rittenberg, as well as the entire art, marketing, sales, and publicity teams. I love being a Forever author because I know I will always be in good hands with them.

And of course, a huge thank-you to my incomparable literary agent, Rachel Brooks. I would not have this career without her, and I am endlessly grateful to have her on my side.

I always knew writing this book about a medical condition that I have personal experience with would be hard. But what I didn't expect was that while writing it, I would develop another medical issue that required me to temporarily put my writing on hold. And when I was able to write again, it was with new challenges that required accommodations. I already knew that I should never take my health and my body's abilities for granted, but this tested me. But life really does imitate fiction, and just like Marley in this book, I learned to reach out for support and lean on others to help me get through it. Thank you to my writing and publishing support system—Roselle Lim, Lily Chu, Nisha Sharma, Mona Schroff, Namrata Patel, Jackie Lau, and Jenny Holiday—for being there when I needed to vent.

And most of all, thank you to my family: My kids, Anissa and Khalil, for their patience and understanding. My cats, Darcy and Matcha, for their snuggles and purrs. And most of all, thank you to my husband, Tony, for propping me up, for being my eyes when I needed him, and for repeatedly telling me that I am strong enough to get through this roadblock. I am better now, but I'm not sure I would be better without my people (and my cats). I love you all to the moon and back.

ABOUT THE AUTHOR

After a childhood filled with Bollywood, Monty Python, and Jane Austen, **Farah Heron** constantly wove complicated uplifting happily ever afters in her head while pursuing careers in human resources and psychology. She started writing those stories down a few years ago and is thrilled to see her daydreams become books. Farah writes romantic comedies for adults and teens full of huge South Asian families, delectable food, and most importantly, Brown people falling stupidly in love. Farah lives in Toronto with her husband and kids, plus two cats who rule the house.

To learn more, visit:
  FarahHeron.com
  X @FarahHeron
  Instagram @FarahHeronAuthor
  Facebook.com/FarahHeronAuthor